J_Carter

FOLLOW  •••

# THE BUY-IN
## A Novel

3:45     4:49

You     Gotta Take a Shot...

For information:
AF.FORD MEDIA, LLC
15826 S LaGrange Road, Ste. 265
Orland Park, IL 60462

**BOOKS**
An Imprint Division of AF.FORD MEDIA, LLC

Printed in the United States of America

979-8-9880203-2-5  (print)   979-8-9880203-3-2 (ebook)

Cover design and interior design by
AF.FORD MEDIA, LLC

Courteous credits to:
Cover and interior designed using assets from Freepik.com by the following creators:

Freepik for the photography, music player app interface, mobile messaging templates, and Instagram Story templates

pch.vector for emoticons on Instagram frame template

Alicia_Mb for the Simple Instagram Frame Template

jcomp for the curry and cafe photographs

# THE BUY-IN

a novel

Hakeela Buford

The heartsick nineties babies and old souls reluctant to experience (something new),
authors trying to control the(ir own) narratives, marketers selling themselves (short), actors playing roles, and tough customers.
It'll all make sense by the end.

Trust.

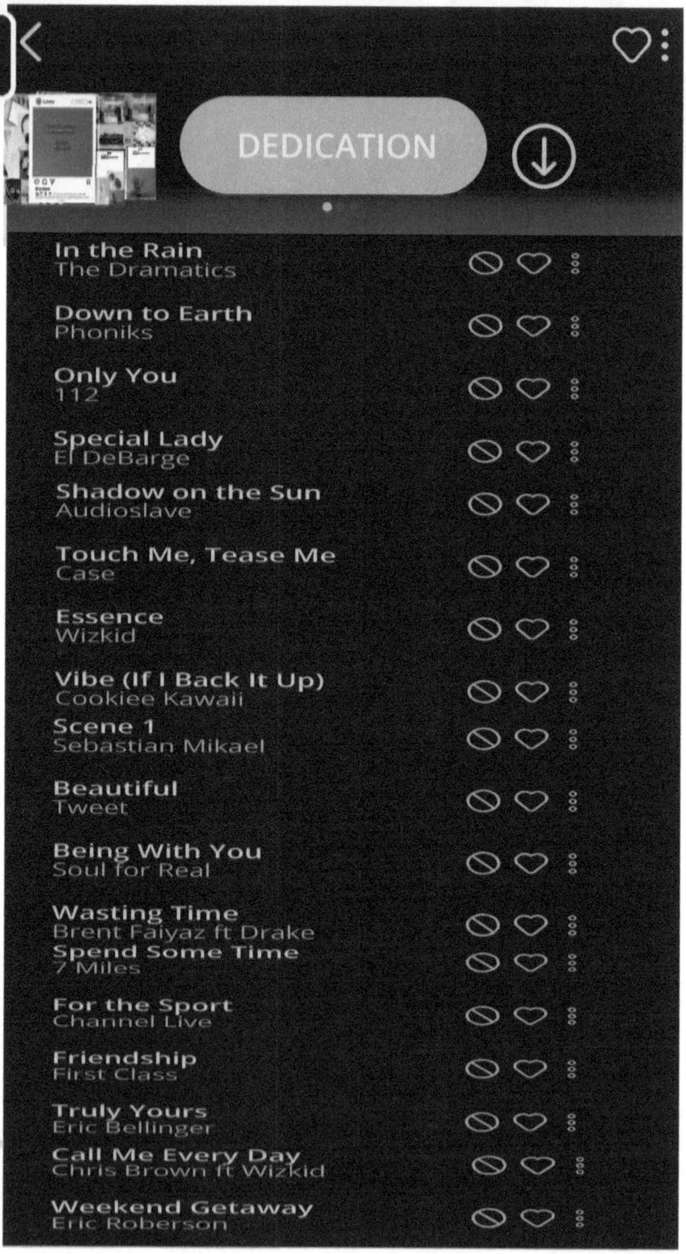

**If Pretty Was a Person**
Hylan Starr ft Wale

**Pretty Girl**
Eric Roberson

**Just Us**
Maze ft Frankie Beverly

**I Want to Be in Luv**
Craig G

**What More Could I Ask For?**
Craig David ft Wretch 32

**Survive**
Kenny Lattimore

**Never Let Me Go**
Mac Ayres ft CARRTOONS

**Start Over**
Musiq Soulchild

**I Found My Smile Again Rmx**
D'Angelo

**Silent Treatment**
The Roots

**Visit Me**
Changing Faces

**Are You Missin' My Love?**
Jesse Powell

**Twice**
Conclave

**Why Does**
112

**All About You**
Ideal

**Sentimental**
Ideal

**One of a Kind Love**
Intro

**Excuse Me Miss**
Jay-Z

**Soulstar**
Musiq Soulchild

**Let Me Be the One**
Intro

**Passin' Me By**
The Pharcyde

**I Used to Love H.E.R.**
Common

**Ferndale**
Elzhi

**Motions**
Raheem DeVaughn

**Reality**
Elusion

**Midnight Blue**
Puma

**Still Wonder**
Alex Isley

**City Lights**
DJ Harrison

**Girl of My Dreams**
Devin Morrison

**Technicolor**
Sunni Colón

*...*
*Should I?...*

*Not yet.*

1:05
Elle DeBarge
U ready?
...as i'll ever be...
Ah but see you agreed to this remember?
..and now I 'm
WHATeva! Liar
You want to see me... Like I want you to, too.
L E T H E R K N O W
A S D F G H I J K
Z X C V B N M
123
space
return

Crap...

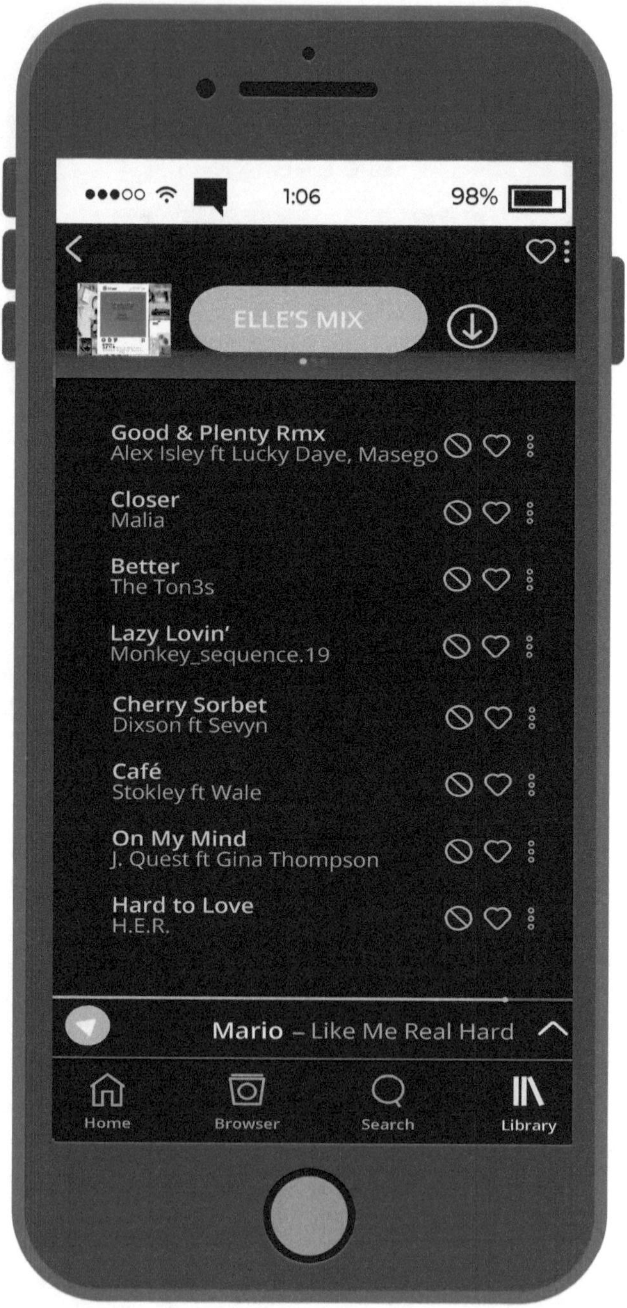

1:06
98%
ELLE'S MIX
Good & Plenty Rmx
Alex Isley ft Lucky Daye, Masego
Closer
Malia
Better
The Ton3s
Lazy Lovin'
Monkey_sequence.19
Cherry Sorbet
Dixson ft Sevyn
Café
Stokley ft Wale
On My Mind
J. Quest ft Gina Thompson
Hard to Love
H.E.R.
Mario – Like Me Real Hard
Home
Browser
Search
Library

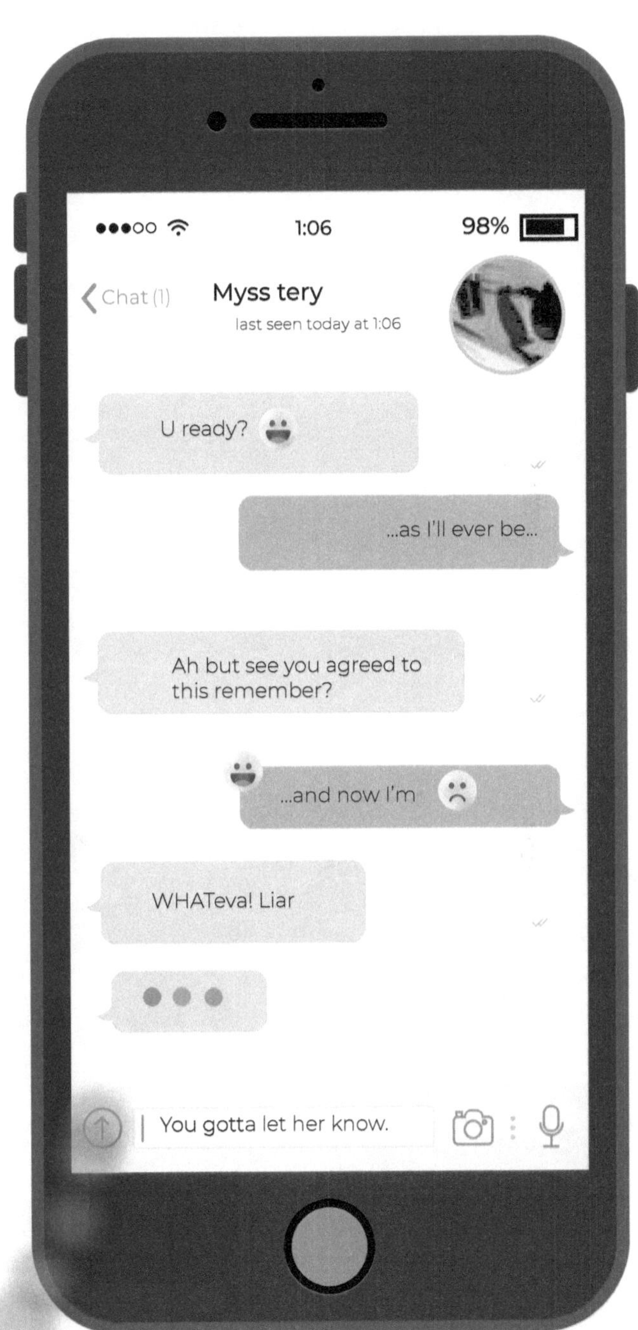
Chat (1)
Myss tery
last seen today at 1:06
U ready?
...as I'll ever be...
Ah but see you agreed to this remember?
...and now I'm
WHATeva! Liar
You gotta let her know.

♡ 1

A RIGHT HAND SPRAWLED A NAME QUICKLY. *REALLY* QUICKLY, mechanically almost, across the first inner page of a book. Right under the title, right under an author's name. The very same name:

*Arielle Smith*

Then the hand released the pen, closed the book. Handed it to a gleaming Cheshire cat of a late-middle-aged woman's ecstatic face as she snatched it up with her manicured paws.

The woman probably thought all of this smiling was going to give her more time at that table. It was all in the creases of her wide-open lipsticked mouth and ultra-white bleached teeth that matched the almost silver speckles of her hair. "Thank you, so excited to read this...for the SECOND time! How do you come up with such *real* work at your tender age? Just *TWENTY*-nine?!"

With her agenda-checking manager/literary agent Kimesha Lee, forty, next to her behind the bookstore table, Arielle Smith returned a soft smile that noticeably contrasted the sharpness of her jutting jaw and the shaved sides of her ponytail-donning hairline. Arielle really did have a hidden mildness, so much so that she leaned away from hitting the lady with a correction. Not like she really felt thirty, her real age, anyway— she never felt her age. So instead...

"Old soul, supposedly...Wise beyond my years?" Arielle loosely proposed.

"I KNOW THAT'S RIGHT!"

Indeed, old Harlequin fiction was always a hit, so Arielle had already played the right marketing card there, and luckily, it had quickly proved to be her niche. *But living the human motions, like my last three relationships, always helped, too. Unfortunately. But don't take my word for it. Ask my three subsequent new wrinkle lines.* But the lady, who was now prancing out of the automatic doors, didn't need to know that. Didn't want to ruin it for a woman who probably didn't even know she still had that kind of bounce left in her ounce since Zapp had last commanded her to on some dancefloor four decades ago.

*Besides, people don't read stories for what's real. They read them for what looks real, wrapped up in words within binding—or tablet devices.*

Arielle finished live-editing her thoughts, as a new book, a new excited reader, landed in front of her. She wouldn't let her personal story impact others—she was a fiction writer, not a memoirist, after all. The sketchy love track record in her *real* life, she figured she could at least profit off of in her fictional ones, her characters and, in turn, her readers stumbling (or bouncing and ouncing) their way into endings way better than her own.

Her own happy endings never lasted long.

"Okay, all complete," Kimesha announced the sudden fifteen minutes later, starting to pack up Arielle's signing pen, unadopted books, and signage.

Arielle came back from her thoughts, looking from Kimesha to her mother, Elizabeth, who was approaching with her rolling suitcase in tow. She slowly rose with a creeping smile.

"All good?" Elizabeth asked as she tucked a book into the suitcase. She'd been visiting for the past week, and had acquired a read for her four-hour flight back to Detroit. Her mom was her rider, for all of her life journeys, her straightforward yet always comforting delivery, character was why she'd offered to tag along today before her flight. But now she was checking her cell phone.

"Yeah, of course," Arielle insisted, finally answering to Elizabeth's wellness check, but more focused on Elizabeth's well-being. "Is that the Uber? I told you I can take you."

"Now, why would you head in the reverse direction of your house to drop me, then go back again? That doesn't make sense," Elizabeth argued.

Arielle grinned with a shake of her head—but her mom had a valid point.

"Like I already told you, I came as an early birthday gift and to see you do your thing for a bit."

"Text me when you get to the airport and then when you make it home." Just as Elizabeth was her rider, Arielle was Elizabeth's, too. She really wished Elizabeth would just relocate closer to her in Las Vegas, yet her mom liked her self-reliance and hated hotter weather—so these visits would have to do.

As she watched Elizabeth efficiently pull her suitcase out of the bookstore, she grinned even more. *That independent lady.*

And Arielle *was* an old soul—and an old soul became world-weary after a certain point. The earthly things they experience becoming tired, played out, *old.*

Hence, what Arielle saw immediately following her third novel's book signing, after slowly pushing her bedroom door open a crack, was *all the way* old:

Her girlfriend under their slip 'n' slide-smooth bamboo bed covers, with a guy. And the two were definitely slippin' and slidin'.

Arielle just stared as they abruptly ended their who-knew-what-round. It hadn't been the first time she'd seen such a scene (though the girlfriend and setting were different, the feeling was the same). Her racing head turned faint; her chest dropped through the soles of her feet. The feelings in her body, her feelings being disposed of. Disposable.

Others in her group, the masculine-of-centers as someone in the group had informed the rest of society at some point in time, were color- and U-Haul-coordinating with wives, puppies, and IG features on Lesbian Couples 'R Us (in front of said U-Haul).

But as for her? She'd been shuttled off to the side, stuck behind the wall that felt like barbed wire rather than dried plaster, to witness her own woman with someone else.

What the woman said as she wrapped herself up in the covers, and the guy quickly pulled on his pants, was so profound.

"You're not on your plane?"

*Ah, yes. My trip TOMORROW. So kind of you to keep track. Well, in a way, this is a day-early simulation of me checking into my hotel,* Arielle mentally wisecracked to fight the less casual feeling rising within. *Kinda like that 'manifestation' ceremony with your brother from another cosmic mother right there. Which in nine months will see the concentrated effort of your collective "YES-YES" affirmations come into fruition if it was performed effectively.*

Yep, this would be the last time she had a relationship with a communications graduate–turned–life coach.

Especially one whose idea of a relationship (with her specifically) was always something else. Emotional *healing* to be ready when the real *twin flame* came around (and other New Age conscious BS brought to you by your friendly social media influencer). At the very least, the girl could've remembered Arielle's real flight date. *But she darn sure remembered my book signing so that she could have my house to herself. MY house.*

But Arielle didn't question, or shout, and she damn sure didn't cry. Instead, she merely turned around and headed back out the door. Might as well, since she was already proverbially kicked to the curb. *MY curb—! Well, really, the city's—Damn, can't even have that.*

And once she hit that still-blazing evening Vegas sun (for the second time in just under five minutes), she let the takeout bag in her hand (with her girlfriend's favorite TexMex) hit the curb (to keep it warm). And soon was in her car, filling her head with The Dramatics crooning out "In the Rain."

Except for her, there was no rain. Only desert.

**KEELA BUFORD**

No more tears, just…washed up. Tired.

She'd make a book out of it later, for older folks always had cautionary stories. Her storytelling would be her *only* love, no longer just her first love, going forward. It was not only the lone thing that she obviously was valuable in—her books had given back to her, too: a finally paid-in-full Stafford Loan just last month, the air-conditioned Ford Expedition she was sitting in, the 1,500-square-foot abode she'd just purchased…and now had just exited.

But first thing tonight, once she walked back inside, she was trashing that annoying AF *sustainable* bedding—and the body pillows. The whole damn set.

*None of it is really sustainable. It's all just a fantasy, just bounded up in some material to make it look so, look real.*

♡ **2**

THE NEXT MORNING, ARIELLE AND KIMESHA LANDED AT THE
rideshare pickup area at LAX, wheelie suitcases in hand, as the Chevy
Malibu from Kimesha's Uber app pulled up in front of them. Arielle
opened the door to:

"The Luxe?" The young-twenties driver greeted them from under
the brim of his Lakers Mitchell & Ness classic snapback.

But even given Arielle's love for all things vintage (such as this
driver's cap, or a '90s cassette, or a pair of Nike Air Max 1s), she had no
capacity right now for anything but what had just emitted from this
talking head, rather than what was atop of it. She looked up her hotel
reservation email confirmation on her cell phone:

*You're staying with us at Freehand Los Angeles!*

She whipped her head at Kimesha with a cocked eyebrow. The
latter apologetically shrugged but gave a quick, courteous nod at the guy
as she settled her things into the backseat.

"I know. *Not* the Freehand just yet. But look, it's a great one-day
conference. For writers to make connections and learn the latest
marketing practices," she finally filled Arielle in as she pushed her
sunglasses up onto the top of her mass of thick, coiffed coils. "And to get
your mind off of yesterday."

Arielle rubbed the bare side of her hairline with a thrust of breath.
She *really* wasn't in the mood for people, even less than usual. This
weekend, she just wanted to *connect* with a drink or two (or twenty) and
Netflix, alone in her hotel room after giving her West Coast cousins three
hours of her face at this restaurant they booked for tonight. Meanwhile,
the equally native Kimesha would be trying to learn (for the umpteenth
time) the generational mussels recipe the right way from her mother. But
of course, she had to throw in some work for Arielle, even on this weekend
vacation. Arielle knew there'd been a catch when Kimesha had decided to
come along.

Just then, another itinerary-related phone message:

*Don't forget A! We STILL holdin to our commitment*

It was Tish, Arielle's old friend from college. And AI was Tish's nickname for her: Arielle Introverted. For, like Iverson, Arielle was quick with the moves—to escape social events specifically.

*No beats happenin without movin*
*And happy G-day to ya lame a$$*

This was their bond. Around music, rhythm, the culture—and sneakers. But right now, it was about Arielle's birthday (partially) and the music, a beatmaking event (most accurately…one that Tish had been harping about for quite a few months). So Arielle tapped a quick text back:

*Just say the word*

Then Tish had the last word:

*Naw this time YOU sayin it*
*Cause obviously that's the only way it's actually gonna happen*

*She ain't neva lied.* Another sigh. Arielle slipped her phone away, only to be reacquainted with a waiting Kimesha who gave an encouraging cuff of Arielle's shoulder.

"Legs that make it through landmines are the stuff of legends."
*Oh, THAT'S what I am.*
"And today, the legend has made it to a MILESTONE!"

Minutes later, Arielle groaned more or less to herself as they stepped away from the check-in table inside the Luxe Sunset Boulevard conference lobby. Because first, she had *this* milestone to cross.

Kimesha pumped along while Arielle lagged, attaching her Market Your Way to Success attendee badge.

"I promise it won't take even an hour out of your plans for tonight. My birthday gift to you."

"But why? I just observe you humans recruiting and booting amongst one another with tragic results, conclude even further that I'm doing this people thing right, then use it to my advantage." Arielle flashed the cover of her latest romance/drama novel, the one from the book signing, under her arm. "Marketing to success."

Kimesha swallowed a chuckle, nudged Arielle further away from the table and the conference crowd in earshot. Didn't want to be a bad influence.

Too late. Suddenly, Arielle heard a slight snicker within her earshot. She and Kimesha both shot a look over, and there she was…

*Elise Nelson*

Arielle's eyes fell on the middle-aged Black woman's badge.

"You're not lyin'," Elise seconded Arielle, in that commonplace communal way that Black women did over a moment of understanding. Even if they didn't know one another, such as in this moment.

Arielle looked at Kimesha, really fighting the smirk pushing into the edges of her mouth. "See? Don't tell me I don't know about my ex-career."

Kimesha rolled her eyes as Elise chuckled with Arielle now. But her managerial scolding was cut short as her cell phone rang, and she waltzed feet away to take the call.

Suddenly, Elise's eyebrows quivered, her eyes shooting down at Arielle's own badge, then back up with certainty. "Arielle *Smith?*"

*Uh-oh.* Arielle nodded to confirm with a modest half-smile. She was still getting used to this occasional recognition when she was out and about. Damn, Kimesha should've been right here to see this moment, so she'd finally see that Arielle didn't need this damn conference. It was nowhere near A-list celebrity (or TikTok?) status, but it was *more* than enough for her. Even in her prior, loosely public role as a senior writer/editor for a mid-sized marketing agency, she'd never received this kind of attention. But one Reedsy Books By Black Authors (cool kids club) inclusion and two freelancing-backed-by-a-hard-earned-savings-account years later, she was suddenly in a new world. A world that she always felt she was tiptoeing through, never quite comfortable. But she was trying.

Elise eyebrows soared. "*Doin' Things Out of Character!* You, right?!"

"Uh-oh, already. That's why I only pop out for my restock of Lipton."

That took Elise out. And since Arielle's eccentric coping responses that only a few often understood had been readily accepted right then, she couldn't lie… Instead, she just smiled. With this fun-loving woman who wasn't finished yet.

"Trust when I say this for all involuntarily celibate queer women out here: That HOT WAX STRIPPIN' at the *end—?!*"

A passing senior-aged conference attendee (and her pursed lips) acknowledged Elise and Arielle, jerked a moment in her tracks.

"For the eyebrows," Arielle recited her one line in this fan's monologue scene, shrugged at the lady. "My book."

The senior cleared her throat. Carried on.

And just like that, back to the moment before:

"*Girl!* You can't read that one too late, or you'll wind up hidin' out from your main pillow in a hotel room with your *body* pillow!" Elise confirmed.

Everyone *did* love a fantasy. Steamy ones especially. Pushing her writing a bit with the subtle *Fifty Shades of Grey* flavor of this appropriately named latest novel was continuing to prove successful.

Elise showed the conference pamphlet, with the lineup of speakers' headshots. Arielle instead gleaned the wrap-up time for the event on it:

*4:00*
*!!*

"You should be on this…rather than *this*," Elise clarified, stomping on the generic hotel rugs, as they neared one of the conference's open presentation rooms, "with us common folk. *BUT* since you are…"

As Elise pulled out her cell phone, Arielle already knew what was coming.

"Can I…?" Elise couldn't be blamed for not finishing since she was already swiping on the phone.

"Oh, yeah. Sure thing," Arielle obliged. *Do I really have a choice?*

Elise went in with no further hesitation and initiated the selfie with a wide smile.

"Thank you!" she exclaimed as she slipped her phone away and nodded at the open door. "Now, lemme go see what I can uncover."

"Happy marketing." Arielle bid her farewell with another obligatory yet amused smile, just as Kimesha found her.

"Ready?"

Arielle rolled her eyes with full spirit and sass (hunty) and headed on down the hall.

Kimesha cracked up. "Uh-oh! That was a little feminine for you, no?"

"Since I'm already doing things outside of my character…"

♡ 3

AND UPON EXITING THE CONFERENCE, SHE HONESTLY COULDN'T SAY SHE'D LEARNED ANYTHING IN THE EIGHT HOURS SHE'D JUST WASTED, except why she could never do a nine-to-five ever again. Between the monotonous, wordy speeches, the basic questions that only further encouraged them, and the Arctic winds gusting out of the vents, Arielle was more than ready for warm food and drinks with her cousins. *Damn, I can't believe I actually just thought that.*

But twenty minutes later, entering the reserved meetup place, a Brazilian-Peruvian fusion restaurant, post- Lyft, she realized that she was late to her own party. In front of Juliana, her free-spirited bartending Irish twin of a cousin, there were two glasses, and one was completely empty. Juliana and her two sisters never wasted time getting their fun started.

Now, within earshot but not yet within their immediate view, she heard the wrap-up of the first of many a festivities she'd no doubt be a witness to tonight: Sinead, the oldest, clowning a guy, about a decade or so older than her, as he backed away from the table.

"Your mouth particles just hit me in the face, *sir*. I'll have to pass," Sinead boomed. People at other tables peered over at the poor guy's departure.

"Talkin' about getting my number but no drinks. That Thuggish Ruggish Bone was probably your bum-ass daddy," she accused her sisters.

"He was *not*. He looks better." Melanie stifled a snicker beside her, as she took a sip of her drink in an uncharacteristically aggressive manner.

"I can count on one hand how many times we've seen him in the last two decades. How sure are we that he even knows what *we* look like?!"

*Oh, yeah, the drinks are already hittin'*, Arielle thought, her mouth practically watering for similar approaching solace. The three sisters *never* talked about their estranged father, who had chosen his freedom twice—when the girls were toddlers and when Juliana was ten—for a girlfriend whose attitude couldn't tolerate their own during one very rare (and short-lived) weekend with him. In place of his presence was his cash (and even *that* was a struggle).

But alas, that all was temporarily in the past again as Arielle landed at the table to grins from all three cousins.

"First drink's on you, Easy E…the rest on us!" Sinead cackled with slightly droopy and glossy eyes. The other two joined in.

"Easy Elle," a loose moniker in honor of the West Coast rapper Eazy-E, referring to Elle's chill, which contrasted with their own hot, comical mess. And the gag was that Arielle was just as mellow in her libation escapades—one shot of nastiness was usually more than enough.

*Usually.*

She sat, smirking, and eyed the menu. Little did they know, *this* weekend the joke would be on them. This weekend she was trying to flood out of herself the past six months of memories, during which she'd allowed her now-ex to become increasingly more unreliable.

This weekend, she was washing it all away, starting with a:

"Coconut rum," she announced to the waitress who'd just arrived. "Actually, two, please?"

Needless to say, the tres amigas instantly quieted, gaped, then—never too quiet, as two Geminis and one Aries—reemerged.

"Cuh! Say *whaaaa….?*" Juliana puttered out, her engine running on caipirinha, and, therefore, landing on a lopsided, toothy grin.

But Sinead's hazy yet unrelenting focus was the hawk on the whole situation. *She's about to ask questions.* Arielle bounced her feet under the table. *Not now, PLEA—*

*BUZZ.*

Arielle sighed with relief as she looked to see a video call on her phone coming in: Marlon and his burly, broad shoulders and full goatee, in what looked like a freight truck. Her ten-years-senior brother now lived in Raleigh with his wife, Latrina, and their daughter, Jada. "Happy thirtieth, sis."

"That's my fave cuh? Let me see him," Sinead directed.

Arielle did as told *very* happily, to deflect from herself.

As Marlon, Sinead, and Juliana chatted, Melanie, the middle and—as usual—most-sober sister, gave a quick wave to Marlon then turned her attention to the waitress, who was back with Arielle's drinks and ready to take their dinner order. "Looks like *I'll* go," she piped up. "Can I get the rib—?"

"Ribeye tobanyaki." Sinead dragged her gaze to the waitress and went first. "Medium-rare, please."

"Well, dang. Tell me I'm the malnourished middle child without tellin' me I'm the malnourished middle child," Melanie muttered, then smiled at the waitress. "Same. Thanks."

The waitress nodded, then looked to Arielle.

Arielle swallowed before beginning. Malnourished Melanie had to use the little energy she had to feed four mouths beyond her own, four male ones. But as for her sisters?

"Uh, can I get the chimchurri rice and—"

"It's chimi-*choor*-e," Sinead intercepted. And no, she wasn't one of the Geminis, but she was just as quick. "And don't think we're not gettin' a storytime before leavin' here to explain this little drinking escapade you got goin' on." She chortled.

*Crap.*

Because she meant it, and Arielle knew it.


True to her word, as the quartet were departing an hour and several drinks later, Sinead pivoted around to Arielle and just stared. Then the second pair of eyes, Melanie's, followed. And then the third...

Arielle exhaled. "We broke up—"

"*Oww.*"

*Yeah, exactly. Ouch—*

"There goes Miss Young lookin' *young* at the ripe age of fifty. Owwwwww," Juliana slurred, looking completely away from Arielle, with a brief twerk of her blessings that a few passing men lingered to receive.

*???*

Then, Juliana's eyes bulged as fast and big as her delayed responses would allow her to. "Y'all! That's PAULA YOUNG!"

"Calm down. These nosy people in here..." Sinead instructed Juliana's hype self—but then took a gander at Paula herself.

Followed by Melanie, then Arielle, turning to look. Indeed, about thirty feet in front of them was—

*Oh, yeah. Paula Young.* A veteran R&B vocalist, who was keeping it rich-casual with a monochromatic pant suit, wedged sandals, and sunglasses in her hand, while stepping away from her own dining booth with...

*...Elise?*

"*Oooh*, I wanna know where she got those shoes," Melanie complimented.

"You know those things are probably more than your rent," Sinead shot her down, still gazing at the legend.

"Unh-*unh*. Miss Young ain't like that! She shops at Target. I've seen her photos with fans there," Juliana counterargued in defense of her favorite celeb.

Meanwhile, Arielle was thinking that this woman who looked like Elise had to be a doppelgänger, seeing as she was wearing different clothes and her hair was also now down. Until the woman crossed her own familiar eyebrows at Arielle, then launched them up, and instantly made her way closer.

"Wow, twice in one day! Is this my sign that I should be your apprentice?" Elise giggled as Paula comically assessed her fan girls, then Elise's fan-girlin', then appraised Arielle up and down.

This new proximity was all Juliana needed (because she most definitely didn't need any more drinks). "Oh em *geee.* I love you, Miss Young."

Paula couldn't help but chuckle. "*Ooh,* you're a troublemaker like me. I see it already."

Suddenly, a tall, slim, chef-suited man with no hair on the top of his head (it was all on his chin) came up behind Paula and put an arm around her shoulder. She whipped around initially with a sharply cocked brow, then a vivacious, welcoming laugh and hand on the hip.

"Boy, I was about to say, '*Who* is the silly fool to come up touchin' me?!'" The two embraced. "Thank you, baby. It was all delish."

The man gave a polite nod to them all, before settling back on Paula. "No, thank *you* for finally coming…About time."

Paula tittered some more. "I know. Look at this place! My daughter's gonna kill me once I tell her."

"Ah, you should've brought her."

Paula rolled her eyes playfully. "The baby has her *own* baby now, okay? She can bring herself if she really wants to."

The man chuckled and nodded back towards the open cooking space behind him. "Well, look, gotta get back to it. But don't be a stranger. I'll get you the best seats again, no reservations. Hear?"

As he walked away, Paula wasted no time waltzing back around to Elise and Arielle. "Okay, now back to *THIS* reunion."

The cousins all chuckled without inhibition, whereas, Arielle was still trying not to bring too much attention to herself, knowing that for the second time she'd been saved by the bell. Still, the writer in her observed the scene, receiving firsthand confirmation about Paula Young's down-to-earth nature that groupie Juliana was always soliciting, unasked.

Elise continued her introduction. "This is my new favorite *bestselling, African-American, FEMALE, QUEER* author who I met at that conference earlier," Elise explained.

Paula looked at Arielle, who mustered a nod and a grin. "How's it goin'?"

"And today's her thirtieth birf-*dayyyy,*" Juliana helped.

Paula slowly nodded herself, another survey. "*AND* a birthday girl!" She joined in. "Listen, just don't have a midlife crisis like my daughter did."

After another round of laughs, Arielle included (right now, happy for this increasingly comical LA moment's reprieve), Juliana reached for her phone. "Can I—?"

"Girl, come on." Paula waved her in like a mother, before they all settled into a selfie.

As they pulled away, another group of random fans/diners swiftly decided this was as good a chance as any to cash in on the moment. And likewise, "Unh-huh. Quickly," Paula accepted, let them snap a photo with her, too.

Once it was back to just the first two parties, Elise added, "One last thing: This girl can write damn good, Paula. I'm tellin' you. Maybe even the content you need."

*Uhhhhh..???*

Arielle immediately shot a glance at Elise. While Sinead, Melanie, and especially Juliana shot widened eyes at *her...*

And then there was Paula.

"Okay. Let's do it."

Juliana's jaw dropped more than her current BAC level ever could.

Arielle coughed. "Uh...apologies, but...I don't really—"

Elise jumped in. "I just met you at a marketing conference, right? And you said you used to be in that field?"

"...Copywriting. Within the Marketing department."

"Even better." Paula already was going into her rose-gold Coach leather clutch for her cell phone. "I have something MAJOR releasin' soon. That's all you gettin' until you and I talk more," Paula informed Arielle, then gave her biggest fan a smirk. "And maybe this one right here will get the first sample after."

Juliana bounced with glee.

"No, not a new album. *Yet.*"

And just like that, Juliana flatlined.

Paula began marking off in her calendar app. "Three days from now: three-thirty or four?" She gave a steady eye on Arielle, her stylus pen on the ready as if this was a contract form right then and there.

"Three-thirty-*five* or four," Elise corrected. "You have a three o'clock business call and like to take a five in-between."

"My assistant." Paula graciously acknowledged Elise before going right back to the stylus—and Arielle.

"...I, uh, actually have an engagement. A signing in—"

"She's only here for the weekend." Sinead made it plainer.

"Then I'll be seeing you in *ONE* day," Paula confirmed. Then as she began heading out: "You ladies take care."

"You too, Miss *Youuung.*" Juliana swayed on her stilettos, waving.

Meanwhile, Elise saved Arielle's cell number into her phone ("I'll call you with her address."), gave her a thumbs-up, then followed Paula out of the front exit doors.

*What in the HELL just happened?*

"*SO*, as I was saying: You ain't had enough of these goofy girls yet?"

Arielle could've dulled at Sinead's return to her ex. But instead, she had a distracting inkling that tomorrow would be the start to something bigger. She felt it abruptly in her gut.

And no, it wasn't due to the two helpings of rum.

♡ 4

"I'M A SCORPIO, BABY!"

Paula felt the need to rep her own astro-stats as she pivoted around toward her front hallway. "*WITH* an Aquarius moon. Come to me bravely from the head, not at my head. Or I'm *turnin'* my head, okay?"

It sounded like the subject of Paula's discussion was someone who was being more unrefined and less inventive with their words to her, someone who didn't care to (or need to) be the latter given their long-standing relationship. It sounded like the target (er, subject) was an irreverently giggling Elise, stapling papers in the den and slipping them into a manila folder. Whatever point Paula was trying to prove, she must've deemed her efforts satisfactory as she sipped a lemon-wedged glass of juice from a straw and opened her front door.

Just outside, Arielle jerked her head up from a text on her phone:

*Txt back or look back in 5 for reinforcement*
*LA native rule #1: All that glitters ain't gold Most of it's really zinc*
*Or white rock*

She wasn't one-hundred percent sure what Sinead's last line meant. But she knew it was most likely alluding to the city's underbelly.

And she also knew, to not land six feet under somewhere herself, she'd better send a text back:

*No reinforcement necessary*
*Thx*

"Uh-oh, she's callin' backup. I done scared her already, Elise!" Paula announced and briefly knocked her head back in a proud chuckle as she pulled the door open and stepped aside for Arielle.

"Glad you're impressin' somebody. Because you surely were failing with your assistant, who keeps you on track," Elise promptly, playfully responded back while continuing her process in the den.

"Just wanted to make sure I had the right house—almost felt like I was nine again in Detroit." Arielle lightly stepped into Paula's entry with its vaulted ceiling, her smirk concealed by a grin.

"*Mm*-kay..." Paula grinned wider as they stepped past the corridor's large staircase and entered the den, where she gave Elise a pointed look. "Quick comebacks *from* the head. Yeah, she's got a way with words."

"Told you," Elise simply stated before looking to Arielle. "Want something to drink?"

Moments later, a water bottle landed by Arielle's laptop just as creative video briefs, product mock-ups, and more marketing bedlam from Paula's hands did.

"As you can see, this is my current situation," Paula casually explained with a chuckle. She spread out all of the artifacts on the desk. "So, first things first. Guess I should finally give up the secret deets and tell you what the heck it is I'm working on."

Arielle grinned, nodded, at the ready with a Google Doc on her laptop. "Who, what, when, where, and how. All I need."

"You just get straight to it, huh?" Paula gave her an assessing eye, an approving eye. "Okay, so, *who* would be me, and *what* would be my new fragrance line: Everlasting Young. Like yours truly." She dramatically motioned to herself as Elise rolled her eyes in passing.

"Now, more seriously, it's a line set to open in a month, starting strictly online and expanding to a flagship boutique on Rodeo Drive down the line. Gotta see if I sink or swim first—my potential drowning won't be as noticeable if I stay virtual at the onset."

Arielle chuckled. Paula was clearly a very personable, bold, yet also humble lady. Okay, *mayyyybe* she could start to see why Juliana was so in awe of her.

Paula continued, "I want Everlasting Young to help striving, inspiring, spiritually happy women *and* equally gay men to continue to be just that. Traits that can be hard to sustain, let alone experience. Well, I'm trying to contain those feelings and experiences within each of my bottled scents. With, of course, well-sourced botanicals and the highest concentration of fresh-smelling essential oils to…" Paula swirled her hand in the air as if concocting right there in mid-air. "Last almost forever, potent, everlasting young, a.k.a. classic, an ever-prime experience. Whether it's for special occasions or just messin' around in a messy bun in your kitchen, just because, just to feel good. And that's the little motto I'm going by, so let me know what you think about it once you start or if I need to switch it up a little."

Arielle had captured it all. "Sounds good to me. It's technically called a mission statement, and I've got it all down, so that everything I write is consistent with it, with your brand."

"Okay, ma'am." Paula snapped her fingers. "More about the why of my fragrances. Well, we have a core set that we're starting off with. They've been selected by my perfume chemist team, based on creating distinctive smells that my fans and followers vocalized in our early development survey from months back. I want people who spray this on every morning, or just before a date, to find not only timeless yet effervescent fragrances, but also find various expressions to keep them forever impassioned and *alive*."

"Got it," Arielle confirmed once again.

"So, what do I need to sell all of this? One, a commercial script for the launch promo, to spread across social media. Two, copy written for the website's About page. Three, product descriptions for each fragrance. The paperwork and launch date have now been locked in and sent to all appropriate parties. So, number four is getting the creative work done for the promo." Paula finally paused, concluded. "*Now*, tell me if I've just *TRULY* scared you off."

Arielle grinned. "Actually, with all that you've given me, I've already thought of a boilerplate if you need a press release. It will sound a lot like the brand mission statement. Shall I add that to my line-up of content to write?" Arielle proposed.

"*Yes*, please. So, we have a total of, what, five pieces of…content?" Paula quickly murmured, counted off with her fingers, and looked back at Arielle. "So, if you have to work on it for a few days, you can send me the files in an e—"

"I'll have it done by tomorrow," Arielle replied politely.

Paula paused, gazed at Arielle, then back at Elise.

"So, translation: 'Don't call me, I'll call you when I've finished this in my sleep.'" Paula cracked up as Elise joined in.

Arielle modestly grinned with a roundabout confirming shrug.

Just then, the doorbell rang.

Paula hopped up. "Oo! There goes my baby."

Paula bustled to the door and opened it, and in sprung long pigtails with a purple backpack attached.

"*Mee-MAW!*" The little one, who couldn't be more than three or four, screamed in delight as Paula lifted her and kissed her forehead.

"Look at you all decked out!" Paula beamed as the girl bounced back down to the ground and immediately dove into her bag.

"*Ummm*, Miss Cori, you forgot someone," Elise declared, placing a hand on her hip as she ambled up with a rising smirk.

Cori sprang up and ran into Elise's ready open arms. "Oh! Hi, Lise."

"Em-hmm. 'Cause you know you're not gettin' any of my cupcakes if you play me," Elise kidded as she ruffled Cori's hair lightly. "Got some hang-time with you today, lil' diva."

"Unh-*huh*. Just rude—and super excited about her new little game she basically bullied me into gettin'."

That wasn't Elise's voice, Arielle assessed without looking. It also hadn't been Mee-Maw Paula's...even though it was uncannily similar to hers...

Arielle casually looked up from her archaic laptop (It STILL hadn't shut down, but it was still reliable, and Arielle was cheap...and old.).

And there, stepping in was a young woman who looked to be in her early thirties.

She looked...*familiar*. Arielle briefly shuffled cards of association in her mind, then found it: from the droves of photos Juliana had shared of Paula on red carpets and such. In many a lineup, she'd been present beside Paula, in various growing ages but still the same face: her daughter Jae'cy.

"Okay, EVERYbody's cute today." Paula smacked her lips, noting Jae'cy's outfit from head to toe: loose yet thick wavy tresses draping the shoulders of a wine-red cut-out-front long-sleeve, paired with open-toe bootie heels.

"O*kay*?!" Elise parroted.

As Jae'cy rolled her eyes at Paula, then made her way over to Elise for a quick hug, Arielle blinked then shifted her eyes away. In the process of doing so, she could swear another set of eyes were on her—an instinctually learned hyperawareness thanks to childhood trauma (a.k.a. bullying). But more of that another day, shutting off her laptop (finally).

"*Ooo*...you're gonna get hooked up with Mee-Maw," Paula baby-talked to Cori, scooping down to her. "We'll make some popcorn, watch movies, and do our *nails*."

Cori leaped around in delight. "YAAAY!"

Jae'cy must've been thinking the same about her upcoming freedom as she pivoted back around and to the door, Paula shooting right in behind her for a bear hug.

Jae'cy patted Paula's back lightly a few times then lowered her arms. "Ma, I love you, but I gotta go. It starts in thirty minutes, and you know how traffic is."

Arielle couldn't help but to think that for someone who was presumably living their (famed) passion, her face and tone seemed more like a child going to school.

Paula lightly slapped Jae'cy's tush, Arielle cutting her eyes back away briefly.

"You got this," Paula attested, showing her own backside. "And got it from the best."

"Thanks, I'll keep that in mind when hard times come, and I'm on music video sets," Jae'cy sputtered out a sarcastic chuckle.

"Good luck, Hitta!" Elise supported.

"Break legs, Mommy!" Cori sprung up, flinging her handheld game console onto (thankfully) her backpack, which turned the room's initial gasps to chuckles.

*Yeah, I could do the same to Elise's for getting me into this mess.* Arielle slipped her laptop into her backpack. When she peered up again at the room, Jae'cy was bending down to accept Cori's affectionate wrap around her neck.

"Thank you, baby," Jae'cy responded, then kissed her little one on the cheek. "*Mm*WAH."

Just then, with her grandbaby wrapped in someone else's brief attention, Paula's attention picked up on the sound of Arielle's zipping backpack.

"Oh! I'm so rude, forgive me."

*Damn.* Arielle shuffled internally; she was *really* trying to be low-profile. Always. And this weekend was increasingly working against her attempts.

Paula then made an intentional look at the rising Jae'cy. "I already told this freshly thirty-year-old here about your midlife crisis that's got you *stayin'* trying to be twenty-nine."Jae'cy turned her head slightly in Arielle's direction.

When Arielle met her eyes, there was that microsecond of silent awkwardness that two introduced young people always gave one another. Then whoever was the less socially inept (or at least somewhat less rude) party would say something...

"You're now in the *Dirty* Thirty club?"

Arielle nodded, delivered a mellow grin.

"Happy birthday." It was a courteous line but a very casual-cool delivery.

Therefore, Arielle decided to attempt social appropriateness for once in her life. And simply, equitably said, "Thank you, thank you."

"*NOW...*" Paula folded her arms with another pan over Jae'cy. "See how she just stands in that rather than running backward to somethin' that's outta reach?"

"Yeah-yeah," Jae'cy simply, loosely agreed as she affectedly jogged to the front door. "Okay, bye." And was gone.

"That chile," Paula exhaled, then nuzzled up playfully against Cori's face. "How you keep her in check, Cee-Cee. Hmm?"

Cori giggled.

Pulling her backpack on, Arielle suddenly recalled (involuntarily, subconsciously) something Juliana had felt the random need to tell her in one of her fangirlin' shares: "She's different from her momma. Spotted her at a low-key party I went to before. She kinda carries herself more…chill, slightly more mature it looks like than most people our age. But she's…cool. She cool."

*Yeah, looks like Juliana was right again.*

Jae'cy also appeared to be inexplicable, mysterious…And behind money-makin' romances, what Arielle enjoyed most were mysteries. Really wanted to explore that genre in her new stories, in fact.

*'Cause romance is out for me right now…*Yep, instantly, Arielle was up and for the door. That door…

*But the current mystery is, why do I now feel uneasy like I did coming home after my book signing a few days ago?*

♡ 5

AND JUST LIKE THAT, AFTER SOME MUCH-NEEDED ALONE TIME IN HER HOTEL—almost all of which she'd spent working and appropriately informing a shocked Kimesha of this new side work—she was right back in Paula's den the next afternoon. This would be a very quick session, given that Arielle had a flight and Paula had an engagement.

Elise and Paula were locked on the words sprawled across Paula's computer screen, a Google Doc from Arielle. Nine pages of everything Paula had requested, and been delivered.

Paula looked up at the idly standing Arielle, who had been eying the wall clock across the way. The door that she hoped to soon open and leave out of. No knocks to the two ladies, but Arielle really needed a break.

"So, I hope you know that you're now officially on my freelance team," Paula told her.

Arielle inhaled deeply but humbly chuckled. "Uh...okay. Thanks."

Paula looked back at Elise, who only said what she'd been saying since day one: "Told ya... And *now*, I'm tellin' you something else." She nudged her head at the wall clock.

Arielle seized the moment to quietly zip up her backpack.

Paula popped up. "Oh, shoot! RIGHT, the charity ball!" She glanced back at Arielle as she landed a socked foot on the first step—and Arielle's Pumas headed for front door. "I'll be in touch regarding next steps. Keep that phone on you."

Arielle revealed her phone, with a hushed "Yes, ma'am," which made Paula and Elise chuckle. And speaking of the phone:

*4:00!*

Her flight left in an hour and a half. She quickly requested a pick-up in her Lyft app, hand hitting the doorknob. But the knob twisted out of Arielle's slack grip. She stepped back just in time as Jae'cy entered.

Jae'cy paused, looked at her, with a subtle, tension-reactive widened eye.

Arielle nodded loosely, stepping aside.

"Cee-Cee baby!" Saved by Paula, who was now calling out in the middle of the staircase. "She's here."

Cori came prancing in with her backpack from another unseen room around the corner of the dining room-adjacent wall. "Mommy!"

As Jae'cy bent down in her white Jordans, velour hooded jogging suit, and side-parted ponytail (*Very '90s "round the way,"* Arielle noted), opening her arms, another person stepped inside, all astute cleanliness to his frame, with perfect dewiness to his face.

Paula tipped her head back as the man entered. "Looks like we're both just in time to have *enough* time for this quick magic makeover. How was the ride?"

"Crazy jampacked as usual," the man who must've been her makeup artist easily exhaled as he revealed a MAC cosmetics carry-all.

"*Hey,* Miss J," he addressed Jae'cy as he made his way to the staircase.

"*Heyyy,* Mister Reese," she singsonged back smoothly while guiding Cori to the door.

But Paula remained square on the steps as Reese continued up, looking at Jae'cy.

Arielle glanced down at her buzzing phone. *YES. A Lyft's five minutes away.* And then, in a quick text reply to Sinead:

*Nope still don't need it. Because I'm leav—*

"*So?*" Paula fished.

Jae'cy hid a grin, looking back over her shoulder. "I got the part."

"Told you," Paula said, throwing an air kiss, to which the recipient wrinkled up her nose. "Love you. We'll talk later. 'Cause now *I* gotta go." As she trucked up the rest of the stairs, . "And lock the door behind you!"

Jae'cy sarcastically departed, "Thanks, because I was thinkin' of just leavin' it wide open."

And open it was.

Arielle quietly sliding outside, with an exit nod at Elise. She exhaled as she touched the pathway.

"Oh! Can we get donuts, Mommy?"

"*Emmm...*We'll see."

Arielle instantly saw to it to walk a little bit quick—

"She's a trip, right?"

Arielle knew who *she* was and what Jae'cy meant. She inhaled deeply, then turned around.

Jae'cy was strolling, a settled walk as Cori bounced alongside. *Still cool,* Arielle confirmed—with a...flutter (???) in her belly. *Well, yeah, that happens when you don't grab breakfast...*

Arielle pulled her backpack strap up on her shoulder, even though it hadn't fallen.

Just like Jae'cy's mouth hadn't. Instead, it rose in one corner, faintly.

*But actresses have many faces, right?* Arielle tried to put the observer in her away and match the platonic face looking at her, beside a black-on-black Range Rover Sport in the driveway, to which Cori was now skipping.

"I hope she didn't scare you," Jae'cy joked casually with a little chuckle.

*Em, smart car taste, too.* Arielle silently admired its sleek black rims, which she knew had a pretty solid yet rational price tag. But she grinned. "Oh, no. Reminds me of home, all of my aunties."

As Jae'cy loosely lifted an eyebrow, Arielle noticed for the first time how lushly big her brown eyes were. *Okay, that's enough, Elle.*

"You're from Saint Louis, too?"

"Detroit. But Midwest recognizes Midwest," Arielle replied evenly...glancing down at her cell phone:

*Your Lyft driver was reassigned*
*?!?*

Arielle hoped she'd make it to the airport in time.
But alas, Arielle now knew her wish for instant departure (and to not analyze) were futile. So...*le sigh...* "I hear that lil' twang in you all's voices, too."

"Yeah-yeah," Jae'cy admitted with an eyeroll, contrasted by a proud, full smile. "My friends always tease me, like, 'Say soda. See, you don't even sound right when you do it.'"

*But you sure sound like a chatterer.* It was another surprise to Arielle—not in a bad way. Just a new mystery.

And indeed, Jae'cy suddenly twirled her car keys with an indiscriminate look off in the distance: the age-old blasé female body language. She had it down to a science. Because with her almond-shaped eyes atop of commanding cheekbones, and a leggy, full body, she most certainly had more than enough suitors (of *all* persuasions) in her face every day.

"I've been here all my life, but practically all of my family is in Saint Louis, and I'd go every summer growin' up, so..."

"Keyword: summer. That's why I had to move from Detroit to somewhere with more sun than ice. Well, until Lake Mead begins to pack its own bags."

When Jae'cy looked at her questioningly, Arielle said, "Vegas."

Then, *there* came silence.

And then, Arielle's Lyft pulled up.

Arielle peeped the now-open Range Rover as Cori relentlessly worked on the seatbelt in her backseat booster. Then she looked back again at Jae'cy, and they tipped their heads.

Arielle almost chuckled at the timing, but stopped as she swore she saw that same small widening of Jae'cy's eyes. "Uh, congrats on the role."

"Thank you," Jae'cy replied. Coolly. As Arielle expected.

And as she headed off while Cori struck her painted fingernails out to Jae'cy, who began tightening the girl's buckle strap...

"Look what Mee-Maw did!"

"*Ooo. Very* cute."

...Arielle shivered as she touched the metallic back door of the Lyft. Even though it was Cali in September, not Detroit or Saint Louis— or any other place in the Midwest.

She settled in the backseat as the Lyft driver, a young light-skinned Black guy, squinted his equally fair hazel, light-flickering irises to a blinding sight that wasn't the sun right then. "So, this her spot, huh?" he commented, noting Jae'cy more than Jae'cy's Range Rover as she got into the driver's seat. "With the matte Gammas, too?! She*EEez.*"

Ironically, Arielle felt certain that he was from Detroit, the Midwest himself. She heard it all in his tone.

Finally, he came back down to Earth, his Cherokee, and his passenger in the back seat, beginning to pull off. "LAX?"

"Yeah."

And that was a 'yeah' specifically for his second question, not telling him that his first was incorrect—because who knew what stalkers lurked out here.

*But Jae'cy knows the difference between glitter and real gold by now.* With her being more of a LA resident than a Midwest native like Arielle and this driver. That could be another reason for her "screening" kind of vibe. Who knew.

But what Arielle did know was that she was finally headed to the airport, getting back to her *own* stomping ground.

*So, Elle? The journalistic, editorial side of you from your past life, the one you were so ready to get away from? Yeah, act like you remember that.*

♡ 6



BUT THE WEEKEND STILL FOLLOWED HER, RIGHT INTO HER LIVING ROOM, as she took her hard-earned seat in front of her laptop to play some Solitaire like the old lady she was before starting this new manuscript. Maybe she'd call it *Bamboo and Other Things Not to Do.* Since her ex was no longer a person in her mind.

All columns were suited and booted in color and ascending order. Just a final card to place down—

On Juliana's forehead that popped up (in front of racks of liquor) on the laptop screen. *"Heyyy,* Melle-O girl!"

Yep. Another nickname.

"Glad to see that your antisocial behind is alive and home. But now, *I'M* about to be dead. *'Caaause…"*

Juliana showed her cell phone on this self-imposed webcam call she was conducting during downtime at the bar, revealing a post on Paula's Instagram: a snapshot of Arielle's marketing copy in its Google Doc on Paula's laptop, with Arielle's name visibly showing as the Doc owner. Arielle silently read the post's caption:

*Working on the final touches for something SUPER big #comingsoon #blkexcellence #liveyourlife #EverlastingYoung #andyesiwasthinkinofmygirlChakawhilecreatingthis*

"O-*KAY,* cuh!" Juliana glance-examined the photo again. "Oo, WAIT! Did you meet her—?!"

"I met her daughter," Arielle flatly said.

Juliana enlarged her glee; Arielle downgraded her gaze. But Juliana still caught it—even through the damn screen. And she cheesed slower, slicker. "You followin' her now, too?"

Just as Tish in the peanut gallery popped up on Arielle's phone in a WhatsApp call with a simple impish smile and a point to the very same Paula post on her computer screen behind her.

Arielle practically spat her Lipton out while starting up a new round of Solitaire. *Man, is everyone celebrity-obsessed???! I thought you didn't even like "soft" R&B, Tish?* So, Tish, exit stage left. Arielle swiped her away (one troll was more than enough). *Now, back to the first one.* "I'm a writer. It's not part of my mystique."

"Elle, come *ONNN,"* Juliana bemoaned.

"Allow me to explain to you for the fiftieth time: The social interaction I've just had? For you, it was a weekend. For me, it was a weekend to last me the rest of the year's weekends. And it will."

No response surprisingly... Arielle peered over from her new game...

...to find Juliana now showing a just-made Story/post—on Jae'cy's Insta:

*Calling all marketing/writer professionals: Show me what ya got!*
*Plz* 

Then Juliana (a.k.a. @JuliDaJewel) slid her finger down and pointed to a comment on the post: **Scan it. Now.**

*JuliDaJewel*     *Check out Arielle Smith @ElWordSmith*

Arielle let the current Solitaire card fend for itself, maximizing Juliana's literal screen time so they could see one another *very* clearly. "Delete it. Now."

Juliana refreshed the post. "Re-*laaax*. The girl asked for some marketing—"

But then she paused. Because her comment had disappeared.

She shot her eyes back at Arielle, who leaned back in her seat with a pacified stare and a sip of her Lipton as she logged out of Juliana's Instagram account. *Yeah, marketing's MY field; bartending's yours. So, you just focus on fixing people's martinis over there and not my deficient social life over here.* "Forgot you had me promote your birthday party last year, huh?"

Juliana rolled her eyes with a cackle of defeat. "I can't believe you saved my login!"

"You play too much," Arielle countered.

"The only one playin' is YOU! This is about your name and brand!" She chuckled to a floored decrescendo. "*Giiirl!* She probably doesn't even check all of her comments anyway. None of them do."

But Arielle wasn't smiling.

Juliana shook her head slowly, more solemn now. "Elle, you *really* have to stop the whole fatalistic thing. If she noticed it, she noticed it...." She paused her speech temporarily—but not her gaze. Waiting until Arielle slid her eyes back over from the new columns of cards on her screen, all out of order, currently out of her control.

"She probably already has before today, anyway..." Juliana instigated in her conclusion, with her own swig of a Blackberry IZZE.

Arielle sniggered—but it was low, weak, exasperated. She knew what her cousin was trying to imply not so discreetly and she was not having it. Even if Jae'cy did more than likely see Arielle's non-straightness, so what? If the girl wasn't bi or something herself, more than likely many of her friends and network were, since she lived in Cali. She was just looking for some creative help…that Arielle wasn't looking to extend right now.

"Girl, let me free you from this grand five minutes of captivity before you contaminate me with your vibe even through this damn Wi-Fi. I can't get my future baby daddy with these affirmations you be vibratin'."

"You had one but cut him out of your future. Remember?" Arielle knew how to end this chat *real* quick.

Now, Juliana's vibe did drop—along with her characteristic bombastic tone. "Don't start…"

"I've never seen a guy like Rashad so intent about you—or your de-*PLOR*-able living room. You know you appreciated—"

"What I *don't* appreciate, like I openly tell everyone, is anyone crampin' my style. So that hashes that."

Arielle didn't bother. Juliana didn't want to hear about her ex-boyfriend of five years, the longest relationship she'd ever had…which ended in a marriage proposal that she ghosted. *Because someone crampin' your style wouldn't keep your home spick and span the way you want it. The way you've had it for so long.*

"Well then, me and my vibe are done. With you and your other human friends."

Juliana practically snorted. "Ha. Not for long."

Arielle stiffened. Juliana twirled a pen in her hand with a new cock of her eyebrow.

"*You* betta manifest not havin' to come to some type of launch party in the next few weeks," Juliana informed.

Arielle knocked her head back against her office chair, but unfortunately remained conscious, and Juliana fully released her laugh. "*Yes*, girl! Us LA people have a networking event even when you get a background role on a three-hundred-viewed YouTube series!"

With that, Juliana was gone.

Alas, Arielle was now free of the chaotic assault to which she'd just been subjected. But her own remaining chaos was staring right back at her on the screen: those unorganized columns of cards.

She began to slide one down—

*Buzz…*

She felt like a damsel in a thriller who'd thought she'd made her grand escape only to spot the back door unlocked. Or a bootleg remake of *Scream*. *Scary Movie*. One of dem.

On her cell phone was a new message alert (from Instagram):

*Your work comes to life next month young lady. Oct 29 (also my bday!), 6 p, Los Caballos. Bring a friend if you'd like!*

*How about a stand-in?* Like they did in Hollywood? Maybe Juliana.

She decided to leave the message unanswered for now. She could AT LEAST control how soon to respond to Paula's Everlasting Young launch party invite. She was genuinely happy for the birthday girl, but going out to celebrate that happiness? Yeah, not so much. And with that, Arielle tended to her game.

Er.

*RING.*

Make that Tish's phone call.

*This girl is relentless.* On the third ring, Arielle accepted.

"You know, since we've been outta college, you've gotten rude as hell."

"My bad, the connection dropped."

"Why you ain't tell me you're workin' with celebs now?!"

"You follow her?" Arielle was very confused as to why the all things rap, Freddie Gibbs–luvin' Tish had any interest in following—

"It's Paula YOUNG!"

*Of course.*

"And my girl plays her out every day. But look—All Imma say is this: I don't know what lucky stars lined up for you for this opportunity, but don't lose it. There's a reason for it, AI."

"People get married and become prophets, gotta love it." Arielle wearily grinned.

"There's a reason," Tish simply repeated her adage.

"Then I'll tell her *you're* the one who wants to sing back-up on her next album."

"Because you'll be too busy tryin' some lines out with her daughter in a minute, huh?"

Arielle bared teeth to the unseen Tish, who breezily chuckled.

"Ight, enough of that. *When* are we snagging the tickets?! You KNOW those things sell out fast each year. And I just checked this morning, and next year's IS sold out already! Time's wast—!"

"I bought them."

"…Yeah?"

"This morning…For after next year. 'Cause—"

"They sold out waitin' on your stallin' self, fool!"

Both laughed.

"You excited?"

*Who knows what I am right now.* Besides having more lined up in this short passing of time, an *interesting* time, to say the least. "We'll see in two years."

In one year, who knew what would happen, let alone two.

"Well, this is a start," Tish confidently stated.

*Wasn't that the truth.*

"Yeah."

*But to what?*

## ♡ 7

WELL, THE QUICKER, CLEARER START WAS A NEW MANUSCRIPT.

All dedicated writers had their own productive, creative systems. Some were midday writers; others rose with the birds. Arielle didn't technically wake with the birds so much as the birds came to join her at her living room-office windowsill like clockwork each 4 a.m., after her night of typing. She was the night owl.

In school, and later her corporate days, she'd always had to force herself to get up at the crack of dawn like the morning birds.


But she still had one aspect of the Paula job to fulfill. One that unfortunately had her hitting the airport rather than her pillow at four.

*This damn—*

"Party! Party. Party-issa-party. *AYYY!*"

At least someone else was excited.

Now, outside in the night-lit downtown skyrise where tons of cars and limos were, she just wanted the Hennessey stench that had just infiltrated twelve inches into her face to slide back six.

When it finally did, in its Louis Vuitton, gold cufflinked and chained (and grilled), bearded body, Arielle didn't immediately scurry to a safe space. Because there wasn't one.

Outside this launch party's tall site was Balenciaga, Gucci, Louboutin—and that was just the high-profile names by clothes. The bodies they donned were equally high-profile: all kinds of musicians, actors, reality stars (...)....And then Paula, sashaying right on over in her midnight-blue Alexander Wang V-neck gown and diamonds.

Arielle decided that if this thing pressed on too late into *actual* midnight, which it more than likely would, she was sneaking up out of here. She had her writing system, after all.

But right now? Paula was pulling her toward the red carpet rollout photo spot, about forty feet away. "*Oooh,* okay," she voiced favorably en route, as she scanned Arielle's black satin dress shirt, tapered, slim-fit slacks, and Bordeaux Aldo oxfords. "Someone cleans up nice!"

*Yeah, because typically, right now, I'd be in sweatpants or gym shorts in front of my laptop.*

Arielle's outfit definitely wasn't luxury, but it was evidently worthy of a spotting with the high-profiler, as Paula landed them in a melee of cameras on the red carpet—along with many other stars. "This is the *writer!*" Paula boasted.

Arielle stuck her hands in her pants pockets but nodded collectedly, not so much at any one of them individually but rather indiscriminately, the whole rather than the parts. An old anxiety-reducing public speaking trick she'd mastered in high school.

But even she recognized some of them: one IG model in a bikini of a dress, and an actor her mom crushed over in some soap opera when she was a kid. She'd be sure to report to her mom that he looked to be maintaining his age (judging by the black, non-receding hair and tight stomach) and his bachelor card (no marriage band)—yet had maybe lost two inches of height (Did the camera make people taller, too?). And—

Her vision was halted by camera flashes. A flood of them.

She didn't know which way she was looking at that point, but she *did* feel another face. A face peering artfully at her—

*FLASH!*

What had to be a thousand eye blinks later, now out of the spotlight in one sense, Arielle had sudden Instagram follows she didn't ask for. Primarily, one came from Elise just as they were stepping off the red carpet for the venue.

"As you know, or are about to, I'm tryna get like you. So I'm wondering, since you seem to have a successful blueprint with your books, if you'd mine helping me with my first..."

"Yeah, sure," Arielle obliged. She wondered if the woman knew how uncomfortable she was, and that talking books would put her back in her comfort zone.

"THANK you." Elise halted at the venue doors and made the most extreme, indebted bow that Arielle couldn't help but chuckle at.

Then, who woulda thought it, her mom Elizabeth's soap opera beau—Gary Perkins, he greeted her as—was introduced by way of Paula and then made his own proposition. She'd be sure to inform Elizabeth that it was: "Some magic, to be honest." More specifically, he had an upcoming limited sketch series on YouTube—more details to be discussed later.

Eventually inside, Arielle found a place to chill, by a wall next to some others who were in their own buzz-filled world. Looking across the large venue, filled with Paula, her team, and close family and friends, she saw a huge wall screen playing the polished footage of the Everlasting Young promo video. The opening revealed all shapes, sizes, ages, and creeds adorning themselves in fragrance, including Jae'cy. Awaking, walking, working, and partying...to the last scene: a red carpet landing on, of course, Paula—and her closing words: "You've arrived, everlasting young. Like me."

Arielle couldn't lie, the video came out great. Including her script, which she had been a bit uncertain would succeed, because it had been a while since she'd written business-oriented creative copy. But a story was a story! And not to brag, but if she couldn't do anything else right, she could devise some fiction.

At the video's end, some scenes and sights of this very night played out over backing music (and Arielle thanked GOD and/or the videographers that she didn't pop up). Dancing, convening, and laughing over drinks; Paula stopping for quick chatter, girl-hyping, or requested selfies; red-carpet snapshots of various guests.

Then Paula with her gelled bun and chandelier earrings, Jae'cy behind her, talking to a handsome media reporter with a beat face:

"How are you, *Everlasting Young?*"

"*There* you go. You know how to conduct on these carpets."

"Indeed, *yesss,*" the reporter cooed back, glancing from Jae'cy back to Paula. "Tell us: How are you feelin' tonight?!"

"I feel great! Happy, *excited.* This creation has been a true labor of love that I hope everyone else will love, too."

"I know that's right. And most importantly, what are you wearing, Miss Paula?"

Paula did a swivel in her gown. "Oh, just a lil' Alex Wang. My boo."

*Dang, since you 'conduct,' at some point in this conversation, are you gonna ask anything to—?*

"And *you,* Miss Paula's Daughter?"

Jae'cy stepped up a bit, her own impressive outfit coming into view: a black, long-sleeved satin gown. She gave a playful shoulder shimmy. "Can't go wrong with Saint Laurent. You know?"

"*Oooh,* okay. It's like that?" The reporter good-humoredly encouraged her bravado.

"Please. She got *THAT* from me," Paula insisted...but not quite focusing Jae'cy's way.

"*Yesssss,* she get it from her momma!" the reporter proclaimed.

Jae'cy smiled at the entertained reporter...then slid a look at Paula with a split-second drop of her smile.

*Em, looked like a slight side-eye there,* Arielle observed, deeper than the others around the space who had just easily laughed like the reporter.

"Both of you beautiful ladies I'm sure come from a line of fine MOMMAS!"

**Scan the beginning of Chapter 7.**

*But looks like a sour note might've just popped up for Miss Paula, too.* Arielle spotted a faint shuffle of Paula's stance and a sharper smile.

"I see it in y'all, the fierceness and love!" The unaware reporter fanned a hand at them, and they both just shared an appreciative smile.

And as Arielle started copping feels on the ninety-degree border of the wall giving way to a hallway...

"And what are you doing these days?" That was directed to Jae'cy.

"Em, let's see. Right now, I'm beginning a new film..."
But Arielle *had* to check her phone:
*11:00!!!*


She was going to the hotel...right after going to the restroom.

Striding past designer-laced stars and behind-the-scenes faces, Arielle found herself still humored by many of them not looking as spectacular or tall in person.

Above her head appeared ceiling signage designating her to one direction for the ladies room versus the right side...

Set her eyes back down, about to turn lef—
Dang.
Another dead end.

Not by wall but by person: Jae'cy. Bent down behind a plant vase doing...*something.*

Arielle could've turned around, but she really had to go to the restroom, which was just beside her.

As Arielle got closer, she became increasingly curious—and amused. Jae'cy couldn't be sneaking in some white rock up her nostril, right out in the open, could she? (Arielle had seen it all since moving to the West Coast.) No, she (and her mauve-polished, one-inch fingernails) was feeling for something on the multicolored carpet. The dim-lit ambiance didn't help.

"Y'all do Easter egg hunts a lil' different in Cali, huh?"

Jae'cy halted her hand, lifting her head. And a moment of natural surprise played out. But Arielle thought she might have seen some upward motion in Jae'cy's mouth just before the girl squinted at the ground.

"Unfortunately, this one is for something a little bit dissimilar..." Jae'cy vaguely shared.

At this point, the suspense was just unmatched, and Arielle just *had* to uncover what was up...or down.

She crouched to the ground, joining her in the investigation. Suddenly, she pointed at an area around the base of a large planter. "Is this it?"

Arielle quietly noted Jae'cy slide her squinting gaze over to spot what Arielle's finger was aimed at.

But Arielle could see it all: that micro gesture and a clear, thin, circular disc.

Jae'cy moved forward to the section of the floor being addressed, darn near her nose almost touching the ground, she was so close. *Oh yeah. She's really on hard times.* Arielle had to turn away to dispel her amusement.

Jae'cy clicked her tongue as cool confirmation, a tilt of her head forty-five degrees in Arielle's direction at least. "*Annnd* I have no way of cleaning it…You must have that good ole twenty-twenty."

"Yeah, somethin' like that."

"Must be nice," Jae'cy stated as she picked up the lens and scrunched up her nose at the collected specks of dust in it.

"Yeah…especially when I remember to have my contact solution on me."

Jae'cy shot her 10/20 eyes up first, then the rest of her head followed the remaining forty-five degrees to Arielle's face…This time, a mellow simper showed on both sides of Arielle's mouth.

Jae'cy shook her head—but cracked into a chuckle as she slowly rose and inspected her lens.

"The older I get, the more I consider Lasik," Arielle said as she stood back up, too.

"I'm sayin'. This is a real-life struggle."

"But nothing like *that* one."

Jae'cy tracked Arielle's side-eye at a rickety lady whose heels were walking her like a puppy. She let out a discernible halt of breath before bowing her head away from the poor woman.

"This place has treated me *much* better, though," Arielle continued. "I've added like fifty connects to my Insta."

Jae'cy's smile ascended more. "I'm surprised I didn't see Paula's busybody self pullin' you around all night."

"Your mother is a real one. I haven't really been doing the whole content marketing thing anymore since leavin' the nine-to-five life, but I'll never turn down a side hustle."

"Right?!" Jae'cy had a full smile, cheeky and childlike almost. Arielle conjectured that it was one she didn't show often, because this was her first time seeing it. "*Multiple* streams of income. That's my next move, too." Then her mouth retracted inward again. Just like that. "Once I get to building it."

"What are you trying to do?" Arielle inquired, inexplicably deciding to add on to a conversation for the first time in her life, elongating it.

"I went to culinary school," Jae'cy explained, and Arielle thought her tone seemed higher, livelier than when announcing her audition. Then it dropped below her lower feminine register for a dramatic aside. "I'm not only gifted in mimicking. You need *all* kinds of hustles out here." She tipped her head at the space around them, the designer-coated people. Including the wobbling wild Tom Fords that had gotten closer...

"Accurate—"

"Well, FINALLY caught up to you!"

Oop. The head tip must've been the accidental dog whistle.

Jae'cy slowly turned her head, Arielle even slower, to the struggling lady and her massive beam at Jae'cy. Arielle slid her eyes down from the pounds of foundation to those six-inch heels.

And without even looking Arielle's way, although Arielle peered hers, Jae'cy's naturally high yet paradoxically soft cheekbones slowly arose a bit, all the while keeping an intentional, collected eye on the woman.

"Miss Gorgeous! You and your momma are the little celebrities tonight...among *us* celebrities!" The woman cackled. "I saw that recent cameo you made in...what was that? 'Days to Depend On?'"

"Mm-*hm*. Yes, ma'am," Jae'cy confirmed, with a way that was subtly unique, gave her an underlying difference from a lot of their female peers.  It was the polished, polite smile she'd just delivered that was more customary to a forty-something's face, rather than the thirty-something one it was presenting on right now. Maybe being the only child, under the wing of her mother. Matter of fact, the thirty-something's entire currently Saint Laurent gown–adorned body was dressed like a more mature crowd, but the body itself wasn't quite as discreet. Fully exhibiting ready curves.

*Yes, ma'am. Yes, inde—*

Arielle had to shift her eyes away to random passersby to turn off her natural investigator mode.

"You *GO*, girl! And your little lady is getting *so* BIG!"

"Thank you, thank you. Yes, she *isss*..." Jae'cy drew that out with a head tilt in a way that seemed to suggest that the little lady was also getting to be something *else*.

"Well, I won't keep you. Just wanted to say hello. I'll be seeing you at some more of these."

Jae'cy gave a civil smile, with teeth this time. "Alright, take care."

And she was gone, And as Arielle cut her gaze away briefly from Jae'cy's to hide a grin, a scratch to the freshly shaven back of her undercut head...

Jae'cy summarized: "LA. *Anyways*. You write stories, right?"

"Yeah. Just wrapped up a press tour on my latest book."

"So, *maybe...*" Jae'cy chewed her lip in consideration. "If you're game for connect number fifty-*one...*"

Arielle tipped her head, a quick grin. "Most def."

*MOST DEF?!!!!!!!!!!!!!!!*

*This is not how you get solo time, Elle.* At most, she'd have an annual two-month book promo run from Kimesha's snagged deals. Autograph signings here, an interview or two there at a local book shop— or NPR if she was feelin' fancy. But her largest job was just sitting with her laptop and Lipton five months straight before moving on to her editor, Rachelle Albertson.

But *something,* as she watched Jae'cy pull out her cell phone from her matching black Saint Laurent clutch (it seemed to be her color), made her cool with this. With an equally cool, chill person.

"My momma's gonna start preachin' about this sooner or later anyway. Like 'You keep sayin' you wanna do this, so do it—*and* stick with it!'"

*The girl was right;* she could imitate perfectly.

Arielle began giving her the details. "Okay... It's 'El—'"

"WordSmith."

Arielle looked over at her with a cock of her brow. Jae'cy halfway grinned as she showed her cell phone, a comment from IG on her marketing request post:

*Check out Arielle Smith @ElWordSmith*

Arielle winced. She wasn't an actress herself, but she was about to die trying.

*And now, Juliana most DEFINITELY would. I TOLD her not to—!*

"Yeah, I remember someone hypin' you up, then disappearing. But little do they know, it doesn't disappear from my notifications."

*Of course.*

"Oh, and this helped, too..." On her phone screen now was Paula's most recent Instagram post, revealing the group red carpet photo from tonight, everyone (including Jae'cy—and Arielle) tagged with the caption closing it all out:

*@ElWordSmith This young lady is a true godsend and my team is only continuing to build from here!*

Arielle blinked wryly.

"Yeah, she's put you *all* the way on blast now." Jae'cy's surprisingly brightening eyes made it just a *wee* bit less demoralizing.

"Just like she used to at my school concerts, shouting my name and clapping—during the *middle* of my clarinet solos!"

Arielle grinned, relieved that the attention had passed without too much suspicion. "Aw man."

"*Then* tried to persuade me earlier today into bein' okay with her tryna pull a similar stunt tonight, with her whole birthday song and cake cutting."

Arielle hoped the stretch of her spine didn't show up on the outside, the pseudo-journalist in her peaking again. "It's your birthday, too?"

"Last week," Jae'cy confirmed casually with a lackadaisical roll of her eyes. "But unlike my mother and her Gemini Rising, I know how to keep some things from the front-page news like a *true* Scorpio."

"Yeah, ALWAYS hidin'!"

*Okay, yep. Time for the restroom.*

With the help of her heels, Jae'cy looked a little over Arielle's head at a young woman decked in a long-sleeve, belly-bearing shirt and pants set, heels, and full face and hair, courtesy of layered extensions. A naturally pretty girl, but her hair and heavily contoured face kind of distracted from it, in Arielle's furtive opinion, whereas Jae'cy's own lightly concealed face and classic pulled-back hair only accentuated her appeal.

But Arielle's clandestine assessment was quickly pushed aside as she observed the internal dialogue of the woman at *her* appearance: quickly running over Arielle's tapered edges, nose and labret piercings, low ponytail, then back up to her bare face. In quick conclusion, this woman's gaze fell somewhat...but with a flicker of something. Arielle, though catching it, just tipped her head cool. She knew what that micro gesture meant, saw it almost every day in other female faces like hers. Saw it in all of her exes. And was well over it: superficial fascination.

The woman breezily completed her perusal and sashayed over to Jae'cy, hip-bumping her. "I've been lookin' for you, trick, 'cause I *just* found Alonzo up in this mob. You know, my old photographer friend from art school with the editorial gig at *Mahogany* for that film issue they're finally about to roll out?"

"Girl, what inside knowledge *don't* you have?" Jae'cy giggled.

"You'll *neee*-ver know," her friend singsonged, taking one of Jae'cy's forearms as her own arm whipped up her cell phone for a selfie. "Guess where I and this beauty—*JUST* like her mother contrary to some of y'all haters' delusions—are?"

"For starters, how about not having the clue in the video?" Jae'cy piped in, nudged her eyebrows up at the ceiling restroom signage—that included the venue's name—above them.

The woman's eyes bulged as she tracked the cue then chuckled.

"You stay gettin' things that should *stay* behind the scenes into *the scene.* Good thing you leave the real camera work to friends," Jae'cy kidded, giggled to completion.

"Okay, looks like you keep getting paged, Miss Carter, so…"

Arielle started to backpedal. To the restroom.

Jae'cy stopped her with an easy grin and a tip of her head at the woman beside her. "Oh, yeah. This hot mess is Breyah McClerran. She's my stylist–slash–assurance that I'll stay relevant in Hollywood as *more* than 'Paula's daughter.'"

Breyah glanced over proudly, with a little jut out of a hip.

Arielle gave a nod.

"But yeah, I'll hit you up when I have everything ready," Jae'cy concluded.

Arielle nodded. "Cool." Much like Jae'cy had reverted to being.

And as Jae'cy headed away—arm in arm with Breyah, leading the way—Arielle couldn't help but exhale.

*Nothing but networks—and I'm just trying to find the exit…*

♡ **8**

SHE GOT TO IT, IN HER HOTEL ROOM, AS USUAL. WAS STILL UP IN THE EARLY A.M., as usual, typing up one final line to close out a chapter. Like all of her stories, the new one was pseudo-autobiographical in the sense of pulling from her real-life experiences. It was a writer rite: dropping in personal nuggets.

The latest nugget she'd revealed so far in this story?

Having a thing for noncommittal or otherwise emotionally unavailable women. But of course, it wasn't her. *Nooo,* it was her protagonist—in this case, Ash, short for Ashley.

The plot? Ash, a cremation tech, is trying not to turn into ashes herself after getting caught up with a woman who's overheard some law enforcement–involved underhanded information at a *gentleman's* club where she worked. Not to mention, in the past, the woman slept with a key person in the whole scheme: a critical person who more than likely is a cop and is now targeting Ash for what she might know about all of the mysterious bodies and their unsolved murders that had been piling into her crematory for the past six months. The six months since she's met the woman…

The name? *Ash Must Fall Down.* It was a thriller with themes of the unexpected and unknown needing to be tackled, no matter how uncomfortable.

As she yawned away from the laptop screen, her eyes connected with her cell phone. She stared at it.

*I should at least have professional courtesy…*

She opened her Instagram app and pulled up Paula's page, going to the post from just hours ago: the selfie with Paula. A few quick taps on the keypad produced:

*Couldn't have been more ecstatic to see this come to life!*

Short and to the point, but with an exclamation point to make it seem much more triumphant and agreeable than she felt on the inside. Corporate Grammar 101—which she'd thought she'd left behind for real narrative language and syntax.

But then she released a tight breath, for Paula was really easy to communicate with, and her project, too, was much more fun than the financial and consumer-packaged goods of her editorial days.

As she kept scrolling for who knew what reason after posting her comment, she hoped that the clientele list she'd suddenly gained wouldn't get any longer or more high-profile…but she did make a stop. It was technically a repost, according to Paula's caption that her eyes landed on:

*I'm sorry. But this memory HAD to come outta the vault. I STILL say I won!*

And then the original post caption:

*Who did it better??? #youngsyungmama or #youngGRANDmama #nationallazymomsday*

So naturally, Arielle looked at the corresponding bilateral collage photo. The left photo showed a silk-headscarved, PJed Paula in her large master bedroom king bed, beaming with open arms in the direction of her boyfriend, Kadeem (Arielle gathered that from the comments section), a fit, handsome older man who had to be a trainer (probably how they met). He was extending a smoothie…but it looked like her open arms were for Cori, behind him, Because she had the food tray with strawberry-dolloped French toast, egg whites, and two strips of turkey bacon. Cori was cheesing proudly.

The right photo showed Jae'cy in a booth at a diner, kissing a smiling Cori's forehead as she held a handmade card with the words "Have fun today, Mommy! Love, Cori." But there was someone else on the other side of Jae'cy, a guy who looked to be her age…and a bit of a clown. It was just something in his very toothy grilled grin, metal-studded eyeglass frames, and two big gold chains. Just…too much.

*Le sigh.*

Arielle dropped down to the comments for the *#youngsyungmama* versus *#youngGRANDmama* convo, beginning presumably with a relative based on the shared last name of Young:

*Honestly…(Still) looks like Cori won*

And Jae'cy responded underneath:

*Which means I did (AGAIN) #thatsYUNGMAMASbaby*

A slew of laughing and thumbs-up reactions ensued, and then a verdict was finally presented by Elise:

*Talk to 'em, Yung J!* 💪 *#allowhertoreintroduceherself*
*#sryboss #dontfireme #orcutmypay #weliveincali*
*#andmybestselleraintfinishedyet #norstarted*

Arielle smirked, then looked back up at Jae—
*Stop, you're acting like Juliana.*
So Arielle put the phone down.  More stalking would be creepy and at some point, the writer's temptation had to be shut off. Anyway, the sparrows were now here.
Plus, she had a flight home in just under six hours.


As she settled into her window seat, she looked down at her cell phone notifications. Sinead always made it a point to send her a threatening "Text me or I'm bringin' SWAT" message whenever Arielle traveled. The SWAT being her and her Smith & Wesson artillery team.

But Sinead's text wasn't what made her own snooping spree last night look less extra. Instead, as the final passengers boarded, one settling beside her, she was focused on a notification on an Instagram post she'd randomly made in passing a vinyl record shop (!) in the airport.  The particular album she'd spotlighted in her hand? *The Miseducation of Lauryn Hill.* The specific part of the album shown in the post image? Its track listing on the back cover, NOT the front cover. Her caption?

IYKYK Some of you may know what this is and how I feel about this. But do you know which is my favorite song on it? Whoever gives the right answer first, my gift to you will be a free signed copy of my latest release. (Okay, I'll give a hint: If you've read one of my earlier books, you'll know.)
#thinkijusttimetraveled
#sointhatcaseLAXcaniget30dollarsbackfromthisequallyridicouslypricedplaneti
cket #OhCalifornia #toknowyouistobeconfused
#icanttellwhichismoreoverpriced
#theplaneticketorthealbumbutdefinitelynotmybook #unlessitsinthisairporttoo
#midwestgirlinawildwestworld #iykyk

It wasn't her usual kind of post, when she actually posted at all. And it wasn't any ounce of profound (although Kimesha's ecstatic reaction would be "Amazing marketing!"). But a certain handle— @J_Carter—had reacted with a heartened like.

Granted, since Instagram showed followings' most recent posts in the live feed as soon as one hopped on their app, that wasn't anything profound either. But it did prove Juliana wrong about just how social media observant public figures really were.

…Especially when she saw a second like from Jae'cy on another post she'd made. Two months ago.

Granted, it was her second most recent post, since she only shared content maybe once every quarter or just before a book release ("NOT amazing marketing!"). But still, considering the post was a selfie of her and her now-ex at a Suns game, her attention rose.

Arielle couldn't help but laugh. One, had she *not* just done the same activity on Paula's social page just earlier this morning, viewing content out of just simple leisurely inquisitiveness? But even more, Jae'cy had unwittingly reminded her to put that Suns post (and then some) where it belonged.

She completed her mass deletion of all things exes just as the flight attendant was beginning the opening announcements—Arielle's cue to stow her phone and put her seat back.

And finally, she looked out at LA growing smaller and smaller as the blue sky rose, and her eyes shut.

♡ 9

AND ONCE ARIELLE HAD RETURNED HOME, SHE HAD SLEPT. HARD. So hard and good that it was pretty much the only highlight of that (subsequently quick) day. But she took advantage of it because she hadn't been booked with any business meetings by Kimesha.

However, soon she had to go back to adulting.

Starting with a video call from Kimesha, who was "just checking to see how the new work is going."

"Yep, already diving into the next chapter—"

"No, the *new* project...with the singer? Paula Young?"

"Oh, yeah," Arielle paused, then fiddled a random pen in her hand that she'd just picked up on her desk. "Actually, now I have *two*. Her and her..." She chuckled a bit. "Daughter."

"Oh, yeah? ...Jae'cy Carter."

Arielle would never understand this starstruck business...or at least, didn't want to.

Kimesha took a moment, inquisitiveness in full mode. "...And how's that going? Must be something new in that water over there that has you so people-chummy lately?"

As Arielle scanned the comments under the airport-prompted contest post on her laptop (because she knew Kimesha would be encouraging that next), she felt Kimesha's eyes on her. While responding to one follower's winning comment on said post to get their shipment details for the signed book, she just mustered up a sarcastic laugh. "Just taking on work as goodwill. They're actually a nice group of people. Looks like I still know how to write for marketing."

It wasn't enough. Clearly, as she looked back up at Kimesha and that same look.

"I see..."

*Do you?*

Because now, Arielle, was seeing something else as she continued her deflection via Instagram scrolling...right to one subject of Kimesha's current unspoken inquiry on her feed.

"Well, it's a bit refreshing, honestly. For a moment there, I was worried about my client's outside life. So, enjoy the rest of your day. Unless you have some more things to do for your LA...*friends*."

And with that, Kimesha was gone. *Le sigh.*

But there was still the post Arielle's attention had directed to;

Jae'cy was sharing a mango sorbet smoothie with Cori, both sipping from separate straws, but their shared almond eyes up and big at the camera. Arielle hadn't noticed until then how much they looked alike.

She paused a second in deliberation, then saw the five hundred other hearts as reactions...

Tapped on the heart (doin' it for the kids).

Then hit the X up outta there.


But that didn't put an end to what followed.

Someway, somehow, this became a pattern: Jae'cy liking a post (Arielle at a book signing), Arielle doing the same on one of Jae'cy's (Jae'cy behind-the-scenes, goofing off with castmates as the film she'd auditioned for began production). This meant that Arielle was now engaging more on social media! Kimesha "practically had a coronary when seein' you in my feed more!"

Before she knew it, she was flying back in to LA to work with Gary on the live sketch shoot in downtown LA that he'd propositioned to her at the Everlasting Young launch party. He knew this type of approach, a same-day sketch *with* writing, was a bit unconventional, but he wanted to create a new experience. And Elizabeth, as she informed Arielle over the phone en route, wanted his phone number. Arielle's goal on the other hand was simply to make her 11:40 p.m. flight after this gig.

But she'd taken on this writing favor, the four sketches Gary had assigned for her to write on set today, because any advertising proceeds Gary gained from the show's premiere views would go to a breast cancer charity in honor of his recently deceased sister.

At one point, she looked up from her phone during a mini-break. While Gary and two other actors enacted her latest lines on the set, lo and behold, Paula came waltzing in with Elise...and Jae'cy.

*Gary did mention "star-studded cameos,"* Arielle thought, and Paula was one of his friends in the industry. But Jae'cy?

Well...she *was* an actress. Arielle remembered their last meeting in the star-studded halls of Paula's Everlasting Young launch party. But instead of the high-profile garments of that night, this morning Jae'cy was in fitted French terry sweats, some Filas, an open cropped denim jacket, and straightened hair. The perfect kickback look. *Yep...*the waistband of the sweats kicking back, relaxing low on her—

"What's my lines, girl?!" Paula shouted as she hugged Arielle. Followed by Elise...

When Arielle peeled apart from her, Jae'cy was hanging mellow on the outer edge.

*Time for a hi, a nod, something, Elle.* Because Jae'cy had just given her a closed-mouth grin.

"What's goin' on?" Arielle opted for a simple greeting and nod.

"Deeper show biz education today," Paula enlightened, lightly hip-bumping Jae'cy. "Ain't that right?"

Jae'cy rolled her eyes, then chuckled. "Uh, *I'm* the actress. Just F.Y.I."

*But (yep, back to observation)* Jae'cy's second chuckle floated out a bit lighter, as if she was trying to play it cool rather than just *being* cool as usual. And trying to shake something else away?

"Well, today we *both* are the thespians. Let the best woman win," Paula ribbed back. "'Cause you musta forgot what music videos are."

"Good, at least *y'all* remember what your job is!" Gary chimed in as he came trotting over. He then looked to Arielle and her propped-open laptop with the next upcoming sketch's story-setting dialogue, based on the very general scenario Gary had given her: "a mom and her grown daughter—whose behind she can *STILL* whip."

And in this particular sketch's case, the ending would play on the adage, "I brought you into this world, and I can take you out." The actors would take all of Arielle's scriptwriting, quickly read it over, and then run with it, to reach the sketch's end through their wit and creativity.

As she watched the group walk off toward dressing rooms to prep for the sketch, she couldn't help but smirk because the ending, her ending to this scenario, was about to be *so* right...

Moments later, delivered in their contemporary costumes, Paula/Momma, Gary/Poppa, and Jae'cy/Grown Baby Girl. Paula sold it, striking out a hip at the set's kitchen counter while *death*-staring an eyebrow-cocking Jae'cy as Gary slide-exited stage left. Then, based on whatever unseen mother-daughter happenstance had just occurred—more than likely, a smart-mouth altercation—Paula gave the ominous words: "I *wish* you would try me."

And so, Jae'cy, in fact, tried her once again. "Whatchu gonna do?"

That simple line was performed with the most spot-on neck-rolling, eyebrow-cocking, and lip-smacking sass.

Arielle then watched her ending approach as Paula wound her hand behind her head—and not for a high-five. "Girl, I'll take you back to—"

"And cut!" Gary called out, signaling the quick costume and scene change. To which, all the actors jogged off the set, crew changed the scene to a hanging disco ball and set up strobe lights. This would be shown as a "live" jump cut in the published version, executed as an eye-blink special effects disappearance of Jae'cy followed by a jumping match cut appearance of the new set with the help of the editing team.

When Paula and Gary scurried by Arielle and hopped back onto the set in 'fros, bell-bottoms, and platforms, Paula came right back to that scolding, hand-cocked-back position. She then propelled the hand forward where Jae'cy would've been, essentially swinging into the air with such speed and force that her rear went into Gary.

"Careful, we've already got Baby Girl," Gary imparted with a grin.

As Paula gasped at her now round (prosthetic) stomach, Arielle whipped her head back to stream in a can of Lipton.

That was when Arielle caught someone in her peripheral: Jae'cy, strolling over in her own clothes again, plus a ponytail and a water bottle, eyes on Paula, Gary, and another actor engaged in their scene.

Arielle lowered her tea, gulped. She had planned on cutting out since Gary had told her she'd be free after this last sketch. But alas…

Jae'cy turned her head toward Arielle, who had to acknowledge that at least Jae'cy wasn't one of those overwhelming social types, and it was now only 8:30 p.m.

"So, *uhhhh*…who wrote me out so early?" Jae'cy came to a casual stop beside her and smirked.

Arielle skewed her mouth to hide her smile, with a little click of the tongue. "Sorry. Show business."

Jae'cy cracked into a chuckle, just a *wee* bit louder than Arielle had yet heard her laugh. "It's cool, I probably killed the jokes anyway. This is my first go at live sketch."

"What's your usual, like, genre?"

"So far?" Jae'cy thought, drummed her bottle cap with long fingernails. "Indies, dramas."

"Well, there's a first time for everything, right?" Arielle gazed at her. For her first time since meeting Jae'cy, since meeting anyone, being more uncomfortable with the possibility of *not* receiving a look back versus receiving it. A silent tap on her Lipton lid.

Then Jae'cy met her eyes, with a blink of her own dark eyes, Arielle still not having a read on them and the darkness of the studio not helping. "Yeah,…I guess so."

Arielle crossed her arms, turned her head back to the set with another click of her tongue. "Kinda like something else that you've yet to…" *Inform me of since your mom's launch party. And of exactly what the venture is and exactly how I'll play a part in helping you with it.*

Jae'cy, intuiting her verbal cue and body language, said, "I didn't forget."

"Okay, that's a wrap!" The AD came by, yanking off her headset. Arielle had even forgotten that the girl was there.

Then Paula and Gary came over, and Elise, emerging from the changing area, with a planner and bottled water.

Gary slapped a hand on Arielle's shoulder. "Thanks, good work!"

As Arielle tipped her head wordlessly with a quick grin, she could've sworn she felt a certain pair of eyes on her....

"Dinner, ladies?" Paula asked, scanning from Arielle to Gary. "And gent."

"Uh…"

Jae'cy interjected, "Ma, she probably has plans."

Arielle nodded to approve that message, with a modest smile. "A flight."

"Oo! Okay. Well, it was nice seeing you again. And I'm gonna send you the details for another quick little write-up I need for one of my new seasonal products. A spring mandarin and bergamot one. Hear?"

"This one won't be followed by another party attendance, will it? Because I preferably would like to keep that part of marketing in my past life." *And because…no. Side money, yes. But social engagements need not be included.*

"Look—can't even blame ya because 75 percent of the time I only tour and go to these shows because I have to!" Paula cackled then confirmed, "So, to answer your question, no mingling necessary."

Arielle nodded once more, firmer this time. "Then, yes, ma'am."

As Paula pumped onward, Elise suddenly whipped around. "And *I'm* going to send you my draft. Finally started the first chapter!"

As Elise wheeled back around, Arielle rotated her head slowly over to Jae'cy's returning gaze. Arielle refolded her arms, back to the business.

Jae'cy immediately glided her head then body away, waving her off with the additional participation of her swinging ponytail mane. "*BYE!*"

"You can't get BUY-in without ever buying into yourself first…. And some actual vision boards, a strategic brief, a retail space in the works always helps, too." Arielle smiled lightly but with steady eye contact.

Jae'cy just stared a second… "That's normal talk for you?"

Arielle shrugged. "Some old habits never die." *Such as my Pew Research Center email subscription from corporate, obviously, because…* "But almost 25 percent can and *do* die with the right, ready strategy…And a ready customer."

Jae'cy shifted her chin subtly over before the rest of any other part of her body.

Yet when Arielle grinned, she revealed a simper.

"Oh, that's what I am now? A sales pitch, huh?" Jae'cy challenged good-naturedly.

"Well, I'd prefer the word 'business.'"

Jae'cy squinted. "And what's in it for you?"

Arielle actually had to think about that, because her mouth was moving faster than her common sense.

"...Discovering that I don't hate my past as much I thought, apparently...because my client list for marketing keeps growing in this city."

Jae'cy laughed.

"But also...the only way you'll get buyers is by standing out. And the only way you stand out is by adding value," Arielle continued, strangely more introspective. "I wanna add value." And, subsequently, she felt herself palpitate.

Jae'cy was focused on her more intently now.

"I know about something called reputation management. I make your work through my writing look good, which in turn will make *my* name look good. And—"

Jae'cy squealed. "Ah, THAT'S it! Noise marketing."

"It's a win-win to me," Arielle conceded. "But you sure you don't speak my old language, Marketing 101?" *Because I'm about to figure out yours,* Arielle finally decided, her curiosity finally making her submit.

She wanted to see more of what was under Jae'cy's many faces. *You never know, Elle. It might come in handy with another story down the line....*

Then she cracked a sly grin, joined Jae'cy in the moment...until it fell into laughter.

"Yeah, I can see that this city has already tainted you."

Arielle decided to plead the fifth, and started to swing on her backpack. Anyway, Jae'cy was now looking down at her phone.

"Em...then maybe you can rub some of that confidence on me, to meet this guy."

Arielle took a look at Jae'cy's phone...revealing the very same restauranteur in the same exact restaurant where she first met Paula, his self-named eatery behind him in his Instagram profile photo: Capri. "Oh, yeah. Him."

"*He's* only one of the most hustler-spirit, crazy-talented chefs out here," Jae'cy snorted faintly, biting her lip.

*She's nervous. Clearly more than she was before her audition when I first met her...*

"I just wanna be a big kid like him..."

Arielle wasn't nearly as passionate about culinary things as she was music and sneakers, but she never knocked anyone's goals. Plus, she'd noted, in Capri's restaurant on her birthday, in a framed review on the way out, that he was an inner-city Miami native with paternal West Indian lineage, who had sent himself through Kendall College of Culinary Arts in Chicago. But with his flair for the non-traditional, after moving to California he found a godsend in one trusting African-American production company in need of last-minute event catering…an event with a guest list of even more Black Hollywooders, Paula included. From there, it had been like wildfire; he'd become incessantly booked for personal catering. Before he knew it, he'd opened his trailblazing fusion eatery and had only bloomed from there.

*So it makes sense why she looks up to him.* And it was cool to her, witnessing more layers of Jae'cy unfold: the cool kid trying to be like another cool(er) kid.

"So looks like you got some growin' to do, too," Arielle told her.

Jae'cy struck a reflexive, twitchy half-smile while sliding her phone away. Then, from the other exit, that same bifocaled, grill-bearing guy from her Lazy Mom's Day post entered, like he'd stepped right out of the photo, completely on-brand with his blinding luxury jewelry and Adidas tracksuit.

"That was quick," Jae'cy greeted him.

"Yeah. And I'm parked on this side."

Jae'cy suddenly gazed back at Arielle with a tilted kind of gesture. *Stiff*, Arielle thought.

"This is my boyfriend, Deonte," Jae'cy introduced, glancing at him. "This is Arielle, who wrote my mom's TikTok video."

*Oooo, I reallllly don't need any new introductions.*

Deonte bounced his head at her, seeming carefree to Arielle; she nodded back, noting the wide-open grin, unlike what she'd typically get from guys around their girls. He was just…*too* lighthearted, in her opinion. *Doesn't really seem like a match.*

"Ay, what's up?"

And with that, he was checking his cell phone. Jae'cy tipped her head back at Arielle as she started walking backward toward the exit.

Arielle reciprocated with her own head. But *in* her head…

*And he can't even pay attention for two minutes? Second flag on the play.*

Jae'cy must've concurred, fully turning to the exit, with Deonte quickly typing last words then sliding his phone into his back pocket to get the door.

"So, you've been at the shop all day?" Jae'cy sustained their convo.

"ALL mornin'. We got orders comin' in like *crazy* for the new shirts..."

*They weren't lyin'*, Arielle thought as she made way to the other exit. *Everyone has a hustle here. And now, I'm heading home to mine. Even if Miss @J_Carter, for whatever reason, is stalling on hers.*

But Arielle figured the scene would be continued. She and Jae'cy had just settled on that. So obviously, there was something both determined they'd be getting out of this...whatever *this* was—and whenever it officially started.

And what did Arielle know? Maybe it already had. Actresses and their tricks, Arielle could learn a thing or two for her stories.

Right?

♡ **10**

REGARDLESS, JAE'CY WAS STILL DEFINITELY MAKING SURE TO DO EVERYTHING *BUT* plan a business meeting. But even in Arielle's own business to which she'd returned, Jae'cy appeared.

It started at the top of the year, with a Zoom mentoring session she was about to finish up with Elise. She was actually a bit of a natural, for someone who "only took one English Composition class at a community college—and didn't even finish it." She could've fooled Arielle, because her story, a pseudo-memoir told through the lens of the fictional main character, was very enjoyable. Arielle thought Elise's relatable and raw narrative voice about low-income beginnings would resonate with many, and was honored to assist her.

As Elise jotted down some writing tip from Arielle in her notebook, just above her cranium came Jae'cy's, looking around for something in the background of her mother's den. Based on her sunglasses, silver hoops, long but light kimono, and thong sandals, Arielle surmised she was on her way to some kind of pool or water party.

"Hey, have you seen an extra USB drive? My mom said it might be in one of these file cabinets. Hard to miss, one of those big external drives with its own cord and looks kinda ratchet 'cause—"

"*HEY.* Please excuse this rudeness during our *meeting,*" Elise said to Arielle, who just chuckled. "Even if it is about to wrap up."

That was when Jae'cy whipped her head over her shoulder, freezing as she realized. Then she proceeded to apologetically, affectedly tiptoe out of the room. "I'll come back."

"*Man.* She's everywhere," Arielle jested.

Jae'cy gasped in offense, then gave a proper hair flip. And it might as well have been an AK-47. "Can't stay relevant in ya house."

*Well, damn.*

She hadn't meant to make an attack on Arielle (who was, in fact, a homebody when she had the opportunity to be). Or maybe she had. And if so, Arielle could've struck back with a statement about Jae'cy's business materials not yet being seen by anyone. But then she couldn't.

Because Jae'cy was already gone.

But she was back at the start of June. As Arielle was ending a Zoom interview with a literary magazine for their next month's young author spotlight video, she noticed another heart: this time, on her profile photo, to which she'd added a rainbow filter for Pride Month.

But when she checked Jae'cy's own page, there was no new post regarding any kind of teasing sneak peek or snapshot of business meetings, no talk of anything culinary-related. Nada.

But best believe the latest selfies were in full throttle. Some with Cori. Many more of herself or with friends, all lightly filtered straight poses into the camera. And the occasional few of Deonte at his shop pop-up events. *Ah, so he's a clothing creator. Makes sense.*

However, Arielle *did* notice a post around a short film that Jae'cy appeared to be in, judging by the trailer and Jae'cy's caption announcing that the film's debut would be in the upcoming LA Shorts Fest.

Alas, paying their ongoing social media deed forward, Arielle hit the heart.

But Jae'cy wasn't so endearing later that same week, while Arielle was making a new vegetarian restaurant run she'd convinced meat-eating Kimesha to partake in as an exchange for forcing her out of the house to discuss book buzz techniques. Arielle showcased her vegan calamari with a new (to her) Instagram feature: the story. It was at Kimesha's advising, to keep relevant and entice possible newcomers—even when she wasn't discussing book updates.

In her words: "Not every post has to be about business. It can just be you showing how you're like them and, accessible even after you eventually take their money—so that you can continue to take their money."

Arielle understood that from her old marketing days but stubbornly had been avoiding it. She didn't want to showcase herself, to have anything accessed beyond her fiction, after she accessed said readers' cash.

But (another) alas, she posted:

*Still have no idea how I use this (feature). But at least I did THIS right.*

Then she placed an animated arrow (after Kimesha's direction) toward the direction of her calamari in the Story video.

"Oh, and add a few emojis."

At this point, Arielle just wanted to get to the grub, so she quickly dropped in the restaurant location as a pin, along with a fork emoji then a bowl of noodles. She'd thought the story share had been decent—until she got a notification, a DM, not long after lowering her cell phone back onto the restaurant table.

"See? Already getting success," Kimesha declared, as she dabbled her fork in her fake lo mein.

But the DMer thought otherwise:

*But did you do it right REALLY?*

Arielle froze mid-bite at the snarky, gloating thought, fork idle in the air.

Kimesha looked up in confusion, maybe part concern. Or maybe she didn't want one of her largest moneymakers dying on her. It was business, after all.

Either way, the insult (er, comment) continued:

*Looks like the food I used to feed my cat...And then it got kidney failure. #idonthaveacat #butitwouldhavegottenthatwithTHAT*

The commentor? @J_Carter

When Arielle lowered her fork and picked up her phone, Kimesha cocked a pleased, surprised eyebrow (but the thing she hadn't yet lifted was that fork next to her lo mein).

*Just for THAT I'm sendin you side dish recipes every week*

Arielle didn't pick up her fork after posting the comment, as she tried to predict Jae'cy's response; she felt Kimesha's side-eye on her during the process, but didn't care. She was partaking in social media parlay as the manager had requested, and she knew it was about to get real...entertaining.

Sure enough, a second later:

*And I'll have a perfect seasoned roast to accompany each one.*
*DM them to me.* 🐾

"Havin' fun over there?"

Arielle heard Kimesha and placed down her phone. "Figuring that out right now..."


And as requested (or challenged?), Arielle messaged Jae'cy just about a week later, while passing by Chex Mix in her neighborhood store during a grocery trip.

The recipe?

Puppy chow.

*Since she thinks herself funny but is ignoring this other business she coincidentally HASN'T been talking about, she can waste time eating a powdered sugar, chocolate, peanut butter, and Chex Mix grade-school delicacy. Because, obviously, she wasn't caring about trying to get on the level of Capri.*

Jae'cy messaged back with a trio of laughing emojis and then an expected snapback:

> *Don't have a dog either. And my boyfriend doesn't count. #buthedpassonthistoo #whatisEarthBalance #dontyoumeanLandOLakes #thisgradeschoolrecipe #youcandobetter #yourpageincluded*

*Speaking of someone doing better…*Arielle redirected in her mind as she redirected to a new aisle: snacks, which were her thing. Jae'cy didn't know how perfect a segue she'd just given Arielle, to do what she really wanted to do in the first place:

> *Well, uh…I don't exactly see any of your developing menus in the audience.* 

And then, Arielle had to park at the corner of the chips aisle for Jae'cy's attack:

> *Ok, Inspector Gadget. Whatchu gonna do? Tell my Momma?* 

And then shots were fired from both sides:

> *No, I'm tellin' YOU. That's good enough.*

> *Real Gs move in silence* 💀

> *Yeah but Lil Wayne has something to show for it…More than lasagna*  *(or its silent g). Anyone can make that.*

Now, with one small point on her side, Arielle moved on to grab a reward: some Fritos.

Or maybe not so fast, a new round from the opponent:

*Ok, ok I'll have you know that I'm actually meetin with my
business team this wknd so I'll be ready in like a week to collab...
But daaaang homie you're persistent*

*That's the only way to be, the marketing in me*

*Ok gotta go cyber mom, make sure to report this back to my real momma
but tell her to keep my infractions light* 😮
*I'll* 👁 🐻 *u ltr*

*You got it*

♡ 11

BUT JAE'CY REALLY MEANT IT, DMing Arielle not much longer than two weeks later to meet up virtually. They both currently had majorly conflicting busy schedules: Jae'cy was flying out to Orlando for a few reshoots in that same film she'd been cast in around September; Arielle had to get through some developmental editing with Rachelle at the publishing house. With Rachelle being a seasoned editor with high-acclaimed authors in her clientele, each new book always required Arielle to hermit even more intensely than normal to correct all of the loose ends before prerelease. Rachelle wouldn't have it any other way, so *Ash Must Fall Down* wouldn't be any different.

So, a Zoom would have to be from Arielle's living room desk. Unfortunately, though, someone else *would* be rolling up to this house today (besides Elizabeth, who had arrived yesterday morning). She temporarily deflated at the thought of it as she readied her Zoom background. That someone would be Bamboo (yep, Arielle was at that level of petty now) coming to get her last belongings a whole nine months later. She was lucky Arielle's heart chakra wasn't *too* perforated at this point in her life not to have taken the girl's bike to Goodwill.

Arielle had already unlocked the front door for Bamboo to enter (whenever she decided she'd be stopping by in the next few hours) and for them to mutually be unbothered. Arielle was set on not thinking about that moment until it arrived…hopefully after this Zoom.

Just then, Jae'cy's face popped up in the Zoom window, with a gloriously sunny palm tree background, a real one, and Cartier sunglass frames resting on her head.

"Uh-oh, I'm hatin'," Arielle greeted.

"I am too. This might be my one and only time to do this while I'm here."

Arielle chuckled while Jae'cy straightened up and pulled out a stack of papers from a folder so smoothly that Arielle was silently impressed. She might have been a procrastinator, but she could still get right to work.

"So, I'm thinking that I need some basic starting pieces. Menu descriptions. A main, like, catchphrase. Like what *my* tag will be…" She began, and with that, the conversation flowed easily.

"The proper term is tagline," Arielle harmlessly shared, mechanically.

"Okay, rub it in," Jae'cy commented back.

"Sorry, I was just explaining—"

"And *I'm* just playin'," Jae'cy clarified, this time with a smile. That brighter, wider smile that Arielle had come to realize was an intriguing, mystical mix of bubbly and relaxed.

Arielle grinned back. Sure, she had palm trees right outside her living room window, too, but Jae'cy was feelin' herself. *This girl is funny.* And while still noting that settling smile...*But why does my stomach feel funny?*

The good-natured kickoff tone helped pave the tone smoothly over to business. Arielle was almost having fun, she realized, as Jae'cy went on to elaborate, while still skimming the top page in her stack of papers. "Now, don't judge me. But I always have to write stuff like this down like some type of old lady because—"

"It helps it stick better," Arielle chimed in, already nodding with a knowing smile.

"Yesss. See, this is why we're here today. You get me. And so, we got THIS," Jae'cy emoted, "'Cause time's a tickin'."

"Then: Who, what, when, where, and why. Give me the story. Who it's for, and how you're going to win them over," Arielle directed, ready to take notes.

"Oh, no pen and paper?"

"Not when time's a tickin'."

Jae'cy chuckled yet instantly perched into a resolute posture, as if a director had just yelled action somewhere. Arielle couldn't lie, Jae'cy's layered and mutable capability was fascinating.

"Okay, so...Honest Bites, Honest Bites," Jae'cy began, tapping her fancy fingernails on the edge of the paper stack. "That's the name of the restaurant. Well, more like a café. Down South meets West Coast, you know?"

*What I know is that the torture you women put yourself through should have a bigger payoff than awkward hand motions that will surely lead to carpal tunnel down the line,* Arielle stifled a grin. The alternating salmon and seafoam green of each fingertip was distracting. Arielle always appreciated a woman who cared for her appearance—

*Okay, focus, Elle. Stay with the present story right here.* And so, she got to typing.

"Okay, that covers the who and what," Jae'cy continued, now flipping to the second page of her paperwork. "I want to launch in two months, in LA, with next month being a soft launch.... So, of course, how do I bring the people in is the key question, right?"

"Well, there are a few *other* questions we should ask at this point, to get the message locked in. Who exactly are you trying to reach? Why should they want to know more about you and what you offer? How will you be relatable?" Arielle proffered.

"Right!" Jae'cy now read off the page, a pop of true passion on her face. And not owed to the sun that was beaming down on her. "So, my spot will be all about giving some real, transparent, healthy but also honestly *real good* soulful food. And on a deeper level, a tribute to my brutally honest, tough love grannies. My mom's Tennessee-born mother Bettie and my paternal grandmother Helen from Cali who I'd always be up under in the kitchen. I will bring all of those flavors of experiences, tastes, love into this new kitchen. *For* everyone and their own down-home ancestors and kitchen memories...and for us, the forerunners of the newest generation, who are currently unimpressed by today's attempted lies across the board, from politics to gossip to food, and are chucking them away with one social news *bite* at a time." Jae'cy paused for Arielle to appreciate that last play on words.

"Got it, got it," Arielle confirmed with a nod Jae'cy's way.

"Cool. Yeah, so it's go time. Just all of the logistics left to do. Finding real cooks. Because we've received some...interesting résumés, let's just say. Then there's the final paperwork for the commercial property, the physical site. It's beachside—"

"Very nice," Arielle responded, then advised, "But how about—of course, if it's possible for you—giving yourself two months at least instead of just one to make sure everything is in its ready state? You know, because what if you uncover the need to add more dishes or add *more* to your dishes, based on the taste-testing feedback at the soft launch? And you know how appraisals sometimes can go for property."

"True..."

Arielle noted how receptive Jae'cy was, chewing her inner cheek as she stared off a second.

"I'll connect with my team on it. But that's why I have made the location for the soft launch as my house first anyway. Plus, wanna test everything on my family and friends first. I'll be able to handle their feedback a bit better before the real deal."

"It's your baby, I get it. We'll just need a strong buzz. A press release, word-of-mouth, friends or invited tasters to spread the word with social media BITES," Arielle emphasized.

Jae'cy chuckled anew. "Thank you. Yeah, this has not been easy, but I'm doin' it for my heavenly queens. Gettin' their legacy out there with the help of YOUR writing." Jae'cy employed a tilt of her head, which made Arielle grin.

*She certainly has the charm. That's for sure.* A key factor for actresses and CEOs.

Arielle had recorded it all dutifully, typed some notes on the spot. Especially around the café's inspiration (and how Jae'cy's face had lit up more while discussing the two ancestors).

"So, I take it you were Grandma's girl," Arielle primed. The investigator in her could never pass up a good story. Besides, all this information would help her form the perfect relationship-building brand positioning statement, jumping off of the slogan that had already chirped in her head. One that would connect to any age, creed, or ethnicity of this café's possible audience: "Honest bites, made from honest love."

"I was the *only* girl!" Jae'cy chuckled a hint wistfully. "On both sides, for a minute. The first one…"

"Me too!"

Arielle internally flinched at a new sound in the room, yet felt instant relief after the recognition that followed. No, not Bamboo yet. Arielle exhaled a bit as she looked over her shoulder to incoming Elizabeth, pumping by behind Arielle with a mop and pail in hand. She quickly, warmly glanced at Jae'cy on the computer screen. "So, we cherish it, cherish every moment with the ones we love, right?" Paula established before a sudden strike up in her tonality and a bit longer of a gaze. "And you are such a *beautiful* young lady!" Then she looked at Arielle and Arielle's off-chuckle, registering that it might be—"A business call? Oh, sorry."

Arielle just waved it off because, in her mom's defense, she forgot to inform her about it. And furthermore, Elizabeth was already

pacing away.

Arielle noticed Jae'cy's amused grin. "Uh…my mom."

"I take it that your cleaning is not up to her par."

But an additional distraction arrived just then: Bamboo. As she stepped into the living room, she must've heard something in Jae'cy's speech, because she slowed as her eyes slid over Arielle.

Arielle blinked sluggishly before turning her head back to Jae'cy. She tried a quick, professional smile. "Uh, excuse me, please. One second."

Jae'cy instantly, tactfully, nodded.

Arielle had no sooner whirled around in her swivel office chair, hop-glid over to Bamboo, and moved her past Jae'cy on screen, past the kitchen (thankfully, Elizabeth was not there presently), and through the hallway that led to the garage where the stuff was waiting.

"I told you I'd left it all in here. I never changed the garage door code," Arielle informed her.

"I was wondering why you orchestrated this whole thing like it was a secret mission," Bamboo taunted. "Hiding your celeb crushes...you writers are so weird." She cackled so hard that Arielle hoped a stalk wouldn't strike her eye.

"This is business," Arielle responded as monotonously as possible, leading Bamboo's arm to the bike. "*This* is your bike that looks like it needs a new chain, like I told you months ago." Then she pressed open on the garage keypad. "And this is the end."

Bamboo looked at her, her leer retreating. Because for the first time ever, Arielle wasn't giving her the only thing she'd ever truly wanted: attention for her pretty girl privilege. And *that* was why Arielle had compromised her preferences (including that of her bedding arrangements) and self-respect. But not today.

"Take care," she said politely.

Bamboo stared at her a second, not knowing what to do. Finally, she narrowed her eyes, snuck up a new smirk, and wheeled her bike out.

Arielle maybe should've been suspicious of the expression of that exit, but she figured Bamboo would just get burned first before she burned Arielle—another time. Arielle didn't play with fire; trees played that role. And everyone knew how that fun always played out. With that, Arielle hit the keypad once again for the door to close. Their door closing. *Hopefully, this time for good.*

Arielle resounded that in her head as she made way back through the garage/laundry room hallway and past the kitchen, coming back into the living room. Jae'cy's face appeared to be questioning who Bamboo might've been, but she respectfully decided not to speak on it.

She only knocked up her shoulders, although with a hint of tactful softness, and lifted her business materials to clip them. "I don't know if I've been traumatized by my momma's eyebrows and firm faces, but uh...I think sis was tellin' me that I need to pick up these papers and head out for this *other* pick-up I have to report to in twenty minutes. *SO...*"

Arielle couldn't help but to bust up, loud, releasing the last bit of the past.

Jae'cy gave a light, playful grin. "So, yeah. This was really cool. I think it's gonna be cool, too."

"Yeah, you got this."

Jae'cy suddenly appeared to go meek, maybe even uncertain, bowing her head then nodding it a time or two. "I hope so. *BUT* before I go..."

*Oh, crap.* There was sure to be another big request; she could tell by the hold of the gaze and the quivery smile.

Jae'cy read Arielle's stiffened expression and chuckled. "Just a low-key event. The soft launch! Not *too* many folks there. I'll have some menu items I'm thinking of, but want to get some honest feedback before setting it in stone."

"Oh, some honest bites?" Arielle flashed her eyebrows for the intentional pun.

"Ha ha. Yes, that's the point. Glad we're on the same page," Jae'cy hid a grin as she started to put her things into her purse. "So, I'll give you more details on exact time, location...*ALLA that* before then." She looked up, steady, as she zipped up her purse. Confident like her mother but somehow more mellow. "Cool?" But that didn't mean she wasn't just as effective as Paula.

"Oh, I was actually supposed to answer because that *wasn't a* rhetorical question?"

Jae'cy winced, chuckled politely. "Em, an actual invite, or, more importantly, a forewarning before that invite would've been appreciated, huh? Sorry, I've got a lot of moving parts going on right now, so—"

"Just playin'," Arielle interjected, revealing a light grin.

Which made Jae'cy do the same.

Arielle nodded. "I'll have the social ad script, press release, and menu descriptions to you in about a week."

"Okay, *BYE!*" Jae'cy settled with a flash of teeth, then hopped up and off the camera.

*Yep, she's a little boss in the making. . And honestly,* Arielle thought with that smile still retained as she closed the Zoom app, *I really respect it.*

"All good?" Elizabeth had trotted back in again, then just stood there a second. .

"Yeah, of course," Arielle said. "Why?" *Am I palpitating from your gallons of Clorox you've just brought into the room?*

"Oh, just thought maybe you were still on your meeting. Because it looks like you were reacting to something."

And with that, Elizabeth started to wipe the wall-mounted flat screen TV...

...That even from some feet away, Arielle could see her own face in. And indeed, she still wore a lopsided grin, as if having heard a good, snarky joke. The kind that bubbled up to the surface before relaxing on the punchline.

♡ 12

AND THAT SMILE STAYED PLASTERED ON after she'd successfully passed on her manuscript with an A-plus verdict from her tough yet attentive editor this morning—after only *one* round of rewriting versus the usual three.

When she told Head Boss Sinead, who'd picked her up from the airport and who she'd be staying with across town in Glendale, she was greeted with a congrats. And then tossed a leather jacket right before she left out the house that evening. "It gets cold at night on the West Coast, girl! But you betta bring it back 'cause that cost me my whole paycheck way back when I got it."

"AND you could've taken my car, if you weren't scared to drive someone else's."

*And now I'm also scared to wear someone else's jacket. Thanks.* Arielle nervously stepped out Sinead's front door and into the pepper-haired Uber chauffeur's backseat.

And then, a half-hour later, she was prepping to exit it... *In five, four, three, two...*

"Alriiight," the older lady kindly farewelled her, looking back from her driver's seat after slowing down to the front of a two-story modern brick and stucco home in a row of more like it—with a line-up of crammed-in vehicles. That was when Arielle noticed how the woman resembled her deceased grandmother.

"Stay safe."

*Stay safe.* That was the prayer Arielle abruptly chanted in her mind—twice. The first was for the senior woman, hoping that she only did day shifts on these streets. The second was for herself, to trek this upcoming moment successfully. Arielle clutched Sinead's jacket like a security blanket.

Then inhaled, looked to her cell phone, hit $20 where she'd usually hit $5 on the tip (so maybe the lady could end her shift a little bit earlier), then mustered a light smile. "You too."

With that, she rose up with the leather jacket draped over her shoulder, sliding her eyes to the two-story stucco abode as if she'd never seen such material before. Like undomesticated, untrained eyes, unfamiliar in the ways of people. She stepped forward as wheels whizzed slowly by.

*Man, right now, I could really use my grandma.* The one who always accepted her eccentric adolescent nature, laughing and clapping at every odd living room "concert" till Arielle was ten...and then she was gone.

Landing at the doorstep, Arielle pressed the doorbell button. *Here goes.*

The door swung open, and there was Jae'cy, hair half up in a top bun, with an olive-green tube top, cropped, tapered pants, and white open-toe sandals. She smiled coolly, scanning Arielle's own casual short-sleeve navy mesh polo and slim-cut denim jeans—and just *one* gold rope necklace.

*Well,* Arielle thought quickly to herself while offering up an easy grin, *at least the grooming is off to the right start.*

But maybe that wasn't enough. Jae'cy's eyes swooped away from Arielle's face, as if suddenly detecting a hint of the wild. Then she fiddled her hands in the air in a seeming train of conflicted thought.

Jae'cy tried for a smile, which made it hard for Arielle to know what her human fate was just yet. "You didn't bring your..."

*Stand-in?*

"Friend?"

*You want more feral creatures of the trees inside? Better hide your boyfriend.*

Arielle inhaled roughly. "My friend?"

"The one I saw at your house." Jae'cy smiled anew, almost forcibly. Arielle figured her asking about it now was her way of trying to delicately express congenial hopes that everything was good on Arielle's side.

"Oh...No. I don't bring my plants with me," Arielle flatly stated, as if that was a solid response, meanwhile stuffing her phone away in her pocket.

Jae'cy opened her mouth, seemingly at a loss for words to clarify who she knew Arielle was oddly referring to. But she didn't immediately speak, paused in that silence as if to switch gears. Knowing even with her 10/20 vision that there hadn't been a hint of any plant in the Zoom background. "Didn't know you had a green thumb," she quipped as easily as she'd interrogated in that same breath.

"I didn't either. So I tested it out. Turns out I just have five fingers." Arielle subtly flared her nostrils but then quickly contained them. "And not a good garden hose."

Jae'cy's mouth quivered and a solitary chuckle uttered from her as Arielle let go of her irritation...in reaction to Jae'cy's roundabout manner of making her feel maybe just *slightly* less bothered and more removed from Bamboo. It was weird how that worked.

Arielle noticed a rolled T-shirt in Jae'cy's hand with screen-printed green words: "Honest Bites." The "T" in the latter word was drawn as a fork, with a piece of thin-sliced meat on the tip.

Meat...Arielle laughed internally at the sick and cruel coincidence. Sidebar: She was meat-averse in two ways. One, as a vegan. And two...Well...she was gay. "Deonte designed you freebies for today like I suggested, huh?"

Jae'cy lost the smile, turning her eyes up to the ceiling, as if she saw a random speck of dust drift by, small and virtually pointless.

Shoot, might've been Deonte. Looked like it was safe to say that Deonte was out of Jae'cy's line of vision now.

"Err..." And Jae'cy had just confirmed it.

Arielle chuckled tensely, shaking her head. "Okay, this...'conversation' is over." Indeed, because even though she'd only observed that relationship all of two or three minutes, Arielle was honestly happy for Jae'cy. In her eyes, this was another reason to celebrate today. *All of that gold and silver blinding everyone in his presence was about as annoying as Bamboo. But hey, at least Jae'cy got shirts out of her situation.*

"*RIGHT!*" Jae'cy emoted in her tone more than her facial expression, which Arielle interpreted as keeping it light (not to be confused with light-hearted)—and keeping it moving. And with that, Arielle stepped inside.

As Jae'cy strolled and talked, Arielle quietly spied the whole lot around her, taking in the scope of it all—

"So, yeah. The cooks just revealed everything. They've *only* been here since six..."

—the hallway, the current music that Arielle knew by sound, the grimy one-dimensional monophonic beat...

"We have all kinds of flavors for all kinds of palates—" Jae'cy paused for effect, cut a glance back at Arielle. "Dietary restrictions."

But she also paused because they'd come to a long table towards the end of a corridor, with a heap of mock aprons with names on them, one being Arielle's:

*An Honestly Dope Writer*

Jae'cy picked it up and extended it. "Your meal ticket to a possible prize at the end of the night if you're called during the raffle," she divulged proudly about the aprons.

"Oh, clever-clever."

Jae'cy put a satisfied hand on her hip before moving forward—as Arielle, while supportively adorning the apron in one of her pockets, making sure the name showed, clenched her abdominal muscles tight. They'd just landed on the people.

Lots of people, overwhelmingly from their age group. They were talking, drinking, and laughing, wearing their own aprons (some wearing it, others draped over their shoulders), rompers, short sets, baby tees, or just straight-up bras. Nike, Gucci, Reebok, Yeezy slides, Prada adorned their feet.

"I just *knooow* my momma is havin' a whole scene right now 'cause I left her stirring a batch of sauce in the kitchen with a whole hairnet." Jae'cy drew out a low but rich laugh.

And sure enough, there came Paula waltzing up, hairnet in hand, eyes on Arielle's apron. "Uh, when'd this happen?"

"Oh, she just got here," Jae'cy simply reported.

"Girl, that is *not* what I'm referring to, and you know it," Paula dismissed, waved off Jae'cy. "*So,* she finally got serious about this whole thing," Paula averred, checking out Arielle, who chuckled humbly, whereas Jae'cy just shook her head with a roll of her eyes. "Good. Glad she took heed and I can finally, *HOPEFULLY*, take a *seat*," Paula stressed, an eyebrow back at Jae'cy, for double meaning on every day prior to today and this day itself, playfully throwing the hairnet at Jae'cy.

"Here we go. I *knew* that was next," Jae'cy chuckled herself—but a bit fainter this time around.

Like a cascade to silence. Much like the one Arielle had witnessed at Gary's sketch taping.

Suddenly, a woman who appeared to be the same one on Facebook that Arielle had predicted was a cousin or some type of kinfolk to Paula came to a trotting stop beside her.

"Hey, baby," the woman hugged Jae'cy. "How'd you like that new training guide I emailed you? Gotta get it right before claimin' it as 'written by Doctor Loren Young-Richards.'"

"Educational," Jae'cy rejoined easily with a smile.

Loren cracked up in a way so uncannily akin to Paula that she had to be her sister. "You didn't read a lick. Just know, we *all* need technology—especially safe Internet and network servers."

"Hey, ma'am," Loren addressed Paula next, popping a glossed paper menu directly up in her face. "Um, did you see that they're spoilin' us with *tempura* today?"

Paula promptly deemed the two other ladies insignificant, shooting over her shoulder as she headed back in the direction from which she'd just come, "Welp. Looks like Imma have to call up my trainer tomorrow morning."

"Or put *on* a trainer in the meantime…and hope the other one doesn't reprimand you," Loren suggested, winked.

"Oh, a lil' hard motivation ain't eva hurt…Unless it's supposed to," Paula instantly whipped (and winked) back.

"No pain, no gain! *There* you go!" Loren squealed. "And not talkin' mom's ideology with us when we were growing up."

Paula rolled her eyes with a smirk…somewhat subdued.

Arielle shifted an eye at Jae'cy, replaying curiously how Paula's smile had seemed a bit hard-pressed attempt at the mention of her mother. And now, as she thought a bit more, she replayed a similar subtle look she'd spotted on Paula's face when motherhood had been brought up by the red carpet interviewer at her perfume launch party.…

Bringing her back to the current (just innuendo-filled) moment, Jae'cy summed up with, "Those crazy ladies. Hopefully, that doesn't pass down." Then Jae'cy's eyes lifted over Arielle's shoulder with a new spotting, a new smirk rising. "And here comes another one."

Arielle looked back to see Breyah emerging with an affected gape at Jae'cy. There was a little swagger in her walk, even in her turquoise midi party dress and shimmery matching eye shadow, the whole nine. (As in all of an entire makeup aisle number nine.)

"I heard that, trick!"

"Good, your ears are workin' betta than your eyes did a minute ago."

"GIRL! I don't know why you thought I was going to measure out some Louisiana hot sauce into cups of fried drumsticks and wings anyway. That's that *real* boughetto, Quiet Storm!"

That got "Quiet Storm" to reveal a fuller, playful grin and a giggle at her age-old nickname, stemming from the start of her and Breyah's relationship as theater mates in high school. With their scores now equal, the pair called a truce with a laugh. Arielle, seasoned from her involuntary days of refereeing Juliana (The Whiner), Melanie (The Punching Bag after a failed go at The Referee), and Sinead (The Boss), called her side.

"Imma go where the magic is…" Arielle trailed, pointing in the direction of the kitchen, from which everyone was coming and going.

Jae'cy tee-heed then Breyah followed.

"You know what's up. *Perfect* segue," Breyah commented, moving her gaze briefly to Arielle, retaining a smile.

*Yep, it's my specialty.*

In the kitchen, she reconnoitered the rest of the room while sustaining her trained neutral gaze, with a straightforward goal: the food. And even then, she already felt some eyes on her. There were way too many people, and she'd have to float around from one pocket to the next. It was what she'd done at social events for as long as she could remember, after one too many awkward high school games and hangouts where she'd somehow get pulled into deep conversations by the extroverted classmates who were always inexplicably drawn to her "mystique." That would soon be understood as introversion.

Yep, so segue she did and would do again, to yet another space in this place—after hitting up the food. But not before probably being brought into a tête-à-tête by a much older person or two, because that was the other draw she always had. But at least with that group, it made sense: she had grown up with older people. Her grandma, her mother's uncle, who stayed with them during his terminal illness. Arielle would always visit him in his room and chatter away.

So, she'd give it about an hour or two, or whenever the sun had finally set—whichever came first. And then, she'd do what was known as her Slide Out, after people had a few libations and others were starting to depart.

*Yep, go to the restroom and then not return...*

Arielle paused, and not because she'd reached the long row of food trays with their respective names on the island in the large kitchen. No, she had randomly gazed down at her apron and realized she'd have to at least stay until after the raffle...which typically was at the end of the event or very close to it.

*F—!*

"Hard to decide, right?"

Arielle turned her head around to an older woman holding an empty plate. The woman smiled breezily, seemed to be a young at heart, bohemian type, judging by the colorful clothes (a long geometric-print skirt) and adornments (bangles, wood hoop jewelry, and locs). Arielle predicted that she had to be another relative, invited by default rather than status.

"Yeah," Arielle pushed out a grin. "So many options..."

"Well, let's eeny, meeny, miny, moe it, and see what we catch. How about that?"

"Sounds like a plan."

The woman then took some small chicken pieces, drizzled with red. That must've been the "Louisiana."

Well, Arielle wasn't from there, but she *was... "Plant-Based."* She moved over to those marked trays accordingly.

She decided not to overthink the possible cross-contamination and just went for the lime-infused candied yams. One, because she loved candied yams and was interested in what these different 'lime-infused' guys would taste like. And two, she figured she'd get the response her latent hypochondria was yearning for in the form of a rumbling stomach followed by an actual, emergency restroom trip, which would be her perfect opportunity to Slide Out. In both ways.

# KEELA BUFORD

Screw it, she was cashing in on the pan-seared vegan crab cakes, too.

Comically enough, she and the woman met with a mutual gaze at the other end of the kitchen island, both of their plates jam-packed.

"Mission accomplished," the woman cackled with a raised palm.

Arielle lightly connected her palm, even laughed a bit herself, and then the woman was on her way. "Have a *celebrated* rest of this culminating summer solstice!"

Oh yeah, Zen Auntie most definitely wouldn't have gotten the invite if she hadn't been someone's auntie. "You too."

Arielle reached the patio sliding doors, connecting with the handle. Sliding the door open, she peered around at the sextet or so (a damn mob) of late twenties, early thirties, primarily dudes. Understated and not-so-understated assessing dudes—and not in an interested way, surely because of the exotic-looking bra-wearing girls at their sides. Arielle had been on this type of display before, and not exactly for the appreciation of her high, sharp cheekbones, jaw, and undercut. Instead, the opposite. Yes, Cali, NY, and ATL were known as the LGBTQ-plus American havens. But whether she was in her old Midwest roots or West Coast-adjacent Vegas, Arielle's brand of gay mysteriously always brought unhappy guests. It was an unfortunate talent. The much more masculine, yet much sleeker-faced Tish had explained to her once that it had to do with that jawline Arielle owned that made her look more serious, standoffish, or unfriendly. "And your quietness don't help!"

Alas, these girls (probably "bicurious," the usual) scanned that face, the undercut, cheekbones, with a complex mix of stealth eye-sliding, a silenced snicker, or a snaky smirk. Then they all shared a collective answer to their next unspoken inquiry: about her enigmatic entry into their quarters, as exposed on her apron. The role that now felt more like a scarlet letter.

She just shifted her eyes away and deleted herself for them. Right out to the pool.

Unfortunately, other people were having their own personal parties, quite evidently a bit (or a lot) tipsy. But the backyard hideaway improved as she landed eyes on Elise, with someone (a very androgynous-looking, tall female) beside her at a patio table across the pool. And honestly, as Elise motioned her over, although she would never admit it, Arielle felt a sense of happiness, of reception. Relief that the rest of the night had instantly become easier. *Ole girl beside her is about as jaw-less as Tish, but at least she's not getting side-eyes. Let's blend in.*

A small, known group was always Arielle's preferred modus operandi at things like this. A control group, so to speak. She'd still do her eventual Slide Out—*oh, fasho,* as Sinead loved to say in her proper native West Coast tongue. But with the way Elise could talk, it would go by *QUICKLY.*

And it did.

After Elise had introduced the person beside her (the "friend," who she happened to keep connecting eyes with—they had to be that mid-stage where neither party had yet bravely proposed an official relationship title), they'd moved on to all kinds of topics. As she started to share the latest, her recent near-death experience while rowing with said friend, the outside DJ interjected over his dropped track:

"Ight, y'all! It's time for the second-top thing most of y'all showed up for. It don't matter where we hail from or land, we always posted for somethin' free, you feel me?"

"*RIGHT!*" the crowd boomed in agreement.

Even in the typical West Coast ethnically blended space, it wasn't hard to figure out who "we" were.

"Ay, ay! But real quick real quick, I need y'all to do these two simple things for me with them devices in ya hand. Step one: download and open this right *here,*" the DJ directed, pointing to the TV monitor beside him that began to play an Honest Bites app video (which Arielle wrote the copy for). Arielle had pitched the idea as a way to not only market Jae'cy's business but also to pull in followers right from the get-go, so they'd hopefully share the news of the café opening. "And step two: tap 'Begin' on the poll that pops up once you enter the app and tell us what your favorite *AND* least favorite bites were tonight—*honestly.* Honest Bites wants ya honest feedback, ight?"

They agreeably tapped on their phones. Arielle knew exactly what she was voting for. And exactly where she would post herself, after she headed inside. But right now—

"Come on, come on! Yeah, y'all cute but today is not your video. I know: in Cali, *shocking,*" Breyah announced, bouncing to the beat of the inside DJ's low, looped instrumental, motioning with her microphone like a crossing guard for the start of the raffle.

People laughed, and made sure to land around the long stage in the living room, where Jae'cy and her café staff were setting a few last prizes on a filled table.

"So, let's follow one simple instruction we all learned in kindergarten, if your school wasn't ratchet. *If* your name's called, you say, 'Here!' Capeesh?" Breyah was really feelin' this MC situation.

"Bre, *GO!*" A young female, presumably her friend, giggled out. "You get one presenter role at the BET Awards and now have lost yo mind."

"Okay," Breyah submitted, clearing her throat, dipping a hand into a bowl of folded paper scraps. She unfolded one to read, rolled her eyes, smirked. "Michi Davidson...of course."

One of the tall, assessing guys from earlier in the day showed much more glee than he'd given Arielle, slinging his apron over his shoulder, then flexing like it was some kind of MMA title belt. His friends pushed his puffed chest, his girl looking like the ultimate proud winner's wife.

Arielle couldn't help but crack a grin with everyone else, including Jae'cy as she extended an envelope down to Breyah.

"Boy, just come get this—" Breyah paused to glance back at Jae'cy. "What's his award for being always extra, Jay?"

"Fifty dollars to court Nike."

And the guy accepted, proudly, smile spreading wider as he walked up, took the Nike gift card, and put it in his pocket.

*Hunh. Maybe I should've gone with the black Air Max Motion 2s or low Air Force 1 '07s instead of my PUMA Motorsports.*

Wait, maybe that would've just made him *more* hostile.

Arielle moved on...a PUMA'd foot or so closer to the front door hallway, so grateful that the raffle was in the room right by it. She had told Elise she was heading to the restroom and was on her way.

Breyah moved on to a "Jordana Noelle," who looked like the singer that her name sounded like, sashaying to the foot of the stage and curtsying with her gift bag. A congratulating peer tried to twerk on her as she passed back, but Paula came out of nowhere, shutting that down with a firm hold on the girl's arm, then a slick nudge of her head at a corner that Arielle at first thought meant a timeout. Instead, there, a group of playing yet snooping kids, Cori included, resided.

Breyah instigated with a tilted head and a nonverbal "Oo-wee" exhale. Then she carried on, and Arielle did the same, continuing toward the front door hall for her impending Lyft...

"Al*righty* then...Chase..."

One name after another was called. With each, Arielle got closer to the door. And then there was the last, lone ranger on the raffle table: a mini-spa kit.

"Addison Brews."

Appropriately awarded to a woman of forty-plus years, based on her mannerisms and clothes.

*Ah, well...no prizes for the feral animal. Guess not getting kicked out or stoned was mine.*

But Arielle had a bigger prize awaiting her behind door number one anyway: going home (with a takeaway container of those lime candied yams she'd grabbed from a cool older lady chef on the "way back from the restroom"). Well, more specifically, Sinead's house. But it was still just three people—Sinead and her two kids, Sasha and Gavin—versus what had to be at least a hundred right now. A currently distracted and celebrating (or good-naturedly bemoaning) hundred who watched Breyah turn to Jae'cy and extend the mic.

"Any ending words for the night, Miss New C-E-O?"

"GO, JAY!" More cheering and clapping.

"Yung Hitta!" That was Elise.

*Yep, time to—*

But with her last peer at Jae'cy before her getaway, Jae'cy's humble smile around the room had just randomly landed right on her.

*Crap.*

Jae'cy looked...like a "just given her first clarinet solo" type of humble. A type of child-like vulnerability.

*I've gotta stop making up these storylines.*

Although she suddenly froze at the realization that she'd truly spotted something for once in those murky eyes of Jae'cy's.

But she *could* at least tip her head awkwardly in exiting...and Jae'cy faintly nudged up her eyebrows. Not in a sluggish, tipsy way but alert, sober. The girl had straight up caught her before she'd disappeared. So much for hoping.

There was no way to slide out (a.k.a. be inconspicuous) now, just had to step out, as she heard Jae'cy address the crowd.

"Yes, first off: *daaang*...you all could've left something for me. A hush puppy, a bone, toothpick. *Somethin'.*"

Arielle could hear the laughter boom over the instrumental from inside even from the front porch steps. Only then, she exhaled as she hit the lawn and pulled up a Spotify album by beatmaker Phoniks, coming on back *Down to Earth.*

And then, at the end of it, the Lyft vehicle pulled up.


When she walked in Sinead's front door forty minutes later, Sinead looked up from channel- surfing, then down at Arielle's Styrofoam-holding hand. Arielle instantly, sharply inhaled.

*Crap. Her—*

"No thanks, don't eat strangers' food. Not even famous ones. But...where the *hell* is my jacket, Easy E?"

♡ 13

*F—!!*

The only thing to do was go right back, to the last place she wanted to be. Arielle couldn't even, for once, process her oldies currently playing on Spotify via Bluetooth because her old ass was trying to figure out how the hell to get to point B. Sinead had let Arielle use her ride for this second, jacket-retrieving trek.

And as Arielle slowed down in front of the same brick and stucco place, she gulped.

The cars were gone. *All* of them.

Arielle pulled into an empty curbside about a house down to not be creepy. She started to pull back off but knew what awaited her back at Sinead's would be even scarier if she did.

So, she sat there for a second, staring out the windshield, and letting out a slow breath. Finally, she got out and walked back up that walkway, to that front door, that doorbell. Arielle heard its melody reverberate.

*Yep, time to go. The last thing I need is this girl thinkin' I'm trying to—*

"I was about to say, 'I don't know what crazy person is coming by this late to the party, but he or *she* is about to get another kinda prize." Jae'cy chuckled in the now-open doorway.

"You get all kinds of prizes in Hollywood, huh?" Arielle grinned, twitchily.

"I had a woman stalk me like two months ago!"

Arielle internally cringed—then outwardly. "…That's craazy…"

"Well, technically, she was my mom's, but she couldn't find her as easily online. Ya know, because she's the big *celebrity*." Jae'cy popped her lips in affected ambivalence—yet blinked a bit too sharply in contrast. Alas, she pulled the door back a bit more. "Anyways, what's up?"

"I forgot a jacket. It's—"

Jae'cy stepped off to the side for a clear entry. Arielle stood, mouth open, staring cluelessly.

"Black. Mm-hm. I thought I saw you come in with one and was going to let you know in a sec," she revealed. "Yeppers, the Durty *Thirty* hittin' you quicker than that door did behind you an hour ago! Ya *slippin'*."

As Arielle began to chuckle, Jae'cy noted something else: "But looks like you didn't forget to hop outta here with that food"

"Did you put some Louisiana voodoo in the yams, too? It's cool, we can keep it between us."

Jae'cy snickered. "I don't know if you're referring to the hot sauce or my Gran's roots. Either way, you're off. But *ooh*, my first customer is a boujie vegan? *Mm*-kay," she proposed, promenading down the hall.

And Arielle just wavered at the door, stuffing her hands into her pockets.

Jae'cy slowed, looked over her shoulder, and crossed her eyebrows with a grin. "Uh, you gonna come in?"

*Noooo. Because if I don't get back to Sinead with her ish…*

Arielle stepped inside, digging her fingers deeper into her thighs as self-inflicted punishment for her hasty departure that had left her needing to return to the scene.

As she slowly gained upon Jae'cy in the *very* empty living room… "Friends. How many of us *don't* have them?"

Jae'cy grinned a tad at the restyled Whodini reference as she led the way to the kitchen. The MC was a tough crowd. "All of my *friends* are mommas, busy bosses, and/or wives now. Literally or symbolically. So they have curfews. Breyah *just* left because she has business per usual in the AM. And my mom took my little helper with her." She took to a stool at the kitchen island, where Sinead's jacket was residing. "So, cleaning duty solo."

And that was when her phone rang. "Hey, Michi. You good?" That was Arielle's cue to eye the many still lingering plastic cups, plates, and napkins. Arielle wasn't OCD (completely), but she had a thing about dirty dishes; she couldn't help herself from tossing them into the big trash bags propped up against the kitchen island… "Uh, yeah…I'm good. Why wouldn't I be?…"

*But I ain't.*

"Uh, no. I *definitely* didn't. I don't even have time right now with this large mess y'all left in my house. So, yeah…Sorry, my guy," Jae'cy chuckled at and farewelled the unheard (and sounding like having been dismissed) Michi. Then turned her attention back to Arielle. "Uh, don't you have a flight right now? Since you're somethin' like a busy boss yourself?"

Arielle slowed, briefly coming out of her locked-in state, after picking up a couple *nasty* napkins. "Not until tomorrow afternoon… And I don't have any wives. Just cousins."

Jae'cy guffawed, the kind where the hand had to connect with the belly of a bent-back body. It was the most sincere one Arielle had seen yet, which made her pause fully this time.

But best believe her hand was finding a bottle of Lysol.

"And looks like I just have Michi! He said I messaged him because someone had weirdly pulled up to my house."

Arielle gulped.

"But sir, I am too busy up in here to be checkin' out windows and my phone, so he must've had one too many drinks tonight," Jae'cy dismissed all of that scene with a chuckle.

And with that, back to the Lysol: It felt very, very light. As Arielle pointed the bottle at the now cleared but still contaminated island top, and pressed it a few times with no luck, she learned why.

Jae'cy rolled her eyes. "My mom and some of her cleanin' before she left."

*So how come she didn't get those paper napkins?*

"Let me go grab another one."

Arielle didn't even nod as Jae'cy stepped out, too busy spotting some dirty plastic plates at the sink that just had to go. It was one thing for kids to leave things all over. But *adults?*

Before she knew it, she had connected her cell phone's Spotify app to the large Bluetooth speaker that was slipshod on top of a plastic silverware packaging container, and music mildly filled the space. It was always her cleaning-up ritual to get the job done. And this kitchen, which could've fit about three or four of her own in it, was indeed a job. She hated seeing messes and realized that it would mean she wouldn't be returning Sinead's jacket as quickly as she'd thought.

Jae'cy still hadn't made it back by the time the third song started: "Only You" by 112, vintage '90s R&B at its finest. The song was in the middle of its magic as she took a money shot into the trash with some balled-up paper towels.

Unbeknownst to her, Jae'cy had started to re-enter, stepping in closer as the song suddenly elevated. The male singers lifted their range a note or two, one layered over the other in smooth harmony. As Jae'cy quietly watched, skewing her mouth to one side in an artificial cringe, the still-unaware Arielle shot an eyebrow up and eyes down to her cell phone.

"Oo, it's like *that?*" Arielle commented, slightly turning up the song in the Spotify app. "You ain't have to do all *that—*"

A Lysol spray bottle tapped Arielle's shoulder, and she whipped around to find Jae'cy, who bowed her head a second to hide a smirk. When she looked back up, she said, "Yeah, you don't have to do all *THAT* either."

"Oh, that's old folks music. You don't know about that."

Arielle jabbed, chuckled coolly just as she took the Lysol bottle and as the singing men began to dismiss themselves ironically on cue, the music slowly fading out...and giving way to another old jam: El DeBarge's opening wail for a "Special Lady."

But as she started spraying the kitchen island, her eyes floated up to the top of Jae'cy's head, noticing that *all* of her hair was now up in that high bun. The girl had done taken advantage and taken a break.

"*Uh.* I'm an eighties baby!" Jae'cy giggled.

"Good to know," Arielle flatly commenced, beginning to wipe the island, "but you got the decade wrong. Thanks for your time, trap-loving contestant."

Jae'cy arched a brow, mouth dropping open. "You know what I mean—" She halted, crossing her arms, and squinted with a new concealed grin at Arielle. "When were *you* born?"

"Gettin' kinda personal," Arielle continued as she went deeper with the island top, stepping right in front of the hands-on-the-hips Jae'cy, who was staring at her. "But 1990." Arielle glanced up with a squint of her own. "What were you? Eighty-nine or somethin'? Does that even count?"

"Eighty-*eight*. So, that means I actually *grew* up in the nineties versus being born in it."

"You probably don't even know even half of that era's obscure cuts, but fine. We'll let you into our group since everyone always wants to be. Can't blame you, our music is the best, but—"

Jae'cy giggled away. "Girl, *BYEEE*! If we're bein' honest, it's neither of our decades. It's the seventies...Miss DeBarge."

Arielle halted. Was that another clowning moment? A spot-on jab where it hurt the most, at her old soul and taste in music as the great El DeBarge did indeed dive into his second verse with all of his passion, talent, and falsetto might?

The *gall.*

She shot her eyes up to Jae'cy, who shot back a challenging, playful flicker.

"Like I said, I grew up in the nineties. And you must've forgot who my mom is," Jae'cy explained then tipped her head at the Bluetooth speaker. "But girl, you sure you didn't have a 'friend' pop up in that Zoom last month? Because that's a lot of repressed vibes goin' on."

Arielle hid her own rising smile, taking back to the island top. It still was so entertainingly bewildering how openly sizzling Jae'cy could be when she wanted—and quick with the ripostes, too.

"Okay, I'll give you that.... But I also think you just used your fake twenty-twenty from over there to read my cell phone screen," Arielle jested. "And who's to say I'm not getting into a creative zone for my next story. You know, like you 'actors.'"

"Unh-unh, don't do that," Jae'cy 'reprimanded.'

Arielle slowed her cleaning momentarily and gave a wry, light chuckle. "No, really. The inspiration is lacking this time around. For this next story. Kinda buggin' me actually…" *And confusing me as to why I'm having trouble.*

"What is it about? The story?" Jae'cy actually matched her, a true question rather than the riposte. But a little playful grin was still there.

"I'm trying for, like, a thriller, I think. And…" Arielle trailed, paused a second, looking Jae'cy's way. *Ah, she's a Scorpio, this is her language.* "It may be centered around an ongoing homicide case or ring of cases. And I'm just trying to have the conversations by some of the criminal investigators, detectives, you know, sound as natural as possible."

Jae'cy skewed her mouth to the side in rumination. She tapped her hands on her hip a second. "I think I have something from a film I was in. Actually, the one I just wrapped up. A thriller, too. My character actually had some forensics books in her dorm room as props that I was able to bring home with me. So, I'll see what I can find once I get the chance to…Ya know…as an *actress.*"

"Oh, cool," Arielle replied genuinely, but then got back to business. "*But* I think you're playin' about your zodiac sign because you're a little feisty on the low."

"Who says Scorpios can't be as big and bad as fire signs?!" Jae'cy's eyes flickered distinctly that time, almost like true fire, made less alarming only by her grin.

*Yep, she was right. Scary just like a Scorpio.*

"Plus, I'm a Sadge rising."

"*Ah,*" Arielle instantly resolved, snapped her finger with a nod. No further explanation was needed. (She couldn't say the same for some weird red tinge floating in a plastic cup on the counter. *That* had to be some Louisiana.)

Jae'cy appeared lightweight offended—or, on second thought, entertained and ready for a(nother) argument, re-folding her arms with a steady eye. "You're surprisingly a lil' sharp with the tongue, too, so what's your stars lookin' like?"

"I'm a Virgo, ruled by Mercury. Seems like you already know a little somethin' about all of that, so I'll leave it at…that."

Jae'cy's eyes were really twinkling at this point. "But you like to go against the grain a little bit, I see. And in a stubborn way, like a Scorpio. However, not as *dark* with it, even with all of the pride. Also not so dramatically attention-seeking about it, like a Leo. *Soo,* I'm thinkin' …Aquarius rising?"

*Once again, Scorpios proving why they're creepy as…*

"Em…maybe," Arielle colorlessly answered. "*Now…*since we've trekked into each other's astro-equivalent of social security numbers, shall we get back to the show? Miss Hovah?" She ran her Lysol bottle-decked hand over the residual mess still in the room, which made Jae'cy chuckle fully anew.

Then as Arielle took a broom g from beside the fridge, she started sweeping into piles around Ja'ecy, who had a ready dustpan.

"It started off as a joke, from Elise. I can look kinda standoffish."

*Really!*

"And I love rap. *And* since my first name sounds like Jay Z—"

"Yung J," Arielle joined. "And *then* the irony of it all is me unintentionally naming my child after his middle name."

"…You sure *you're* not a stalker?"

Jae'cy took then rammed the broom onto the top of one of Arielle's Motorsports, to which Arielle fittingly hopped back with matched speed.


But before her Motorsports even hit the ground once again, she heard Jae'cy clear her throat.

Arielle turned back, and there was the leather jacket in Jae'cy's hand, which she extended, cocking a brow and shaking her head in her open front doorway.

Arielle tipped her head then stepped up to get it. "I swear I'm usually more responsible than this."

Jae'cy laughed, light and cool. Yet she blinked humbly, Arielle spotting that clarinet girl once again…and wondering if, back then, she had weaved and bent, similarly unsure, her first time doing something new. "Thanks for coming."

"Sure thing…" Arielle just as modestly responded, then popped out a shrug. "A Black person doesn't turn down lime-infused yams."

"Oh, not even a vegan one?"

"Not according to your DJ." Then her voice dropped. "With y'all hood boujee selves."

"Come on, you have to embrace some of the vibes that hit. Admit it!" Jae'cy squealed.

Arielle pled the fifth.

Then there was a true silence.

Arielle tipped her head again, more like a lunge…because Virgo.

"Check you later… Hope you remember your way back to your cousin's." And with that, Jae'cy made the closing for the both of them, then turned back to her front door.

As Arielle got into said cousin's car, something was slowly rising in volume in her head.

And then it hit her. Happiness…and something else.

And once again, even more now, she didn't want to admit it. But she thought it.

Couldn't help but to, like a brand-new internal thought loop. Louder than the one she had on the way over, louder than any music today…

…

"Damn."

♡ 14

THE VERY NEXT MORNING, Jae'cy sent her a text just as she was stepping into LAX.

It was a video, with no words, of Jae'cy pulling up a couple of books to the camera, with the books' spines, titles visible to the viewer. They were the books about crime forensics that she'd mentioned.

*Looks like she had time sooner than later.*

In eerily perfect pre-recorded timing, Jae'cy said, "I actually did a quick dig and found them. I'll be passing the airport soon if you're there and wanna grab them."

They texted about where to meet up, and Jae'cy was there, discreetly rolling down her passenger side window and extending the books through the crack like some kind of drug deal. Her next stop would actually be her café (checking on the last line of furnishings before Honest Bites' opening day).In her sunglasses, she then sipped her red-hued smoothie and savored it with a concluding rub of her lips.

*Dang, don't make it look so good*, Arielle thought. She took the books with a smile.

"Welp, don't want you to lose your plane seat, too, like you almost did that jacket, so," Jae'cy ribbed, tucking her smoothie away. "But I take it your cousin doesn't play."

"And even if she did, I still wouldn't want to play with *her*."

"Uh-oh." Jae'cy almost coughed up a bit of her smoothie.

Just then, a woman passed by, eyeing Arielle up-and-down. Arielle reciprocated thoughtlessly (she was a lesbian after all), a mutual, subtle realization of the other. The woman walked on with her small duffel bag into the airport.

Even with the shades covering her eyes, Arielle could still read Jae'cy's expression. The girl was checkin' her checkin' the other her. It was all in her motionless focus, then the slow rise of an eyebrow over the rim of her shades.

"Well, uh..."

"Good luck on landin'...*that* role," Jae'cy finished, a rousing smile sliding across her face.

"Ha." Arielle spoke the laugh because she truly wasn't feelin' *that*: entertaining the action of putting on any of those kinds of feelings for a female. After her more than bad luck, her picking game needed a tune-up first. Maybe she should hook up with a vegan farmer next...or, at the very least, someone who knew herbs, spices, food—

Arielle shot her eyes away from Jae'cy, feeling a feeling...

Her pants pocket vibrating. She checked to discover it was an incoming call from Kimesha.

"Imma actually be in your stompin' grounds next month for my own new role. A *confirmed* one," Jae'cy ribbed.

Arielle winced, clutching her chest, her ribs affectedly. "*Oooh.* Enough, enough." But then...

"Hit me up," Arielle proposed.

"Yeah, if you remember who I am. 'Cause, you know, that memory is a lil' shaky."

Arielle hid a smile as she put the books in her travel backpack. "You're 'Jae'cy Carter,'" she copied Jae'cy's voice and tone, which made Jae'cy smack her lips and hide a grin.

"Unh-*unnnh. Bye.*"

Jae'cy rolled up her passenger side window then peeled off the curbside, and Arielle called Kimesha back, heading inside.

"So, I know you'll have to hop off for TSA and all, but just a quick update: Got you lined up for a couple guest columnist articles, to add to your organic advertising buzz for this new book. You'll want to mention it on all of your socials."

"With how many emojis?"

"Fifteen astonished faces. Because obviously someone woke up on the right side of the bed for once..."

As they hung up, she thought, *I guess it is time to acknowledge this happiness fully. A genuine good working...er, friendship. Yes, friendship.*

Arielle clutched her travel bag strap around her chest. Obviously, she was liking this, because she'd invited another hangout—on her own turf this time.

Looked like she had maybe a bit of time in her own busy life, too. *Because a good story might be emerging, indeed.* As she walked under airport signage en route to TSA...*Guess it has to be set in LA.*

♡ 15

AND LINK UP THEY DID THE VERY NEXT MONTH AS DISCUSSED.

But what they somehow hadn't discussed yet until that very date was… *Where and, most importantly, when are we meeting—?*

*Headed your way rn*

*Uhhh…*Arielle stared at the just-received message on her cell phone, taking a brief moment away from her story at her computer desk.

*errr…just after you tell me which way that is supposed to be lol*

Arielle pondered. *Well, the girl doesn't just want to be cooped up in here, so since I invited myself to be a good ole hostess…*

*Live n Color?*

It was a relatively established club. Well-known, but not too overly frequented. A perfect place to lay back and listen to music, sometimes live, sometimes with a featured painter making art in real-time. But always—

*Lots of throwback cuts*

*Ofc* 💀 😄

With the spot in close proximity to Arielle, she made it before Jae'cy's rideshare and scoped out the scene. Yep, laid-back like she'd anticipated. There were people here and there, a pretty mixed crowd in a pretty vast lounge, but not packed to the walls. *Speaking of walls.* Arielle found a free table by one, just off-center of the performance area. *Yes.* No performers tonight, but a painter was propping up a canvas and the visiting DJ was setting up to take lead for the night. *Better be a good set—*
"No drinks *yet?!*"

Arielle looked over her shoulder to see Jae'cy approaching with a tone-setting, bouncy grin.

"Was waiting on your suggestions."

"You're the hostess, ma'am."

"And my cousin's the bartender, so…" Arielle went to her phone as Jae'cy laughed and observed in humored cluelessness, taking a seat in the chair beside her.

Juliana worked later shifts on the weekends but also had a slow period around this time. Who better to ask for suggestions.

There popped up Juliana in Arielle's video messaging app, wiping off her workstation in a presently quiet space. "What up, cuh? Are you *ACTUALLY* outside on a weekend?! I'm so proud of—!"

Then she became even more ecstatic or briefly catatonic, hand-wiping ceasing for a suddenly bigger priority. "Girl, is that—!?"

Jae'cy kindly waved, chuckled. "Heyyy."

As Juliana turned her gaped face back to Arielle, Arielle brought her back down to Earth. "We won't keep you, but what was that one drink you tricked me into that time at your house last summer? It had like lemons and—"

"Uhhh, yeah, girl," Juliana mocked, shook her head from Arielle to Jae'cy then back to Arielle. "That would be called *pink lemonade vodka.*"

And just then, a server came on the ready, Arielle tipping her head at her phone. "What she said."

Two minutes (and two pink lemonades) later…

"Mm-*HM*," Jae'cy emoted, complimented Juliana over a slow, savoring sip then swallow. "Not my usual mix…Or I'm just really thirsty for some other stimulus after hearing nothing but shouts and clapboards for the past ten hours."

"*Ayyyy.*"

*This girl was making the most out of these five minutes.* Juliana almost twerked right there on the vide—Wait, nope, she actually did.

"Oh, meant to say this minutes ago. You look *real* familiar, like I've seen you somewhere recently?" Jae'cy gandered at Juliana.

Arielle almost lost her drink, coughing awkwardly.

*Oooh, I hope this girl doesn't help Jae'cy connect the dots as to that IG referral she made way back when.*

"*Ayyy,* girl. You probably have. You know LA smaller than my size fives."

Arielle shot her eyes over to Juliana who was doing what she did best on the video once again.

And that was when Arielle's prayer was answered; an unmistakable *boom* beat hit the room: "Touch Me Tease Me" by Case.

"Welp, signing off," Juliana saluted, a mixer bottle now in hand and a twinkle in her eye. "Grown folks gotta get back to work. And some other folks gotta…"Jae'cy slid her slightly droopy-lidded eyes across the open dance floor area, where people were beginning to gather and dance. Even in the dark, Arielle could see she was a bit buzzed, but that was all.

Then Jae'cy stood up, moving to the music. Soon, she was really into it, laughing and swaying in perfect rhythm with the melody as she made her way toward the dance floor. Even sooner, guys—of all backgrounds—were looking. *Shiii*…even their dates were at this point.

And so was Juliana, who'd suddenly stuck around a little longer, all eyes on Jae'cy's hips a little too closely—and not exactly for comparison.

Arielle shifted *her* eyes to her (second) drink. "Uh, I don't think she's…"

Juliana was basically running her fingers over her mixer bottle now.

"A Gemini."

She was auditioning to be in the LGBT like, "Put me in, coach."

"Have fun, cuhhh," Juliana faded out into black on the cell phone screen as a person came up to her bar. "Gotta make some actual dollar bills now off my mixology knowledge…Then might throw a couple her way."

*What? And the rest hopefully to a maid?* But then, Arielle truly had to humor herself…Because, she couldn't tell if it was the lemonade lemonadin' or all of the bodies in the room, but all of a sudden, a wave of humidity hit her in this desert state. Honestly, she wished it was a case of approaching premature menopause.

But she knew it wasn't.

She and the guys were looking at the cause, right there. And suddenly, the almond eyes stared at her with a flash of a grin and a beckoning hand motion.

Arielle cringed. *No please don't call—*

"*DE*-BARGE!"

Many heads looked Arielle's way.

*Damn, there really are a lot of Black people in Vegas now.*

"Over here. *Now!*" Jae'cy, the almond eyes' owner, iterated.

*Man, she sounds and acts like her mom.* Arielle exhaled as Jae'cy gyrated over, her whole brown-jumpsuited body a smooth, round motion. Yes, including the hips.

Arielle clutched her cup, took in a deep slurp from her straw. And the next instant, Arielle found herself in the middle of the dance floor, mostly just rhythmically moving from side to side. But Jae'cy determined that wasn't enough, pulling her by the hand. Maybe even a bit endearingly innocent. *A side she doesn't too often show.*

Either way, time was of the "Essence" as prophesied by WizKid over the emerging, *much* slower melody. (Arielle didn't follow a lot of current music, but she knew the first time hearing his hypnotic Afrobeats a year back that she had to keep pace.)

But now, the music had her subtly gulping on a drink she'd long gone swallowed.

For it was...

Now just steps away...

...Turned inches...

...Face to face, smiling and laughing...

"Oh, you know *THIS* one, too?!!"

Jae'cy's big, shining eyes, wide full-lipped smile, handclaps and finger snaps. And those whinin—

"I...have to use the restroom." Arielle bounced her eyes aside as fast as she could and Jae'cy responded by lowering her hands and slowing down hips that didn't need to be made in Nigeria to prove their capabilities.

*What is goin' on with me???* But she knew—Arielle knew exactly what was goin' on.

Her resolution to stay away from women for a while was being attacked by a voice saying "Risk it all." And right then, that proposition (the hips, the lips, the thighs, the eyes, gazing back at her) wasn't looking too—

*Restroom. NOW.*

She had to Slide Out, even if just temporarily. She pushed open the restroom door, and the AC allowed her to exhale finally...then feel damp coolness.

Yep, there were way too many bodies in here.

But she'd eventually, now that the "Vibe" had changed to Cookiee Kawaii, have to go back out there to them.

To one...

...Who, back at the table as the artist finished up their first painting (a heart burning), asked, "Isn't it like *super* hot in here now?! Or is it just me?"

♡ 16

JAE'CY LET OUT HER OWN BREATH OF RELIEF AS SHE LEFT HER HOTEL ROOM BATHROOM, curls fallen, makeup removed, lashes, too. She ambled past Arielle to grab the remote from the desk she was sitting at. Having dropped Jae'cy off here to ensure her arrival on her film set the next day, Arielle was surprised to see that Jae'cy still looked like the same person in bare face. Arielle had seen some scary cases where she'd thought a stranger had snuck into her bed during the night. Case in point, the woman who'd turned into bamboo.

"Your cousin is funny! She doesn't even *need* the drinks!"

"Yeah...she *really* doesn't."

Jae'cy chuckled while working unsatisfactorily at her jumpsuit's back zipper in front of the full-length mirror. Poor thing wasn't even close, her fingers nowhere by the top zipper. And Arielle couldn't tell which had the pink lemonade: her struggling at the mirror or the mirror leaning against the wall. Arielle had to briefly look to the random commercial playing to keep from snickering.

"Miss DeBarge, I saw that. You could actually help."

Arielle rose. "Y'all women," she commented on Jae'cy's nails. "Just unnecessary."

"*Just* unzip it, please. Didn't ask for any of the side comments."

"Then y'all equally bogus, too, with that nice nasty."

"Nice nasty!" Jae'cy trailed out a laugh. "And wait—'*Bogus?!*' Girl, you really do live in the past."

Arielle twitchily grinned. But not for what had just been said. For what was about to come...

Arielle completed the favor, pulling the zipper down until just before the middle of Jae'cy's back appeared. Jae'cy could handle it from there. *She HAS to.* "There you go, queen. Anything else needed from the pauper?"

"Nope, you're all done servin' me. For now." Jae'cy trailed out another chuckle.

Arielle only blinked...as Jae'cy managed the rest of her back zipper: Down the valley of her back...To a new hill...

Arielle lifted her gaze to the mirror, where Jae'cy's vision had already settled on hers. Then Jae'cy widened those eyes a bit subtly—yet also with acute reactiveness that her other movements tonight hadn't even come close to achieving.

Arielle hop-stepped away with an affected, nervous chuckle. "*Unh*-unh. I know that face. No more requests."

Jae'cy let out a giggle as she headed back into the bathroom...then another as she reemerged (in a surprisingly simple gym tee that must've been from high school, along with kickaround shorts). Arielle tried to focus on the Court TV, trying *so* hard right now to become a remote jury member.

"Lookin' a lil' uncomfortable there," Jae'cy jested as she alighted onto the bed. "Must be a complex case."

Arielle peered over at her. "I have outside clothes on." There was one thing Arielle didn't play about, and that was germs. It was what she hated the most about traveling and having to stay in hotels.

Jae'cy crossed her eyebrows in fascinated confusion, then gave her attention to her cell phone..."*You* put some better clothes on, emaciated-lookin'—!"

Arielle peered again at Jae'cy, who suddenly had a glassiness in the eyes that Arielle felt instead of saw.

Jae'cy showed her cell phone. "Look at this."

Arielle slowly arose, sat next to Jae'cy, then beheld the cell phone screen, which hosted a full-body selfie of Jae'cy in a hip-hugging short set. And then a host of fawning comments:

*It's like that???* 👀 👀

*You betta* 💥 🔥 😍

*Face card neva declines* 😍

*When you slidin' thru over to me next?*

Then THE comment:

*Uh...hopefully after she slides back over them dinner rolls she keep stealin from her momma (Who STILL looks betta than her)* 😩 😫

Followed by Jae'cy's response, one Arielle wouldn't say she didn't expect as Jae'cy read it aloud...

"You're right. 'Cause you're already my sidepiece, bih!"

*...But, man, is THAT what you really had to go with though?*

Arielle looked up at Jae'cy.

Jae'cy lost her icy grin. And gained a cocked eyebrow. "Now, what's *your* problem?"

*I could ask you the same. Why you need validation, when that cool exterior of yours portrays otherwise.* Arielle studied Jae'cy. She honestly was feeling annoyed, even though she was just starting to get the privilege of seeing a side of Jae'cy that she didn't give to the public. And she wished that Jae'cy could see just how awesome that was, *she* was. Not as a "celebrity" or "Paula Young's daughter." Just as Jae'cy, and be ten toes down in that.

Because if not, that was how a person got tripped up, tripped themselves up.

"That's how the social media game *still* is?"

"Goofies still trippin' in our DMs and posts, we have to show them the jungle they landed themselves in. Me and Breyah were JUST talkin' about this earlier."

Arielle believed that "a formula of entertaining foolishness with foolishness equals nothing else but more foolishness." And whoops, she'd just said so aloud.

"Okay, I'll let you talk to them next time then, Aristotle," Jae'cy pushed out a short chuckle. "About their favorite subject, which is obviously me because my old boyfriends *definitely* didn't have any complaints."

The current crime of passion trial playing on the TV couldn't have been more darkly ironic.

"So, how come you're not with any of them now?"

Jae'cy flared her nostrils in a way that Arielle had to admit made her internally flitter a bit. The most chill girls were always the most chilling. Maybe because they kept so much inside. Who knew what they held in there?

But in Jae'cy's eyes, Arielle began to see more clearly some ideas. The ones that helped her write her own stories. Ones she preferred to keep on paper in "characters."

Arielle headed to the desk for her keys. That was enough psychoanalysis for today—even for a writer.

"Oh, now you're in your feelings? These bums do this for a livin'."

Arielle looked over. "But you're the actress. You can be *anything*...a chef...and more."

Jae'cy held her gaze. Her eyes were the most focused they'd ever been. Arielle gazed a second longer, releasing a low, silently compassionate although still annoyed breath, then bid her farewell with a barely there nod.

Jae'cy let out a snigger, while her eyebrows furrowed. She leaned back against the headboard, folding her arms, glassy eyes flickering. And not in a good way. "Lighten up!"

Arielle wryly smiled, trying to keep cool from the heat that was rising in her. "I can do lightheartedness, but I can't do mindlessness. Whether in romantic relationships or friendships. Not even as a kid, and definitely not now. If that makes me uptight, then," Arielle yielded, shrugged somberly, "so be it."

Jae'cy paused, quieted, and turned her head to Arielle, who maintained her gaze, to see if Jae'cy was finally taking her seriously. Jae'cy inhaled stiffly, chewing her inner cheek, then looked away.

With that, Arielle gave a last tip of the head. *I'm staying neutral. This is just business, and I should've just dropped her off.* "Have a good shoot tomorrow and a safe flight."

"Whatever, girl. It is *not* that deep."

Arielle opened and then shut the door. To the deep that could've been but was too busy trying to swim away.

*Must be an LA thing, to keep it shallow and a show.*

It was all well and good anyway; in the end, Arielle had just been taxed out.And wanted her damn money back.

Jae'cy had shown her shadow side, and it was a fermented thing, mixed with some yeast, water, juice…and suppressed pain. The universal thing that made people sway, lack the ability to stay ten toes down.

*Yep, everyone back to their own.*

Starting with Arielle. With her favored drink of choice.

♡ **17**

"TAKE *SEVENTEEN*! Geez!"

The announcement caused all types of high laughter, from Tish and her wife, her very round-bellied wife, Erica, with a huge half-blue, half-pink painted box in front of them.

The big kid, Arielle's homie was about to have the first kid of her own. Arielle couldn't believe it when she'd gotten the call.

After first visiting Elizabeth, Arielle had made her way across town to a solid middle-class 'burb of Detroit where her once adamantly "I'm never settlin' down" friend had, in fact, recently settled. The green lawn in the backyard was something Tish had never had, coming up in a tiny apartment in the inner-city. Arielle was proud of her.

But she was sure ready to head back out west to the dry heat she kind of liked now. She could just feel fluids prepped to drop any time now as she baked in this humid stickiness.

"It's a…"

Raylen, Tish's niece, was now a full-blown girl…goofily prancing around with the box.

"I'm so glad my bro took care of it," Tish always used to say to Arielle and their group of same-major (Media Communications) college friends. That was her answer to the whole kids question back then, her parents being good enough with at least one of their children giving them grandkids. And thus, Tish was good enough with just being the fun auntie, taking in Raylen as the daughter she didn't have by always letting her tag along at the park when she'd go shoot hoops. But that was the only kind of bond (bind) Tish ever welcomed, because relationships only meant strings attached ("nails and bolts" was Tish's specific, explanatory wording). Only meant love and the possible chaos it could bring.

As Raylen played around with the non-nailed down box, it was clear that she was definitely silly. She get it from her auntie. Tish finally struck up an eyebrow at her and Raylen giggled as she obediently placed her hands on the box lid, pulled back, and…

Nothing but blue balloons floated up to the sky.

Tish rocketed a fist up into the air while Erica rolled her eyes. Arielle took it that her favorite color was pink.

"Yessir! Baby Drew it is," Tish ignited first.

"BOY!" the crowd catapulted right behind her.

Erica must not have been too disappointed, though, because she giggled lightly and took Tish's cheek gently in one of her hands, Tish looking back down at her. Erica had artfully and wordlessly conquered Tish, and she kissed her.

Arielle cut her eyes away to her phone. Yep, it was time to Slide Out to the airport. Back home, her new book's beta reading phase was readily approaching. It would be a bit different for her fans, this thriller/action-oriented tale. But with the usual wit of her trusty main character, she believed her fellowship would be content.

This time, at least, she'd foretold the event host about the exact time of her departure.

"Still breakin' ankles, AI?!" That had been Tish's response to not Allen Iverson, but to Arielle Introverted. However, Tish wasn't really one to talk. She, herself, could rival the great AI and his fast, deflecting handles, because she used to be just as speedy in diverting from even second dates with girls back in school.

But now the ex-bachelorette had hung up her (player) jersey—or placed it away in a box, after removing the nails and bolts.

"You never know, AI. The next one might be your box of plenty," Tish had chuckled into her ear.

But all Arielle could hear was that, damn, Erica had made even Tish's characteristic hyena-esque laugh different. More self-possessed, cool, collected. Tame. Maybe even...

Human.

*Dang, lost another one to the game.* Arielle wryly smiled in memory of that not-so-distant conversation. *Well, hope you have better luck than me, Tish. Or a much better piece of armor around that heart of yours...Or a much better game still left in that player's jersey if need be.*

Then Arielle's "smile" became tighter. *Of course she has better game: breaking hearts rather than ankles. Because she was always the one breaking hearts back in the day.*

Arielle blinked all of that away, because she'd suddenly felt a slight tinge of...envy?

Fear.

*Psh, no... Just have to get to this flight. And—*

*BUZZ.*

*To this phone ringing. Sigh.*

Always something to get to, to get away from something else. Yep, Arielle stood firm on that as she then equally held true to her age-old ways, passing the front lawn of Tish's two-story brick home to await her rideshare.

So, in the meantime...

*BUZZ.*

She finally reached for the phone, but when her eyes met the screen, her suddenly sullen face turned even more so.

It was now on the third ring. Time to make a decision...

"Hello?"

"Ma'am, I am just calling to say I'm alive...obviously," Jae'cy responded, with a light laugh.

Arielle could tell that it was a forced laugh, because its tone was the same awkward, lagging beat as the words before it. Arielle delayed a reply because, quite frankly, she had a lot and nothing at all that she wanted to say. She really didn't like the feeling of having so many words and so few places to put them. Words were something she could usually control—the *only* thing she could.

Then she exhaled, just let it go. Why was she getting so worked up over a girl who was just business? She'd already vowed to operate on a non-emotional plane.

*...But I said I might get a story out of this...*

"Hopefully...or this is a cause of concern right now."

Jae'cy chuckled again, still low and light in delivery but purer now. The tension was broken. Arielle smiled a bit, cooperatively.

"*Annnd...*" Jae'cy paused. She wasn't here, and Arielle wasn't there, but Arielle could see it right now in her head from observing the gesture many times in person: Jae'cy knocking her head to the side casually with a slight smile, before defensively, warily admitting something intimate.

The memory of that face now gave way to slowly developing photographic recall. It was proving hard to grasp the entire face, but she could clearly see snapshots of its parts. *Dang, such a tough case.*

Jae'cy continued, "Secondly, I know that I am a work in progress, and...it might start with putting down the mimosas."

Arielle mustered up a small, surprised smile. At least Jae'cy had self-reflection, but she wouldn't be naive about it. "...And putting down people with your other hitter."

Still, she was one to want to work with someone's potential, like the literary version of a miner: finding diamonds, the perfect jewel, in the rough. Sometimes, it was a hit (for her professionally, at least). And other times...Well, that was *another* story.

"But, I'm a certain Greek man's ghostwriter, not a bartender, so I can't really help you on the moderation policing. And even if I was, I still couldn't because...then I'd be a Greek bartender. So..."

Jae'cy now was squealing, Arielle chuckling lightly with her.

"Well then, as I work on my *new* beginning... can you at least assist me during my *grand opening*?"

This time, there was no Paula-esque declarative wording within the question mark. It was, for once, a true request.

*Well, that's…new,* Arielle thought. She hadn't even realized she'd felt disrespected until she noticed, now, how she didn't feel disrespected anymore.

And that felt good to Arielle, to be more valued. And *that* was new, too.

And so, although she didn't explain to Jae'cy that she'd actually be coming into LA anyway for Sinead's birthday (just a relaxed family-only breakfast and hangout at her spot, shockingly, and hence why she was coming), she obliged. "Okay, but I won't be arriving until later."

Now that respect was being shown more, she wanted to keep it that way. And of course, with respect being a two-way street, since she'd helped with the café launch, it was only right to complete the business of it, even if social events weren't her thing. It was no different than the momentary fraternizing she used to do at company events back in her marketing days.

"Great, DeBarge! I'll send the deets. See you there with sneakers and *without* Stacy Adams and impromptu doo-wop on the stage. We don't need that service from you, already got our performers. Comprendes?"

And after Jae'cy parted with a good-natured "Bye," Arielle hung up with a snicker. *She better have a box of plenty more goodies. Like those yams.*

♡ **18**

"HERE WE ARE AT THE OPENING OF THE LATEST FUSION EATERY TO GRACE LA!" rang out from an urban news reporter and her camera crew in front of a packed food tent and a procession of public figures, celebs, and other fans and supporters. And by way of a walkway connecting it, there was a beach, volleyball net, and pop-up stage where a rapper was entertaining to a crowd across the street.

"None other than Honest Bites Café, the creation of none other than award-winning Paula Young's daughter Jae'cy Carter. If you're not familiar with Jae'cy, you sure will be after you try *these* right here!" In the reporter's hands was a takeout container of the Louisiana wings. Of which she had to take a bite. "And as you see, Paula Young herself is performing for this big turnout here at her daughter's beachside festivities to raise earnings for Honest Bites' neighboring charity organization."

"Here you are!" a cashier under the tent announced, then speedily deployed two trays of air-fried, Cajun-spiced potato wedges and those infamous Louisiana jerk wings to a customer at the front of that long line. Beside them was the strip of business suites, the first being the nonprofit that Jae'cy had mentioned to her during their first meeting, and who the fundraising would be helping today. Then there was the café with a grand opening banner running across its entrance, and a sign that said

*HONEST BITES.*

Arielle read that and then the space around her as she arrived and passed by, forgoing any food right now from a still-full stomach at Sinead's brunch (the girl had actually kindly made her a Just Egg veggie scramble). Of course, she would be taking a to-go container of her usual before leaving here. But first—

"Ight, ight! Listen up! Yeah, I know. *Another* favor. But it's for a good cause, you feel me? We need each and every one of y'all to COP somethin' to eat..." The same commanding DJ from the last open-air scenario boomed over the speakers, dropping his track low in his set-up, on the sidelines of the beach volleyball court across the street via the walkway. "Fifteen percent of all orders will go toward this hardworking group of gents and ladies that is fightin' for the well-being of our next generation of young gents and ladies..." The DJ pointed to a quintet of middle-aged men and women in matching nonprofit logo tees, standing beside him and looking to the applauding crowd with humble smiles.

Arielle had already been virtually acquainted with the nonprofit through a link that Jae'cy had provided. And so, she passed by that, too,..

...strolling by people of all ages on the walkway who were holding drinks and plates. Looking instead at what she was slowly approaching...as she heard Paula and a fellow singer begin a duet on the pop-up stage now some feet ahead of her. Mostly older folks in the crowd, but a few younger people, too, were all clapping along, shouting out professions of love (the men) or "You go, girl!" (the women) as Paula winked back at them from the stage. Seeing Paula live in action for herself, Arielle was wondering why she hadn't hopped on Juliana's fangirl train a long time ago....

But that also wasn't what Arielle stopped at, instead stopping because she'd now been spotted by Jae'cy, Breyah, Michi, and friends watching the stage on the outskirts of it...and after a quick snap with a fan/supporter...

Jae'cy motioned Arielle over. And all eyes fell on her.

*Nope, still not that DeBarge.*

But damn, where was he right now when one needed his high "ooh baby" to Paula's sudden alto "mm" for deflection? Wasn't this Cali???

Arielle exhaled low as she made it over, for she'd just entered the inner circle. And she *didn't* like it.

The crowd was in chinos and loafers, cargos, skinny jeans, rompers, dresses, and fresh white Nikes or wedges. But Jae'cy was doing her own thing, casual but chic in newly installed long braids, free-flowing down her button-up shirt, sleeves cuffed, paired with a necklace and shorts and strapped sandals. But the point remained that the legs were leggin', Arielle spied, then jumped her eyes back up to Jae'cy just in time for a—

"Hey, there," Jae'cy welcomed Arielle, and the rest of the crew either nodded (the guys, excluding Michi) or smiled a bit (the girls, including Breyah).

Luckily for Arielle, the vibe immediately seemed more open this time around (excluding Michi) as the gang just the same returned their attention to the food, sunshine, and that spectacular music by—

"Your momma, Paula. She thinks she's doin' somethin' up there," said an older guy coming from the direction of the stage, who, upon greater inspection, Arielle realized from social media was Paula's boyfriend, Kadeem. He flashed a grin under sunglasses and a cap.

"Ha-ha," Jae'cy responded with a playful eye roll. "Let's save the jokes for after the end of this set *that* is five times harder than those so-called Olympic sets you have her doing at the gym."

"Your attitude still needs work, but your menu's a success. So Imma…" Kadeem moved onward with a chuckle.

*One point for Jae'cy*, Arielle humored herself in thought as she dodged an incoming look of displeasure from Michi to tend to her white (!) Nikes that had some sand on them.

And also intentionally took the opportunity to scope out the rest of the people at the party, particularly any queer women like herself… She did. Ones with some nice kicks on. We're talkin' Gucci and Yeezys. Arielle peeped that, peeped Michi, then peeped her literally dusty simple Nikes. She couldn't win for losing with this guy…It had to be something deeper than shoes or appearances, must've been something about *her*…

*Wouldn't be the first time.*

"Any plans after this, J?" He brought his attention elsewhere, at least for now.

Jae'cy, seemingly clueless to this not-so-kind friend of hers as she people-watched, replied, "Em. Nope, now that I'm a really working, working momma, I'll be going on home to take care of some business."

Then she purposely turned an eye at him, a rousing smile. "And maybe I'll find you some, too."

"Daaaaang!" Breyah started and the rest finished the quick laugh, now all eyes on Michi.

"She got you, bro."

*Two points for Jae'cy.*

And with that, Michi put up the deuce wordlessly. Too prideful to show defeat—his girl, or one of his girls since she was a new one, Arielle noted, was with him. "WE'RE headin' to the food, too."

*Now that THAT'S done. Even though ole boy looked like he wanted to cry just now, on to someone else—*

"Lil' rugrat!" Jae'cy's voice proclaimed.

Running by was a giggling Cori chasing a little boy seemingly around the same age. But the thing was, as Arielle now noted the boy didn't appear to be havin' it. And so, he bolted off, living her in the dust (sand). Naturally, Cori pouted, folding her arms.

As Jae'cy shook her head playfully, Arielle was somehow transported back to her own childhood. Moments she thought— admittedly, a little sourly—about every now and then and how right then in that particular moment it felt so much like the present, looking and pointing right back at her.

Naturally, Breyah and the gang chuckled good-naturedly. But for some reason, a reason that strangely crawled under her skin, Arielle didn't think *that* was the greatest move. Correction: She knew it wasn't the greatest move.

And sure enough, as she'd intuited, that was the worst thing they could've done. Because in Cori's eyes, and ears, all she'd translated from that was—

"You're humilitian me!"

*These kids sure were advanced these days.* Granted, this particular kid was trying to say "humiliated," but those were a lot of well-enunciated syllables even still that she'd accomplished even if her emotional regulation still wasn't quite there yet. The best Arielle could come up with at Cori's age was "You suck!" because she was a wee bit temperamental back then, and having a teenage brother ten years older certainly didn't help.

But more than humiliated, Cori was—

"...Wa HAAAA!"

Now crying. Bawling, sniffling, the works. Lips trembling and curled down, making her look more like a newborn again rather than the approaching-five-year-old that she now was. But there was always that very, very little part of us still tucked away inside, even in the littlest of us.

Arielle knew. She *knew.* And she saw it in Cori, the usually sassy little girl, whose lips now only quivered more with the largest heaves. All over what one moment could do.

Jae'cy held her arms out. "Aw, Rumpa. No one's making fun of you."

"Unh-huh! You just DID!"

"Baby, don't be like—"

"They weren't laughing *at* you," came another, heroic voice. *Yes, save the day.*

*Wait a minute...*

*NO. No-no-no.*

But naturally, everyone else now had heard the voice, too—and were looking her way. Not Jae'cy's way, Arielle's way.

She was truly actin' out of character, but something about seeing that baby face so...close to the skin. The young needed to be protected.

Arielle said again, a bit louder, "They weren't judging you. Promise." And then suddenly she found she had the baby in her arms. Yes, Cori was now on Arielle's hip.

*AWK-waaard.*

Jae'cy helped by leading Arielle and a now head-burying Cori to the sidewalk. "This girl is very competitive."

*You don't say.*

"And—" Jae'cy mouthed: "She's sleepy."

She needn't have mouthed it, because Cori was blowing out Arielle's eardrums. "Anything sweet and cold?" Arielle followed along. (The first—sweet—part of the request was for Cori, the second—cold—was for her.)

Funny enough, as if it was really as much of a chaotic club scene as it felt, Jae'cy duly nodded in seamless comprehension, already pumping toward the café and by a temporarily doting, offstage Paula and her slice of cake.

"Uh-oh. What's goin' on with Mee-Maw's baby?"

But before Jae'cy could explain further, an editorial photographer was coming up for the prized "celeb mother and daughter" photo.

Paula gave a sweet wink to the photographer. "Sorry, baby. But as you can see, my baby has to tend to hers. Take a break to enjoy some of this good stuff right here." She showcased the cake.

And with that the photographer dutifully obliged with a smile and carried on, just as Kadeem arrived and playfully nudged Paula then nudged his head down at her cake.

Paula rolled her eyes and gave a defying lick of her fork. "I know, I know, hallway monitor. But the lil' FUPA," Paula presumed, modeled her figure with her hand on her flat tummy, FUPA no more. "Courtesy of my child and Sara Lee has long sunk so you can pipe on down, too." Then she sashayed off with a grinning Kadeem…who then helped himself to a piece of the cake.


Three cherry-rimmed lemonades later, the three sat on barstools against a wall in the spacious café, Cori now reduced to a damp-eyed, sniffly countenance.

Then she scrunched up her nose.

"I don't like it!" she whimpered, pushing the straw away.

"Em-em." Jae'cy softly struck up an eyebrow, much like the tone of her voice: a gentle but evident mother's chastisement. For being hurt didn't warrant being bratty.

Arielle seized the preoccupied mother-daughter moment to quietly pick up her own cup (heavy on the ice) and press it against her shoulder. Amidst her fallout, Cori's fingernails had dug into her.

Then she pulled the cherry off the rim of the glass, popped it in her mouth.

Now Cori was in the process of turning her head (and sniffles) in her direction. Both Arielle and Jae'cy watched her, giving her the attention she wanted. Noting how she resembled a mini-Paula, Arielle chuckled on the low.

Jae'cy wiped the tears from the little one's big cheeks. "She is a *whole* mess."

Arielle realized Jae'cy's voice became so much higher when she was really tickled. Then her eyes, looking more *unadulter*ated than Arielle had witnessed them ever before, landed on Arielle.

*SCREECH!!*

The stool legs' shifted against the floor as Cori suddenly dismounted and shimmied down.

And Arielle cut her eyes to the walls: painted designs of vintage LA and rural South images, two framed photos high above the mounted menu board. They had plaques underneath, naming Jae'cy's maternal and paternal grandmothers. Looking back at Jae'cy as Cori took off, seemingly recovered, she said sincerely, "Good job."

Jae'cy fluttered a bit, ever so subtly, but Arielle caught it. "Thank you…my mom really helped today, setting up included. But she won't be doin' the same tonight because she has a 'date.'"

"Testing out trainers with her…trainer?"

Jae'cy squealed; Arielle put herself on timeout with a new sip.

"And some more Olympic…sets?"

Okay, this time a real, longer sip.

"*DIS!*-missed."

Jae'cy just as soon settled anew. And then, there was a slight quiver of just one corner of her mouth.

Arielle gulped while waiting for what she didn't want to see.

*Oh, no. Please, not the—*

Flicker in the gaze.

Arielle hung her head. Because, additionally, a trap beat had started thumping inside as a food prep employee exited the automatic sliding doors with a new pan of victuals for the crowd. *Put Paula's cake down and put her back on the stage. Please put her back on.*

"Oh, the first time you were *MORE* than happy to assist the up-and-comers, DeBarge, so what's the problem now?!" Jae'cy smacked her lips.

"Anyway, I could appreciate the helping hand again for something. Well, really just someone who knows how to taste."

Arielle thought she'd just choked on a cherry pit.

♡ 19

AND NOW, LESS THAN THREE HOURS LATER, what could she say? Cherries were her favorite fruit.

And apparently Paula's. Arielle noted from the counter in Paula's kitchen, something like a Zombie Apocalypse mound of bags of cherries as Paula tossed the present one in her possession inside the fridge, then popped one of the pieces in her mouth.

And then popped something else into the air.

"Soooo, y'all cute for each other?" Jae'cy didn't stop stirring her…concoction. (Arielle was scared to know what exactly was in there—it seemed like it might be a mighty strong chicken, putting up the good fight.)

And so did Arielle's esophagus. She coughed out a low chuckle as Jae'cy emitted a sound of pretty much the same effect while returning to her normal tempo.

"Uh, negative, Ma. I'm not even her type."

"What she said."

Jae'cy and Arielle were the only ones still laughing—and who had only been laughing at all.

Paula wasn't helping tonight, but she'd kindly lent her house for the cooking session. She raised an unconvinced brow but moved on in her shimmery pants set, pearled up from wrists to neck to ears, as her cell phone rang.

"…Mm-kay…'Cause I was sayin', we don't have to keep it that way. We can keep it REAL in here. Lashes off, bras," Paula informed just as casually as she checked her phone then grabbed her purse off the island stool. "*And* other pretenses. Okay? All of that is for outside."

Then she moved her words to her phone as she moved on out of the room. "Sir, I'm steppin' out now. Don't rush me; this isn't an a.m. date with kettlebells…"

Jae'cy continued stirring, then headed to the fridge, bending into it.

Arielle's smile quivered a bit, looking. Then she quickly straightened up, as Jae'cy shimmy-turned to her with one arm full of bell peppers, the other nestling coconut cream and coconut milk. "A creamy base or a more fluid one?"

"And *no*, there won't be cheese, eggs, or anything that walks on four legs."

"What about two?" Arielle looked at Jae'cy's legs heading to a spice cabinet, and cut her eyes away to her cherries.

Cori suddenly hopped in, and up on a stool, pushing a coloring page into Arielle's face that was actually pretty darn good for a kid who'd just learned how to hold a pencil maybe two years ago.

Arielle leaped her eyes up dramatically and asked, "How much you charge for lessons?"

Cori gave a full belly laugh. But this was no laughing matter to the third person in the room.

"That's what I'm gonna be asking the summer school if someone doesn't finish *her science* lesson." Jae'cy only revealed a scant smirk at the end.

Cori's mouth, shoulders, and voice dropped faster than the ill-fated Lake Mead as she begrudgingly took to a worksheet directly in front of her. That was when Arielle caught a glimpse of the bane of the little one's existence: Pluto, the reject planet.

As Cori began to look up at Arielle for some divine intervention, a.k.a. big person help, Arielle spotted a heart-shaped white area on the celestial body in the science assignment's aerial view photo. Then her eyes pivoted down to a lone yet complex paragraph of the homework project and, reading it aloud, wondered how it was kindergarten-appropriate: "Here is Pluto as recorded from NASA's New Horizons spacecraft. Its heart-shaped saltwater mass is comprehensively inhabited with poisonous ice. What do you think about that?"

Cori expectedly just continued to stare.

"So, all this time, Pluto was human?" Arielle sarcastically questioned.

Cori tittered again. In the adult dark comedy version of it all, Arielle was working to have her responsive mouth show synonymous amusement rather than the tension it was truly feeling at that moment, thinking about human nature. And once again, the only fellow big person in the room was the tougher one in the crowd: Jae'cy turned to a cupboard with a stiff arm and a light—very light—snicker.

Looked like the assignment would need more work. So, clearing her throat, Arielle straightened a bit and looked more studiously at the paper. And Cori listened. "Now, knowing everything that you do about Pluto, say aloud the most favorite thing you've learned."

"Mm..." Cori twiddled some of her coily tufts, swung her nearest leg right next to Arielle. "It's a dwarf?"

"And what does that mean?" Arielle continued to read the prompted guided practice instructions from the assignment.

"It doesn't belong!" Cori giggled hysterically once again.

And Arielle felt another twitch, another thought on human nature...and its views on those who didn't quite seem to fit. "But serious really quick. School *is* serious. And I know you're seriously smart, too. So, be serious *and* smart, okay?"

Cori paused. *Welp, guess the comedian had to end the show eventually.* And even with her attention on Cori on this parental-like stage she'd just mysteriously put herself on, Arielle felt the slight turn of Jae'cy's head in their direction.

Cori nodded quietly, then just as before, in kid-fashion, skipped on back off to whatever happy land kids mentally had the privilege to dwell in while adults were deported from it.

But maybe Jae'cy had been able to sneak back into her own old Kiddie Land just then, Arielle shifted her eyes over to see Jae'cy savoring a spoonful of whatever she'd just taken from the simmering pot. "*Oooh* yeah. You did that, Yung J," she told herself. Then her eyes glided over to Arielle.

Arielle decided it was time to get off the stage—but not without some kind of closing.

"My bad."

Jae'cy slowed her stirring a bit. "For what?"

*For what?? I just lightweight disciplined your kid...* "Don't really know where that life lesson came from..."

Jae'cy wiped her hands on a towel, slowly, wordlessly. "No, you're right. She's *too* smart for her own good sometimes."

"I just want the best for people."

"Never would've guessed." Jae'cy roused up a smile. "Nah, it's good—she's gettin' older now. That's what my mom and I have been talking about. How it's time for her to understand bigger commitments...so she just got a lesson on it, from a good teacher."

*Oh, wow. Was that actually a compliment from Yung Hitta? How did that just happen?*

"And I don't just let anyone talk to my kid, so..." She chuckled lightly. Arielle assessed Jae'cy's posture, which had turned directly to face Arielle. "So...doing more of that is perfectly fine by me."

Arielle inhaled, swallowed, then nodded.

Because although she had always been unsure about parenting (of course, not thinking about this situation in that kind of way!), a guardian type of role was something she *could* imagine.

"'Cause Mama's teachin' is a lil' bit different and involves actions instead of words," Jae'cy exhaled her proclamation, dramatically.

"Uh-oh. Well, I want her to dodge some of my childhood fate," Arielle responded, while having some "belt and Elizabeth" flashbacks.

where she'd show out or stubbornly not listen. Single mother trials and tribulations. "So whenever that's about to happen, just let this substitute step in." Then she pointed to herself.

"Okay, I'm holdin' you to it."

…Arielle thought on that statement, that commitment, as Jae'cy turned back to the stove.

"Now, back to this." Jae'cy dipped a new spoon into the pot, and then cupped it over to Arielle. "Bell pepper sauce. Vegan. Promise."

Arielle tried it. No after note (she'd just learned that word from Jae'cy a second ago). *Dang, that's good.* She didn't even know her eyes had been closed until she opened them, and there was Jae'cy cocking an eyebrow up at her, arms folded in waiting.

*And yet, my stomach just got queasy.* Arielle forced herself to focus back on the taste…

And then she felt the heat flow down—an after note, possibly some cayenne.

"Okay…" Arielle rubbed her lips together. "You know a lil' somethin' somethin'."

Indeed, she did. Knew how to give just the right amount of tantalizing spice. To make the liquid heat even stronger.

"I know this," Jae'cy affirmed, popping out a hip and a proud grin, then twirling back around to the stove. She whipped her head around to reveal a bag of asparagus. "And *this* is next."

Arielle went back to her bowl of cherries pronto. Just because she was vegan didn't mean she liked all plants. "Okay, just watch," Jae'cy finalized as she returned to the stove, making a point to fixate on Arielle's head. "…And then watch me work the same kind of magic with that hair."

That made Arielle stop the antics—stop breathing temporarily, too. But the other one had already moved on, had released the nasty green things into a new pot.

Thirty minutes and four or five ill-favored tracks later, Arielle couldn't believe it: the last sole survivor, the final asparagus stalk, was about to meet its fate.

Jae'cy stole a glance, just as the stalk disappeared into Arielle's mouth.

Arielle smirked as she rose with her plate…and as Jae'cy passed by with a fine-tooth hair comb and gel, MO3's "Outside (Better Days)" playing through Paula's Bluetooth speakers.

Nonetheless, when she turned around from the trash, a slow, cool glance met her in return.

"It was ight."

"Yeah, *IGHT!*" Jae'cy chuckled as she uncapped the gel jar. "Your hair's gonna just look *'ight'* in a minute."

"Betta than whatever that noise is," Arielle nodded back at the speakers. "Leave the music to the Aristotles, chef."

"Um, excuse *me*," Jae'cy interjected, curling the comb back to herself pridefully. "You musta forgot about Yung J. So, for your info, if you *listen* to the words of this song, it's about complex emotions of the present trying to live with that of the future. What lies outside? Change or fate? And how you're trying to go forward with all of that on the journey in mind. Hopin' that the journey itself isn't cut short."

Arielle still wasn't all the way transformed but secretly liked Jae'cy's equal passion for music—even if it wasn't on an equal instrumentation level. And so, she refrained from further verbal combat.

"If you'd actually listen to some new stuff sometime, you'd learn that a person can always acquire something from other walks of life…Even a philosopher."

Arielle slid an eye over. "I bet you revel in converting people to your side, don't you?"

"Don't *you*?" Jae'cy grinned devilishly.

*What is that supposed to—?* Arielle hid a grin.

"So, listen," she said, "I am a jack of all trades, and one of those trades is doin' hair. But all of my boyfriends, they never even let me try a line-up on them. Nuthin'. They're just as choosy as the ladies about their hair, don't believe the hype. So I was wonderin'…" She finished her proposal by revealing the comb and waggling it. "Pleaaaase?"

*Oh, this one is crazy.*

Arielle comically noted that and the fact that she *did* enjoy having her hair played with. So, she then took a seat down on the floor between Jae'cy with a shake of her head and a sigh. "You look *way* too excited right now."

"Yesssssss!" Jae'cy wasted no time in removing Arielle's ponytail holder.

"Oh, so now my dyke ass is the next best thing?"

Jae'cy temporarily dropped her comb, chuckled. Full-belly. Like mother, like daughter.

Arielle felt like an audience member admitted to an exclusive show that was about to unfold. She almost didn't know how to react. Maybe this thriller she was building was coming a bit *too* quickly.

Much like the low-budget horror film showing an unknown intruder's boots enter a dark home that she'd flipped to via the idle remote by Jae'cy's thigh. She had to do something to keep occupied.

Jae'cy picked the comb back up and ruffled out Arielle's thick hair. "What we thinkin'? Straight back? Cornrows, zig-zaggin', stitch freestyled? I gotchu," she assured, running a finger or two through Arielle's hair. "...Passion twists?"

"I dare you."

Jae'cy busted up, then demonstrated real shock. "Hooooold up. You actually know about that?"

"I know what to avoid. Yes," Arielle responded while keeping another grin under wraps. "And my fifteen-year-old niece helps, too." Then she shrugged. "But nah, I really don't—"

"Care," Jae'cy parroted divinely, shook her head. "Mm-hmm."

"But can I..." Arielle pointed at the unfolding film on the TV they were staring at. "Continue my purveying of this masterpiece...?"

"Go for it. I don't even really watch TV."

"And yet you're an actress...interestin—*ow*." Arielle winced, craning her neck around at Jae'cy to make her pain clear to the person who committed it.

The same person who peeped Arielle's still staring eyes, then nudged her before looking back up at the screen from which an actress's scream emitted. But the effort of ignoring Arielle showed in the fullness of her lips, quivering up to a smirk while containing a chuckle.

Arielle still hadn't turned her head. Still looking at the other sight in front of her..."What's happening?"

Jae'cy gestured with the comb's tip like a knife, ready for another assault. Arielle remembered real quick what Jae'cy's zodiac sign was— and turned right back around to the screen.

"Mm-*hmm*, now just play your role and watch."

Back to the film's action. Within twenty minutes (almost as swift as Jae'cy's hair braiding was), a limp arm came flapping down off the edge of a mattress. Even the villain now had an easy victory as the family dog in a jump cut on the screen jerked upward and charged out of the kitchen door for its own deducible fate.

*Speaking of out the door...*

Figuratively, Arielle did the same, clicking instantly on the remote to some random, but uncanny, documentary on the psychology of dogs.

Jae'cy squealed as she braided. "*Oo*, a lightweight once the dog gets put into question!"

Nonetheless, some kindness in her Scorpio-Sagittarius heart kicked in, and she flipped to a channel full of entertainment reality shows.

"Alright, my turn," she announced, clicking on a bachelor's dating program. "Michi—"

Arielle instantly coughed away a snicker.

Jae'cy caught it with her ears then her eyes but continued with a covert grin herself. "Told me to catch this right before he left today at the gala. He's finally gettin' 'on the map' as his secret corny old butt always says."

"Oo, sounds like we could be friends…But looks like he's 'No new friends' so…"

Jae'cy cooed out a laugh while starting on a new braid, the second to last. "Michi is just…Michi. He's a Cancer, so a lil' moody every now and then."

"…Ah."

Jae'cy giggled louder now. "Sounds like you're not convinced."

"Oh. No. Just providin' a mood."

Jae'cy erupted into an amused fit as Michi appeared in a solo intro shot on the screen, talking to the camera.

"I'm Michi. Thirty-two. And I've been known as a player."

Arielle snickered. "Who wrote this?"

"But he's got the shoulders, though! The shoulders! That's what us ladies care about."

"We know, we know," Arielle dragged out while holding back a grin as she rolled her eyes. "The tall, dark, and handsome."

Just then, Jae'cy popped up as a cameo along with Breyah and more friends, a few that had been at the launch party earlier. They were inaudibly talking at a day yacht party before it broke into a solo soundbite clip of her discussing Michi's 'everlasting bachelor' image.

However, Arielle's peripheral view suddenly became clouded by Jae'cy live in the flesh, the girl having bent her body over to check Arielle with a cocked brow and full study. "And what? Yours is lemme guess…The five-foot-five, cute and slim curvy, super exotic slash ambiguous."

Arielle slid her eyes away from the TV, from the Jae'cy on screen, and she coughed out yet another snicker, but much tighter. "Not even."

"Right, sure."

"That isn't my type," Arielle retorted with just a bit more volume but chuckled harder in amusement at Jae'cy's disbelief.

"Mm-*hm*…Then what is?"

"…Five-eight or taller. To match me." For a reason she couldn't explain, Arielle wrestled her fingers ever so subtly as if she were trying to get them to fit, even when they were in-born in her, her true body…Must've been that Scorpio penetrative effect, to make one second guess the truth of their own words. The best investigator out of anyone…even writers. "Sustenance in the body. Grown, personality and age-wise, preferably more than me. And recognizable as Black."

Every last one of those fit…the opposite of the type of person Jae'cy was adamant on.

Jae'cy squinted, but it looked more like a twitch one had when sudden dust hit—or a thought.

"I low-key—" Arielle paused herself to spasmodically grin, grapple her fingers even more... "Or I guess *high*-key now, like studs."

Jae'cy almost jiggle-giggle stabbed Arielle in the eye with that south-dipping, fine-tooth comb-holding hand. "First of all, who still says that?! And second, you're a *lie*!"

"I do."

But her lopsided grin might've dispensed some of her credibility. Honestly, Arielle did call herself more so androgynous minus the heels and makeup (which she'd prefer her girl to wear). But she thought about how Tish actually did like and date another stud back in school for a minute—actually one of her longest minutes with a girl at that time—And how no one had thought a minute about it. Other than, "Damn, that was for a *minute*!"

Behind her back of course.

"You *DEFINITELY* don't. But okay."

But this particular girl here was calling Arielle out about her attractions right in her face.

"How do you know what I like?"

Jae'cy quieted, rested on the end of the last braid left in her hand, as she pondered...And unquestionably was still not believing it...but rather figuring out what that *"it"* truly was.

Arielle shrugged, felt like she suddenly had to offer more. "Like I said: Height and age."

"Oh. So, a parent?" Jae'cy wisecracked.

"Suga momma...whatever," Arielle instantly rejoined with another shrug to play the game. "If the shoe fits...Just a real one I can walk in my *own* shoes with," she continued, concluded more somberly though, for reasons unknown. Maybe because she felt she still had to, while being on those pillows in front of studying eyes. And so, she inhaled then finally granted them access to hers. "A mature journey." Yes, although, Arielle preferred women her age or older, her ex before last had been two years younger. If she felt a vibe, and the gap wasn't too big, she'd give a person the time of the day. Long as, at the end of the day, there was a vibe, a maturity. One she hadn't yet perfectly found...or wasn't quite ready to look for in a different way...

The moment silenced. Both looking, no more quick-witted deliveries, no more quips.

Jae'cy abruptly poked her mouth to the side to be comical again, back to braiding. "Mm-*kaaaaay*...Tell me any ole thing, so I don't jack yo head up."

Arielle boomed out a chuckle at her not letting up…and hence, why she was still on this floor getting corporal punishment.

"And 'accidentally' forget to add some *edge control* on top of it…But I think I have a cute friend in mind I can hook you up with."

"That's cute for your friend. And her edges."

Jae'cy squealed.

Yet Arielle was *not* playing. "But I'm good where I am right now. Thanks."

"O*kaaay*. Suit yourself," Jae'cy, this one (surprising) time, easily conceded, finishing up the last of Arielle's long braid. As she smoothed it out with her hands to beautify it a bit, she ran the fingers down the lengthy road, closer to Arielle's neck….shoulder…mid-back valley…

"All done."

Then just the quiet.

Both still just looking at one another.

Kind of like a moment ago but longer, kind of like the moment before that at the hotel but without the mirror. And without any vodka mixed in the drinks, just two glasses of their finished plain lemonade resting on Paula's kitchen island.

And then—

"ARE YOU READY FOR SOME FUN?!!"

Cori and her handheld learning game

Arielle tersely blinked a few times, then turned her head to the little girl as she bounced onto the other solo perpendicular couch. But Cori had her curious attention instead on Michi and a woman now gazing googly-eyed at one another across a table in a restaurant on the TV.

In the next second, Cori moved her head from Jae'cy (softly brushing in edge control) to Arielle (dazing at the screen).

"Are you girl—"

*Oh, no. No, no, no, no. Noooo.*

"Friends?"

Arielle felt her stomach drop. She stifled an uncomfortable grin, and then they looked back at Jae'cy, who widened her eyes. Arielle broke the silence with a mellow chuckle.

Jae'cy smiled at Cori. "Uh, no, baby. Elle is my friend who *is* a girl. Like your friends at school."

Cori moved her head back to the TV with a shrug. "Okay." And then she bounced right off of the couch and pranced over to the fridge.

Arielle spoke, low. "What is going *on* today?"

"Mommy, I'm hungry!"

Jae'cy rose with a light, laidback exhalation. "Welp, time to feed this little growin' woman."

Like the kind(er) hostess she was surprisingly proving herself to be today, she walked Arielle to the front door. When she caught a glimpse of herself in the hallway mirror, she couldn't help but pause in observation: seven braids in simple straight-back rows. Had to keep it masculine-of-center and alla that. But Jae'cy had pulled out a couple of baby hairs in the front.

"Okay,...you did that," Arielle verified while finishing up some side-profile glances like she was at a video shoot. "Now, let me go show some girl that this time love's for real."

"*BYE*, Elle!" Jae'cy swung the door open with a titter.

And that was when Jae'cy got even more kind. Far too kind—no Jay Z.

Smiling, as Arielle turned from the mirror...and saw the opening of her arms. "Thanks for all of your continued help."

Arielle wavered there a second, because she wasn't usually the hugging type (her family practically had to force her). But this time...

She twitched on a smile, then took a step forward. Opened her arms.

And received the hug and its chuckle. "And letting me touch that head."

And then, a kiss.

Touching Arielle's cheek with her lips. After they pulled away, that was all Arielle saw.

"Sure...no problem..."

And then, she saw those almond eyes, looking back at her. No flicker, just full. Sweet. That was new.

*And that was, Elle, what you've—*

Arielle had gotten distracted of her next moves (having landed down the porch steps outside) because...of the approaching presence of someone new.

He was an average tall guy, with chains like Deonte but less of them, more complementary. Where Deonte seemed flashy for the performance, this guy did it for the award...that he already knew he was going to get. And Arielle knew as he came closer that he was related to Cori. His distinctive, thick black hair trying to be tamed under his brushed waves as he tipped his head cool at Arielle showed resemblance to Cori's boundless mane.

"Daddy's girl. *There* she go," he smoothly said, strolling right on by Arielle and then by Jae'cy. He crouched down to Cori who peered from behind Jae'cy, a hand on her mother's thigh, backpack on.

Cori smiled, close-mouthed, then finally revealed some teeth and dimples.

*Based on that facial expression, he must be the weekend parent tops.* Arielle's investigation mode had involuntarily kicked in.

She also figured he had to be of some kind of Caribbean or Afro-Latino blood, based on the mahogany skin and sleek hair. Not to mention catching him in a social media post or two, (once again, thanks to Juliana's pop culture news bites) with some kind of Caribbean flag—

*AD,* Arielle just then randomly recalled. Or Adrian, his full first name. He was an urban celeb events promoter. And that was all she knew—or cared to know.

That was when Arielle decided this was all the socializing she needed today, so just as Jae'cy ironically glanced her way, she nodded toward the door.

"See you later," Jae'cy imparted casually. Arielle perceived that it had to be a practiced move she gave in parting to reporters all of the time based on how instantly it had come on.

But based on how Jae'cy turned her attention even more flatly to AD immediately thereafter, Arielle realized the shift in her energy and tonality was for AD, not Arielle. Jae'cy was irritated and trying to have control over it.

And quite frankly, not doing a great job—Jae'cy looked pissed. "She hasn't eaten yet," she told AD. "Because you said you'd be here at six."

Arielle, for fear that she, too, would be reprimanded, stepped farther out of earshot, glancing at her cell phone: *6:45*

*Damn.*

AD just picked Cori up with an exhale and a sluggish nod. "My bad…"

Maybe he said something more…and maybe he didn't. Arielle had already stepped away. But even from the few seconds she'd just seen, Arielle more or less could glean their old storyline. *The too cool for school connection must've been how Jae'cy and he first vibed. But all of those pretenses shouldn't matter when you have a kid. She just wants her parents, both of them.* Arielle would know…because that was all she'd wanted, too.

But before truly pushing the observations aside for the day, Arielle couldn't fight the image that flashed into her head of Jae'cy's indeed scarily angry yet also tired face, and how just seconds before AD's appearance, she had looked so relaxed. *Probably why she hadn't even mentioned you nor your supposed arrival today. Because it looks like you've fallen short before.*

But what did Arielle really know? It wasn't like Jae'cy had ever talked with her about AD and the circumstances of their co-parenting dynamic. Not like it would've made sense for Jae'cy to do so, considering nothing that happened between them. And AD could've just been a busy man, handling his professional business; event planning could be very consuming, surely.

*Enough of all that. Let me get my end to this crazy cousin of mine's house before she comes to perform a "wellness check."* Because that probably would be more terrifying than the last glimpse Arielle had of Jae'cy's face as it practically burned a hole through AD's head.

But truly? What Jae'cy's face had looked like just *before* AD arrived, when it was just them two, might've been what made her chest suddenly flutter the most.

Arielle couldn't figure out which woman was scarier.

♡ 20

UPDATE: *ALL* WOMEN WERE SCARY. They were bad news—and kept trying to create news where there wasn't any to be had.

A trio of them surrounded Arielle, just hours later. There had been a lot of eating today already, and now she was being force-fed by her cousins. She kept staring at the door, just feet away.

And with purpose, all three of them—Melanie, Sinead, and Juliana—eyed the braids that were matching Juliana's and Sinead's own.

"Uh-oh! Who's the connect?" Melanie asked. As the only one of the three who typically minded her own business (because all sons and a husband), she was out of the loop.

But she was sho nuff about to be brought into it: "The same one she's been *connecting* with each time she connects her feet on the pavement outside our airport."

"That *star* chick."

Then Juliana smirked, and Sinead sipped. Respectively disrespectfully.

"It's not like that. They're talking about Paula Young's daughter," Arielle reported correctly, more so to Melanie.

"What does that have to do with *anything*?" Sinead pontificated more than asked. "I have a laundry list of *'famous'* dudes on the scene whose lines I still haven't picked up. To star in their next baby momma saga, I'll pass."

"Me too!" Juliana piped in, a bit too animatedly. Then she squinted with a light twinkle in her eye. "And you know good well y'all go by better pet names than that with each other."

"I can't believe this saga continues," Arielle said wryly as she sipped her cocktail. By nine p.m., her sense of humor had dropped along with the sun.

Time to deflect.

"Wait, I thought *you* wanted to be someone's baby momma?" Arielle narrowed her eyes at Juliana.

Juliana hovered her glass at her mouth while staring intently at Arielle above the rim. "Don't deflect."

*Don't be a hazard to your renter's insurance.*

Arielle exhaled with another low chuckle and a shake of her head.

"And don't worry about me. I'm not new to this, I'm true to this," Juliana clarified, setting her glass down and her eyes back up to Arielle. "Anyway, she's cute! You're cute *and* gay…Thinkin' they're gonna be greeted with a plate of Mrs. Fields when they decide to 'try out' girls like it's some food, and instead these chicks are throwin' out stale Nabisco's. It's not all sweet and rainbows out here. So, just be careful… 'Cause, I've seen some thangs." Those eyes hadn't left Arielle yet. And neither had Melanie's and Sinead's.

Arielle peered at the door. *Dang, is it getting farther away?*

"*ANY*way…" Juliana moved on, toying her drink's rim with a slow Cheshire grin.

Arielle shot up as Sinead drank another shot up. "Regardless of how old as hell this is: Imma head out."

Sinead almost spat out her drink as her other two sisters burst up over theirs.

"Nice guys finish last, Elle!" Juliana called out.

"Girls, too! Even with their good cookies!"

Now, the whole restaurant was ignoring their lasagna and burgers.

"It's time to stop simpin' so you can be a *REAL* starter."

*Yep, just like A.I.* Arielle was already *pushing* that Exit door.


Arielle was so happy she'd booked a hotel for some downtime. Pulling out her phone for what felt like the first time that day, she saw new IG notifications from followers and comments on a post made the other day, a screenshotted excerpt from her graphic designer of her first promo interview with Goodreads for her latest upcoming book, *Ash Must Fall Down*.

She typed out a comment to one fan's inquiry—*Subscribe to my newsletter to get all of the signing dates!*—to hopefully address the others just like it.

Right as she sent the comment off, there came a notification at the top of her cell phone screen with a fresh email's subject line:

*Suspicious Login Attempt*

From Instagram.

Well, that *was* suspicious.

Arielle stared quizzically at the message; she always routinely changed her password with the most random mix of character stuffing. Then she'd clear everything out before logging out. She could only think that maybe Juliana was calling herself being slick and trying to play matchmaker with some DM exchanges to a love prospect for her. But Arielle never gave out her passwords.

Arielle pondered it a second longer, then chalked it up to some kind of scam, phishing.

And then took it as a sign to just exit stage X (after changing up her password).

Minding her own business…if the writer in her would let her.

♡ **21**

GETTING BACK HOME TO VEGAS MEANT time in her mortgaged four walls. The comforts of her taupe-accented walls, mahogany floating bookshelves, and chaise lounge greeted her in the living room. Minimalism blended with a modern artsy vibe, her favorite aesthetic. But she headed to her bedroom. Time to sleep in, all in her cozy bed. Just relax and—

*Shi….!* She'd forgotten something. Again.

"Your masterclass on Teachable? Yeah, remember that? The film crew's arriving at your house at one sharp. Then we'll take the live feed to Udemy. Don't forget," Kimesha had relayed to Arielle earlier as Arielle was completing a morning bike ride around her neighborhood park.

No sooner than she had stepped out of her shower and gotten dressed, then the small indie production team were rolling up into her living room. With efficiency, they set up the lights and cameras, adjusted the streaming settings on Teachable, put the lav mic on her, and finally tested out the audio and video. Arielle was holding a writing workshop that could be purchased at any time down the line by interested viewers—the latest marketing push from by Kimesha.

The only difference this time, and that admittedly made her feel chill, was that Arielle was speaking to an audience about her stories. Speaking about her true passion, words, right in her home, right at home.

The videographer and sound mixer were all set for her to start, counting off the cue, then tipping their heads her way.

"What is the key to any story?" Arielle kickstarted her mission statement of sorts, to bring the audience in. "The marriage between character and plot, both impacting the other. To really illustrate this idea to you, let's first begin our story with each other here today by discussing character development, the character arc. And let's look at this through the lens of one particular character."

Okay, yeah. She already had a rhythm going.

"My lead, Tarran, in one of my earliest novels. She's an illustration of this trope: the character you love to hate…and by the end, you find out you never really hated her at all, you just really wanted her to win. And I want to see you all, you amazing writers and your stories, win, too. So, with even more winning techniques I want to share in this quick journey we're sharing together, let's move on to…"

And move on, she did. Touching on various other ways to build one's hero's (character's) journey, with the use of excerpts from her own stories and some well-known movie references.

Arielle thought, as the recording stopped, *This was actually kinda fun.* Arielle didn't mind teaching people about the art of creating. She even smiled a bit, staring at her braided reflection in the screen, just before the camera team shut it off.

To only return to another screen not too long after…


"You were kinda flat."

That was how Jae'cy greeted her in place of a "Hi" as she landed in Arielle's Zoom room for their content strategy meeting the following afternoon. Arielle would be presenting a competitor analysis report of other mid-sized healthy eatery peers and social media tactics they were using. She'd suggested this report for Honest Bites' social listening maintenance, seeing where one was startin' to slip and slip away from followers with their calls-to-action and content. Not listening to one's loyal base about what more they wanted from a business could cost that business their loyalty, their following, their brand. No one knew that more than a public figure, and that was why this one had suggested they talk the report out together in a meeting before she had a clothes-fitting session with Breyah. This same one who was now calling Arielle "flat."

"Uh…" Arielle knew the comment couldn't have been in reference to this meeting's Google Slides deck she'd emailed Jae'cy earlier this morning. She decided to just start the meeting recording (Jae'cy's request, so she could keep reference of it) while awaiting more details.

"In your class. The example, with the main character. You forgot to mention the reason readers bought into her slightly toxic personality and still loved her all along in *Doin' Things Out of Character.* Because of the *buy-in,* the audience wanted to see what was in it for them to care and invest in the lead. You forgot to mention it was because she was so relatable," Jae'cy filled her in then clicked her tongue. "Em-em-em. Ya *slippin'*!'"

"So…should I give you an A for that?" Arielle didn't know whether to feel some type of way about the fact that Jae'cy's callout was correct or the fact that she'd—

"Watched the whole thing. So, yep, I'll take an A. Or a discount on the next payment I give you." Jae'cy laughed. "Don't look so shocked!"

Just then, Jae'cy got up from her seat to get a drink off her kitchen counter, body coming in full view on the laptop screen. "I *do* like learning new things…just wanted to make sure you weren't keepin' any hidden gems from me."

*The only thing I'm trying to hide is…*Arielle peeped Jae'cy's biker shorts, knotted tee…trailed her gaze back up to find Jae'cy's lips as they started up again in a grin, smack dab in full center on the camera.

*…the same thing you're trying to hide.*

"I'm starting to think you have selective memory loss, though. Like Cori when she doesn't want to do somethin' after I've told her to."

Arielle clenched her stomach. "She's a…character."

Jae'cy rolled her eyes, but hid a grin. "Who you all dressed up for today, though?" She was addressing Arielle's salmon-pink mesh short-sleeve polo and fresh haircut. "Gotta Motown reunion concert for your fans?"

"Yeah, busy just like you are, too." Arielle grinned as she pulled up the competitive analysis deck she'd made. "And *this*," she modeled her polo to a humored, 'underwhelmed' Jae'cy, "is what real classiness looks like rather than all that play makeup your friends are out there showing on IG and TikTok." Arielle laughed inside at the cringey posing straight-faced, intentionally parted lips and equally affected unrealistic 'doe-eyed' blinks that felt like one per second into their phone cameras that many chicks loved to do these days on social videos.

"So, I take it you only date *Jet* "Beauty of the Week" pinups."

Arielle couldn't help but snicker; that was a perfect comeback.

In that *straight-faced*, eye-gazing silence, Arielle could see that maybe Jae'cy was seeing into her.

*Relatable.* If this wasn't the perfect example of a mirror being placed in front of you…Or a camera, recording all, as this Zoom meeting was right now.

"No, I just like women *real.*"

Jae'cy's eyes moved to her cell phone, swiping on it. "Elle, Elle, Elle. I don't know," she finally sighed affectedly, shook her head. "You are such an interesting case to me. But you're gonna have to make some adjustments with the prospects you got, or else no one will buy what you're sellin'."

"Nah, it's why I left Marketing. And write books that oddly…sell. It's like people and me only relate when we're the most apart," Arielle countered loosely back, but she had already started to look off idly elsewhere herself. "Gotta love life's irony…"

When Jae'cy spoke again, it was low, almost like *she* was telling a secret. "That's my territory…. Me and the audience, always separated by a screen that I can't even see. But it's there, and if I'm not watchful, I keep acting, even off the set, like it's still around."

Arielle listened. "Always in an act?"

Jae'cy squinted harder with a tight swallow. *She just shared something big with me.* Not her friends, Breyah, her mom. Definitely not a casting director. *Me...and, I think, only me.*

That hit in a...weird way. Arielle could sense the need of comic relief, their usual play, to clear the way for the both of them as Jae'cy immediately orated a comment from an IG post, in an affected tone and diction:

*"Hey, is she datin that stud writer?"*

Arielle grinned wider as they looked at the remark, on a post from one of the young ladies at Jae'cy's official grand opening. Arielle hadn't noticed the cameras at the event, but that comment would go down in history. "Stud, huh? That's a first, I'll take it."

Jae'cy gave a terse chortle with a sky-high, firm brow. "But *I* won't." Jae'cy responded aloud: "I think every woman has appreciated another woman before. BUT *no* need to jump to conclusions in this day and age."

Arielle furtively bit her lip then just had to look over. *What else was on this unfolding agenda of things unstated today?* Granted, Arielle had had her suspicions. But it was *very* surprising that Jae'cy had just "revealed" them to her.

Arielle cracked a lopsided half-smile. She'd let baby girl have her moment. (Indeed, no need to jump to conclusions—but it was a universal fact that every girl was at least bi-curious.)

Then, there were two ways she could go right now: Dig deeper (*But remember, even though we've got cool and friendly terms between us, this is still a client, Elle*). Or put it all down and away (*Because she's a CLIENT, ELLE.*). Or somewhere in the middle...

*Since I've got you talkin' today, let me take advantage because I might not get this chance again.*

"Hmm...so, I'm curious," Arielle started, then pulled up a hand to her chin with a squint. "Lemme guess, your type is five-foot-five, slim-curvy, cute, super ethnically ambiguous, and most def *not* handsome in this case?"

Jae'cy affectedly shrugged as she cast away her attention back to her phone. "I *meeeean*..."

Arielle waved her off. "Girl, I ain't finna play with you. *Or* y'all's play makeup," she finalized as she stood up and pulled out her own cell phone. *Now she's got me doin' one of her moves.* Because it was getting a bit...

"Oh, you're bored now?" Jae'cy jested.

"I have a...date." *Welp, that was a new one for early leave excuses.* Yet, unlike her nine-to-five yesteryear TGIF tactics, this one was true. Juliana's many talents while bartending was making love connections for one of her newer, younger colleagues, Taylor, who was a hustling bi-state (CA and NV) set designer, aspiring to move from the small, no-budget film scene to the big screen. What better opportunity than to set her up on a date with the Vegas-dwelling Arielle during her upcoming gig that was going to be in production there?

Arielle finally peered at Jae'cy as she slipped her phone back into her pocket.

Jae'cy seemed to pause...and then smacked her lips. "That tour life *POPPIN'* now, huh?! Gotta keep the muses comin' for that next top-seller. Em-*kaaay*."

*Why do I oddly feel guilty?* Arielle tucked a hand into that same pocket, unintentionally smooth and debonair like a music video pose. She flashed an awkward grin for the camera known as Jae'cy. "Looks like she's in her twenties. Someone my cousin—she calls herself a matchmaker."

Jae'cy snapped her fingers followed by a little twirl of her hand. "Uh-oh! Make sure you edumacate baby girl on the grown folks' oldies. But before you kick me to the curb, let me see the kid!"

*Valid.* Arielle sighed low and slow, then edged up her cell phone, which revealed @TaylorMade's IG profile page. Because of course she had prescreened what this girl was all about.

Jae'cy looked. Truly.

*Sheesh, do YOU wanna take her on the date?* Arielle "joked." But without a grin.

Jae'cy finally, affectedly snapped a finger at the profile photo of Taylor: five-foot-five, slim curvy, super exotic-ambiguous. "*Oh*, she's cute."

However, a more immediate truth suddenly redirected Arielle's attention back to the present: Thirty minutes had passed, and the real business hadn't even taken place. And even more, neither of them, even reminded the other...The first 'just business' hiccup. "Looks like you're slippin', too, though," Arielle imparted as she noted Jae'cy likewise rising from her seat (Breyah had just entered Jae'cy's house, waving at Arielle in the background). And even with a screen in between them, Arielle could've sworn she caught Jae'cy's face pick back up from some quiet place it had just fell—and not because of spunky Breyah's arrival.

*Can't be caught slippin'.* Especially with business...

"We should go over the competitor analysis."

And that did it; Jae'cy caught on. "I looked your stuff over. You said you can do it all through my HootSuite, TikTok, and IG logins, right?"

Arielle nodded. *So why then did you ask me to meet?*

And so, then Jae'cy did the same. Just business...

*Like all of the other meetups? And why did I come?*

Arielle said nothing more, and neither did Jae'cy. Maybe because it *was* just business. *Or maybe because I gotta get to this OTHER girl.*

Or maybe, because by stating more, one would end up stating what hadn't been stated.

Caught slippin'. In this room of proverbial mirrors.

♡ 22

FORTY MINUTES LATER, Arielle was now at a soul bistro, this spacious spot full of portraits of rap, R&B, and jazz artists.

"Well, it's technically a trap-inspired kitchen. They play tracks requested by the crowd while you eat. Now, Taylor's really out here doing her thing; she's not just one of these little girls. Be sure to acknowledge that. 'Cause your ass can't be awkward or mean. This my reputation we're talkin' about." (That had been Juliana the Matchmaker's debrief on the way over.)

But she wouldn't be mean (not awkward, not guaranteed). She couldn't hurt the young soul's heart by reneging; that was how bad karma happened. And nobody had time for that. But also, because…something about stepping out of that Zoom room and into this one felt…refreshing. It could've been caused by the '70s vinyl placards on the walls or the throwback jam playing over the speakers.

Or because Taylor, as she increasingly approached the table for two in the center, had on a ready smile with two ready glasses of ice water. *The least I can do is contribute to the conversation as an active listener.*

And so, not long after sitting, she'd learned a middle name. ("But some call me Naomi. Listen, get you people in your crew who make you feel six feet and delusional. We gotta live out here!") And a favorite song, as it began to play next, that she'd try to forget as soon as she stepped out of here. ("Oo! 'Callin' all my friends with benefits!' This STILL *slaps!*")

Then, Arielle shared what Juliana had told her earlier in preparation. "You got a chance to pitch in on a music video set recently, right?"

"Oh, I'm headed for the *real* sets."

And Taylor/Naomi was definitely dressed the part as well. She had on a suede dusky-brown bolero hat atop chin-length curly honey tresses. Asymmetrical chunky off-the-ear wing pendants, bronze ankh pendant around her neck. Cut-off denim shorts covered by a vintage flannel about the waist and ending with brown suede booties.

It actually was a nice look, but Arielle was still judging the dialogue.

"But *yesss.* I'm workin' my way up," Taylor confirmed, with a slight tilt of her head, toying with her pendant like she was tapping into her ancestors and spirit guides from *A Different World.* Then she perched up her head. "But what about you and that commercial spot with Paula *YOUNG?!* I love her sound. I might be...*young*," she chuckled. "But I know my oldies!"

Arielle eyed the window across from them, the sun setting. It had been going okay, but now... Maybe—Arielle wrestled the straw of her ice water—*she was right.* "She" being Jae'cy. Maybe, she was right: It was someone's bedtime. Because Paula, at just forty-nine, wasn't really in the oldies group but rather slightly old school/neo-soul at best.

Arielle lowered her glass of water, then *had* to ask. "Uh, sorry, my cousin didn't tell me your age..."

"I'm twenty-six."

Arielle deflated internally. *Yep, definitely time to tuck in.*

Taylor must've read the body language. Or the spirit guides had. "But I'm wise for my years."

*Great. Now she's trying to qualify herself. I must look how I feel.* Arielle put on a polite grin. But, she had to admit she did like that, at least Taylor was willing to claim Paula Young's group as music, and that was much better than most.

*No. Maybe* she was wise enough...

And this time, "she" *was* Taylor.

Taylor shot a smile back. Impulsive, speedy, and sure.

Young.

Arielle shook her head with a light chuckle.

"What?"

"Nothing." She'd let the spirit guides illuminate her.

Plus, right on time, a waitress, was approaching so Arielle turned her gaze to the menu. "Want some mozzarella sticks to start off?"

"*Oo.* That could be the meal right there!" Arielle watched Taylor take to her own menu like there was a coloring page inside.

Impulsive, speedy.

*And sure.*

But *maybe* that wasn't too bad. Look at how far that had gotten her as yet.

♡ **23**

*A NEW DAY, A NEW KIMESHA BOOKING DONE* after a promo interview at the largest and most frequented Las Vegas valley bookstore.

And twelve sleeping hours later, she was now on her boxer-briefed butt in front of her living room TV, just chill—

*BUZZ.*

Arielle slumped her head back, misjudging the rear of the chaise lounge that ended up being the wall. She grimaced lightly and began to give her attention to her cell phone. "Come on, Mesha. You promised nothing until tomorrow—"

She paused to read the short text message:

*Gonna swing by your way in a sec about something if that's cool*

Arielle obliged with "Cool" but followed up with a "Tell me why you're hitting me up on my Saturday off-day though." Random DMs with jibes were their thing, but a random message out of the blue for pop-up visits was new. *Maybe she's in town again for some kind of film.*

But instead, Jae'cy informed her that she was attending a one-day restauranter seminar in Vegas.

And when she pulled up in her shades that she then slid atop her straightened hair, a corner of her mouth was on the ready. "So, how was the beginning of your new love story?"

Arielle ignored the question with one of her own. "Why are you here?"

Jae'cy began to open her mouth for an answer but was stopped short by her ringing phone. "Sorry—one sec. Got something big to ask." Putting up a quick, apologetic finger of wait at Arielle, as Arielle tapped quietly at her countertop.

"Hey, Miss Rumpa!" Jae'cy cooed, as she helped herself to the living room couch (*like she's been here before*). It was in an exclamatory yet soft voice that told Arielle that Cori was on the other end.

"Yes, I will be back soon, okay?" Jae'cy further responded. Then when she continued with a "Hey..." it was easier-on-the-tone, which would've seemed like a soothing to one's tyke at the revelation of a parent being MIA a bit longer. But there was just something *else* there.

"...Yeah, we can take her once I land there..."

*Ahhh.* This new tone was of parents talking—two of them. Arielle suddenly felt like she was sitting in someone else's house instead of her own.

Arielle dropped down back on her kitchen island stool—

"Okay, *sooo…*" Those new words emerged behind her as Jae'cy rose from the couch and strolled over to Arielle. "Sorry about that again. Back to this. The *other* reason I'm here…" Jae'cy recommenced. "I want you to be my…partner."

Arielle instantly glimpsed, stared really, over her shoulder at an amused Jae'cy, her eyebrow cocked.

*"Partner," what a choice in words. Even for a girl who recently "confessed" that she isn't exactly so straight. But hey, at least she was talking business…or at least, so far that's what it sounds like…*

"I'm working on a new script for a short film," Jae'cy clarified. "And I need good perspective for the supporting role. She has a bit more assertiveness…gusto—"

"And more than likely bi or something. Okay, I'm followin' you." *But to where exactly? First that…hug. But now…this???*

Jae'cy resumed with a confirming chuckle, "You're of a more…" She hand-gestured. "'Unconventional' female vein, so I think your insights would be invaluable. But even more, very authentic and realistic. *And* I'm thinking to that point, your words transgress—"

*Oh, she was on a roll.* Getting out all of the thoughts that had clearly been inside her mind for a while. An intellectual, analytical mind surprisingly, like Arielle. And she liked that. *Okay, focus, Elle. We're back to work again…*Yet, Arielle found herself back on those lightly furrowed eyebrows on this suddenly cerebral face of Jae'cy's. It was kinda adorable. Arielle felt a slight grin coming on and didn't hide it. Wanted to see if Jae'cy would spot it during this thesis she had goin' on.

"So many types of writing formats. It's why me and my mom started working with you in the first place: that *wordsmithin.'*" She paused. "Sooo, if you're game, this could be a long-term business venture, along with more Honest Bites marketing stuff."

Jae'cy finally took a breather.

"Alright," Arielle confirmed, with a little shrug.

"Cool. Because first things first, I have a commercial next month."

"HA."

Jae'cy's attention then randomly fell on the magnetic calendar on Arielle's fridge. "Music Hop: The Key of Love?" Jae'cy read the words aloud then turned to Arielle. "What's that?"

*Something my scary ass signed up for that I'm still thinking about reneging—*

"It's, uh, just like this annual one-day workshop that a national urban music collective does. A different site, theme, and wild card each time. This year will be mostly about love-based tracks, everything from opera to R&B, and flipped into hip-hop—and it's in my city this time. So, all of us would get to play around with some vinyl and spin it."

"It's in two weeks!"

"*If* it doesn't get halted," Arielle murmured.

"It might not happen?"

"It might not happen with *me*."

"Why?" Jae'cy asked.

*Probably thinkin' in her head, "This girl." Well, that would be right, 'cause this girl's staying at home, and Tish and Marlon will just have to deal.*

"You seem invested. Maybe I'll let you go in my place."

"Shoot, I'll go *with* you!" Jae'cy counterargued, already tapping and swiping something now in her cell phone. "Looks like there are two tickets left. It sounds like something cool. Different." She looked at Arielle. "And makin' you a little nervous because of it."

*Still reading me like an open book.*

"So you need a lil' emotional support."

"My brother, Marlon, and friend, Tish, are comin'." Arielle couldn't tell if the knot in her stomach was from pre-event nerves, her subtle other passion she'd been holding off all her life really for fear of getting poor feedback. "You don't have any…film days around then?"

"Nope. Currently, the latest shoot wraps up before then, so I'm—" Jae'cy abruptly paused, clicking her tongue. "Oh, shoot. I don't have anyone for Cori that weekend. My mom has a singing gig." She looked at her cell phone. "And her dad's out of town…"

"Bring her, too," Arielle proposed, shrugged. Cori would have fun. What kid didn't have fun making noise? She knew she did on her brother's drum set in the basement when she was young.

Arielle observed Jae'cy, scrolling on that phone. Slowly.

"She can talk you OUT! Ionno," Jae'cy finally responded.

"Teachable moments. And I'm the good one. The *nice* one."

"Right, right. Forgot." Jae'cy's guard seemed to fall, evidenced by the lowering of her shoulders and the lift of one side of her mouth. "Kids always come to this thing. Everyone, all ages."

Jae'cy gazed at the calendar.

*Girl, just say yes.*

*Because, man…*

*I really want her to. For real.*

Arielle dropped her gaze to her hands. Her wrestling hands.

She wanted, like she'd been trying to deny, to spend time with Jae'cy. And *that* was why she always came when Jae'cy asked. *And she,* Arielle thought, while looking at, waiting for Jae'cy to confirm, *feels the same.*

*As JUST friends*...Arielle only wrestled more.

"Ight, don't say I didn't warn you," Jae'cy announced. "Including if your girlfriend gets mad."

"She is *not* my girlfriend."

Jae'cy cracked up. All giggles, all jiggles.

Like a kid.

"Well, so she doesn't get *too* suspicious...Taylor's a set designer, right? Tell her to come to my Honest Bites commercial shoot. She'll get experience AND the connections that everyone in LA truly only cares about. All hands on deck is needed."


And when Taylor came into town some days later for a college film production gig, when they linked up, her eyes popped at Arielle's relay of the message with a: "You're *LYIN.*'"

♡ **24**

"YOU *LYIN'*!" Post-commercial wrap-up, this echo came from cheesing guys, hoopers and rappers vetted by AD, hovering around some IG model's post on Michi's cell phone in the eating area. Around them, other actors and crew were packing up, as Arielle booted up her laptop at one of the wallside tables. It was like a game of telephone, but with DMs.

But they lowered their lascivious, practically salivating faces, as AD passed by.

Jae'cy briefly stopped her chitchatting with Breyah and looked to him with a key fob: "This is what all adults have to use now. Some new security thing at her school, so just make sure—"

"Gonna swing by Carl's Jr. afterwards 'cause that's her thing right now." He finished the conversation—on his own terms. As always. "Will bring her back after school Monday." And with that, he left.

Arielle opened a blank document on her laptop, tending to business.

*And* Breyah, who'd been today's costume designer, turned to Arielle and pointed at her laptop. "Forgot my card reader for my phone. Can I...?"

"Oh, sure," Arielle allowed as she rose and headed for a water bottle at the other end of the counter. There was still some time to kill, the rest of the place to disburse, before she and Jae'cy got to the second line of work today: Jae'cy's film script.

Her eyes then fell on Jae'cy, who was pulling her hair up into that characteristic "getting down to business" high bun, which, in Arielle's opinion, heightened her self-contained look, especially with her conservative makeup. And it also showcased more of her face, the steadfast cheekbones.

Jae'cy patted the bun a quick second (*She always does that.*) to address any stray hairs, then her fingers rested on the top of the bun while her eyes moved up, and paused on Arielle.

"*Annnd* back to you. 'Preciate it!"

Arielle looked to Breyah who was already trotting on back over to a table by Jae'cy. "You're all set, queen," Breyah informed Jae'cy while placing her Canon camera gear into its own bag. "Sent you today's looks just in case we need to reshoot. And thank you for trustin' ya girl not only with the fashions BUT! Also, with photographing this set *holdin'* the fashions. Courtesy of camera training sessions with Alonzo."

Arielle returned to her laptop and sighed. A nuisance had popped up on the screen: an update request dialog box from her VPN servicer. *Didn't I just do this yesterday?*

She clicked yes to the update install as Breyah suddenly glanced back at her, then jumped her eyes over to Jae'cy with a chuckle.

Welp, looked like Arielle had spoken those last words aloud.

"I'll call you later." Breyah now sashayed off, swinging her hips left-and-right.

"Me, too," came Taylor from the back room with her belongings and with a coquettish smile at Arielle, which she then widened at Jae'cy before exiting. "Thanks again for this opportunity!"

Everyone else left not too long after.

As Jae'cy settled on the stool next to her, Arielle breathed out a light "pfft." On her phone was a text from Young Grasshopper, a.k.a. Taylor. "Well, looks like I've been summoned...to this rooftop...*thing?*" *There she goes: hoppin'.*

"Ooh, chaperoning?" Jae'cy mentioned casually. Scorpionic stoicism at its finest.

Arielle, shook her head with a wry, but not too forceful, grin as she tucked her phone away and returned to her laptop, clicking open the scriptwriting software she'd recently installed.

"Shut up."

Jae'cy cracked up.

But then..."Just remember that our millennials' hearts don't heal as fast."

Arielle furrowed her eyebrows. "Whoa—what?" *Didn't you encourage me to "give her five minutes"?*

"*What* I know is how these LA girls *and* boys and everyone in between can be sometimes. Even when you know them through true sources," Jae'cy countered, expounded. "People can move differently all of a sudden...I'd know."

"Okay, Yung Hitta."

*For real though. Whyyyy are you now talking to me like a—?*

The tension she had just felt between her and Jae'cy was that of two people in another kind of relationship. A tension that had started to rise since the last Zoom call just before her date. Arielle knew she needed to mitigate that...

"Jae'cy, if there's..."

*But damn, not right now, Elle??* She rubbed the side of her face a moment to dispel the unnerving smile that was rising.

"If there's something you need to say…" *About anything…and everything.* "Just say it—"

Jae'cy laughed. Short, tensely. Like something brewing underneath. "All I'm sayin' is just watch you and her."

Arielle would have to come back to that. She *had* to, because she knew, at this point, they were playing themselves. Playing like there wasn't something brewing between them…

But right now, an extension of that, something else about what Jae'cy had stated at the end rang true… *I know, too. About people moving differently, without warning…* And Arielle, at that moment, mystically felt *that* was what needed to be tackled first—it distracted her so that she had no choice but to recognize it. She felt it as a deep rumble in her belly; like the greatest pain one had when having been neglected for so long— and not just of food. And with the greatest pain, there came the greatest anger—"hangry" wasn't a term for nothing.

"I know that I have to be cautious of how I move." She looked at Jae'cy, who looked only, intently, at the blank doc on the laptop screen. "Even though I've failed with that before."

Arielle turned her vision down to her lap, fiddling with her cell phone. "Especially with a youngin…You know they can't hold water…"

Jae'cy turned her head fully back to Arielle for the first time since the beginning of this conversation. "Or think before they act…"

*Nope, still looking for more.* It was the damn Scorpio energy. Doing what it did best. Causing an action by just being present and watching…for the moment when secrets emerged.

"I asked this girl once in first grade—" Arielle started and temporarily halted, broke into a wry, tight, upset grin. Compelled by Jae'cy's own female alchemy, which was much more penetrative than Taylor's. And now, it had her speaking up *again.*

"Uh, I asked her if she wanted to help cowrite this song with me for…" Arielle hesitated, her smile erased. "*Another* girl we liked…in eighth grade."

"Uh-oh," Jae'cy cooed (her Plutonic behind would at this hidden info). "So, you've chased the cougars since you were a cub?"

Arielle smirked—but very faintly. "Ha. Yeah, and soon I was *truly* out in the wilderness. She helped alright—helped pass the song around the class after I showed her the final version."

Arielle wasn't sure what exactly Jae'cy was thinking or looking like right then because, quite frankly, she *couldn't* look. Was too busy looking backward, into a memory she'd tried to forget that had always followed her. The little girl who needed a hero to save the day but didn't get one. But she finally glanced up, just for a second. "You gotta remember, this was still the mid-nineties…"

Then she glanced off as Jae'cy stared quietly but very fixedly. Arielle had to look away.

"*Soo*...the song ends up in my teacher's hands, and next thing I know, the girl's brought in after I'm forced to confess who it was for. Which turns into her mean muggin' me in the hallway after school as I'm heading home. And the finale was my mom getting notified that night and then telling me it '*wasn't right.*' So, needless to say, that whole marketing strategy didn't get ANY new customers."

Arielle noticed her hands were fiercely clutching her phone in her hands. "I don't know," she continued, shrugged. "Looking back on it now, it helped me artfully play the closet game for the longest." She chuckled, low. Shaky.

Then nothing more.

"...That's not funny."

Arielle fluttered, mouth quivering, then slid her eyes over to see Jae'cy's straight face. The irony.

"You know? Like Cori said?"

Arielle shifted to the laptop screen, setting up the screenplay. "Right, never mind. On to *your* story..."

Jae'cy gazed at her a second longer; Arielle could feel it even with her face toward the screen. Her tense, talented sixth sense, a twist on trauma. Jae'cy still wasn't smiling, but observing.

Finally, Jae'cy looked away and to the screen. Perhaps collecting all that she needed at that moment.

She said, "I'm thinkin' I want to do a thriller. I don't know, piggyback on the last film I was in a little bit."

Arielle's hands were ready on the keyboard, but no direction or even a title had been given to her. She shifted her eyes over to the chief in command, who rubbed her neck and squinted as if in sudden screen fatigue.

"I have no idea why I got the idea to start this while *ALSO* contemplating opening a second Honest Bites location," Jae'cy spoke up, moaning affectedly.

"Oh, dope. You definitely should," Arielle gently insisted. *Man, she was really continuing to build her dream out.* Arielle would always support that.

"We shall seeee," Jae'cy transitioned, cool. "But *first*...as Exhibit A shows, my crazy busy mental block." Jae'cy limply pointed and affectedly whimpered at the all-white screen. Then she laughed, and then went back to staring at that screen once again.

It was Arielle's turn to do what she did best: getting a person's tale through analytical, artful inquiry. "The best way you can form your positioning words in marketing? It's much like acting and film; both worlds are about delivering a strong story, whether it's a social media post or a line in a script. To do this, you put yourself in the other person's shoes. So, let's try this: Put yourself in the shoes of a child, *you* as a child."

Jae'cy immediately examined Arielle's face with a slow rub of her fingers against her forehead, and overall confusion at those choice of words.

So, Arielle painted the picture a bit more. "Why is food so important to us? Because more than nourishing, it also comforts, reminds us of home, right? And one of the first things we think of when we think of home is the one we grew up in."

Jae'cy allowed a slightly inhibited, fragile smile. But reception, a knowing.

"What would you do if you could wake up as a child tomorrow? Before responsibilities, taxes, Cali mortgages." Jae'cy playfully rolled her eyes, then began to reflect, looking downward. It took a second or two. But whatever she had dived for, she had caught a grasp of it, a slow smile rising. "When I was twelve..."

Jae'cy peeked at Arielle, as if the words to be spoken were the long-lost treasures she was unsure she wanted to share. "Pushin' that teen realm, but I'm tuned in."

Jae'cy began again, but fainter, diving deeper in. "I had always been a bit of a daredevil. *Or,*" her smile quivered a bit, "as my mother calls it, a '*hopper,*' just experiencing things, from one to the next. And so, me and my cousins—all of us are girls, born like back-to-back, so we were called The Three Musketeers. When we were visiting Saint Louis one summer, as usual...we snuck out and drove my uncle's ATVs in his open field. He had this huge house and land out in the boonies. And so, uh, me trying to be cool and *different—*"

Jae'cy paused, speech dipping like her smile. She gave a little squint up into the distance. Or maybe not so distant.

Arielle quietly, clandestinely, but acutely listened...and followed Jae'cy's line of vision to the wall inches above them, right ahead of the menu...landing on a photo of Jae'cy, Cori,...and Paula in the center dominating a magazine cover. Framed next to the two other matriarch portraits of Jae'cy's grandmothers, Bettie and Helen. Arielle remembered that pair but didn't recall this new publication addition from the last time she was here.

She explored the magazine cover story's main cover line:

*The Duchess and Her Heirs: Songstress Paula Young on Fame, Fads, and Family*

Followed by the subheading:

*Will They Follow in Her Footsteps?*

"Wanting to stand out...I tried going really fast and—"

"Gassed yourself up." It was old millennial slang, but it was way too appropriate for this moment, so Arielle went with it. Plus, it was good seeing Jae'cy return to a smile after her more somber stare at her mother...and all of the lifelong comparisons to her that Arielle was sure came with it. The look on Jae'cy's face had said it all...even though she wasn't aware she'd just shared it with Arielle. *At least she was saying THIS much...Saying so much as of late even in its fragmented pieces...*

"For REAL," Jae'cy chuckled lightly, eyes floating back down, back to the story. "So I decided to round the trail...and the next thing I knew, I went from seein' a ditch to seein' my cousins' faces above me lookin' down.... Luckily, nothing got wrecked. But needless to say, we *walked* home after that.

"Then my Granny Bettie, who by this time was living with my only uncle left in Saint Louis, heard us sneaking in from the rocks before we heard *her*. Her and her repeating track three of some Sweet Honey in the Rock song," Jae'cy glanced over to clarify—and then some. "It was her favorite group. I'm sure you've heard of them."

Arielle only admitted by way of a soft shrug and simper...Didn't want to disrupt this new moment with their usual jesting. The story, all about the story.

"And, I'm not gonna lie, to this day, I can't tell if my knockin' knees right then came completely from being rocked on that ATV. But she looked past our guilty-as-hell eyes, past my guilty dirt-stained and scuffed knees. Past our..." Jae'cy floated her eyes back up to the photographs with a new, tighter squint, making it hard for Arielle to know who or what she was agonizing over. "...young, wild womanhood and just right to her butterscotch pie on the kitchen table. And that's when we all exhaled," Jae'cy recounted with her own exhale...and a smile. "All she wanted to do was give us what she'd unsuccessfully tried to give her daughters when they were young and wild, and yet, that they never could quite replicate because they turned to cooking up albums and dissertations instead: Her famous age-old butterscotch."

Then Jae'cy's eyes reopened into their natural crescents, and Arielle could exactly see where her gaze had landed: away from Paula and herself, to herself and Cori.

"But she taught me, and I learned how...and Cori will too."

She finally returned her eyes to Arielle. "I hadn't remembered that in so long..."

Arielle simply smiled gently, and Jae'cy fluttered back.

"So, now that you climbed up out of that ditch, young and wild..." Arielle gave a nod at the laptop screen and slid it over toward Jae'cy.

Jae'cy chewed the inside of her mouth. Then, like a neural shock, or electric, Jae'cy sprung up with a perch of her fingers on the keyboard and a shaky smile. "Just do it, right?"

And so, she dove in, much like she did into her rock's, her grandmother's, comfort food. Dove right into a title:

*Butterscotch: (Sweet) On The Rocks We Dwell*

*Just like her.* An old root had just gently prodded her branches, so she would confidently know that she could land on her feet even if she might fall. What life lived bravely was really supposed to be about.

"A cookbook," Jae'cy announced. "That's what we're making. I'm even talkin' recipes I said I'd never share. And you'll make sure the backstories behind each work," Jae'cy decreed more than requested, but her steady gaze made it seem more like an order to herself. One that Arielle was going to make sure she stuck to.

Little did she know, this was music to Arielle's ears.

Because if there was anything that Arielle loved more than words, it was uncovering mysteries...and seeing Jae'cy unmask more of her mystery, who she was, what she truly loved, what was on the inside, had Arielle quietly in awe. She'd signed up for this for the story, after all. Not to mention, it was a story Jae'cy's fans could appreciate, making her more relatable, which could only mean a more loyal and new following for her as well. *Now, she's not just sharing with me—she'll be sharing recipes, something everyone can experience.*

Arielle raised a glass, or rather her water bottle. Jae'cy hid a rising smile with a shake of her head...but she then raised up her own.

"Cheers to new stories," Arielle established.

Cheers to them. Finally agreeing for once on the same tune.

♡ 25

AS FOR HER AND THE DJ TWO HOURS LATER? ALL THE WAY OUT OF SYNC.

First, though, she and Jae'cy had gotten into the foundation of the cookbook concept. Fully in rhythm—just for the day—they fleshed out the synopsis and some recipes Jae'cy was sure she wanted to showcase.

"If the Honest Bites creator is creating a cookbook, 'honest bites made with honest love' has officially become 'how to bring winning comfort meals from the heart to the table.' That's your cookbook's story," Arielle suggested as they sat side by side at that Honest Bites counter.

"Okay, I'm with it," Jae'cy approved.

"Cool, so…" Arielle pitched the next major lineup of business, scrolling on Google, and Jae'cy peered in to read alongside her. "Says here that the average cookbook has about three to four hundred recipes."

"Oooh, baby!" Jae'cy clicked her tongue and shook her head.

But this was nothing but a cakewalk for a writer. Arielle chuckled. "You'll just tackle it in parts; that's how I do my book chapters. Let's aim for three hundred recipes, so as not to scare you. Pick out fifty recipes a month for the next six months, with a story behind each one, and just like that, you'll have a cookbook."

But Jae'cy didn't look as confident, still staring at Google's daunting number.

"And you'll use this spreadsheet I'm emailing to you to place in each one as you pick them." Arielle grinned. "Okay?"

"Oooo-*kaaaay*," Jae'cy finally agreed.

And as Arielle and Jae'cy finally stepped out of Honest Bites' automatic sliding doors just as the sunset was starting, Arielle heading to Sinead's car while Jae'cy went to her own, she gave Jae'cy as assignment for their next meet-up: to begin the first recipe's backstory.

"Okay, which one?" Jae'cy tilted her head as she slid her sunglasses onto her face.

"The butterscotch, of course," Arielle had clarified with a smile…just as a beep came on her phone.

Even with half of her face now covered, Arielle could tell Jae'cy had heard the beep. Jae'cy nodded silently before disappearing into her car.

And since then, she'd been just as ghost.

Well, except for a selfie (rooftop edition) of Arielle and Taylor that she'd hearted that same night.

For her part, Arielle had downed two too many tequilas, to challenge Young Grasshopper about who was "too uptight."

But after that, now a week later…nothing. Arielle knew Jae'cy wasn't on any kind of social media sabbatical because she'd paid the deed forward on one of Jae'cy's latest social media posts: a solo walk video captioned "Mommy breaks be like…" with just simple shades, braided-out hair, a peace sign. She had to give Jae'cy credit: she wasn't afraid to be bare to the world. At least, in one way…

*But she was definitely withholding some kind of backstory right now that didn't relate to any type of food. Because why else was she suddenly MIA?*

Turns out it was because she was doing the celebrity-socialite thing. Being everywhere, as usual.

Starting with a cameo on a series.

Arielle caught it while Juliana flew into her city for a random-ass visit ("'Cause I wanna kick it with my cuz!"), streaming series-flipping to a stop on one on the TV from her self-appointed position in Arielle's chaise furniture. "Oh, here comes your girl, cuh!"

Arielle peered over from her demoted, seated position at her desk to see Breyah getting foot care at a spa. The camera cut to her over-animated face talking in a solo confessional on some kind of LA designers reality show.

"So, I'm just chillin' in the back, about to get into my Zen on ya girl's born day, enjoying anotha revolution around this sun. And guess whose pretty butt comes surprisin' me, knowin' I need it after wack boyfriend numero four?" Breyah exclaimed, "My boo, Jae'cy!"

Then appeared Jae'cy, peeking into the spa room, then coming to a summoned place in the empty foot station beside Breyah with a "*Heyyyy* birthday girl" and reveal of a gift bag. But instead of bouncing in acceptance, Arielle noted Breyah's down smile.

"So…" Jae'cy slowly stepped into the elephant in the room as she did her now bare feet into the foot basin. "What happened this time?"

"This time?" Breyah snickered, and Arielle noted the flare of her nostrils. "Must be nice having everything in your world going perfect."

"Whoa, hold up." Jae'cy's smile faded…but the concern was still there.

Back briefly in the confessional, Breyah commented, "My best fran always knows how to cheer me up, though. Even when I'm bein' dramatic."

"I'm sorry, J," Breyah instantly recanted, sighed back at the spa. "It's just...trying to balance dating with my clientele, and having that side constantly growing and blossoming, while on the *OTHER* side..." Breyah just let out another larger sigh.

"But think about how far we've come from our young twenties days. Back when we didn't really have *either* side mapped out. Now look at us. Killing our dreams...And soon, the person of our dreams will be right there rockin' with us, too."

Breyah leaned her head back against her seat, bemoaned. "I thought Mister IG the other night was the *person of my dreams*! Turns out he was just a nightmare."

"Of *course*, he was, Bre! You betta just be lucky you didn't get catfished! Or some gift that unfortunately keeps on givin'." Jae'cy chuckled.

"Girl, I think I still *was* catfished! You can tell all of his sponsorships have clearly been based on his six-pack because *upstairs?* Not so much."

"Yeah, it's hard out here for us," Jae'cy expressed a bonding statement. To make Breyah feel good, of course.

It failed.

"Please. You have options. You *always* have options. You just *always* choose the ones you know you ain't feelin' and act like you don't see the ones who you might truly be down for and who might be down for you." Breyah paused. "Must be nice."

Now, Arielle was all the way tuned in as much as Juliana was. Maybe even more.

"Girl, whatever. You got one more time today, and then I'm takin' *THAT* gift back."

And the two girlfriends moved on with laughter.

"Okay, BUT...Where is our spa lady?!" Breyah picked the energy back up, as said spa staff member re-entered with ready, warm towels.

"YESSS!" Breyah immediately responded, but especially for the Reese's she'd just pulled out of the gift bag. Then pulled Jae'cy into a hug. "Thank you!"

"Yeah-yeah.'


And then (she was) in Arielle's kitchen...

As Arielle was munching on some avocado toast and checking her latest IG business-related notifications, there Jae'cy came up on her feed with a new post, a shared post (a clip) of Jae'cy's *Mahogany* magazine feature and interview from Breyah's page, evidenced by the caption:

*Thanks, boo, for letting me dress ya. @J_Carter is on her way up, y'all*

And naturally, Arielle clicked, meeting a face of butterscotch, Jae'cy's, with a plunge V-neck diamond gown for the magazine cover that was snapshotted on the screen…

Arielle read the headline:

*Jae'cy Carter's Honest Bites: On Her Recipes for Rising Success and Being a Liberated, Empowered Woman*

Then the interview snippet appeared. "So, thank you, for sitting down with me!" the columnist said with a clasp of her hands and twinkling smile. "First things first: congrats Black Queen of Her Own Company, which has been getting doubled patronage at the café month over month, no?"

Quickly, a duo of B-roll footage showed an urban news reporter and her crew walking and talking with Jae'cy as she showed them around her jampacked café filled with patrons of all ages, genders, and ethnic backgrounds eating at tables, checking out, and ordering. Then it was back to the present interview:

"Yes, thank you. I'm so grateful, to my sponsors and team. As, yes, a double minority—Black and female—I'm truly shocked at how much my café has grown, actually," Jae'cy shared with her own polite smile.

Arielle hoped maybe she herself had been one of the first to push Jae'cy to even start Honest Bites…to believe in her vision…

"You know?" the columnist commented. "That brings me to a great point: We like to think that we, as women, now have ultimate agency over the stories we want to tell about our gender and sexual identity and expression. But what do you think? What is your idea of a free, *empowered*…"

Right then, Jae'cy smirked discreetly.

"Woman?"

Arielle might have asked the same question herself.

Jae'cy cleared her throat. Then she seemed to notice the columnist was grinning almost slyly. Jae'cy's mouth twitched.

"Well, I can't speak on what agency is for another woman. But *as* a woman, I can add to its definition, and show that we come in all forms. Not just physically but also in mind and…behavior, too. And for me, I've always been an accepting person. Especially since I've been around creators and artists all my life, people who every day challenge

136

and change the standard. So, I think that's inspired me, and it's why I like to think that I live each day in what feels right and good for *me*."

This seemed to get wheels turning in the correspondent's head, perching a hand up to her chin and flashing a grin as her multiple hoops in each earlobe swung. "*Ooh. Elaboration is advocation.*"

Jae'cy chuckled. "I just don't box myself in, and I admire women who are just as unapologetically liberated."

And finally, she was in the bookstore...

As Arielle and Kimesha were departing from her promotional book discussion/interview, passing by the magazine racks.

That butterscotch again, front and center.

Arielle felt herself smirk while replaying Jae'cy's last words in the interview. *Unapologetically liberated, huh?* But it wasn't like Jae'cy was the first in the female species to show it; Arielle was staring beyond what was being said to what was being seen behind it.

And she couldn't pipe down the journalist in her.

And Kimesha couldn't either, seeing it all on Arielle's dazed face. "Uh-oh...Are we—?"

"No."

But...yes...

Because Jae'cy in that gown.

It was...

*Damn.*

*What am I doing?*

Arielle moved into action, as she reentered her home about thirty minutes later, her fingers tapping on her phone's keypad:

> *Hey, kinda concerned that I haven't been verbally assaulted*
> *in the past few weeks*
> *text 1 to lmk you received this*
> *dial if you wanna resume our tradition (and prove you're still alive)*

Arielle scratched the back of her neck—an itch that wasn't really there.

She chewed at her lip. For a moment, there was nothing.

Then, a new message icon popped up.

She tapped to incoming replies coming in.

> *1*
> *You are so dramatic*
> *2*
> *I'll call u soon*

And then…nothing. Not another text. And certainly not a call. For days.

Only Jae'cy's last batch of established recipe selections reached Arielle, by email, for her editorial input.

Now, in the late afternoon days later, Arielle had one foot out her front door when her cell phone rang.

"*Yes*, I'm still coming," Arielle affectedly sighed into it without a look at the incoming caller. Elizabeth, the impending Birthday Woman, was probably calling in her typical caring fashion to see if Arielle still could comfortably come pick her up from the airport tomorrow, given her busy schedule. Case-in-point, how twenty minutes ago, Arielle had moped around her closet for a decent polo for this website optimization lunch today with Kimesha and advertisers. She'd just surprisingly reached a pretty modest number of sales with this new genre crossover, but she wasn't loving having to leave her house.

"Let me guess. More people."

The voice that uncannily remarked was definitely not Kimesha's. Or her mom's.

Arielle paused, key in the keyhole, and just stared at it as if frozen stiff from a ghost spotting.

"Uh-oh," the voice continued. "Maybe *I'm* the one who should be concerned now. Anyone there on the other side?"

Arielle locked the door, then pivoted around to her driveway. "Well, you got that creepy Scorpio thing goin' on. So, you might be havin' a channelin.'"

Jae'cy giggled. *Ah, yes. The tradition is back like it never left…even though you temporarily disappeared…which I've learned is your thing…Like mine.* But Jae'cy's edge was that she could delude much more effectively than Arielle ever could.

"*Anyway*, I got your feedback on the first recipes. Do you have a good Wi-Fi setup workin' for you in that afterlife?"

"Call the spirit guides—they'll show you the exact location. It's pretty fly, not gonna lie." If Jae'cy wasn't stopping, she wasn't.

"Okay, silly," Jae'cy surrendered. "I'm calling to see when we can link back up because I think I'm ready for the backstories. Of course, starting with the twist on my granny's butterscotch—"

Okay, that all was most definitely fine and dandy, but why was Arielle suddenly melting like butterscotch?

She chalked it up to the desert heat and settled into her car. "I have some time in the a.m. weekend after next."

There was a pause. Which made Arielle follow suit, key in the ignition. "Uh-oh, you must've just received a new download. If *sooo...*" She started rummaging in her glove compartment. "Can you—or they—tell me where my notebook is? Because I know I had it with me last night."

Jae'cy burst up, back to life...or the third dimension. "Em-*hmm*. You too busy for even your OWN job these days, huh? What, chaperonin' your friend at the slot machines again?"

"Ha-ha. *Any*-way, we're makin' it a Zoom or what?" Arielle redirected as she backed her car out of the driveway—and hopefully out of the dead-end Jae'cy just tried to corner her into. She did not want to discuss the latest status on any "friend."

"*Oooh* yeah. You're real brand new now."

"People still use that?" Arielle smirked as she pulled out onto the main street outside her housing community.

"If *you're* still using 'fly,' then you can *fly* on over here. Or drive. It only takes like four hours. Ya know, just a lil' friendly advice to dodge that whole people thing."

"Oo, but see *that's* the thing," Arielle jabbed back. "I won't be avoiding one person still...you."

"Girl, you know you want to see me!" Jae'cy countered immediately, full of overestimated confidence. Just like a damn Sadge rising.

Arielle's hand slipped a bit on the wheel as she turned a corner. Checked it.

*Damn, let me turn on the AC.*

"Let's do...just before noon?... Like, a week after...because my schedule opens up again after that...a week after your Music Hop event."

*Dang, she'd remembered.* But Arielle knew she was happy about the event...even if time had just snuck up on her. She looked at today's date on her phone. And yep, the Music Hop was only a few days away.

Arielle nodded silently first, then vocalized. "If you're really good at your side hobby, you'll see that I just said yes."

"*BYE*, DeBarge." There was a giggle, then a click.

Then a—*HONK!* Arielle fluttered, staring at the green light that she could've sworn was still red.

Arielle suddenly shut off her car audio, the Spotify that was programmed to autoplay when she connected to Bluetooth, presently on her '70s love playlist from last listen. *No, nothing needed from the Stylistics right now. Thanks.*

Arielle's mind was in its own playlist of thoughts. *She is one strange mystery to me...but that's exactly what I'm signed up for.*

*And that's why I'm always so intrigued and uncertain all at the same time. And still can't stay away.*

        And because, she hadn't forgotten about that kiss.

♡ 26

THE MAIN EVENT, THE MUSIC HOP, WAS NEAR. BUT FIRST—
    "PLEASE WELCOME TO THE STAGE, ARIELLE SMITH!"
There was another big event. One that felt almost as unnerving. Arielle exhaled backstage just as Kimesha tipped her head to the platform, the lights, the panelist host. *THE PEOPLE.* The opening day at this symposium's Authors Guild–partnering conference for minority writers: "Where Is the Love?: Minorities in Romance, Science Fiction, and Action."

In one way, she *was* excited. This was a highly publicized conference celebrating creators breaking story stereotypes, such as Black people cast solely in comedies or economical strife. What she wasn't excited about was that this was her first-ever live talk with a large audience and mass broadcasting. A book signing? No prob, just a quick signature and salutation. A streamed master's class? *Cool beans, all done at home at my computer.* One-on-ones with a magazine columnist or content specialist for her book on their landing page or upcoming e-newsletter? Also cool. She was once in their shoes, familiar territory.

But Arielle had always known that this thing, her writing, was just as much personal as it was public. Today, she and the people were not separated by a book or a screen.

Kimesha was right: This event was a sign that she'd really reached self-sufficiency, wouldn't have to return to a nine-to-five, to someone else's rules. When she'd first started this author journey, this was what she'd wanted, but doubted she'd obtain: being financially and professionally free. But having to share more of *her*? Em...

At this point, Kimesha just gave her a soft but deliberate push to move forward.

With everything, there was a trade-off. If she didn't want to be told when, where, and how to work, then she'd have to make *this* work. "This is gonna elevate you!" Kimesha had said, Arielle reminded herself mentally as she climbed the platform steps. *If it doesn't kill you first...*

Luckily, she wasn't the only author speaker onstage; there were three other panel speakers (one whom she'd brushed shoulders with before, at the very least, in the same virtual aisles of their Amazon genres:

African-American, romance, etc.). And she was the final chair to fill, to the viewing delight of the many fans and aspiring writers awaiting.

As that seat got closer and closer, she just stared at it, as the applause came closer. But as she descended into it, into the initial nerve-wracking seconds of any new experience, she came into a new feeling, into the flow of the unfolding event. And at that point, she made a judgment: *Ight, you've made it this far.*

That was, until the discussion opened up to the crowd. One eyebrow-pierced, curly-haired young Black woman was handed a mic and rose. "Yes, my question is for Arielle," she inducted with confidence. "As a fellow LGBT—"

*Could've fooled me.*

"Dramatist—"

*AND! a dramatist.* Arielle knew this fellow "masculine of center" woman was *really* about to get into the meat now.

"Getting my feet wet in this popular space where unique marketing, as you certainly know, is *so* integral…How do I write more…authentically?"

Arielle thought about how to answer the question. Because, unfortunately, she knew the answer, but was hoping that she could speak on it in such a way that this seat didn't start to burn….

*Let's give it a go, Elle…* "I think a lot of us writers transcribe the world that we know. It makes sense. We're good at it, and it's something we have to give ourselves grace about because it's what we're—and I mean all of us, as people—are taught to be good at: to peddle what we know. But then we have to not block ourselves from *pedaling* one page further, even if it starts to feel unknown, and pen what we uncover. That way, we become master marketers: ones who always take new risks. Otherwise, we'll get tired of what we're selling."

The woman nodded evenly, silently, lowering the mic, and Arielle nodded back.

*Cool, looks like that was enough for her to chew on.* Arielle was glad that the woman hadn't followed up with a boundary-piercing question like those she'd seen in some panels—

"Going to dive in there real quick. GREAT question!"

*Great.*

Apparently, the host, though, had some more of that meat's bone to pick. "But I'd like to build on your answer a bit."

The young woman descended into her seat. Arielle's, on the other hand, began to rise—in temperature.

The host skated her eyeglasses over to Arielle like the scariest of librarians—or make that a warden. The woman, Gracie Wilson, was a prominent socialite-influencer in Black Hollywood circles, with a considerable following. And therefore, Arielle just knew that she was surely about to influence this right here. "So, that brings up the age-old concept of writing from a place of pain, does it not? Isn't that what they say gives us creators our best work?"

"Well, I think you write *into* your pain," Arielle spoke aloud. *And I'm finna write myself out of this one.*

"You can start to reengineer your mind to approach it in that way. Meaning, to learn that pain is something you're not forever inhabiting but rather temporarily visiting, then eventually you leave," Arielle replied to Gracie, then peered at all of the other thousands of eyes in front of her. "And that's how you get to that happy ending you all love."

The crowd chuckled. It was a universal truth that all conscious sentient beings knew: Happiness was what everyone wanted. Needed. And when really in hunger of it, forcibly created it whether through partying or playing up or writing a certain narrative...

Arielle hoped that was all the truths that they'd need from her for the day.

But Gracie still looked to be wanting *another* truth to unveil... "Indeed!" She clapped for a second. A second. "Do you think that's the reason you've moved away from the 'getting the girl' trope? *That* ending too hard to attain?"

Sure, Arielle could've given Gracie the gracious benefit of the doubt, that she was speaking about Arielle's *Ash Must Fall Down,* which focused on wins other than her typical romantic wins. But Arielle knew better, ergo Gracie's very active social media presence.

Regardless, since she had committed to this...

"Well, I—"

"Don't speak so soon." Kimesha had somehow craftily summoned a mic. "Wait for the new chapter in the *NEW* book."

*Thanks, Kimesha,* Arielle thought, then exhaled a breath she hadn't realized she'd been holding.

The crowd laughed as Kimesha slid her eyes over to Arielle, widening them discreetly as Arielle's sweat cooled. However, something had stuck out to Arielle about the moment. Not with Kimesha, but with Gracie and what she'd insinuated. What could she be getting at? Talking about her personal life, that was why Arielle preferred to let her work do the talking for her and not actually talk about the work because some people took liberties to be messy. But in her other book talks, albeit of a much smaller attendance usually, that kind of weird insinuation had never been the case. *So, why now?* It was weird; it was feeling like the start of something here in the public brewing but she couldn't yet make out what...

Either way, her most immediate concern came roughly thirty minutes later when the panel was over and the same young woman from the audience who'd kickstarted the uncomfortable conversation was approaching Arielle as she headed toward the lobby. *Ah, nah. Not another quest—*

"Thanks for those words up there. I needed them." Judging by the subtle yet stiff clutch of her crossbody bag, Arielle guess that her need was more than just professional. As with all writers, the need was emotional. Words to live by, to live. A need...

And that was why Arielle wrote. To help others meet their need...One that might sometimes be painful, but only at first. Until they bravely reached the end. She couldn't lie, this slightly more baring experience, with people face-to-face, hadn't been *too* bad. It had actually been good.

At least, for someone else.

Arielle grinned at, encouraged the woman. "Your upcoming story is gonna be real, right?"

The woman chuckled. Then nodded. "Definitely."

This was what she wrote for.

AND THEN, THERE IT SUDDENLY WAS: THE MUSIC HOP. Before its mid-day start, Arielle was picking up her very first love, Elizabeth, from the airport.

Arielle pulled up outside Delta and got out to assist the approaching Elizabeth and her rolling suitcase. Arielle hadn't told her to reschedule her trip months back because she wasn't even sure she'd be going to this event. And now here they were.

Driving away from the airport, Arielle explained her weekend plans.

Elizabeth delivered her own agenda: "Makes no difference to me. You already know having an empty house will let me get into my own party up in those dusty cabinets I didn't get to last time I was here."

Arielle grinned. Her mother's practical love was endearing, if annoying at times. But she cared about her, always had.

Her phone vibrated.

"Want me to answer?" Elizabeth offered while already nearing Arielle's phone, nestled in the cupholder. "The name says…J?" Elizabeth read the phone incoming caller screen then read Arielle's face. "Want me to put it on speaker?"

"Em. Yeah," Arielle answered, focusing on the road. "Thanks."

Elizabeth dutifully obliged, the call opening.

"Hey, what's up?" Arielle said.

"*So,* my flight got a lil' pushed back—LA at its finest," Jae'cy updated with the very audible sound of airplanes as her background. "But we should land there around—"

"ONE, Mommy."

Elizabeth chuckled at the adorable busybody, Arielle grinning, too.

Then Elizabeth took it a step further. "So I take it you have your boss with you today?"

Jae'cy shared a quick sighing laugh. "Help me."

Arielle smirked at the conversation (*that was supposed to be mine???*). "My mom, Elizabeth, is here with me. She's here for—"

"You're the lady from the last time, right? On Zoom?"

"Yes, that was me. How are you?"

"I'm wonderful…" Elizabeth paused this time, her next move, a long, assessing look, for Arielle alone.

*Crap, a red light.* Arielle shifted her focus back to the phone. "…And yourself?"

"I'm good—as long as I listen to this little one here."

"I know that's right." The new friends chuckled. And Arielle twitchily grinned, gripping the wheel. As she made a right turn, she seized another opportunity to peep her mother, who was too busy engaging with Jae'cy to give Arielle any more meaningful looks.


When Jae'cy pulled up into Arielle's attached garage in her rented sedan, her conversation with Elizabeth resurrected like it'd never stopped.

"Okay, Miss Boss, I see ya," Elizabeth and her broom acknowledged Cori, in her two high-bunned tuffs of hair and overalls, then moved right along to Jae'cy and her ponytail, sunglasses, baby tee, and jeans, before Arielle even could. "And you're even prettier in person."

"Aw, thank you." Jae'cy suddenly looked coy…but still with poise.

An interesting study, *always.* Arielle gave a nod at Jae'cy's smile greeting her.

"Well, let me get back to what I was tackling." Elizabeth headed to the interior of the house.

"Cleaning up after your baby, huh?"

"I know she needs her behind whipped for all of this dust she left for me up on these cupboards," Elizabeth simply summarized as she was already off to the trenches.

"Uh-oh," Jae'cy chuckled.

And Cori squealed.

*Thanks, Mom. Thanks.* Arielle skirted her attention with a restrained grin over at Jae'cy and Cori.

"Aww, stop. Your mom is sweet. Now, MINE is spicy." Jae'cy shook her head with purpose, which made her hoops swing lightly…and the natural gloss on her lips shimmer.

"So, stopped at our hotel to check in and all of that. We're still good on time, right?"

"Uh, yeah, told Tish and Marlon we—uh…" Arielle started. *I actually haven't told them anything. They don't even know that she's coming with me, but they better not play with me—*

"Meeting them there," Jae'cy offered.

Arielle nodded, then turned her attention to Cori, backpedaling to her SUV with a grin as Jae'cy retrieved Cori's car seat in the sedan. "Ready?" *'Cause, man, one of us has to be.*

"YES!" Cori bounced right over.

They all settled in. Then, as Arielle worked with the key in the ignition (???), she glanced at Jae'cy.

"The first step is 'Go.' First emotional support tip of the day."

Arielle chuckled. "Yeah." *Baby, I'm gonna need that humor today.*

Jae'cy started summoning Spotify as Arielle backed out of the garage. "Alright, me and Rumpa are ready to DJ the pre-party. What we got UP-tempo in this tracklist?"

Tish and Marlon were cracking up about who knew what as Arielle, Jae'cy, and Cori walked up to them in the Music Hop's large lobby. But judging by how quickly they straightened up, pulling back their shoulders and their grins, Arielle knew what they wanted to say once she was solo.

*Just keep it movin', y'all. Right on over to the festivities.*

These clowns irked her sometimes, but she was glad to see them in-person. It had been a while. Between Tish and her newfound wife and mommy life and Marlon's ongoing family and trucking work, adultin' had them all quite busy. But it never kept them from their innate goofiness. Arielle couldn't tell which of the two of them slapped her back the hardest.

"AI, you puttin' on some tone?!" Tish said as she observed Arielle's light sculpt in the arms.

Although Arielle didn't work out as consistently as she should, it didn't take long for her to show results.

"Looks like you're ready to join me at the gym next time you fly down to see me," Marlon encouraged.

"Ha. We'll see. Let's just see about this other event right now, though." Arielle tipped her head at masses of people entering the open doors. But she knew there was still one more conversation she had to have.

She inhaled then extended a hand between Marlon and Tish then Jae'cy and Cori.

"Y'all, this is—"

"Ay," Marlon interrupted, snapping his finger at Jae'cy. Like Elizabeth, he was more extroverted. But it was nice having a bit of home in him and Tish with her today. "I think I seen you in a movie on Netflix the other day!"

Jae'cy fake-cringed. "Ooh, I know *exactly* which one you're talkin' about."

Marlon started rollin'. "Ay, a B movie is more than most people ever get. Gotta start somewhere."

"I guess..." Jae'cy chuckled, quite humble, really,

"It was actually kinda decent," Marlon added. "Some of the scenes got me."

Tish extended a hand to Cori. "Hi, there." To which Cori swayed.

"Loves attention, that one. Just forewarning," Jae'cy reported with a shake of her head.

Next thing, Cori was all of the talk. She started pulling Jae'cy's forearm in the direction of other dashing and trotting kids. "Come on!"

Everyone followed suit...but Tish hung back and nudged Arielle discreetly, side-eying her. "Tish, please."

*But she was right. Elle, knew it.*

They entered the large workshop space where various breakout sections were, small groups of attendees already being led to their respective sections with various instructors at each.

Jae'cy glanced back over her shoulder at Arielle with a grin that showcased her cheekbones. "Uh, how come I look like this is my event instead of yours?"

"Yeah, AI." Tish picked up her pace as Jae'cy turned back around, approaching a signup section at the welcome table just outside of the large conference room door where the event was located. But she gave another furtive eye at Arielle.

Arielle sighed, then pushed Tish towards the signup. "Go. Now."

Tish cracked up, moving on.

It was time to focus on music for a second, get signed in at the welcome table, get assigned to an open booth (the twist of this annual event: you'd be assigned a booth, not pick your own), and there, you'd find a selection of crated vinyl around a specific artist, genre, and/or era. Working with the tools given to you, and mixing it on Rane ONE DJ Controller machines. One in each booth.

After signing up then moving to the large conference door, one of the workshop staff members approached them, extended his arms around the space and announced, "So quick rules: As you can see, we keep each booth to two or three partners max., so you guys can split into groups of two and three. Your choice, but *we* pick the booth you go to..."

*All except for two sections are left,* Arielle mentally counted.

"So, who would like to go with who?..."

Tish flashed a grin at her.

Actually, everyone was looking at her, as if they were waiting on something.

*Did I miss something?*

"Two in your party have just elected to pair up..."

Arielle watched the staff member's hand extend to Tish and Marlon, and then to one of the two empty booths on the opposite side of the room that was decorated in Adele album cover art. *No way. There's NO way both of them can be happy with some soft R&B...* But Marlon and Tish were already trotting off to that side, while flashing a mischievous grin on the sly her way.

*And Elle, be real. You know you're happy that it's now just—*

"The three of you are taking on 'The Challenge'!" The staff member grinned, extended his hand to the second empty booth just some feet ahead of them, with cover art of various hip-hop albums. "We have about three of these booths per workshop, and we call them this because your job will be actually even *more* interesting," the staff member explained as he walked them over. "The samples you'll be using are ones that are notable for being obscure and unexpected for hip-hop tracks. Everything from Action Bronson's 'Contemporary Man' sampling 'Sussudio' by Phil Collins to Busta's 'Gimme Some More' using 'Psycho' by Bernard Herrmann."

"Oo, fun," Jae'cy pitched in, even bouncing her shoulders a bit.

The staff member chuckled as he landed them at their destination. "So you have to not only test new skills, doing the mixing in general, but also test how well you can pick out sounds from old tracks, selecting the accurate sampled tracks to be mixed that match the hip-hop song in which it appears."

"Oo, don't look so tense," Jae'cy chuckled at Arielle as she perched her hands excitably in wait on the Rane ONE table in the booth. "We got this."

*Maybe she was right, this was gonna pan out just fine.* As the booth instructor explained the process, assigning the initial hip-hop track they'd have to emulate by first identifying the sample he started playing over their booth speakers, Arielle had already dropped down to the crate of vinyl in front of her.

"That's J Dilla," Arielle ascribed instantly to the first challenge tune playing.

"That would be correct." The instructor nodded with approval. "One of the best to ever do it."

"Definitely," Arielle agreed, picking up the sample vinyl and placing it on the chopping block, the Rane ONE where the magic would begin.

"Oh, she's ready," the instructor chortled.

And so was Cori, hopping over to the Rane ONE with big, curious eyes. Arielle sheepishly grinned, almost like a daze. She hadn't seen a DJ controller machine up close since childhood, in Marlon's room.

"So, who wants to be the demo person?"

Jae'cy and Arielle tipped their heads in-sync to Cori.

Minutes later, after the instructor's run-through and then three separate machine tests within their group, he parted to let them see what they were made of.

Arielle shook her head sharply, honed into the new creative process. But she felt herself in this moment. And her hands were moving in the small crate of vinyl in their booth, picking up a vinyl cover, soundtrack for some kind of film called *Fantastic Planet*.

Jae'cy was amused yet gripped, watching their sudden group leader. "Okay, I'm impressed, DeBarge."

Arielle shrugged. "I recall everything. All I did was listen to music growing up. Used to sneak into my brother's room and get up in his CD collection, when he'd go out with friends."

And somehow, as she was schoolin' Jae'cy on her musicmaking background, she was also insentiently, just naturally, helping Cori's hands correctly place down one of the new vinyls onto the Rane ONE for the new challenge song that was now playing over the speaker in their booth.

"From Nas to Black Moon to Bahamadia."

Jae'cy started to tinker around on the Rane ONE, to no success, hovering undecidedly over the various awaiting bright-colored effect buttons...

"And he won't ever admit to it, but..."

*Sure hope she did better with the clarinet.* Arielle stifled a chuckle in observation, then helped Jae'cy out, taking one of Jae'cy's fingers and guiding it to one button: START.

"Some Sade up in there, too."

Jae'cy chuckled, a bit like a quiver, a bit of a quivery retraction of her hand. Arielle heard it and felt it ever so finely. Almost as fine as her ear trying to detect the right switch and flow of the beat as she tried out another effect button on the Rane ONE.

"So, since you've had this hiding in your back pocket so long, how come you've never flexed a lil' something until now?" Jae'cy asked...while slipping her hands into her back jeans pocket.

Arielle continued to mix but answered fully, or as much as she could while being cognizant of the little one beside them. "Remember what happened to me the last time I got excited showing something to somebody?"

Jae'cy's eyes floated over to Arielle, whose eyes floated up from those concealed hands up...Up to the glossy lips on that awaiting face. And then, and only then, the eyes that fluttered faintly.

As the music played over the speaker, as the sample skipped, as Cori giggled (due to her 'mixing' on the Rane ONE and hence the sample skipping)...

"Exactly," Arielle took to digging through the small crate of more crazy bizarre vinyl. *Damn, I want to kiss her. But what about Cori? Has she even told the girl what she's got going on with AD or...? No, because she's—*

"Okay, that's it today, folks!" a staff member announced in the center of the big room. "Your certificates will be emailed to you."

Attendees all over started to slap one another's back in a well-completed effort for today or clap appreciatively at the staff as they started to depart.

Tish and Marlon popped up. "Ay, look. The wife just called me, I gotta see what it's about," Tish announced, pointing toward the exit. "But we gotta talk about today, though!" Tish eyed Arielle on that.

"And that's my cue to call my own misses," Marlon followed suit. "So I'll be by later." Indeed, as part of their annual birthday tradition for their mother, they'd be surprising her to a Stylistics concert tomorrow.

"Aw yeah, gotta see my Momma Liz!" Tish shouted out.

*You guys are so full of it.* "Later," Arielle proffered.

Then Tish and Marlon were gone.

"Mommy, can we eat?"

"I'll see what's around before we head back to the hotel, okay?" Jae'cy started up, fixing one of Cori's overall straps.

As Arielle fixed herself to...

"I know a good spot nearby," Arielle extended.

*Nah, I just led.* Arielle didn't know when the switch in her had happened. It was probably over the course of peering at Jae'cy's face, the sun kissing that skin and bouncing off those shimmery, brown-glossed lips on the way over. Or when she'd felt Jae'cy's hands while leading her to the right button on the RANE, to the start. Or...

*No, it had started before today, much longer ago than today.* But today had been the climax: She knew she wanted to stretch out their time together—and wanted Jae'cy to clearly know it, too. *She has the whole day. And I do, too...*

...Jae'cy peeked up as she smoothed out some flyaways on top of Cori's hopping, excited head.

"Great!" Cori harped back, atop her stool at Arielle's kitchen island with a full mouth, a nearly depleted cup of arroz con pollo and an open can of Materva in front of her. That was her response to Arielle's asking her verdict on the Cuban spot they'd gotten takeout from.

"But mine looks better than yours," Cori completed, noting Arielle's indeed simple salsa, beans, and sauteed onions in comparison to her jampacked chicken strips, veggies, and the rest.

"And you'd be right," Arielle conceded.

Jae'cy chuckled, having to pause midway to a sip of her drink.

"Elle's fun."

"I agree, baby."

Arielle grinned to herself. She'd become a softie for the little tyke herself, even though she'd grown about two inches since they'd first met.

"Because she makes you smile."

Arielle's smile dropped. *Oh no, kid. You can't give away my tricks, though. But not because of me.* Arielle now knew, long knew, that she was no longer fighting the feelings she had since she'd been failing miserably. So, no, the denial of this child's valid observations were no longer was because of Arielle; it was because... *Your mother in the audience isn't ready for it.*

So, of course, the vibe instantly got tense. For one.

"Uh, yeah..." Jae'cy smiled anew, while toying with her pop can. "Well, different people bring out different sides of you, baby."

"Is that why you only talk to Daddy but don't laugh?"

*But this girl's not lettin' up...And I'm happy for it.*

"Daddy and I have you around. That takes serious faces for the baby." Jae'cy got playfully in Cori's face with a nose touch that made Cori giggle.

But only briefly. Back to the interrogation. "I'm here now, and you're smiling. Daddy doesn't make you laugh. Elle does."

Arielle shifted a look over at Jae'cy, much like Cori just had. Awaiting a response, just like the little one.

Because she *did* want to know what the deal was, too. *Were* they co-parenting?

And Jae'cy only kept her gaze on the child. *But she can tell I'm looking.* She was shifting her drum on the rim of her pop can, to a beat that only she could translate.

Then she took those drumming fingers to Cori's tummy and started tickling her. "It's because you always steal all of the giggles. Thought about that? *Huh?*"

Cori couldn't think at all because she was laughing too hard.

Elizabeth came trotting in on a mission toward the fridge. "I know this kitchen better still look the same way I left it about thirty minutes ago," she said, with a bite into her apple. And that was when, as Elizabeth was making way back to which she came, Cori's child attention span caught something on Elizabeth: various gemstones on her ringed hands.

"Those are pretty!"

"Why thank you! Got some more if you wanna see 'em."

Cori was already hopping off the stool and hopping over.

"Oh, boy," Jae'cy softly giggled. "The girl loves all of that stuff then the next minute is bouncing off of everything."

Elizabeth simply grinned at Jae'cy. But lingered on Arielle.

And with that, the new friends walked out.

Taking the sound with them...

Jae'cy peeped Arielle.

Arielle stared back...

"So...today was a date."

*She knows that wasn't a question.* Especially when it would've been maybe more accurate that night at Live n Color, when it was so apparent what was building between them. But even then, it wouldn't have counted—because back then it wasn't officially stated... "Not when you invite yourself."

Jae'cy quivered on a smile. *So she knows what the answer is.*

"...But you forget that I just paid for this food."

Jae'cy giggled. "So, *that* was the date!" And that, too, wasn't exactly a question.

"Only if you want it to be." *It was the truth.*

Arielle lost her teasing, her quirk, her grin. Gained something else. An assertion.

Jae'cy lost her teasing, her spunk, her smile. Gained something else. An unanswered question.

And then one of her own, shifting her eyes to a returning person:

"What do you say? Back to the hotel?" That was directed at Cori.

She'd just skipped back into the kitchen, heading to the interior garage door as Elizabeth returned with her apple core.

Arielle lifted a parting hand, smiling at Cori first...Then Jae'cy...

"See ya later," Jae'cy waved bye, mostly to Elizabeth whose eyes she fluttered over to. "Nice meeting you. For *real* this time!"

"You, too. The both of you take care on your morning flight, hear?" Elizabeth imparted.

"We will. Thanks."

Then just like that, there was just the closed door. Arielle pulled in her lips. Elizabeth looked from Arielle to the door, then back to the door, then back to Arielle.

"She's one of your clients, huh?"

Arielle took to cleaning a spot on the island countertop that wasn't dirty in the slightest. Elizabeth had made sure of it. "Yep."

"She seems like a really nice young lady."

"Yeah, she is." *Yep, that's all I got.* Silence...

"Well, that's good...Glad it's a nice relationship."

"What is?" Marlon stepped in via the garage hall door from which Jae'cy and Cori had just left...and thus, the "confused" face he had on wasn't really convincing.

Luckily, his attention turned to greeting Elizabeth, a peck on the cheek, then a reveal of his phone. Which made Elizabeth crack up in delight and then show it to Arielle.

There, in all of her plaid-uniformed, wide-mouthed, snaggle-toothed, first-grade school picture glory was Arielle on Marlon's Facebook page, captioned:

*Remember this? Lbs*

"How come you don't smile like that anymore?" Elizabeth asked.

"You seen her face lately?" Marlon jested as he helped himself to the fridge.

"Because if I cause any more civil unrest, I might get banned from society for good." Arielle smirked limply at the girl she once was.

Alas, she revealed a grin, gummy wide, just like her mother missed. "Is this good?"

"I think giving you and her a couple of minutes longer to talk would've been even better."

Arielle snickered. Okay, it was time to catch a day-early flight, for Elizabeth. "Mom, let's not..."

Arielle lost her grin.

"But something tells me that it would've been a long conversation that was long overdue, too." And now, Elizabeth had lost hers. "That's *real* social unrest."

"Yeah, 'cause you was *REAL* restless today." Marlon came back into the kitchen with a handful of chips. Her Fritos.

Arielle knocked her head to the side with a moan.

"Yeah, I seen it on that big head of yours," Marlon boasted, stuffing another handful into his mouth. "Me and Tish seen it. BOTH of y'all."

*So, what you want, titan? My head as the prize???*

"And she sees it, too..." That was all Elizabeth ended on. So vague, yet so clear.

Arielle pulled together her best casual nod. Then watched as Elizabeth then Marlon left the room.

Arielle exhaled a tense breath, leaned back against the fridge. Thank goodness Elizabeth never pushed her. But she was also a mother who'd lived and seen some things, including Arielle and Marlon's father stepping out. Yet, Elizabeth never said painful words about him to Marlon and Arielle, only showed up every day in her and Marlon's lives.

Although it was admirable to Arielle, it was definitely not something she wanted to have to go through: braving pain from love. And that was when the long-buried truth hit her: She had never really been in love. 'Cause real love didn't exist. Or real love meant pain. That was what her childhood had told her and now she was still telling it to herself with no question, and as if it was truth. And that was why she was *just* now allowing herself to feel it in one way: to herself. But not outwardly, to the world. Because then that would mean crystallizing it. Make it physical. Make it something susceptible to the world...and its pain.

Arielle re-conjured the vision, the past from moments ago: if she looked hard enough, she saw the snaggle-toothed girl still there, the huge cheeks now replaced by high cheekbones.

The same girl. Under the surface.

A woman like her mother understood that. And so, she'd just left it at that.

But as for another woman...

*BEEP-BEEP.*

Arielle's eyes floated down to her illuminated cell phone on her kitchen countertop.

Then she walked over to it.

And picked it up.

With a new question awaiting in the form of a video call:

Jae'cy panned the view to a knocked-out Cori in the back of the sedan. Then Jae'cy's face appeared, smiling. "As you can see...she had a blast. The both of us..." Then she blinked more shyly. "Do it again, sometime?"

And Arielle nodded. "Only if you want to."

So many long overdue questions.

But one solitary truth.

At this point, she had suddenly become more direct with Jae'cy. Some things long overdue...And so,

*Yep, definitely back in LA...*

♡ **28**

INDEED, A WEEK LATER, AT TEN-SOMETHING AT NIGHT, she was getting out of a Dodge Camaro.

*Man,* this girl moved fast.

Taylor hopped up in step with Arielle in a business district in downtown LA. And as they walked down it, Arielle felt another buzz.

Mentally…

*You know what you need to do, Elle.*

And physically: Her hand brushed up against by Taylor's.

The girl had done it many times before, even with others, Arielle had observed over the past months. She was just naturally one of those carefree, expressive types. But *this* particular brush…

"Thanks for coming."

Arielle shifted her eyes over, and not a second later, Taylor skated hers in return. And for a moment, there was just silence.

But the young boho never accepted nonspeaking for long. Still had to make commentary on what she felt; just feeling it was not enough.

"So, you always shiver when people touch you?"

"What does that mean, child?"

"Whatchu think, wordsmith?"

Taylor peeped her, shockingly quiet for once, as they increasingly neared the sound of people…

"You're good at sticking to the script, all of the rules, right?" Taylor then lightly, teasingly challenged.

Even with a bit of a flicker…*Like—*

Arielle blinked the inbound thought of what Taylor had just done with her face away. But not the first thought of what Taylor had said, a thought somehow wisely issued by the young soul, challenging her internally about how she indeed played it safe. *And how, right now, is it really doin' anything for you? You've failed with it lately, Elle.*

"But rules are meant to be broken," Taylor continued. "Weren't you in Marketing?"

"Marketing one-on-one:" Arielle responded…but felt a tinge of irritation coming up. Not with Taylor, at the face she'd just seen in hers a moment ago. And at herself for not being able to get it out of her mind. "Optimize only what needs to be optimized. Maintain the rest."

"And so, what are we..." Taylor flashed her brows. "Maintaining?"

If Arielle had wanted to take a moment to do so, which she admittedly quickly determined she didn't anyway, her reply to the question still would've been stunted. Because just as her lips parted, Taylor's did the same. A race to the finish line that entailed...Arielle meeting Taylor's mouth.

*Oh.*

Snap.

As their lips separated, Arielle stared at Taylor in astonishment— not at the act but at her internal response to the act and how fast she'd developed the response. A feeling of "That actually was pretty nice after so many months..." *Or has it been a year now?*

"Y'all cute!"

That was a female's approval as they walked up to a red-carpeted restaurant entrance and met the lights of her Nikon. Just as quickly, her back was suddenly facing them, to capture other incoming guests.

Well, looked like the little grasshopper had graduated to new heights already. Tonight was a music video wrap-up celebration. As Taylor tucked her arm into the crook of Arielle's pocket-stuffed one, passing Michi with a (yet another) random girl on his own arm, Arielle thought, *Alright...*

Then watched Taylor hop-step right into the venue and wink at her and she...grinned back. *I'll give her credit; she's definitely transparent. Very clear cut.* That was something anyone could appreciate.

*And that* was why Arielle had to—

Take Taylor's hand lightly, grip it. And pause in her step as others (including Michi) continued entering.

Taylor naturally paused, too, looked back, looked at Arielle. Looked at the sudden change of expression on her face.

The face that had made the choice to not only accept but take on the kiss and all that was attached behind it. Because at least this, for now, that was more sure she'd thought. Not her usual mode of being, not her usual experience in life, for the first time ever, wrestling with two 'options,' as Tish used to call her days of fun.

But for Arielle, she didn't view these as 'options', fun. In just the next instant, she viewed these things as disgust with herself, disgust that had been brewing for being in this juggling act like she was some kind of young—

She read Taylor's face.

And felt bad. *Oh, to be in my twenties again. When all of this mess I'm pullin' would've been fine.*

But she'd come out tonight to be mature and only do what was right by letting Taylor know in person. And so, at least now, she also felt a *bit* more authentic. "I'm so happy for you, Taylor. Really. Excited for all that's coming your way like tonight and all of your tomorrows. But I gotta go."

And hoped she wouldn't judge herself too harshly for it; looking at it as a needed optimization—at least for now.

"Is everything okay?"

"Yeah, I'm…"

Going from being just 'fine,' aloof, acting like one thing while really feeling another. And being real.

"Honestly, no. Not for me. And it has nothing to do with you. Just know that. Alright?"

And Taylor scrunched up her face in disconcertment more than confusion, which for the first time ever didn't just make her look older. But also, wiser than Arielle previously imagined. Maybe even wiser than her. And if that was possible, Arielle wouldn't even be surprised…much like Taylor, in the very next moment, showed that she wasn't either about this moment…and what moments outside of her could possibly be the cause.

And so, the second part of Arielle's optimization meant one last thing…

♡ **29**

BUT FIRST, WAS THE BACKROOM KITCHEN AT HONEST BITES FOR THE START OF THE BACKSTORIES. Sitting beside Jae'cy at the food prep table (to be sanitized thoroughly afterwards, promise) Arielle squinted even harder at the recipe title that was in front of her on Jae'cy's open Mac in a ready Word doc:

*Massaman Curry*

"What the heck is that?" Arielle looked more and more like she was visually impaired, or constipated, by the minute.

"It's Thai and Indian fusion," Jae'cy explained as she changed to a two-page view on her Mac, so that now the blanker page was beside the text-filled left page that was titled something that finally made sense: *Bettie's Bountiful Butterscotch.*

Then she followed Arielle's new curious, squinted line of vision to an adjacent scaled-down window on Jae'cy's laptop screen: some kind of report with a celebrity's name atop, a red line labeled 'positive' plummeting across months, and a green line labeled 'negative' skyrocketing upwards.

"And *that* would be a Q Score, something Breyah just decided I needed to care about before you pulled up. Want me to spell that out for you, too?"

"Ha. I don't have trouble with writing the words down. But thanks." *That sounds like something I don't wanna let Rachelle know about, though. Goodness gracious, all those red lines were terrifying.*

"Whew, that's good. Because then I'd be a little concerned about your readers, too."

This chick.

Jae'cy continued her previous thought. "But some of us go above just the words themselves. We *feel* the letters, the consonants in every completed whisk. The vowels in every beginning egg crack. Food is culture; the tongue, the explorer."

Arielle decided to just listen. One, the words were eloquent, and two, she knew they'd help with the storytelling.

Jae'cy then got up for a pot on the stove. Took out a sauce spoon, stirred a bit. Since the café was closed today, Jae'cy thought it would be good, as they worked on this recipe, to taste the flavor, especially Arielle. Eating some of it and experiencing it to help Jae'cy know how to provide a backstory on it artistically. Like what does this taste remind you of? And then free-form writing off of that in connection to Jae'cy's memory from her past that she attributed to it. "Culinary practitioners can't help but know how the words taste," Jae'cy swanked, back to the kitchen counter. But dropped them with some attitude. "I keep telling you word pushers—copywriters, salesmen, *promoters,* who are some *more* salesmen—"

*Ooh...* Arielle *now* knew where this was really going today. Why she'd felt some tension. . Then it turned up a notch, by her own volition. "Uh-oh. Everything fine under the lid there, chef?" she infiltrated smoothly.

"What are you talking about?" Jae'cy gave a snicker, stifled, short. Barely there.

"Like someone got you up on the wrong side of the bed." *And I won't lie, I'm trying to see if literally another person has been there. A promoter named—*

"*Someone* said *they* got up a little earlier on their side of the bed and were going to be here almost an hour ago. To also give *their* take on some of the vacant commercial sites I found to be a potential second Honest Bites location."

"Who? Me?" Arielle was confused. *And looking at properties? When did I tell her I'd—?*

"Uhhhh, yeah." Jae'cy was clearly confused as to why she was confused.

*Dang, regardless of the confusion, the common denominator seems to be that my coming was itself what really mattered to her...*

"I thought the plan was noon? So the flight I booked—"

Jae'cy 'dismissed' it with a light shake of her head and a faint smile. From that, Arielle knew there was something else, bigger, lingering there. And within her, too.

Looking to break the tension, she chose Jae'cy's laptop screen as the nearest escape, spotting an Internet tab. She reached over for the keypad, all the while, multitasking—and initiating what the two did best...but with less wavering, more purpose:

"So, today *was* supposed to be a date."

A light but ready snicker. "No, *not* a date."

Arielle clicked on the tab to find a Bay Area commercial real estate webpage showing three starred properties/suites.

"A playdate."

Arielle peeped Jae'cy, whose eyes were only on the laptop screen. But she revealed a light, nervous smirk. "Girl, pick."

Without long thought, just feeling it (like she was doing most of their interactions at this point), Arielle pointed at one of them: *Solid square feet, will give her just enough room but still offer manageability.* "I'd put my focus on this one." …While she focused on Jae'cy's face.

Jae'cy peeped it, then pulled back some hair behind her ear. "Yeah, that's the first one I decided to email, too."

And still brushing behind that ear like a pre-occupation…*Something else lingering…*

Jae'cy re-arose for the pot. *Of course, the food. Why we're here.* Took a scoop out of it, blew the curry to palatable warmth, then as she wheeled around: "Need my little taste tester!"

Cori came skipping in and immediately opened wide. She'd joined today's affair since AD was too busy to keep her this weekend, on his weekend. "As usual…" Jae'cy had informed Arielle.

After Jae'cy spooned the concoction into her mouth, there was a pause, then her face scrunched up in such an animated way that meant it was either too much for her or tooo yummy. But either way, she had her show on her tablet to watch and skipped once again right on away.

Jae'cy snickered and Arielle grinned as Jae'cy then turned a new ready spoon to her.

"Okay, need a *real* verbal take this time."

Arielle opened. And on her tongue, felt the smooth curry…then the spoon…then moving upward, Jae'cy's finger. Her lips brushing against it. Before swallowing. "Good."

Jae'cy instantly, shakily chuckled (*she knows she felt it…*), lifted that finger, and snapped it proudly. Then took a napkin and wiped a corner of Arielle's mouth. "I see."

And that, indeed, got Arielle seeing some things, looking… "Can't wait for some more."

Therefore, finally, Jae'cy too…Looking down at Arielle's mouth. (*Yes.*) For a long while. (*Even better.*) And when her eyes trailed back up, Arielle could've sworn the lighting had just gone dim in the ultrabright room. "I'm sure."

Arielle snaked up a corner of her mouth, then moved. Not even Jae'cy's way, just a move.

And instantly, Jae'cy moved, hopped her eyes away. Turned back to the stove, the pot. Because it was boiling over. *Right.*

Arielle, resisting the wry smile that spread on her face, instead noted the pot on the stove, the sauce bubbles just creeping above the rim. And that was what temporarily preoccupied her from her own mindset, made her surprised: for the first time, Jae'cy was letting something almost boil over, almost out of her control—

Another brush of that hair behind the ear as Jae'cy turned off the stove. *But there's still something more lingering...*

"I was just..." Jae'cy continued, shrugged. "Speaking in general, saying that people stringing words and hoping they look right, is not the same as stirring them, smelling them to certainty." The girl's nostrils were slightly flared as she made her way back to the table. "But unlike you, AD *does* struggle with spelling things out, such as if he'll actually commit to a date and time consistently." Jae'cy shared, low, a little flat. "We'll see how it goes *this* time. Or if he'll break Cori's heart."

Arielle was running different words in her head while running from other thoughts she was trying to keep pushed into the rear of her mind. But she had to get more of a sense for herself of what Jae'cy was really feeling about AD, even if it was personal. Even if it hurt. Even if it was a question, with some truth she didn't want to hear. "Hers...or yours?"

Jae'cy's eyes shifted slowly but intently onto Arielle, and then remained still.

"*wwwWWWAAAHH!*"

Both Arielle and Jae'cy capered into motion.

"This girl..." Jae'cy exhaled, leading them to the breakroom just around the corner. When they got to the scene of the sound, it was a room full of sky high Honest Bites–branded blue...and red on Cori's chin.

Arielle grimaced, already heading to and picking up Cori. She truly did feel the energetic one's pain that she'd experienced herself as an active kid too many times to count.

Judging by the lightweight denim jacket tied around Cori's neck, the depth and girth of the open gash, the tipped-over step-stool right by one of the break tables, and the caped superheroine speeding through the air on the tablet that was on the floor, it wasn't too hard to surmise how the injury had happened.

"Baby, I told you that stuff is only for the big *trained* girls on TV," Jae'cy explained, as she moved quickly for the hall. For her car keys.

Arielle was a few steps ahead, passing the hallway mirror. And that was when, her teary eyes spotting her gash, Cori rocketed up her hysteria, eyes bulging at her chin in the reflection.

"It's okay," Arielle said gently, rocketing toward the door that Jae'cy swung open. "Nothin' some bandages can't fix."

Then she slid a look Jae'cy's way, as she unlocked the car, and they came into step toward it. Both knew that bandage would be more than likely accompanied by some needles and thread.

Jae'cy reached for Cori as she opened the back door of her SUV...

...And Arielle made her way over to the passenger's side. "I get confused about ten minutes in down here," Arielle simply stated. *So, I'll ride with you.*

Jae'cy looked up as she buckled in Cori. Didn't responded but fluttered. Nodded.

*Because we obviously want to play like a merry bunch of three.*

Then Jae'cy got into her driver's seat.

This was their new style of language. As Jae'cy started up her engine...

*The language we've been speaking these past few weeks.* Arielle awaited Jae'cy's reverse, then spotted her slowly peer over. At Arielle's silent but illuminated cell phone in her lap, with one incoming name showing on it. Then drift her eyes back forward.

"If you have to go, it's cool."

"Gonna be there until at least your mom gets there. Or him." *However, I need you to understand this is now not just for you but...* "For Cori. Only if she wants me to." Then Arielle took a glance back at Cori, who instantly connected still anxious eyes right back at her. Arielle turned an intent look right back at Jae'cy. "But looks like she's pretty sure of her decision."

And so, Jae'cy quietly reversed out of the driveway, quietly continuing *the language we've been speaking these past few weeks,* Arielle repeated in her mind. *And maybe since the beginning...*

The language that was seen, felt, audibly teased rather than *truly* also stated. *What else aren't we saying to one another?* Arielle thought but knew the answer as she watched Jae'cy peel forward for Sunset (Boulevard).

*We for sure need to say what this all is between us. For all of us.*

All Arielle ever wanted to do was string words together and give it to her readers.

And yet now, she was in the audience with them.

Riding off into Sunset.

*Because I said I wanted a story. I just didn't know I'd be apart of it.*

Instead, it snuck up on her.

Damn.

♡ 30

"SO I'M GUESSIN' TALKIN' IS OUT?"

*I'd say,* Arielle echoed in her mind while outside Cori's patient room listening to Paula speak to Jae'cy and thinking of the first tense silent movie-like chapter that had just ended in today's sudden adventure:

"*Mee*-Maw!"

"*THERE* goes my baby!"

As Arielle peered into the outpatient door, Paula's attention and eyebrows peaked ever so slightly at Arielle from her standing spot on the other side of Cori's patient bed across from Jae'cy. "And it looks like *you're* doin' your usual, too. You just save the day in all kinds of ways, huh?!" Paula grinned, but also ran eyes across her, then back to Jae'cy.

Arielle mustered up a quick nod and light smile as she remained standing just inside of the room then shifted her gaze to Jae'cy...who slid her eyes over and by Arielle's shoulder.

Naturally, checking back as well, Arielle saw AD already stepping up behind her—then past her. She felt an energetic buzz from the proximity of their bodies, which told her ever so subliminally that she'd overstayed her welcome.

Arielle decided to attribute that buzz to her phone. She pulled it out as AD settled at the head of a chin-bandaged, coloring book–engaged Cori's patient bed, beside Jae'cy, and pecked his brave little patient on the brow.

Arielle blocked out the incoming train in her mind. *I just wanted to make sure Cori was okay. So, now, with father, grandmother, and the whole big happy family in tow...*

Paula unknowingly further fortified Arielle's verdict with *her* knowing, subtle peer at the practical shoulder touch between Jae'cy and AD that made Jae'cy discreetly recoil.

*Yep, and I'm recoiling, too. Better than seeing this right here...*

"I mean...*no* one was watchin' her?" AD stated.

"Oh, you mean like how I've been watching her the past five years?" Jae'cy countered.

*Yep, outta here.* Just had to quickly book a Lyft or Uber to swing back to Jae'cy's and get her car. As she slipped her phone back away, she caught Jae'cy's eye and yet, moved hers onward to the patient in the bed instead—who she'd come here for.

"Bye, Elle."

A wave back. That was how Arielle responded, hoping it hadn't come out as emotional as it had felt in her throat in the next words set to slide out. The kid's father was here and watching right now with already some clear suspicions about her presence. But she also had another hope, a sincere one for this little tyke with the squishy cheeks and spunky personality that had won her over...and to whom she had done the same. "Hope you feel better."

Arielle saw AD's square shoulders turn more toward Cori and Jae'cy. She'd already violated the whole unspoken rule in the room by being present. And now she was breaking an even larger one: trying to be present in a whole other way.

Simply the tone of her words, not even what the actual words had spoken had put her on blast. And so, she went to the open door and got the heck outta dodge.

Temporarily.

"Will you come see me again?"

One of her feet was already out in the hall, but Arielle looked over her shoulder to the waiting eye of Cori. Didn't look at anyone else, didn't need to. Like Arielle had said, she came here for Cori.

And would do so again...when she returned to Jae'cy's to finish the cookbook project. Because, more than business, there was that One. Last. Thing.

And as she felt AD's eyes slide to her, she knew that was why she had to return...

"Sure will."

AND ARIELLE SURE DID ABOUT A WEEK LATER. WATCHING A LIGHTLY STITCHED CORI zip more than skip right toward her. For someone who'd over a week ago almost lost her chin, she was sure bounding pretty damn good.

Then she rebounded, ricocheting to a rocking stop at the kitchen stool where Arielle was finishing up an edit on one of Jae'cy's recipe stories. She almost clocked Arielle in the face, this time.

Arielle grinned to herself while turning away from the monitor and awaiting the next action. *Kids are so doggone hyper.*

"Do you see *this*?" Cori held forth a new charm necklace for Arielle's admiration.

"That's not how you receive a compliment, Rumpa."

Arielle slowly felt her lopsided, raised mouth flatline.

"At all."

"Remember?" Jae'cy ambled in—eyes only on the little one.

From her spot at the kitchen island, Arielle could see to the front door hallway—where AD was headed, his back to her, after having just adjoined Jae'cy with his "At all" parental statement. Then he stepped out of the front door.

*Like a husband going off to work or something.* Arielle cut her gaze to her laptop…yet subtly bounced her leg on the footrest.

"Compliments aren't toys. You earn them, not shop for them," Jae'cy concluded.

AD had apparently come by to get something he'd accidentally left, following an event that they attended with Cori, Arielle surmised as loosely as possible…and hated that her mind had entertained a thought about it at all, and that she had been left by Jae'cy to fill in the blanks, like usual, upon her arrival, to which she'd headed into this kitchen to set up her laptop and prep for their meeting. Rather, Jae'cy's maternal summoning had instantly beckoned the uncomfortable vibes. It had gotten to the point where Jae'cy's verbal jabs felt like actual blows; when she even gave them at all. As soon as she'd entered this house, Arielle knew her assignment would include more than checking for commas. It would include the silences in spaces that were much too long, like an em dash, where they hadn't been before.

At this point, she'd just wanted to get her whole afternoon back, too. But she was always one to uphold her end of the deal. Including the one she'd not too long committed herself to, for herself.

Likewise, Cori was unabashedly making sure Arielle honored this deal right in front of her, fiddling the charm around her neck as she swayed (and awaited) proudly.

This girl was indeed around her Mee-Maw too much.

Arielle's smile returned. "Nice! Where'd you get it?"

"At the carnival."

But before she'd answered, Arielle had already known. Had seen the prized possession in Cori's hand as her other free hand was intertwined in AD's. He on one side of her, and Jae'cy on the other—once again, thanks to her IG. She had seen it just before she tapped out of the app yesterday, following a tagged notification of herself and Taylor entering the wrap-up party.

"No way! You won it?"

But Arielle already knew the answer there, too, as the oblivious Cori nodded proudly. *Well, at least he's giving her more time.* Beyond more concentrated efforts at parenthood, Arielle was sure AD was making his presence known in response to Arielle being at the hospital—with just laidback yet routine physical presence, much like a businessman. Artfully countering competition.

Arielle made a concentrated effort to smile naturally at Cori…but felt her attention covertly trail over to Jae'cy.

"…Her *father* won."

*Yeah…I see that. And bringing home the bacon, too.* The intercepted words were directed at Arielle this time, but when Arielle glanced her way, Jae'cy's back was turned. Granted, she was stirring some mac and cheese in a pot for Cori, but Arielle felt like Jae'cy had delayed the action for this very moment. *Surely, the chef knows that stovetop noodles won't burn in the amount of time it would take to glance my way.*

The way Cori pranced right back out of the room and up the stairs didn't seem like a kid who was hungry. In Arielle's eyes, the meal prep was a diversion.

But she moved on nonetheless, tapping silently on her laptop, eying a new em dash in a new story. A new pause:

Jae'cy had stopped stirring and stood at the fridge, but she didn't seem to be scanning the contents. Maybe trying to figure out another ingredient, another way, another reason not to look…

Both of their fingers concurrently came to a halt.

"What?" Jae'cy stated more than asked, keeping stoic. "You know what, Jae'cy," Arielle, too, stated rather than inquired while keeping a steady gaze on Jae'cy nonetheless. *I can't do another visit like this. And if that means today is my last visit, then so be it. Because honestly, it's started to feel less and less like just business for a while now.* "Even Cori knows what, and it's confusing her."

Jae'cy returned to the stove, stirring. "We're just working on making sure both of us are present in Cori's life."

Then stirred quicker.

One thing was for sure, Arielle quietly noted: *The pasta definitely wasn't sticking.*

"...That photo was his auntie's doin'. She kinda saw us walk through the entrance gate together the other day—even though we rode in separate cars and just happened to arrive right at the same time. And she ran with it."

"I just don't understand why you don't look happier, now that he's trying to play his role fully. Isn't that what you've wanted?"

*Go deeper, Elle.*

"That way, to keep us from getting deeper with one another?"

The words reverberated in Arielle's ears. She knew it had to be doing the same for Jae'cy...

...who then revolved her head, cocked up a brow with a low snigger. "What are you doing? Stalking my page?"

*"How can I not?!"* Arielle, from out of nowhere, bellowed back. She hated when this happened, when she ignited from something that had been boiling deep underneath the surface, even unbeknownst to herself. An internal volcano, which, once it started to emit, nothing or no one could stop. Not even herself. *I'm tired of the stating things without actually stating them! I'm tired of you not being honest!* "How?! When the news pops up on my doorstep every time I look at my phone?"

"Kind of like the news of you and her does on mine?"

That made the lava pause. Then Arielle spoke up again. *You know you didn't want to hear about that anymore, Jae'cy. You proved it when you stopped liking my posts.*"

Jae'cy turned, giving Arielle a full view of her dubious, bemused face. "From the one who barely cares about social media," she sneered.

Jae'cy concluded her eyeroll, then turned and started spooning out macaroni into a Minions plastic bowl. "I've been busy."

"And so have I, but I still texted," Arielle countered once again. "But I'm just an option. I get it." Her eyes hit the laptop, and reflected in it, she saw herself clenching her jaw. She hated that she'd allowed this feeling to enter. Once again, on the sidelines.

And Jae'cy, upon peeking over, too, in stealth assessment, saw those eyes glisten.

"…That's not true," she argued, but her volume level was turned down. She added a tiny teaspoonful of noodles into the bowl, not really filling it.

*What kind of half-a…?* "Of course it is!" Arielle ignited once again. *I've been keeping this in because I knew at the time it would be better left unsaid. You were just a client, and it was just business. But now? It's more than that. And me not saying anything is making this grow more and more into everything that is not easy to control.* "Come on. We're in two different worlds. You, in the smart mansion. *Me?*" She abruptly thrust out a snicker. "Just a weirdo peddling books for pennies and more old-ass cassettes."

"That's *not* the reason," Jae'cy spoke up.

Arielle noticed her nostrils flare ever so slightly. Maybe they could finally get somewhere. With nothing to stop it, she would see that this conversation was fully fleshed out.

"How else can I be good enough for TL-DRs but not regular conversation these past few weeks?!" This girl had her so mad that she was now throwing out marketing-used abbreviations like some kind of bilingual mother tongue profanity.

"That's not how it is…"

"So then, explain to me. Because I'm a bit confused. Since, you know, I'm always out of the loop."

"DeBarge, wrap up your show…" Jae'cy was practically tugging at the teaspoon utensil in a clear desire to get away and deliver it to Cori.

"Not before you tell me why you give me one sign then another: Business, but also not business."

Jae'cy had gone quiet, gripping that bowl of pasta; Arielle had gone livid, pacing and sardonically snickering.

"A date. But *nooo, NOT* a date."

Gripping and pacing…

"Kiss me. BUT THEN—!"

"I DON'T KNOW!!"

Jae'cy whipped her head then body around, her eyes welling up. Arielle huffed silently, staring.

The wall clock didn't stop ticking, Cori didn't suddenly let out a cry from the second level and the two of them didn't stop gazing at one another.

Until Jae'cy sharply blinked, then looked to that clock. It was almost like she was counting down to something. Arielle read her face, waiting for what lines were about to appear next.…

"…When I'm with—" Jae'cy began, then hugged herself. As her eyebrows started to quiver and twitch in all kinds of subtle confused directions, she worked to find her way in her words, in this foreign space.

"When I'm with someone else, it's a...weird nagging thing that is just...*there*, no matter what I try to do.... And when it's you, it only gets wider." She rubbed her arms as if a pain were pulsating there. "And...it's something I've never felt."

*And there it is. THIS was why she asked me to come today. This was why she'd asked me to come all of the other days. She wanted to see me in person, wanted to be close....*

*And I wanted it, too. And that's why I always obliged.*

Arielle released a long, deep, tight breath that had been buried inside for quite some time, before today.

The quietness returned. This time, Arielle didn't hear any clocks, or faint sounds of some animated movie or cartoon playing on a second-level TV.

Instead, she thought some more about what she had really heard in between the lines. Reading all of the language. But still, she didn't want to jump the gun. Maybe afraid of it misfiring, back on herself...

So she tried a test, shooting out some softer, more coaxing words for the anxious emotion they both had, much like the post-fallen Cori...

"...Well, you got some Band-Aids? We can work this out..."

Jae'cy instantly peeled her eyes up. Arielle tried a smile. Jae'cy fluttered, then slowly lifted a corner of her mouth. Finally, she released a low, delicate chuckle.

The air became a slight Midwest chill, distinctly felt, vulnerable as their eyes reconnected and spoke everything they didn't openly say.

*You said you wouldn't do this again, Elle.* Arielle mentally reprimanded herself with a conflicted mix of irritation and anxiety. Then she suddenly felt tightness in her breath again, for a new inhale. *But it's time to say the things unsaid from your end....*

"What if I told you that..." Arielle spurred on new words, slowly, while observing Jae'cy's wipe at the corner of an eye that was turned away. "For the past months,...I've been wrestling with those things, too?"

Jae'cy went still, peeped over at Arielle. Yet didn't say anything in return.

Arielle decided she'd say it for both of them. "So..." Arielle subtly clenched one of her hands, scared of the plunge she'd said she wouldn't take again. "Now what?"

Jae'cy instantly stifled a sniffle, tautened up. As if she'd just dipped a limb in ice water. She cut her eyes down to the ground and widened them, the rest of her remaining frozen.

Arielle translated that expression as Jae'cy needing time to collect her thoughts. Or as a sign that she'd just breached social norms once again, chasing the wrong thing—even if it might secretly want to be captured.

Because no one could ever admit to loving a beast. Only fascinated bewilderment and curiosity existed behind a barrier or distance...like this kitchen island between them. Arielle knew how this would turn out, had lived the ending many times before.

And so, as she arose with her belongings, on the inside, she was still heated. *YOU wanted a story, Elle. YOU put yourself in this mess, and YOU'RE the only one to blame.*

"I'll start it off. Let's rewind to our places," she prescribed. "You know, like the film sets?"

And then, without a single final glance, she headed for the street from which she came. Where she should've stayed over a year ago.


Before Arielle had a chance to fully exhale, as she stepped a foot into her own four walls, slinging her airport luggage off wherever in her home's front hallway...

*BUZZ.*

*Be careful There's not a more savage girl than a West Coast one*

Ain't that the truth. But Arielle wasn't in the mood for a Gemini seminar by Juliana on taking Ls when she hadn't just too long disenrolled herself from its class less than forty-eight hours ago: the class of Yung Hitta.

Paired with the words of Juliana's sent text, popped up the final F(U) she didn't ask for: A screenshotted blogger photo of a very glowy Jae'cy and AD, Cartier wristwatch-matching, at his daytime fundraising pool party for an urban non-profit client called Jewels in the Rough.

Make that the song lyric caption pulled from AD's embedded IG photo in the blogger post:

*Treat ya jewel to a good cause*
*The way you help her shine deserves a round of applause*

It definitely had nothing to do with the actual cause of the event, but it was clearly witty. He got a C for Crafty; the writer in her had to give him that. The point she subtracted from him, though? Jae'cy did just fine 'shining' on her own...*WHY does she like these flashy dudes???*

*Because she's a 'star', Elle, come on. Blinding, themselves and everyone else, is the name of the game.* Arielle stuck a hard tongue against one of her inner cheeks while then noting the other goal of AD's post: the Cartier sponsorship he'd plugged in. *Yep, bringing home the bacon—with Cartier, too. And that's why he can't even see that she's not even really smiling in that photo.*

Another *BUZZ:*

*Even—& ESPECIALLY—one who's made it*
*She has everything to lose without any hesitance to lose U if needed*

Arielle finally typed back in her phone, nice and quick:

*Heard you the first time Mother Dearest*

But still one more repeated warning came through:

*Elle. BE careful.*

*Dang,* this really had become a *Scary Movie.* And it looked like Juliana actually wouldn't be the first to die after all.
And then the last moment before her ultimate fate....
*BUZZ...*

*Hey*
*Can we meet?*

♡ **32**

*HEY CAN WE MEET?*
Arielle could've sworn that it was Ghostface, and she wasn't talking the slayer of sixteen bars.
She'd heard the haunting voice even in the unspoken words staring back at her on her cell phone.
*She's the very last person you want to hear from right now.*
Arielle bit at her lip, caught in a mix of feels.
*But always the first person, too. Even now.*
Her fingers twitched.

*I can in about 10. Video chat?*


*No*
*In person*

Fair. This definitely is a conversation that warranted a face-to-face. Nonetheless, Arielle clamped her lips up tight, didn't yet respond....
*Where the hell is the ghostWRITER for what has become my life, so I can kill that M-effer once and for all?*
*But before I end this, I want to see how this story might go....*


They agreed to a few days later, Arielle flying in after a business commitment. They met at a park in a smaller city outside of LA that would "hopefully be more lowkey because it's more of a place for families."
*At least the setting is disarming enough,* Arielle deemed as she stepped along the walking path outside the playground area where kids enjoyed themselves. But she still felt her tension rise as she made her way to a particular bench...
She wasn't an actress by any means, but this ish these past few weeks deserved an Oscar.
She stepped forward a final time and met the flip-flops, then eyes, of Jae'cy.

Kids squealing (minus Cori, undoubtedly either with Paula or AD) and birds chirping was luckily the looping soundtrack, or this hush between them would've been so much more awkward.

And then another element of public community spaces filtered in.

"You ladies want *elote*?"

Both of them shifted their eyes from each other to a vendor with his cart nearing them. His easy rather than crazed smile was enough for the two of them to bring down their respective tensions for a second because, *dang*, those red pepper flakes and crème drizzle were sittin' on ready corn cobs. Arielle almost forgot that she was a vegan for a second.

"Eh…and also I have…" The man squinted as he turned his head briefly to some tubs on the top of his cart, one being…

"Toe-few…? To-*futti*?" he pronounced with more effort.

"Oh yeah, this is definitely the West coast," Arielle commented to herself as she obliged with a head tip at the alternative dairy choice. On a street vendor cart of all places.

Both the vendor and Jae'cy chuckled.

"Ten dollars, please?" Best believe, he was getting back to business as he turned his head then hand to Arielle.

*Damn!* Definitely Cali.

But Jae'cy, the native rather than the tourist, wasn't gonna be hustled. "For *both*, right?" she stressed as she went into her wallet then paused. "And regardless, looks like I used my last cash yesterday—"

Arielle extended a ten dollar bill. For once, oddly enough, she had some cash on her. Her mother would've been proud. As she slid her wallet back into her pants pocket, Jae'cy slid a vigilant eye her way.

And even though Arielle felt it, she only connected with the chestnut browns of the guy, who didn't hesitate to grab the cash, and hand over the corn cobs. "*Gracias*," he courteously expressed, then he was off just as quickly as he'd come.

Arielle inhaled discreetly, then turned around. She bit her lip as she extended the non-Tofutti corn, and Jae'cy tilted her head to an oblige as she took hers.

"Oh, you're far too kind."

Arielle nodded as she lowered on the bench. *Yep, and so, here we are.*

Neither immediately spoke; they took a bite or two (or three) of their corn cob that was all the way on point.

But finally, *something* had to be said.

"Haven't put it up on the Gram and *alla* that yet, but…I got an award nomination."

"Yeah?" Arielle almost broke character as she sincerely smiled, truly happy for Jae'cy and how she was knocking things out of the park between her two careers: one more profession, the other more passion.

And also breaking character like Jae'cy, probably unconsciously, was. A quivery smile spreading halfway up her own face as she fondled an earlobe.

*She's nervous.* Sure, the twitchiness could be linked to her first-ever big milestone in the acting world. But Arielle knew it was more so for the next big things to be said, still waiting backstage....

"It's for supporting actress, but..."

"Still big. Come on."

"Yeah...

Spirit Awards. Tonight. It's a pretty big one in the indie world."

"Proud of you. That's the bomb."

"Thanks."

Yep, there was some real uneasiness going on. Because the girl didn't even clown her for using that old slang.

"Only took me four years."

"Hey, for some it takes longer. Or never." *Like this thing we're supposed to be here to discuss.*

"True...so, yeah, gonna throw, like, a little afterparty for it, since it's scheduled right at the end of summer. Make it like a duo bash."

Arielle only nodded, could've stated her assigned role's line. But enough of that. *Time to go off-script.*

And then it arrived, the real thing.

..."I don't want us to continue not really speaking to each other."

Arielle paused, and she just listened as Jae'cy fiddled with her corn wrapper.

"*But* AD and I..."

Arielle looked down at the empty corn cob in her hands.

"We've really started talking this past week. About Cori...wanting to try to provide her with more wholesome guardianship than either of us had growing up. We both think she deserves that, seeing a better parent relationship."

*Boom. And there it is, Elle. The end.*

Once again, the Scorpio sixth sense seemed to strike, Jae'cy looking over at Arielle, which gave Arielle no choice but to do the same back respectfully. Jae'cy inhaled in a shallow way, like another toe-dip test in the water.

"But I don't want *this* friendship, a really dope thing we have that I've grown to enjoy so much when I typically don't really rock all the time with people like that...I don't want *this* to get rocky when I'm already on that kinda road with AD."

*Nah, this side is rocky, too. It's definitely starting to rock.* Arielle placed her corn cob in the trash can next to them; she'd suddenly had enough. Much like the slightly uneven keel of this bench's back legs that she hadn't really noticed until now as she quietly rearranged herself on the seat...But that didn't negate the fact that it more than likely had been rocky for a while.

Much like this...

"I don't know exactly where he and I are going, neither of us do. But I do know that abandoning you right out the window is not the way I want this to go. And so..." Jae'cy peeled her eyes away and down to her corn cob, still toying with the paper.

*And SO, we're—I'M—going to play this friend role again. AGAIN? Come on, Jae'cy. You know that's not going to be successful if it hasn't been already.*

Arielle jerked her eyes down to the asphalt. Where teeth-picking sweet corn and harder to chew rejections dwelled. And she mulled over it all, both unrelated realities that could mystically share one space.

Because Jae'cy still pulled out the pleasant, joyful side of childhood within her, and maybe by toughing this out, they could still have that.

Finally, she looked back up. Then so did Jae'cy.

The shaky but lingering, almost wistful-like smile that slowly spread across Jae'cy's face showed that it was a living arrangement for both, what had to be. Even though they both knew this role, another attempt at it, would cause them pain.

*So long as I'm not going it alone, we'll see how successful we are at this,* Arielle finally, internally committed. For starters, by pulling together a reciprocal smi—

*Wait.*

"...No."

Jae'cy hesitated then looked up at Arielle. Frozen, shocked. Sadly understanding?

Didn't matter. Because Arielle was still standing on her ground. Literally. She had risen, looking upset, even fluttering like Jae'cy just had. But standing.

"No, I don't need any new *friends*. And you don't either. What you and I both need is to take some time apart. And maybe should've from the very beginning. But this moment right here, you could've just kept."

With that, Arielle turned away. Had to, because the beginning morph of Jae'cy's face was something she didn't want to see.

If she saw it, she'd stay.

And she couldn't stay. Not like this.

And in that moment, she realized it would hurt either way: to stay and act like friends or to walk away and act like they no longer knew each other.

And she believed Jae'cy knew it, too.

Because Jae'cy didn't argue it, not like she could. And so, she stayed (silent). And Arielle didn't.

She walked away.

*BUT DAMN, WOULD'VE BEEN NICE TO MAKE IT TO MY HOTEL.*
But no. Instead, hours later, now early evening, she was *just* heading to the hotel. She'd waited on booking a return flight or round trip because, one, she didn't know how long the park scene would've gone, and two, all of the later day flights were long unavailable anyway.

Plus, she'd already figured how the scene was going to go down. And as she'd predicted, connecting up with Juliana (although, she didn't disclose details) immediately thereafter, as she'd imagined she'd want to, provided her some much-needed familial reprieve.

But what she *hadn't* figured, as she turned a street corner for the immediate sight of her awaiting hotel, was to find Michi there.

*Oh, I'm havin' all of the luck today.*

For a minute, he didn't say anything as he clutched the large Fashion Nova bag in his hand. *Ah, yes, probably for the grand Spirit Awards/End of Summer after party tonight. Well…*

Arielle better used her time to tip her head stiffly then begin to step by.

"You know the only reason why she gave you a chance, right?"

Arielle slowed then turned just her head back. There he stood, straight, like his gaze.

"Because you can write."

*No, shit, Sherlock.* That's typically how business worked: one person provided a valuable skill or service to the other person in need of that service or skill.

"Hey, man. I know you don't particularly care for me—"

"Actually," he clarified with a leer, "there were *two* reasons. She told me she saw your work and figured, 'Ay, I can get something out of this.' But she ALSO said that she felt sorry for you. How awkward you seemed."

Arielle wasn't really sure how truthful he was being—whether Jae'cy really said that. But things didn't have to be spoken to be true.

Michi must've been aware of her contemplative face at that moment and knew he could drop in another idea for her to think about. He bent over a little and began to step in motion like someone's reject Alpha Phi. But the way he glared made Arielle quickly lose the inside chuckle. "That *means* she typically likes people with more intelligence about the rhythm of a room, a vibe, a scene. Those who know when to clap, step, step to the right," he elaborated. Then stopped and stared. Hard. "Step...*aside* when they're supposed to."

"Okay..."

"Okay, so then why are you *really* still hangin' around?"

*You know what? That's a damn good question.* And since sometimes the least words packed the most punch...

"That's the same thing she could ask you," Arielle stated instead. Any more words, most naturally, bringing up AD, who wouldn't be too keen on him either, knowing of his hidden pining for his...girl? Situationship? No, speaking on that wasn't necessary, especially when he'd surely seen the ongoing IG timeline, much like her. Just as much as Arielle wasn't chummy with Michi, neither was he with AD. He was Jae'cy's longtime friend...trying to be something more. With (tragically, still) less...of anything Jae'cy might be looking for. Whatever that was...

Coming back up from her thoughts, she noticed that Michi had gone stiff. And now, with Arielle reading his moment of pause, she knew she could drop in another idea for *him* to think about.

"Hopefully, you find what you're looking for, man. And it finds you, too. Whatever it is. Because I know it's more than this."

"Yeah." A snicker. "You, too."

Then Arielle went back to looking for what she knew she exactly wanted most right now: that hotel entrance. For the next-best temporary escape she was looking for before the real one tomorrow morning.


*Sleep.* That was what she'd drowned herself in, more than any liquor or Lipton could, right in her hotel room.

But not for long.

An hour later, Arielle groaned at her cell phone's ringtone. Groaned more than she had at the TV before putting muting it in this room an hour ago after completing her new book's latest chapter on her laptop and a quick video chat with Kimesha on upcoming plans.

After the phone obviously not letting up anytime soon, she finally surrendered to quiet it the heck up, picking it up. And that was when her eyes widened in even more exasperation, at words on her cell phone screen.

Arielle stared at the lit phone, at the incoming caller's name, as it rang another time. She inhaled then pulled it to her ear. A thumping of distant music pulsed in her ear. And then a voice.

"I know I'm the last person you want to hear from right now..."

*Yep.* Arielle floated her eyes up to the muted TV, now playing the news. Wow, even more depressing...But it was much better than what she'd muted.

And no, it wasn't this phone call. *Yet.* Maybe it was wishful thinking on Arielle's part. No, not that Jae'cy was reconsidering. But maybe, just maybe, she was going to allow Arielle to hear her just try to peddle through something uncomfortably here. Let her feel what Arielle was feeling. She at least could do that much. And that was why Arielle continued to play the deafening silent game.

There came a sigh. But not true admission. Instead, "Please just come," Jae'cy insisted, softly. "You *have* to come tonight, Elle."

No DeBarge line, just Elle. A sillier nickname replaced suddenly with a more refined one. Like a clean and proper attempt. Niceties.

And that just ticked Arielle off even more.

"That's where you have it wrong, Jae'cy," Arielle scoffed. "Respectfully. But I don't have to. I don't have to do anything—!" *For you.* But Arielle just erupted into the next train of upset slamming into her brain like some kind of crazy hangover she now felt like she should've subjected herself to, so that maybe she would've never heard this phone. Muted much like the TV. "Understand that, that I don't have to do *anything.* Why should I—?!"

"She's here..."

Arielle felt a throb in her temples, tension, an anger headache, only lightly subsiding..."Who?"

...For maybe another fit to come up again if she wasn't careful...

"Taylor."

Arielle hesitated before responding. But after a second, she realized she didn't really care. Jae'cy didn't know, but Arielle did: Whatever Taylor was now doing was certainly her right, seeing how Arielle had bid her farewell. Right now, Arielle just felt tired.

That was until Jae'cy beckoned her back awake. "Come. If not for anyone, *for you.* So you can see something you need to, that I think you'll want to...Maybe or maybe not including your favorite." The last statement was an order, but not a militant one; it sounded like a mandate of care from a friend. Arielle heard it in Jae'cy's yielding tone. Evident in that waning laugh that was kindly bowing, giving grace. Allowing something else to enter behind it.

A decline or a...

Abruptly, loud squeals and music hit Arielle's eardrum, so much that she had to pull the phone away. *Well, damn. I'm awake now.*

"Come on, bih!" Breyah shouted over the receiver.

Arielle sighed, realizing the phone had disconnected.

And only then, realized that Breyah's usual playful tone hadn't sounded like play at all. And neither had the squeals.

*Something that I need to see?*

*Maybe, especially after that abrupt sound and end.*

♡ 34

AS ARIELLE APPROACHED THE FRONT DOOR after zigzagging through the maze of parked Porsches, Mercedes, Rolls-Royces, and Bugattis in Jae'cy's packed driveway and adjacent sidewalk, she felt a sense of annoyance in realizing that Michi more than likely would be there. Just like another guy in Jae'cy's life would be, too.

*And with that, here go—*

The door opened. And there was Elise, her same girlfriend from the Honest Bites soft launch event behind her.

There was a pause from both sides...then a mutual, respectful nod from the girlfriend to Arielle. And a somewhat shaky smile from Elise's face to Arielle's direction.

It wasn't like they were completely foreign to one another, still working together on Elise's novel. Arielle wouldn't have had it any other way; wasn't like their business had turned sour. And so...

"Congrats again. Like I told you earlier."

"*GIRL*! I'm not the same girl after hittin' 'save' this morning. I almost had an out-of-body experience." Elise smiled purely, much like she'd done in their celebratory Zoom wrap-up just the other day for her finally completed manuscript. "But not like the one all of us almost had up in here! Someone somehow caught the bonfire pit ON REAL FIRE and almost burned the backyard down. But we thankfully got it under control." Elise chuckled out full relief.

Contrarily, Arielle felt herself immediately plateau now, from a peak that wasn't really all that high at this point to be honest. Hit with the realization that maybe what she'd come to see wasn't an emergency after all. *And even if it had been, what would you have done, Elle? Helped out AD with your imaginary cape?*

And now that they were in person unlike the other day, Elise could much more clearly see Arielle's face, the porchlight being further incriminating:

Arielle genuinely smiled, laughed in good will. But also genuinely looked...

Elise stepped in closer, a weaker, more concerned, knowing smile. Took her arm. "You good?"

Of course, she wasn't. They both knew that. But it was the best that could be done right now. Especially when…

There she came in the background.

Arielle naturally seeing her first. Elise's girlfriend sensing it just behind her shoulder as the one closest in the doorway. And then Elise, looking back at her girlfriend as she stepped away as their signal, disappeared.

Then there were two…

As Arielle, even with the grogginess, unconsciously skated her eyes from Jae'cy's tapered pants tucked in open-toe booties, up to a wide-necked waffle knit crop top with a locket and hoops, and nude-glossed lips.

Then she saw Jae'cy slip her cell phone away…behind herself. She didn't really have time to think about it, though, because Jae'cy slowly opened the door wider for her entrance.

*Welp, since I'm here. On to the next situation that my sleep was interrupted for.* And with no words spoken, Jae'cy led the way, and Arielle followed, sliding her hands into her pockets as they passed celebs. All the usual.

Much the same as they trekked through the living room, making their way to the kitchen. As soon as they stepped foot in there, Jae'cy whipped around to Arielle, almost colliding into her. And not because there was any bowl of yams in her hands to bear.

All Arielle saw were Jae'cy's eyes, widening subtly but with an intensity that couldn't be downplayed. At that moment, the greatest depth she'd ever seen in them up until this point. But now, especially now, Arielle's moment she'd been waiting for seemed like it could've waited a bit longer…

*Yep, here goes.* Arielle nervously gave a lopsided grin as she considered that the two of them were pretty darn close in a room of others who were now looking from them. To her…

…To outside.

Arielle slid her eyes back to Jae'cy, whose mouth parted, yet no words escaped, as if she didn't exactly know what to say, or rather, how she wanted to say it. She almost looked like someone breaking terrible, tragic news to someone they loved.

Arielle cut her eyes to the sliding glass door. And there was Michi…along with…

…*Taylor.*

They were in a locked grind, in just as close-to-the-skin post-pool damp swimwear. The girl might have moved fast, but tonight she was taking things *real* slow—clearly, with some help from libations, given her and Michi's low-lidded eyes and plastic cups.

As Arielle started to step toward the door, Jae'cy hopped in her path and placed a hand on her shoulder. "Hey…"

But Arielle kept on nearing the door as Jae'cy's voice and body closely followed from behind… *"Elle."*

As she touched the door, she heard, "She's not worth it."

*Isn't that the truth.*

And then, she pulled it back. Even with the thump of music, the light screech of the opening door still turned heads. It was like some planned performance, choreography, everybody rotating to her in sync. And then they froze, screwed up their mouths in compassionate discomfort, or hid smirks.

AD, over by the DJ booth, met her eyes with a face she couldn't read due to the darkness, and his general cool facade. She probably saw Paula's and Breyah's faces somewhere in that crowd, too. But she didn't much care.

Didn't too much care about any of it, even including Michi's hazy gander falling on her right then. She expected to see a smirk, but instead, he looked about as defeated as she did.

Arielle waited for someone else's gaze to meet hers.

Taylor slowed her grind, lifted her voluminous hair first, then her head, then her eyes. And what do you know? She looked pretty dismal to Arielle, too. Or maybe just hella drunk.

Either way, Arielle wasn't angry at them, couldn't blame them. She'd just seen enough.

*What else is there to see? Their face is my own: None of us with the original person we want*—She turned around to find Jae'cy wavering at the door, biting her lip. *So, gotta press on, right?*

She was just angry that they'd beat her to it.

So, she walked back inside, right on by with a flare of her nostrils. She was going the hell home. Tonight.

She was already on the sidewalk when she heard Jae'cy behind her. "Elle, slow down!"

Arielle only walked faster to her rental car. "This is how you all do, right? Always gotta make moves, no matter who it screws over." *Well, tonight, that's DONE.*

Arielle sniggered, whipped open the driver's door. "But don't worry, I'm a senior citizen, won't be too quick…" Arielle gasped, truly gasped aloud, for a needed catch of breath she didn't know she'd been holding. And something else. Because she suddenly felt wetness trail down her eyes. *DAMN!*

"Elle, look at me."

"Why is this place so wild?!"

"Because *welcome to LA.*"

*Ha, damn straight!* But Arielle wasn't just talking about this city, or any city. She was talking about her situation, story, that always played out this way wherever she went. It just followed her. Right on the back of her neck, making the hairs stand up.

Arielle misjudged her pants pocket in the heat of the moment, the phone falling face forward on the asphalt. She was positive it might be kaput.

"Great, now what are you going to do if someone tries to reach you?"

"Like who? You again? After these past few days, that right there might've been a good sign." Arielle scoffed, her eyes on the car window in front of her...but she snatched up the phone. *Nope, still living to see another day.*

Meanwhile, there was no comeback from Jae'cy this time.

*Exactly.*

Arielle started to drop down into the car when Jae'cy's hand gripped her arm. Arielle snapped back and whipped around as she erupted, "*WHY* are you—!?"

She'd thrown herself around so hard and fast that she bumped right into Jae'cy. Into Jae'cy's face, just millimeters away. Eye to eye, nose to nose, mouth to—

Just then, music from the not-so-far distance resounded: a corny, DeBarge-approved love song.

Arielle dazed speechlessly...

Jae'cy only then diverted her gaze. "Call me when you make it in," she said in a low voice.

Arielle didn't respond.

Jae'cy lifted a brow, not slow and sly like her usual tease, but a light, jerky quiver. "*Call* me." She blinked softly, to let that latest instruction sink in.

Arielle slid her eyes down to her hands as a few female guests departed the house. *Guess they had enough, too.*

Arielle felt Jae'cy slowly step away, felt it by the heat change, the hairs on the back of her neck falling, as a body left another.

"Leaving already, ladies?"

Arielle didn't hear the rest, didn't want to hear the rest. *Because SHE'S the reason for this mess.* Arielle jammed the key into the rental's ignition. *I wouldn't even have started playing girlfriends with that girl if it weren't for— !*

Arielle put her pedal to the metal.

Eff it, her Spotify playlist, too.

♡ **35**

*I'M SO PISSED THAT THERE ISN'T A RED-EYE I CAN CATCH.*

But catching zzzz? Arielle, back in the hotel room, looked up at the bare off-white paneled ceiling...

*RING.*
Arielle groaned. *Nah. Not answerin'—*
*RING.*
*Hold up... Is that the...?* Arielle blinked out of her frustration, then transferred her eyes to the hotel phone resting on the table beside her shut laptop.
*RING.*
Arielle rolled her eyes, getting up from the bed, then picked it up. "Yes?"

"Hi, Miss Smith. We have a Juliana," the Luxe front desk operator spoke back. "Asking to talk to you about something you forgot? Do you permit this call?"

Arielle rolled her eyes even higher. This whole thing was Juliana's fault as much as Jae'cy's. But maybe at least one thing had shifted in her favor today, and that was her cell phone inexplicably blocking Juliana's first call method???

Arielle placed the hotel phone down briefly to look at her cell phone on the bed. Hit the power button and...nothing. The screen was still black; the juice was gone.

*That would do it.*

As she plugged it into the charger, she finally responded, "Uh, yeah...put her through, please."

"One moment."

There was brief elevator-esque music, the usual commercial melody.

And then it stopped.

"...Hel—?"

*Click.*

Arielle furrowed her eyebrows. Now she'd had enough. "What the....?"

She swiftly dialed Juliana from her cell phone. "Hey, what's up? Why'd you—?"

*Knock-knock.*

"*CUH*, was just about to call you! Have you HEARD—?!"

Working at a bar, a social late-night space, it wasn't surprising what Juliana might've discovered this late at night. Probably an inebriated random flashing something in an IG reel or TikTok into her face as she was starting to push them out of the door to close shop. Probably something to do with tonight...

"Elle?" Juliana was now the one confused by the silence.

...But had Arielle slowly lowered her phone, wasn't even sure if she'd hung up. Her eyes were on a new area of sound.

*Knock-knock...*

She neared the door, one step after another, and came into contact with the doorknob.

She clutched it. Opened it.

Met the eyes of...Jae'cy.

And without words, Arielle stepped aside, and Jae'cy stepped inside, shutting the door.

As she did, Arielle caught sight of a rock on Jae'cy's hand. A very shiny rock. *Probably a whole lotta carats, too.* On her ring finger.

Jae'cy turned back around to Arielle, and froze, wavering by the door.

*So, what's for the actual marriage? A whole island in your name?* "...When's the date?"

"Never, probably."

Arielle looked up, Jae'cy switching places with her by talking to a wall behind her.

"He made a big show out of it, asking in front of everyone. And I said..." Jae'cy twisted her mouth to the side, chewing her cheek. "Nothing. The one time all eyes are on me when I have no lines. Because..."

Arielle eyed her; just an audience now, not a character in the drama. *I'm done, now you gotta write this yourself.*

Jae'cy broke into one of those grins that really wasn't a grin but a way to defend against a peek into the cracks. And damn. With that smile, Arielle fell in. Right into the scene.

"He left. Instantly. And well, that basically changed up the whole vibe, and so, everyone left."

"All except for the ring?" Arielle absorbed all of that. Was it the end? Was it going to move into another sequence, a sequel? It was a cliffhanger. And if there was anything that viewers hated, it was an open ending....

"Of course, forgot to take it off..." Jae'cy started with a sour grin but didn't finish with a movement, looking unsure at the ring.

"So, now what?"

Jae'cy froze, mouth parting.

Arielle felt her chest tighten, but that didn't stop her from observing how vulnerable Jae'cy looked right then, suddenly touching her hair so abruptly that the ring almost slid off her hand. *Look at her. She knows she doesn't want to move forward with that dude; he didn't even get the size right...But she doesn't know how to move forward with this either. It's something she's never experienced, a role she's never played.*

*So, you have to step in there, Elle. One last time. Like you know you want to.*

Jae'cy's gaze peered back up to Arielle.

*Like you both know you want to...*

Arielle stepped forward; Jae'cy inhaled instantly.

And so, Arielle inched toward her finger first. That finger, and the ring didn't even protest as it was slid off then placed on a doorside desk.

Then to her face—

"I just wanted to make sure you were okay." Jae'cy surely spoke now, fluttered.

"Sure," Arielle responded.

Then Arielle went in to the deep, from Jae'cy's big dark browns to her matching nude-coated lips. *Damn, they are as soft as they look...*

Went in.

The both of them. If Arielle listened close enough during the rush of it all throbbing in her head, she could've sworn she heard a moan. But at this point, she couldn't tell if it had come from the both of them or just—

"Wai...wait."

After gaining just a bit of distance, with a deep, instant inhale, with a slip of her eyes to the ground, with a barrier of her hand on Arielle's chest, Jae'cy rubbed those lips of hers against one another. Sensing them...*them.* But scared. Didn't know the lines for *this* story.

Jae'cy fluttered, still with an averted look. The actress needed help to lead this narrative where it needed to go.

Arielle shook her head slowly, pensively at Jae'cy. "After holding that arm out in front of you for so long, aren't you tired? Isn't it ready to fall yet?"

Jae'cy trailed her eyes up, quietly, exposed. Another gaze away.

"And once it does, who's gonna be there to catch it?"

Jae'cy rolled her neck, her shoulders tensely. Undoubtedly trying to maintain the controlled front, the *cold* front, as usual... She finally picked her gaze back up and returned it to Arielle.

Arielle moved to the bed, which caused Jae'cy's stage fright to return. She jerked her shoulders back as Arielle cocked a half-smile but stayed steady. "Oh, so my decked-out bed isn't as good as your pillowed-out one?" Arielle addressed her with artful, disarming humor.

Jae'cy finally realized the store-bought sheets (the Target bag right beside it as the clue) on top of the hotel comforter and *dropped her arms* to her sides, head knocking back in full laughter.

Arielle tried to keep the same maintained face, still posing the same question with a quizzical, awaiting expression as she walked closer to the bed, still naturally leading.

"*Giiirl!*" Jae'cy amplified at a level rivaling her dwindling giggle when she could finally speak again. "You make this clownin' you business too easy."

Arielle didn't care, smirked as she kicked back on the bed. Because she knew that she was doing what she did best: writing a scene. All it needed was just one more action to finish it out...

Jae'cy stood there, still holding back. Like she couldn't even trust herself.

It had to be a Hollywood thing, making sure always to be *on*. But Arielle knew better now: it was also self-consciousness. Something Arielle *did* know about, and so like the best teacher, she'd go slow.

*...Actress?*

Jae'cy blinked, softly, as she started to walk forward. Came over and sat down next to Arielle. Took off her purse, then her booties.

And then, they fell together, finally.

Both just gazed with their heads on the pillows, first with residing smirks. Then, as Arielle opened her arms, she lost hers, and Jae'cy did the same. Stretching one arm out behind Jae'cy's head—for Jae'cy to fall, her head meeting the inner nest of Arielle's shoulder.

And they just rested there, Jae'cy's lightly done-up face on Arielle's white polo.

"Shhii..." Arielle broke the air, lightly. "Probably should've covered over my shirt, too."

"So dramatic."

"No, for real. Do y'all, like, sleep in all of...that? Or..."

"It's called bronzer, which can be transfer-proof—"

"Whatever *that* additionally is."

"*It* means it doesn't smear. Other products can be the same, like eyeliner and—"

"Unh-hunh."

"And a whole lotta other stuff you don't care about. Yeah, got it. And yes, I'll take it off in a minute."

"Cool."

"Right on your shirt. Because mine isn't transfer-proof."

"Don't play with me."

Jae'cy jiggled as always when she became severely amused, unknowingly causing more offenses. This time against Arielle's cell phone as one of her feet kicked it. The Spotify app came to life, and "Like Me Real Hard" by Mario started playing.

Jae'cy smile quivered. "See the phone's still working."

"Whoa, there goes that random shuffle." And that was a not-so-random-ass lie.

"Lemme just—"

"No...it's cool."

Arielle moved her attention down...

...and Jae'cy lifted her eyes, full and *right* there. Right here, right now, right beside her. Arielle's stomach flapped, but a writer/director had to maintain the confidence of the scene, no matter how fragile, how tricky it was—that was the only way to get a good story.

And this time, for the first time, Arielle was finally embracing her role in it, too: acting while directing.

Acting...

On the feeling.

Connecting with Jae'cy's deepening eyes. "You sure?"

Jae'cy's nodding head. Then neck. Collarbone.

The crop top's soft knit fabric, revealing an even softer tummy. And a mole, hidden before from Arielle's observational eye.

But not now.

Dwelling just right above the waistband of—

This time, the pause did come from...

*Elle, you BETTER have a good reason for this.* And she did.

Delivering the reason to the hazy gaze floating downward above her. That paradoxically looked as nervously buzzing.

"I'm gonna take you on a date..." Arielle resumed, in a tone that even she had, let alone Jae'cy, never heard from herself. "A real, official one. Preferably after your birthday." (October was right around the corner...If they both could, *would* just stick to this.)

"To a gallery or a play. Something with refinement, mastery, where, while you're pointing out the art, I'm thinking about the living one that's been right next to me. All the way to a restaurant. One of those fancy ones, where we'll eat off small plates with even smaller amounts of food but with so much flavor that now only leaves us hungrier because of it. And that after, while driving away, we both will comment on it. And how we're looking forward to more..."

Jae'cy didn't respond, just gazed. Dazed. Thought about it as Arielle spoke it. Like Arielle solidifying this decision outwardly would make sure they both kept to it. The feelings in the room depended on it.

"More of everything. More with each other," Arielle gandered. "That's what I'm looking forward to." **NOW.**

After a moment, within which Arielle went from speaking to sweating, thinking maybe she'd gone a bit *too* deep…Jae'cy didn't inch back, inhale shakily, rise up for an exit.

She just nodded with a slight flutter to the decision that hadn't been a question. Just a knowing that felt right.

Much like their positions right here, right now.

As Jae'cy nestled back into the resting place of Arielle's arm, it returned to a comfortable silence, lullabying silence: The faint hum of the TV. The light beep of Jae'cy's phone that lit up for a missed call from AD. But for the first time, Arielle felt a bit less mentally occupied by it, knew Jae'cy wasn't answering it anytime soon—at least not tonight. And the low buzz of Arielle's phone, a text from Taylor running atop of the phone screen (*Is it OK to call u?*). And Jae'cy didn't even quietly observe it. At least not tonight….

"How'd the lobby down there not know who you are, though?"

"Good question. Let's ask the vendor cart corn cob guy down at the park."

A soft giggle; a snicker.

"Nope, not on Miss Paula's level. Not yet…But…"

Just the music in there with them…

"Hopefully, the first of more firsts: I got airtime up on the stage tonight…And the second loca—"

"I know…Proud of you."

…Mario was heading to the end of the second verse…

"I was about to call you again to stop you from coming…After she…Tay—"

"I know…"

…Almost there…

"We weren't together anymore. Before tonight."

…And finally, Mario's continued, heightened pleading at the start of the bridge…

"I actually really like this song," one female voice hushed into the air now.

…Singing what they both knew…

"I do, too," rejoined the other.

And sharing that, along with a new light laugh, to a new part they'd just unlocked with one another. With hopefully, more to come.

♡ **36**

AND LIKE THAT, THEY HAD SURVIVED the night.

And now, the morning after...

Arielle wrestled awake. Paused.

Jae'cy was over at the desk, zipping up her last bootie while placing AD's ring into her purse. Still rousing, Arielle watched as Jae'cy now turned around to the bed, her hand reaching for her cell phone at the foot of it. But then, there she stayed in that motion as her eyes landed on Arielle's.

Even with her clothes on, Arielle had never felt so naked with someone.

"I'm surprised the snoring didn't get me up sooner."

"What-*EVER!*" Jae'cy spurted out a giggle, a tension-relieving one. "You'll *never* hear that from me."

"In the future. Or just this time?"

Jae'cy's smile quivered a bit right then; Arielle gandered steadily.

Jae'cy slipped her eyes away as she took to her purse, pulled it on. Then she gave a new, fidgety grin, a new attempt at what used to be teasing, placing her infamous shades on. "Call me when you land." But again, with no nickname behind it.

"And what else do you want the call to be about if I do?" Arielle dared, waiting for Jae'cy to peel down her shades a bit, so that she could at least see those eyes again. *I did what I could do last night, but I can't force someone to act. And I wouldn't want to even if I could.*

"I'll tell you when you call. Gotta think of a way to top alla *that* last night," Jae'cy answered finally from behind her shades. Sounded nervous, and the light, flimsy chuckle behind it confirmed so for Arielle.

Then Jae'cy turned around, walked to the door. Extended that arm. Much like the arm of a second AC with a clapperboard, Arielle realized.

And all she could do was stare at the door as it opened.

Then closed.

*Man, she cut the scene.*

What (or *whose*) narrative was this really now? Arielle was in a pause...but less in frustration, more in thought, a rising fact: Jae'cy was understanding how she cared for Arielle. And vice versa. Last night made that very clear. But she was in her process, still trying to guard that less-cool side.

And now that it was morning…

Arielle arose. Jae'cy had a lot to figure out on her side. And it *was* time to get going herself.

But *man,* she'd gotten that kiss. And almost even more.

And now, she was spoiled by it. Couldn't unsense it.

Because last night was one for the books for her, too. She'd never said what she had and the way she had to *any* woman before. Only the characters in her books ever had. Now she was playing it out in real life.

And then it hit her. *Damn…*

*I've topped myself, too.*

*BUZZ...*

As the Uber turned down a new downtown street, Arielle's eyes fell on Juliana's sudden text on her cell phone:

*Look at this that I just saw in an IG reel!*

And so, Arielle did. Tapped on, then looked at the attached candid video clip in the text conversation.

On it, she saw Jae'cy holding a skipping, ice cream cone–licking Cori's hand as she took a look at her own cell phone. And even under her staple cool appearance, the sunglasses, she appeared to get tighter, lips pursed, with a slow-down in her pace. Not by the energetic Cori, but apparently at something that had proven to be energy-zapping on her phone as she undoubtedly read it.

*Okay, something is going on...*

And Arielle didn't judge that conclusion on Cori's elated expression, bright eyes and sudden inaudible question she posed to Jae'cy, who then shook her head despondently, and in turn, made Cori slump her shoulders. No, Arielle judged it on Jae'cy's despondent head shake *followed by* its turn to the various ice cream parlor diners now looking their way, *her* way.

*BUZZ. BUZZ.*

Jae'cy appeared confused and irritated as she looked back down at her cell phone while quickening her pace to the parlor's exit door.

Much like Arielle did...as her eyes fell on her own cell phone screen.

*She HAS to be looking at the same thing.*

That thing being:

A tagged slideshow post notification by @TheHollyHallPass, an urban entertainment gossip outlet. One of the most elite...and connected. Arielle read the first image's title:

*Trouble in AD and JC Paradise (AGAIN)?*

And the image was more technically a collage: a left-side candid photo and matching right-side cell phone video of AD down on one knee in front of a very stiff-looking Jae'cy in her backyard from last night.

And since Arielle knew that she was somehow involved in this due to being tagged, she swiped to the next image in the slideshow and found a screenshot of one particular celeb's (not so) subliminal IG Story:

*Bros out here playin grown life Kens and really don't think*
*  they girl wanna STILL play wit Barbies???*
*#readitagain #carefuloutherefellas* 😄 😄 😄

*He is soooo showy, passive aggressive, and prideful,* Arielle scoffed, much like Jae'cy seemed to, pressing right by the camera just before she and Cori disappeared from the scene.

It didn't need any explanation for the implication.

It was no other than…

"AD DA PROMOTER
He's promotin' some news, cuh!"

Talking about no other than…

*Elle and Jae'cy sittin' in a tree*
*K I S S I N G*
*If these mofos pull up on my front door you'll soon see*
*You gonna have mo problems than just the one with AD*

*So you ARE hittin that?? KNEW it!*

The first, the call, had come from Juliana (which Arielle ended). The text from Sinead. The third, an IG DM from Tish.

As Arielle blankly stared back at her phone, still in commute in the Uber, she'd really wished they would all just let grown folks be.

Instead, they had all forwarded the HollyHallPass IG post that she was still gazing at:

*Looks like @ADaGreat is announcing his and @J_Carter's relationship is*
*quits – but hers and someone else's ALLEGEDLY is on the way to something*
*more…???* 👀

In the next slide came some onscreen words:

*Remember when Jae'cy said this??? What (or who) you (REALLY) talkin'
about, sis?? 👀 (Spoiler: Peep that lovey dovey look on her face 👀
That LIBERATION don't come from new business and movie deals)*

Along with these words from Jae'cy in a YouTube clip from the
same Mahogany news story interview:

"I've always been an accepting person. Especially since I've been
around creators and artists all my life, people who every day challenge
and change the standard. So, I think that's inspired me, and it's why I like
to think that I live each day in what feels right and good for me."

"Oo. Elaboration is advocation," the Mahogany columnist
stated, perched inward.

Jae'cy chuckled. "I don't box myself in, and I admire women who
are just as unapologetically liberated."

*She did look a little dazed, starry there,* Arielle couldn't lie. She
was briefly dazed herself at the thought: *Damn, was she actually thinking
about me as early as then?*

Arielle sighed as she refocused on the post. Because someone else
had made a bold comment that the post was (understandably, for legal
reasons) tiptoeing around:

*@ElWordSmith Arielle IRIS this you?*

*BUZZ!*

Arielle rolled her eyes as she checked her phone once again, not
even trying to think about the level of digging a person must've gone
through to discover her grandmother-inherited middle moniker. She had
a haunting feeling that this was just the beginning of her personal life
going public.

*IS it you??? 👀*
*Explain cause now who you foolin'?*
*Damn sure nobody with that secret middle name nomo*

*Yep,* Arielle uninspiringly acknowledged and accepted in her
mind as she stared at Sinead's texted screenshot of the random
commentor's exact words she was already looking at. It was.

Her.

Her sudden latest social involvement she didn't ask for. (Welp,
she guessed that she'd really finally "made it.")

Her…

She was thinking about Jae'cy. She knew that this was her world, but this was taking the Wild West to another level.

*Yep, something is definitely going on...*

Arielle's eyes floated up to a new incoming text:

*You made it to the airport yet?*

*And it's just getting started.*

"I MEEEEAN...I DIDN'T KNOW SHE WAS YOUR TYPE."

Arielle sighed at all that awaited behind Jae'cy's front door, where Breyah and Jae'cy were immediately on the other side.

And so, she decided to just listen in for a second, ready herself...

Jae'cy took a moment to respond. But then... "She's not...I prefer Bratz."

Breyah was silent a moment, for the quick sarcasm temporarily dumbfounded her. Then she emitted a tight snicker. "Bih, we're *NOT* doin' this*!*"

"You're right. Because there's nothing to discuss."

"So then why did you put him back on the stage?" Breyah reinstated after a moment.

Another silence. Arielle was sure it was because of Breyah's valid question...

"And poor Deonte never stood a fighting chance—even at six-three and one-ninety."

"That's why I'm staying single from now on. Because I'm obviously not getting the best luck in this relationship thing. Clearly," Jae'cy concluded...or tried to.

"I'm not saying you're supposed to be looking for a spouse tomorrow, a ring. But you *need* to be happy with someone you're with," Breyah stated intently. "Just like I'm tryna be with this new guy I met since moving to San Diego. Since you don't wanna be Cinderella, I'll be!" She tried to joke, heard in her effected chuckle, to make Jae'cy feel better Arielle figured. "But no, I know AD wasn't the Prince Charming for you, so I'm glad you declined."

*DING-DONG.*

*Welp, let's get this goin'...*

"*However*, right now, *YOU'RE* passin' up all the shots that *do* exist. Just play the game right, Quiet Storm. Don't let the game play you," Breyah imparted in a louder, closer volume that let Arielle know they were approaching the front door.

"Oh, like you think *you're* about to do me with my mug?"

"*GIRL!*" Breyah giggled high once again. "You know this is my designated drinking vessel you bought for me here."

"And *here* is where it stays. In my collection."

"See? Always tryna collect things up." Breyah settled just in front of the door, Arielle could hear every word, every spot-on word. "Dishes, high school t-shirts you need to let finally attend their funeral," she continued. "…And feelings."

"And they're just piled up in your house…Don't lose your curb appeal in Hollywood, Jae'cy. 'Cause you and I know it's a market that keeps on movin' farther and farther away. And higher…" Breyah finished, more somberly, real, from a real place as Arielle spotted the doorknob turn.

Breyah, however, still had the most questioning expression in her voice, really expressing the extent of this social media frenzy for the both of them. "What are you gonna do?"

"What *can* I do?"

The door opened a crack, Arielle seeing Breyah first.

Who pondered at that question but fidgeted, shuffled her feet so swiftly and stiffly that it only seemed like one reply was available. "…I guess nothing."

"Media training 101. If I don't make a big deal out of it, they'll have nothing to feed off of much longer."

And then there was Jae'cy in full view. Much like Arielle was now to them.

Breyah respectfully bowed out. No playfulness, just a knowing to let these two have their much-needed solo time. She nodded at the clear-wrapped long-legged jumpsuit laying long and neat on Jae'cy's hallway table, Arielle figured for another upcoming event. "I'll check on you later. And let me know how it fits…okay?" Breyah farewelled Jae'cy with a hug then moved by.

And Arielle moved in, her and Jae'cy gazing at the other. Arielle, now on this side, could see her clearly. She looked…vexed but keeping it together. And rightfully so. *And doing it very well, all in just a basic gym tee, an old high school shirt that indeed looked more like an extra-large than the medium it probably originally was years back. Unbridled down hair, lashes, bronzer, and all other makeup off, in contrast to this morning. Most girls could never…*Arielle then noticed that Cori wasn't around. She'd imagined that either it was a power play and/or ego trip move by AD, to finally keep his commitment. And probably did so with a smirk on his face when he'd come. Or Paula came and got her. But either way, Arielle had to transfer her attention to the more immediate picture. They both did.

"You said you weren't in my world, partner," Jae'cy asked, responded finally. "…How you likin' the *noise* in the cool kids' party now?"

"Well, this has been one of my most interesting days in a while, I'll say that."

"You changed your flight?"

"Changed my mind," Arielle followed behind her, making way to the kitchen. "Gonna stop by an Enterprise or something. Think it might be best right now."

And sure enough, on both of their phones.

*BUZZ. BUZZ.*

Both exhaled wordlessly.

Both staring ominously at the same new IG notification she'd just received. Another messy tagged post on messy The HollyHall Pass.

But this time, they had damn near made a scrapbook of slides, all about:

Elle. There came her face in the first photo slide, her posing on the red carpet at Paula's Everlasting Young launch party...with Jae'cy on the other end of the group shot.

The second slide. With Jae'cy, stepping outside Honest Bites, laptop backpacks and tote purses in respective tow.

The third slide. Featuring el(ote). With Jae'cy at the park. Both sitting on the bench, almost in the way that hips naturally could touch when in close seating proximity on a plane. Like how the cream touched the corn that touched the foil encasing it.

And why not? There was a bonus slide. A far-distance candid shot of Elle singly stepping outside of the Luxe, her face covered by the low brim of her baseball cap...Adjacent to one of Jae'cy, just as solo outside of the hotel, a face covered with black-tinted shades.

There wasn't anything technically stated on a highly explicit level in the photos, such as a kiss or even interlocked hands. But the intention was there. Intention to start some BS. Making a whole album, a whole elongated gossip mill relevancy moment out of this BS.

And the comment section was just as ruthless (and insinuating):

*I knew they were VIBIN vibin...Louder than that music that hit me n my bae when we slid by them at her spot's grand opening like a year ago! #thoseairfriedwingsfyretho*

*I saw her with this girl at a Cuban takeout spot, not many people frequent A hole in the wall typa joint WITH her and AD's kid there And then flaunts her gifts from him days later She's a user 👎 For the streets*

*Nobody in these comments are diggin deeper and need to stick to their day jobs You seriously think THIS is the 'dirt'? 💀 😅*
*They haven't even begun to really mess up these two's backyard yet*

But this unfolding storyline was bigger than alleged two-timing or a public outing. Because for one, as that last comment knowingly warned: a plot could always thicken. For two, quite frankly, neither of those things were new or "taboo" these days and, therefore, not gossip-worthy or trending hot topics anymore. So, the plot *would* have to thicken; there was another end goal at play here. Arielle knew it, could feel it. Which moved this dialogue to number three...

The way Jae'cy's face had just tightened even more let Arielle know what they'd seen up until this point was just the groundwork for a much larger tale...and there were still some more images to go through on this post. Arielle read the caption:

*Who exactly is this low-key 'WordSmith' makin' rounds in Black Hollywood?*

Then she viewed the remaining slideshow images: The first being a side-by-side comparison of Arielle's (yes, Arielle's) Q Scores and Jae'cy's Q Scores in adjacent charts. Her positive score had dipped from 2 to 0 (understandable for an author); the negative one had spiked from 0 to 36. She'd truly gained celebrity status—and then its perks: people quickly coming to discard you just as quickly as they'd come to barely know you.

Em...didn't look too different from her normal life.

But Jae'cy's side was worse. Her own positive score sandwiched up beside Arielle's in the image was at now at a 60 from its just a month ago 70, and her negative score had shot up from 35 (expected for a celebrity's kid—HollyHall's words, not Arielle's) to 55.

Then came press images of Arielle all around LA in a *perfect* chronological timeline, which stood out to her immediately: stepping out behind Paula and Elise with Juliana, Sinead, and Melanie at Capri's...at Paula's perfume launch...on the red carpet at the Honest Bites launch party...stepping arm-in-arm with Taylor into the music video wrap-up club party.

Followed by the very last images in the slideshow...Arielle swiped.

And instantly regretted it.

A different urban news IG page's embedded post as the image showed their caption:

*The WordSmith ALLEGEDLY has devised this whole thing to get her name (and book sales) more out there*

Then their visual "evidence": The first, Jae'cy's IG post requesting marketing pros. Followed by a screenshot snippet of her and Jae'cy's business relationship-setting Lil' Wayne and the silent lasagna talk in her DMs. And then, a screenshotted business marketing site's earnings calendar showing Paula's fragrance line sales in its first week, a Google snapshot of Arielle's books on Amazon with the latest one showing recent reviews for a high 4.5 stars.

But the most suspicious reveal came in the final swipe. Arielle knew it before she even made the ultimate right-to-left motion. *Because the best is always saved for last, right?*

What met her eyes was a screenshot of an IP address lookup results page with a very much so defamatory on-picture caption:

*Oh btw. These images were brought to our attention by a few of our lil' insider friends and brought to you on the low by...*

An animated arrow pointed right at that IP address...A very familiar-looking address.

*Nooooooo way! ME???*

Arielle had to chuckle, harshly, as that was all she could do. "They're playin'." Because the IP address on the lookup site was her own, her laptop's location showing in Vegas on the site's map. Marking her as the assailant, the leaker in this whole thing as a way to get marketing buzz, a.k.a. clout. *Even if that was my thing, I'd never go about it this way!*

No, this wasn't run-of-the-mill silly gossip about someone's attempted comeuppance. This was a defamation train increasingly heading to a bad fate. All to defame. A malicious thing from a malicious person looking to see someone's downfall. Right now, it might've been Arielle as the first victim with the scarlet letter. But she knew, even with her slight taste of Hollywood, that the largest scarlet letter was awaiting to be branded on the most important character in this thing...

The one with the red-hot eyes right in front of her as she finally looked back up. And by the way her mouth was so pursed, yet twitching a bit as if she was working hard to guard everything, confirmed that Jae'cy knew there was much more coming her way next, too.

But for now?

*BUZZ.*

*BUZZ!*

*RIIIIING!*

Arielle exhaled roughly as she dropped her attention back to her phone and was met by Juliana, Sinead, Melanie, Marlon, Tish, and Kimesha chiming in respectively, blowing up Arielle's phone via consecutive texts, calls, and texts after unanswered calls:

*CUH This is crazy!! You think this explains what Jae'cy claimed, like about you comin with her to look at second commercial spots for her and alla that? Someone's been snooping and writing fake convos??!*

*I TOLD you they're all on white rock out here…hit me up if you need to talk*

*Keep positive, cousin. This will pass even if you don't think so RN. You know I'm always a call away* 🩶

*Just stay steady, sis. They like negativity. Don't give it to em*
*But if THEY give U mo problems like threatening yo space hmu so I can give them that Detroit*

*Al, is it time to show 'em how Detroit moves?*

*Just finished the call with the publishing company, we need to put out a PR stmt stat. Let's see how this plays out and if it's time to lawyer up next. But NOW also just received a call from the organization we were supposed to be releasing that Ashes Fall Down deal with in a few weeks. Hold tight.*

Jae'cy's phone was on fire, too, but Jae'cy still hadn't moved, hadn't spoken…

Arielle peeped it, Jae'cy's cell phone that was now just resting on the island countertop. *There's no way she can believe this.* Arielle readied herself anyway, meeting Jae'cy's clenched jaw and stare.

"Come on, Jae'cy," she snickered. "You—"

Jae'cy grabbed Arielle's backpack, snatched out her laptop.

"So, what? You're actually going to believe the gossip? Just looking for a way to not trust ANYBODY, huh?" Arielle was done, was going to let Jae'cy direct her own moves at this point. *If she wants to continuously lead herself to a place farther and farther away from me, from anyone, then so be it.* Arielle folded her arms tight across her chest.

Jae'cy ripped open Arielle's laptop screen, clicked open her VPN network, and shut it off. And, as Arielle continued to witness, she knew very well how to get to what Arielle knew she was going to find: her laptop's true IP address without the VPN on. Arielle imagined it was because of Jae'cy's own secured networks she understandably had set up as a public figure. And sure enough, Jae'cy went to the Apple menu, searched for then pulled up Arielle's network preferences, specifically the Wi-Fi, and finally stopped.

There was the IP address…

Jae'cy slid her eyes back up to the IP address still on her cell phone screen from the HollyHall Pass post.

A match.

"This city really is just a garden of snakes," Jae'cy coolly stated. *Too* cool, sterile. Rehearsed.

Arielle was livid. *She KNOWS she doesn't believe this.*

"Just go."

"Jae—!"

Jae'cy was striding for the hall, for the door. With Arielle's laptop and a grasp and tug of Arielle's arm with her.

*But she wants to believe it. She'll believe this, believe anything before she believes in herself to trust me.*

Arielle sneered outwardly as she gave the woman what she wanted anyway, taking the laptop mid-walk and putting it into her—

*Hold on.* Arielle slowed down her movement a second as she considered. Then she decided to do it: She was going to end this scene with a bang.

"Just admit that you're happy this happened. Because you've *been* wanting a way to guard yourself."

Jae'cy huffed low but gave no comeback, or counterargument.

"Plus, I'm no good for you, right? Michi said it. And you told him the same."

"What?"

"The only reason you decided to give me a try was because you felt bad for me!"

"I never said—!"

"Doesn't matter. Maybe you did, maybe you didn't. But you've probably thought it."

"You know what? I'm not about to explain anything to you." Jae'cy suddenly whipped back around to Arielle with a recollection, a new match to the fire ignited. "No, actually, I can call you out on something, too!"

*What is she talking about??*

Jae'cy's nostrils were flaring madly. "You saying you would meet me and Cori at the ice cream parlor the other day when I asked you on my way there? Then instead of coming late like the first time when you'd stated you be here an hour earlier back when we were first working on the cookbook, you just didn't come at all. The first time was whatever. But *this second time* was a big thing for me, because it was a big thing for her. Because she's the one who asked for you to come." **NOW.**

Arielle furrowed her brows, perplexed at this random mention of her so-called broken promises. Because she never made promises she didn't think she could keep, especially not to kids. "I never told you that."

"You *did*. On Instagram. In our conversation when I asked you, you replied. Then unsent it. But I still could see it in my notifications."

*Aaah, of course.* But this time, it couldn't have been Juliana's work; her cousin was a hot mess but wasn't messy like *that*. And then, dots started connecting in Arielle's head. *So, this was why Cori looked the way she did ay Jae'cy in that ice cream parlor clip. Juliana's hunch was right in that text just now. Someone is playing messenger in the background, acting as me?* And just like that, yep, Arielle knew this web being spun was something now out of her and Jae'cy's control, just two lead actresses playing their part in someone *else's* script. Whether Jae'cy wanted to acknowledge it...or just continue to use it as a mask to conceal her vulnerability cracking open. The actress acting.

"Then how come I don't see that message from you right now?" Arielle showed her cell phone screen to Jae'cy, their DM thread in IG, with no recent messages about ice cream meetups.

"Because I unsent my messages right after that, too. You reneged, again, so—"

"I didn't!"

"So, you're calling me a liar?" Jae'cy didn't ask, only sneered explosively.

"I'm telling you that something is up with all of this. That someone is doing some kind of imposter work."

"I think it's time to lay off the storytelling for a second. Because now you're getting it mixed up with the real world." Jae'cy snickered hard, then pierced with her eyes even harder. "And the real way people move in it."

"Fine. Then I'm just telling you my truth."

"Well, then. That makes the two of us." Jae'cy was still reading Arielle's face tightly. The guard was fully up.

And now, Arielle's was too, her jaw bone clenched. "*You're just* trying to find any evidence of a crime, wanting to find it *so* bad. But the difference between you and me, I call my stories fiction instead of truth."

Jae'cy pushed Arielle to the hallway, to the front door, and out. With a hard, loud slam.

Arielle stared at the door, like a slap across the face. Back on the street.

However, she wouldn't leave without defending herself...

And, even still, caring about Jae'cy, too.

"Way back when we first met, you asked me what I'd get out of it...out of teaming up." Arielle paused—to make sure every word was heard, felt. She knew Jae'cy hadn't departed yet, just as she hadn't. Because whether they liked it or not, they were too deep in this journey, and there was too much at stake. More than words, recipes, leads.

Arielle proceeded, "And, well, I want you to buy into you. Like you had bought into me. So you can finally stop fighting against your biggest audience...your heart."

Arielle slid her eyes away from the door. "Room twenty-four. That's me at Freehand hotel next weekend," Arielle imparted. "Because not only Cori wanted to see me. You did, too."

And with that, she left.

She'd had enough for the day…Getting out of LA ASAP was the wisest thing she could do for now, for so many reasons. Even though she'd be back for business, an author's workshop booked by Kimesha.

♡ 39

*YEP, CALLED IT.* FROM HER FAMILIAR PLACE ON THE CURB just on the corner of Sunset. Arielle opened someone's front passenger seat door.

As she lowered inside, words hit her in dual ways, in dual directions:

"Ooo-*weeeee!* That karma come QUICK these days." That was an emboldened, lime-tipped freestyle stitch braids–donning paparazzo/vlogger paired with a cameraman (yes, really). And a "Twitch IRL" news correspondent inscription right on his tightly clutched mic flag (yes, really).

"Fa *real* though. What is goin' *ON?!*" Juliana aped from her gaping and staring position in the driver's seat.

As Arielle begrudgingly buckled herself in with an exhale, she thought about the *retribution* that she and Jae'cy were, in fact, getting. Arielle wanted to get away from this city as fast as possible. *None of this was deserved.* But with Jae'cy's career fostered more in the spotlight, she was even more at risk.

*Buzz.*

*Great.*

"Girl, I love my hometown, but we are some basic people believin' some fake mess like this!" Juliana said as she pulled away.

Arielle's cell phone showed a new text from Kimesha:

*Call me*
*NOW*

*Not now,* Arielle sighed aloud.

"But drama sells." Juliana was still talking. "'Cause girl, don't you know my DMs and page been blowin' up with follow requests and questions because these people out here have already found out somehow that I'm your cousin?! I had to put my mess on private, almost deactivated it. And you already know Sinead cussed a few of them out on hers. Melanie's smart, stressed-out behind doesn't even have an IG, almost makes *me* wish I had a man and four big-headed little men, too!"

Meanwhile, the Nikon D7500 and lime-tipped paparazzo was getting closer...

"But I ain't gon lie...I'm kinda feelin' these five seconds of fame. And I didn't even have to work for it—I'm *REALLY* one of 'em now."

Arielle looked over at Juliana. And that got *her* point across.

Juliana went in heavy on the gas, just as the hungry, salivating wolves landed at the curb. "Girl, I know. I'm just trying to make you feel semi-better and not let this LA culture chew you up alive 'cause they *will* if you let them."

Arielle slumped her head back against the headrest.

Juliana glanced over, then back to the road. "It's a good thing I finally got this joint tinted...You know what? I'm gonna stop glorifyin' these lames."

*About time.*

Arielle rolled her eyes. But even still... "Thanks for picking me up."

Juliana gave a side gaze at a red light. "Fa sho, cuh."

"But Juliana?...No more matchmak—"

"Fa sho...Just thought it would help you feel better after the ex, give you a chance with someone else."

*BUZZ-BUZZ.*

Luckily, not Arielle's own phone this time.

Arielle peered over. Then tracked Juliana's falling gander and spotted a Facebook post pop up on Juliana's phone. It showed a shared photo post on Sinead's profile of Sinead with a...guy. A very mature-looking guy, in facial expression and wardrobe, smiling. And Sinead too.

"His hair, right? Like, what vintage *Jet* issue in his granddaddy's closet did he pull *that* from?"

Arielle snickered low because Juliana was, as usual, verbally spot-on. But overall, they were both otherwise stunned. Arielle pondered. That explained why she was able to walk out of her house with her life after bringing her car back on a quarter of a tank the last time she'd used it.

"...Wow," Arielle speechlessly resumed the talk. "She's really found..."

"A David Ruffin resurrected from up off of Hollywood Boulevard."

Arielle shook her head and tried so hard to be the bigger person, but a chuckle escaped her again as she was assaulted by black framed eyeglasses and lambchops (yes) from just seconds ago.

"Nah, for real," Juliana redacted, "I'm happy for her. I was wondering if she'd ever find someone who could handle her complicated, mean ass. I guess she deserves it."

This was one long light...Well, time for more conversation...

"...Like you do, too?" Arielle questioned.

"Just worry about your own drama today, miss," Juliana sniggered but low, like her eyes cascading to her lap.

"Rashad gave you so much, Juliana. But what got you with him," Arielle established—then studied, "...is you started seeing your space *too* well when he was around. Like you hadn't seen it in so long. Walls your dad left behi—"

"Unh-unh," Juliana shot out, shot a look over. "Don't put that one-fifty millimeter lens on me, or I'll drop you back down on Sunset to your friend, and the both of y'all can live *snappily* ever after. I'm already in enough stories to last this whole week. Nah, a month." But she wasn't finished, just like pain wasn't when it wasn't healed or discussed with those you loved. "I stopped that melodramatic mess years ago. I told you that already." But obviously her steering wheel material needed the reminder because she was almost digging a hole into it with her nails. "Workin' as a loader at some trucking company after *HOW* many years? Twenty-five? Damn near the same age as me? Unlike him, I've moved *up* and on."

She had indeed, Arielle noted, moved up. Right to the manager role at the bar. But Arielle also believed that her vibrant cousin could put her people skills to better use, better boosting others' esteem, outside of temporary physical enhancers.

However, first, one had to practice what they preached, rather than still fighting anger from her very first male rejection: her dad... *And so, as a result, she hadn't really moved up at all.*

*HONK...*

"...So, how come we're still right here?" Arielle quizzed.

Juliana peeked up at her and then at the light: green.

Juliana proceeded on the gas...

Then looked back over at Arielle...who crept up a slight, gentle corner of her mouth.

"You've always been a lil' off-brand therapist...Just like Melanie. Always dealin' with our crazy asses." But she only smiled, too, softer, vulnerable. "But you *do* know even therapists need some TLC too, right?" Juliana asked directly, gazed directly for as long of a second that she had or could while driving. "Because I know that patience's waning on your side at this point."

Arielle crookedly, damply grinned... "Of course."

And they both knew Juliana was talking about more than...

"Dealing with y'all—"

"CRAZY ASSES!" Juliana giggled right on time for her, though still a bit low.

And then, Arielle joined at the same volume until it dwindled into a new silence.

As they continued.

Driving onward, like they always had to after a shut door.

They weren't Irish twins for nothing.


As Arielle tossed her travel bag on the backseat of Kimesha's Camry (she had money and spent it wisely) back in Vegas:

"It's dropped."

She wasn't talking her latest shares in Amazon and Fendi. (Kimesha was cheap—but she'd spend it all for her cosmetics...and Rihanna.)

She was talking Arielle's developing business partnership with a human trafficking nonprofit. The plan had been to release a dual audio and e-book human trafficking reporting and restoration resource based on *Ash Must Fall Down,* to help the organization's survivors. Kimesha had encouraged the idea since Arielle's story revealed an underground prostitution ring within the gentleman's club.

But her real-life story, notified to the enterprise's CEO by the young staff and some of the survivors, became the new headline of interest...which quickly caused the nonprofit to cancel the launch date that had been scheduled for next week.

As Kimesha told Arielle, "They don't want a 'sexually-nuanced story triggering their survivors back into decline'."

Arielle wasn't Ash, but she had definitely fallen. At least, from this deal. The next draining thought that entered her mind as her head hung low was, *Man, how must this affect Mesha now?*

"Elle, you are a wonderful client. Who, actually, I consider family now. That means you're not going anywhere. And *this* will pass," Kimesha uncannily, firmly responded.

Arielle peered over.

"It *will* pass. Alright?"

Arielle could only quietly nod, sinking back in her thoughts as the car ride moved into pregnant silence.

"Whatever happens, I support you." That timely comment had popped up on Arielle's business Facebook from a devoted reader. And it iterated Kimesha's sentiment. (She had stuck by Arielle like a dope manager to whom Arielle would really have to start showing more gratitude.)

And Elizabeth's. (She would be flying in that night after having received the news from Marlon. And yeah, Arielle would have to show her more gratitude, too.)

And although she wished that she could've felt comfort in all of that, none of those females' intuitively shared, reassuring sentiments could compare to the more incredibly unsettling nature of the gossip mill...and a certain Scorpio she was involved in it with...one who didn't want to let a part of herself fall down. Right then, Arielle could grimly accept why.

"So..." That was all Elizabeth had to say hours later as she stepped inside Arielle's home.

And falling onto the couch and looking up at her living room ceiling as Elizabeth set down her luggage and joined her was all Arielle had to do. *Momma's about to break me down without any effort...* Arielle internally readied herself with a quiet exhale.

So, she knew she was about to tell her mom the tale about this most recent unfortunate events—in a witty way, as was their open tradition. However, always with a tinge of vulnerability, a gateway to deeper conversation underneath. *But this time, I'm not really feeling that. Don't wanna talk even though I'm a hot talking commodity right now.* "Don't get too close. You might come down with an IG."

"A *who?*"

Arielle wearily smirked.

"Oh, that stuff those silly people are saying online." Elizabeth finally caught on.

While Arielle gave herself another moment, within Elizabeth's patient silence. The social media gossip was the least of her concern right now. And Elizabeth knew it. She rejoined the full room rather than just the ceiling, meeting Elizabeth there. "This is all just...complicated. Just..."

"Welcome to relationships," Elizabeth carried the conversation forward. All she'd needed was the keys; now Mama Bear was drivin' this home.

Arielle crossed her eyebrows, wanted to curtail the conversation a bit longer. "Ma, I've had relationships. But this one isn't—"

"*This* one is something. And you know how I know?"

Arielle looked over, Elizabeth's face now much more sensitive, wistful-like.

"That smile I was asking about...the last time I saw it was also the last time you'd planted the biggest kiss on my cheek before heading into school like you'd always used to. The morning of your first-grade yearbook picture. The same day that your teacher called me about—"

*Noooo, Ma.* Arielle cast her eyes back up to the ceiling. But Elizabeth was getting to the grit. Effortlessly. Starting from the ground up, the root.

"You were ashamed about it then. Because you were shamed for it." Her voice cracked, then Elizabeth shook her head. And Arielle was rendered speechless, because her mom rarely cried, and she definitely hadn't the last time this topic came up between them: when Arielle came home frantically, apologizing about the love song incident and Elizabeth responded with muted, conflicted consolation.

"You don't have to be ashamed about it anymore, Arielle. I've seen that little snaggle-toothed, free, *demonstrative* girl smile again...every time you're with her."

Elizabeth grabbed a tissue before any evidence fell on her face. And Arielle was wondering how time had just teleported and when she'd formed the lump she now felt in her throat.

"*So...*" Mama Bear sniffled then asked, "What are you going to do?"

Arielle shrugged. "Cry?" She chuckled it out, like a cough. Much like she'd tried to do back when that paper was passed around the classroom—until she got home and...

*Great.* Next thing she knew, she had a tissue in her hand and her head on Elizabeth's shoulder. "Does this life thing get easier?"

"A little bit. The other half of it, the larger half, is just braving it," Elizabeth replied, stroking the top of Arielle's head. "You know?"

*But I thought I already braved it,* Arielle sighed. Thinking about this woman who drove her mad sometimes. Arielle felt compelled to be more assiduous, more assertive, more demonstrative with her. Thinking about this version of her she'd buried in youth, and how much she liked it. Even if she was still unsure about what the final result would be.

"Just give it some time. Some things need time."

♡ 40



That was the thought Arielle had as she pulled her large Ford SUV into her garage, having dropped her mom at the airport.

Resting in her mind as she'd dismounted, then her black Vans connected to the pavement...meeting a small pair of Taylor's.

No, not the Converses. Literally Taylor. Size five white Adidas Swifts, with leggings and a sleeveless tee topping them all off.

Both of them just stared at the other for a moment inside Arielle's closing garage, as if they hadn't been expecting to meet, even though they had planned it. Two days ago, to be exact. Arielle had figured, *if this girl needs this for her closure, then...hey.*

Taylor had called her up to express that she'd be in town for a Las Vegas–based reality show shooting its pilot episode. The girl had indeed *manifested* her destiny.

"I know. Who would've ever thought, right?" She'd tried to conjure up some kind of amicable conversation over the phone. But Arielle's mind was NOT on the surprising existence of set design for reality shows and the budgeting it limited as Taylor went on to explain.

*No,* Arielle had thought, *only the sky is the limit when Michi is the handy cloud that suddenly swooped in for you to propel from.*

But now, as Taylor saw her sardonic expression in the flesh for the first time since the Spirit Awards after party, she lost the young confrontation approach and looked directly at the focused, morose eyes that were awaiting her.

"I know you think I just saw you as a stepping stone."

*Stone, stool, ladder, high chair. The six more inches you need for Six Flags...*

"...But what if I said that's how you made me feel first?"

*Girl, WHAaat???*

Arielle wasn't sure who'd enlightened Taylor first, her ancestral *Dynasty* from *A Different World* via her third eye or Arielle's *sharper* eye at Taylor just then. But either way, Taylor followed up with some much-needed elucidation.

"Listen—I don't know how true or untrue all that mess is right now," she resumed, her tone gaining a bit of sharpness itself. "But what I do know is what I saw with my *own* eyes all the time:…how yours always changed when you were around *her*."

Bingo.

"Let's just say, I felt like the bait for the prize. Just teasing me in front of the real girl."

Arielle dropped her eyes, looked down at her Vans.

"And I wasn't '*that* girl.' So I figured I'd be the next best thing: *that* girl to make your goal of getting her take a detour. And it was one of the hardest things I've ever done, being somethin' like a distractor, which is *so* goofy. Even harder than landing that video gig with…Michi…and *especially* more than my decline to a gossip vlogger's interview request about this whole thing."

Arielle peered up to find this young lady owning her gaze…and her mistakes. In a very peculiar way, that made Taylor appealing to her in a whole new way, a true, revering way. Arielle respected her openness, slight messiness, and yet maturity and even compassion in the rebound. That was all something Arielle could learn herself, and something that this speedy young one had beat her to. *Of course,* Arielle internally, bittersweetly was amused in a trumped way at that, but then felt immediate guilt follow it up. She had been so entrenched in fear of being hurt that she'd hurt someone else. Needless to say, that made her flatline a bit. Back to listening.

"Because even though I—I'll be honest—saw the opportunity to get some exposure when your cousin first told me about you, I thought you looked cute and cool in your own way in the photos she showed me. And then discovered you were even more beautiful in person," Taylor admitted, "inside and out."

Arielle fluttered. *Man, she really is schoolin' me.*

"But for the first time in my life, I don't think that feeling was reciprocated. And ya girl is a rookie to feelin' *THAT* type a way!" Taylor admitted vulnerably through a dim, low chuckle, a glance away. When she looked back up, she only soundly nodded.

"Well, at least now I know what it feels like on the other side. And it's a feeling, a *knowing* that I'm going to grow in a whole 'nother upward way. Like a few in my past brokenheartedly had to. *So…*" She met Arielle's eyes once again, and then nodded more clearly. "Thank you."

Damn, if that wasn't the kind of evolved response Arielle should've given to all of her exes, at the very least in her own spirit if not directly to them, she didn't know what was.

"And I know this won't make you forgive me any more than all of the other words I just spoke..." Taylor began to step away, but not without leaving something at Arielle's feet. "But I just want to make it clear, even though it's kinda hard to believe what's lie and truth right now: I didn't have any involvement in what's bein' laid out there...Michi either. Because *that* girl? He finds her too beautiful, too."

*No, you made it clear.*

*Too* clear...and as Arielle watched the lil' grasshopper prophet enter her rental car, her Enterprise Merkabah in the driveway, Arielle wished she hadn't. But either way, she'd received the download: Emotions, at times, held each and everybody captive. No matter how cool, uncool, photogenically privileged or not. And spared no egos, delusions. Fears.

The compulsive incoming messages just wouldn't stop as she dazed at Taylor driving off. *But at least you seem to have what you want after all of that, right? Your closure, to remove any "rockiness" on your road to wherever.* Arielle felt her nostrils flare. *YOUR options, business and personally, to pivot to for your convenience. YOUR*--She grimaced and winced together, sourly.

*She's got me on that marketing lingo as profanity tip again.* Not "she" as in Taylor. Arielle exhaled and stepped back into the garage. Had had to go back inside, a retreat, with some music on high. Taylor's face had morphed in her mind to Jae'cy's. Just like it always had. Just like Taylor hadn't too long figured out (that young mind...whose point after all might've been to make old, stuck Arielle see). And that just made her *feel.* Simple as that.

The simplest of things, like simply saying "yes" when you knew your heart wasn't really in it *or* was *so* into it, that new to that kind of feeling, that fervent heartbeat, could end up hurting you, and someone else. Creating the most complex of things afterwards.

Arielle knew that. Man, did she know that. *Especially* after these last few years.

The Merkabah turned a corner and was gone. Taylor didn't need the height, the age, had already ascended.

And meanwhile, even though her mom said to give it time, Arielle was still thinking about, even more now, her. And *them.* That night at the hotel before the morning after brought the turn of events. Then the hotel before *that* in Vegas after the club. But especially, finally, the hotel she should've been at had she not gone to that marketing conference where she first met Elise, just before she met her fate in...*her.*

Great, now Arielle had yet another reason to loathe hotels...but also to like them. A simple thing made complex. And come this increasingly approaching new week of the five-day author's workshop, things were about to get more complex she felt. She just knew it...

"Freehand. Front desk."

There was a pause. *Gotta speak...*

"Can you connect me to Arielle Smith? Room twenty-four?"

"Can't do anything without *your* name." The hotel lobby receptionist definitely wasn't friendly yet not rousing either. But that was a good thing, a sign of possible unawareness.

Much as Jae'cy had hoped.

She had affected her best Midwestern tone, courtesy of cousins and aunties back in Missouri.

But first...a brief rewind.

♡ 41

"YUNG HITTA?"

Jae'cy tried to work up a smile before looking over her shoulder…and there was Elise, who was modeling the most ridiculous pair of shades with Cori into the wall of fold two way standing floor mirrors in the department store they'd somehow randomly ventured inside. *And she has my baby partaking in it.*

Always simple, wholesome, random, down-to-earth adventures with down-to-earth Elise. That was what Jae'cy loved about her. This Stockton-bred young woman of humble but bold California beginnings allowed Jae'cy the ability to come down from the stage and just be. Even though Elise was technically her mother's employee, at this point, nearly a decade in, Elise had become like a sister to Jae'cy, having been on both family and solo trips with her. So the love was real and mutual.

But Jae'cy wasn't lovin' one thing about her that she was seeing right now.

"What's it givin' you?" Elise (and Cori) exhibited the ridiculously big sunglasses Jae'cy's way.

"Definitely no kind of VIP or backstage pass."

"*Daaaannng.* It's like that?" Elise affectedly deflated as Cori giggled. She placed the two pairs of frames rightfully back on the store rack where they *truly* belonged. "Don't get too cute 'cause who else can you be just as epically *unepic* with?"

Jae'cy only smirked as she turned back forward…and then, only then, the smirk fell from her face. Deflated. For real. For she was suddenly hit with the recollection of the only other person she could be just as casual, non-played up with…

*The one you didn't play yourself up to faster and deeper than you ever have with anyone else,* Jae'cy finally consciously admitted and chewed her inner cheek.

She moved on with Cori to the purse section. *As if I need any more of those…*

And halfway froze at a new sight.

Right on the outside corner of the new clothes section, at the foot of a rack was what looked like a tattered device cable, a USB port end to it. As unexpected as it would sound, she'd know that cable anywhere, and not just based on the imprinted manufacturer's name on it. It looked familiar.

It looked like *her*—  **NOW.**

Suddenly, up came Elise's cell phone in Jae'cy's face from another gossip news IG profile.

"Well, the both of *y'all's* dynamic duo sure did make *this* epic, though, 'cause look," Elise groaned.

*I'm trying not to.* And Jae'cy really didn't want to, didn't want to look at Elise, specifically, didn't want to believe the incoming thought about her. Which is why she gave one last look at that cable on the ground, right by where Elise's foot had now planted. The cable that looked uncannily like the one belonging to her old DSLR camera of many years that she'd been looking for over a year now...*Beginning when I'd come over with it one day to my mom's because she wanted to grab some old photos of me, her, Cori, and some family functions on there, Elise.* She now looked at Elise, who looked vexed, glancing from the phone she had in her hand and in Jae'cy's face, although Jae'cy's face stared at her...*The same day I then came back later on from out with friends and asked you if you'd seen it...*Now, Elise was blinking curiously at her.

"All Imma say on all of this is...something about it just doesn't add up. She doesn't seem like that kind of chick. Granted, I've only known her for about two years, but—"

*And I'd like to think you aren't either, Elise. I've known you for longer. Much longer...*

Jae'cy's sudden thought stopped just as Elise's spoken one did because the latter had just spotted the USB cable on the ground.

"Oh—HERE it is!"

*Uh, yeah.* But Jae'cy' couldn't deny, as she watched Elise bend over to it, the relief she felt in her chest, to at least have *one* thing figured out right now in her life. *I knew it was mine...*

"Must've dropped out of my purse a minute ago, but glad it did so I remembered I brought it to give to you," Elise stated, picking the cable up. "Girl, now I see why you lost it! Crazy story—"

*Like everyone's had these past few days, so let's hear it.*

"I found it today, just as I was headed over to meet you. And guess where it was all this time?"

*I'm stumped. Enlighten me.*

"Right up under that big old potted plant just beside your mom's front door!" She handed the cable to Jae'cy. "Unfortunately, didn't see the hard drive it goes to, though. And trust me—"

...

"I looked! For a *minute*."

Elise was proud, smiling; Jae'cy was…up in the air. *Maybe I had left back out with it that day? But if so, then where was the hard drive?* She floated her eyes back up to Elise as she tucked the cord in her purse. *And why did you just now "find" the one of lesser significance (a cable could easily be replaced) and not the other (a hard drive with years of files couldn't)?*

Jae'cy decided to move her attention to the IG page on Elise's awaiting phone to see that it wasn't the HollyHall Pass this time. Oh, *nooo*. It *had* to be another one, always another one.

One that was worse: a highly controversial, long-running (and long lawsuit-laden) celebrity news source…that often times was factual (hence, the lawsuits). And Jae'cy just dazed at the post. There was a collage of wholly false, manipulated screenshotted emails and social media messages from Jae'cy to…

*Taylor?*

The first message was Jae'cy thanking Taylor for her Honest Bites commercial set assistance and hustle-mentality that was 'destined for greatness' (Jae'cy's indeed words). However, the other private communications never happened: Jae'cy's proposition to get Taylor more "set design leads" if she'd get Jae'cy more details *by any means necessary* about the weaknesses of: Arielle and Michi. Calling it "a…mutual sale. Kinda like a B2B."

And the gossip outlet's post caption strung the web altogether:

*Word on the street is—!*

There was much more that the caption had left to say; there were other prior slides in this post that, too, had more say. But Jae'cy had seen enough…for now. And also because, someone else had more to say—

"Ay!" boomed a man's voice.

"You only know what you're shown, right? That's all we ever know from anything. So, we can't really say anything too confidently. So, let's move on, maybe?" Jae'cy resolved to Elise as she released a purse (that she had unconsciously clenched) back onto the rack. The same couldn't be said about her tight jaw as she took ahold of Cori's hand and headed for the front of the store.

But whether or not she wanted to deny it, Jae'cy's Scorpio Sun was now activated and tinkering…

And so was Elise's Aries moon, to the tall, very broad-shouldered guy, mid-thirties, who'd recognized Jae'cy and came leering over. Made sense, she was, of course—

"Paula Young's daughter. Almost finer than her in person, too! I'm shocked. But I'm down to be your next sneaky link," he grossly insinuated with a just as tasteless smirk, chuckle. "Ay, but for real. Can I? Since you're takin' all kinds of applications now, right?"

"Back up, there's a whole child right here! Girl, let's get out of here," Elise now was the one who settled, reversing close up to Jae'cy and Cori and moving them subtly forward with her upper (5'4") body. "Before I become your back-up Robin and change DC to BC, and I ain't talkin' comics." Then she looked at the guy. "After saving the day and molly whopin' you and your friends."

Brick City had never lied, always right in the clutch like any good assistant. Even to the boss's daughter.

"You all live in Lala Land here so willingly, so long," Elise detoured from her short-lived attempt at the higher road (the Aries moon), looking back and shaking her head in pity at the guy as Jae'cy just kept her eyes, head, and feet (and Cori's guarded body) to the exit. "You can't ever tell what's real."

Then she continued to lead Jae'cy and Cori toward evacuation as the perpetrating guy called out. "So, what's the *newest* secret? You're her '*behind the scenes*' PR?" Based on the sneer that slithered up the guy's face as his eyes did the same between her and Jae'cy, he wasn't just implying business.

"Nah. Her front-and-center PR, one step away from returnin' you and your Fade to Black hairline *back* to your touchdown on a Gary, Indiana curb. 'Cause you know you can barely afford your Hollywood one-bedroom, let alone that iPhone." And Elise wasn't done yet. "*OR* that early male pattern baldness."

Jae'cy sourly smiled. Elise was more than a sniper; she was family. Jae'cy hoped…Someone you wanted on your team rather than against it. The guy tried to chuckle it off, affect a stumped scoff of confusion as all eyes now, even Boomers, joined the spectacle and smirked.

And that only further encouraged Elise's fire sign madness, now fully activated.

"P-R. You know? *Punt Receiver?*" Elise clarified mockingly followed by a chortle. "*Wooooooow.* You went big with those shoulders, and you *still* not impressin' girls—or guys—nor casting agents. So *GO home* to Indy and the Pee Wees you stood up six months ago."

Welp, that was probably going to get some choice words back from the media—as well as new material. But it wasn't like Jae'cy laying low would've killed any social media conversation so fast anyway. She *was*, of course, Paula Young's daughter. So Jae'cy couldn't help but to oddly simper as she headed onward past the onlookers. And furtively noting a few of them with similar expressions on their faces, eying Elise in awe, maybe even in support. Jae'cy figured she might have enough backup for the gossip commentary than she'd thought. *All thanks to Elise,* she inwardly joked—had to get amusement out of something these days.

And heaven knew that Jae'cy needed that right now as she reached one exodus and stepped out of the store's automatic sliding doors with Elise into what was next.

She knew Elise was right in her words even though she was still unsure about Elise herself: Wasn't really sure about anything right now to be honest. But what she did know was that she had the rest of the day ahead of her.

And that, as the outside received the two of them, she had to go solo into the next expedition...

♡ 42

STARTING WITH CORI skipping to an all-white, tinted Expedition just some time later.

Jae'cy loosely, distractedly, noted the little one hopping up into the backseat all by herself when just three months back she would've struggled. She was growing up fast…and also looking forward to the loads of Slushies, Doritos, and whatever else she'd sucker her daddy into this weekend.

Speaking of which, he came to a slow stop by foot beside Jae'cy at her front door as Cori shut her rear passenger seat in anticipation.

Jae'cy's eagerness wasn't nearly as high at his arrival, but she was at least happy for Cori getting a bit more precedence over his weekend plans as of right now. And knew this moment was also needed for another reason.

And likewise, AD noiselessly awaited Jae'cy's next move: a slide of her eyes to her hands and then an extension of the diamond ring.

AD sighed—but low, resounding, and, ultimately, accepting. Just like his own hand did the jewelry, right into his palm. He nodded measuredly, then clenched it and slipped it into his jeans.

"If first you don't succeed, *don't* try again?" AD summarized, completed the terms like a contract.

Jae'cy folded her arms across her chest, gazed…much like she did at the end of their first try at a relationship.

"Well, with the obvious answer to *that*," AD snickered low, dismal. "I just have one more question: When you gonna switch up the poker face? 'Cause it's evident at this point that I couldn't get you to. And it looks like she's strugglin' to after me."

Jae'cy pulled back her shoulders, tried to roll her eyes up to the sky but couldn't even make it to the top of the door frame.

She hated being in this seat, but in it, she was. "…I'm sorry," she proffered finally— but transported her eyes to her front door, just knowing a paparazzo was probably presently hiding in a bush somewhere. Paparazzi that his silly post had only encouraged.

"So, if you *WEREN'T* feelin' a bro, why was I told you'd want it without question?"

*HUH???* Jae'cy instantly cut her gaze back to him with a much more furtive, paired tremble in her mouth. Everyone knew about their rocky road and how she'd tried to take things slow, never one to rush into a complete 'yes' on things besides acting roles or a new recipe. Especially after she'd been left so vulnerable post-pregnancy, AD disappearing as soon as Cori had arrived. Giving Jae'cy yet another reason not to trust. Especially not him.

So...her supposedly wanting a ring from him? *A whole marriage??? With YOU just yet???*

"...Who was talkin' that?"

Now, AD sniggered with volume, with purpose, with feeling fully expressed.

Then he shook his head at her in both marked pity and bewilderment as Cori came skipping up to him, wrapping her arms around his leg.

"Why are we still here, Daddy?" Baby girl had hopped out of the car because she was ready to go. And now her bubbly smile was waning to prove it.

AD slid his eyes down to her, bent down, and scooped her up. "I don't even know. Good lookin' out, rida." He extended his fist.

And Cori pounded hers into it immediately and with pretty impressive force, which made AD rumble in a low but pure belly of a chuckle. "Cool...Looks like *we* not in miscommunication."

Jae'cy sighed inwardly.

"...Have a good time, baby," she somehow pulled out of herself for her little one.

AD slyly turned his head back at her over his shoulder as he carried Cori off and smirked. But it was an oddly pitying kind. "Nope, no miscommunication at all."

Jae'cy froze. Then he refocused forward, moving on, to his car. Jae'cy could only watch, mentally preoccupied with what he'd left her with, as he and Cori pulled on and away down the street.

*He'd repeated that for more than a passive-aggressive diss at me. Rather that was like it was irritably for me in another way...*Jae'cy ruminated as she slowly turned back to her front door. *Someone had given him false info...*

So much false info—that was about to be examined. Because she also hadn't forgotten about that USB cable at the store.


*So, back to this.* Jae'cy dazed more, right at her cell phone in her living room while she slowly scrolled. In her contacts...Her most recents...

Paula (*Will call her back in a sec, not quite ready for what she'd have to say.*)…

Elise (*Mm-hm. Need another minute before her, too.*)…

Breyah (*And especially her because her crazy tail will help me feel somewhat better.*)…

Elle DeBar—

She abruptly swiped onward, down the list. Stopping…

on Michi.

Could he have told AD some falsehoods? Like he'd told her that she'd contacted him for his "help' after her Honest Bites soft launch party because of some unknown car outside her house.

*But Michi doesn't talk to AD.*

Of course not. But she also knew, although he'd never stated it, that if ever given the opportunity, he'd try to make her his girl. And so, maybe he'd created an opportunity…

Therefore, there was only one way to find out if he was at least talking to the gossip mills…starting from the beginning: the first truly incriminating post.

She opened her Instagram app and went to that same raggedy IG post with the reveal of Arielle's IP address. *I know she's not your favorite, Michi. But hey, AD and the guys before that weren't either, so…*

She scrolled through the comments for anything that might pop out. Scrolled…stopped.

Her finger was hovering over a new commentator from an hour ago and the comment left by him (??? The person's avatar wasn't a man but was a sports team logo, so she generally assumed. Plus, the person's page, upon clicking on it, was private.):

*Oooo…it's getting weird Check this out*

At the end of that comment was a link…Jae'cy's finger selected, copied, and pasted it into her Internet browser's search bar.

And up came *that other gossip post she'd loosely looked at on Elise's phone…*

But this time, Jae'cy was going to view each slide, for each and every odd thing that might stand out to her. Had to be a reason it was called "weird."

The first slide showed side-by-side images: a selfie of herself and her friend/old co-star Timere two years ago on the set of the Florida suspense indie that gave her the Spirit Awards nomination. And next to that, screenshots of their DMs. *Doctored DMs* showing suggestive comments, which meant, according to the post's words on that slide, she'd "sneak-linked" right in front of AD with him, Arielle…

*…and Michi????*

This wasn't suspense. It was pretense, and it was full of plot holes that some of even her straight-to-YouTube career-beginning films could've done better. These social media claims were getting out of control, and so was the invasion.

But Timere revealed the truth in her next swipe in a screenshot of his own double-image IG post: holding a piece of paper up to the camera simply reading, "Don't believe da hype. J, me and MY GIRL stand by you." Then smiling with his girlfriend beside Jae'cy at her Spirit Awards afterparty. They were quite literally standing by her, everyone friendly, in friendly positioning. No crossed boundaries.

Jae'cy briefly pivoted to her phone messages, found Timere, and texted two words:

*Thank you*

And immediately back:

*I gotchu*

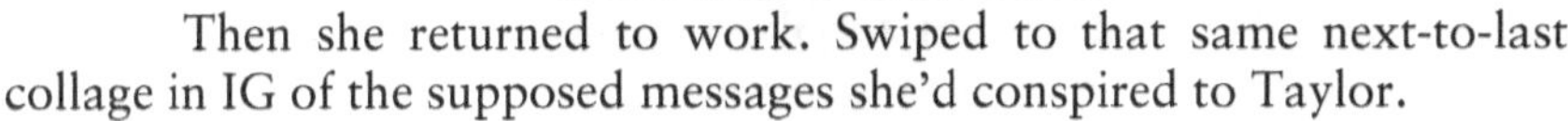


Then she returned to work. Swiped to that same next-to-last collage in IG of the supposed messages she'd conspired to Taylor.

And finally, the last slide's video clip of the YouTube news commentator, her "receipts," and her commentary that was also this gossip post's caption:

*Word on the street is the recent Trust actress actually struggles with trust (Thx preoccupied Mama 'n absent Papa!) but is all good with performance. ALLEGEDLY, beyond just playing undecided with Timere (although he passionately refutes the theory), she 'hired' Taylor to tempt both Arielle and Michi, her longtime bachelor/dance friend who has ALLEGEDLY wanted to be more than that for a while. Like plentyyyy of other guys (and girls have). All this to test out their loyalties all the way. All the while, proof to her on-again/off-again/now completely OFF slightly playboy boyfriend AD that she wasn't loyal herself. Dysfunctional Trust Issues (and celeb narcissism) 101.*

Whoever was crafting these fake DMs and emails knew what they were doing. The stories could easily dupe those not in the know due to how close the post's manufactured dialogue of hers sounded like things she'd actually say…

Jae'cy zeroed in on the comment section, since it appeared to be linking things across these gossip mills…

Scanning by date. Stopped, specifically, on one female commentator's words from two hours ago, hers being the very first words that had been made down there:

*Uh oh Dis rabbit hole gettin deeper y'all...*

Indeed. This post had published two hours ago, at the time she was at the store with Elise. The same time of the woman's comment. Jae'cy stared at that commentor's profile icon. *Hold up...*

Jae'cy went back to the IP address post. Back to the comments section. Scrolled.

Right around the *Oooo...it's getting weird Check this out* comment, there was that same female commentator. With a comment of her own:

*Miss Jae'cy is TRULY an actress, huh?*

And either she was *really* invested in all things celeb gossip with uncanny timing (and plenty of free time) *or* it was someone with a motive, an emotional one.

...She clicked on that female commentator. Examined her very, *very* (too) cute and ethnically ambiguous profile photo.

So much so that even with only five posts, her 500K followers and two million followings would make sense to the human eye. Tons of IG models had made it and earned "sponsors" off of a handful of Facetune-enhanced headshots...

But to the more penetrating eye, Jae'cy's eye, this woman's profile was looking pretty all right—pretty sketchy.

Jae'cy studied the measly five posts to find even more substantiative, meaty evidence, more oddities. There were not only no consistent people commenting, but not one of the commentators was an aunt, cousin, sister, friend. Not even an old college roommate. Jae'cy could tell because none of the comments were personable, no nicknames, inside jokes, girlfriend speech. Just nominal "follow me" posts, heart or eye emojis: flat-out spam or bots. Lastly, the "oldest" post was made three days ago...

...The same day the gossip mill saga began.

In the world of celebrity, it could be hard to pinpoint who, out of so many secret enemies, enviers, weird stalkers, this culprit could truly be. But given Jae'cy's awareness of her trust issues, the only one she could logically think of that would be this familiar with her external expression, manner of speech, and internal expression, her fears, and could've felt slighted in any way would be...one who criticized those trust issues.

And right now, that biggest Achilles heel, fear was about to her biggest strength, justifiable.

Just *one* more part of the investigation to complete...


*2. 8...*

Jae'cy, thanks to her actress-benefiting strong memory, recalled the glimpse of Arielle's VPN details when she'd snatched her laptop and turned the VPN network off to see the laptop's real IP address. But today, her focus was the VPN IP address, since Arielle always had that turned on. She inputted that address into a VPN IP address detection site on her laptop. Her Auntie Loren, an IT professor, had randomly prated about this type of site in the past like she did about other computer things that most times went over Jae'cy's head...

But not this time.

On the site appeared a guesstimated geographic location of Arielle's VPN IP address in a downtown LA area. One that was a known zone for many hotels...

Including the one Arielle told her she'd be at this weekend—*if* the current events hadn't made her lose that opportunity.

Well, there was only one way to find out...

Jae'cy tightened up her jaw, tapped star sixty-nine on her phone keypad before entering the rest of a certain phone number. Then awaited...

"Freehand. Front desk."

"Can you connect me to Arielle Smith? Room twenty-four?"

"Can't do anything without *your* name." The hotel lobby receptionist definitely wasn't friendly yet not rousing either. But that was a good thing, a sign of possible unawareness. She had affected her best Midwestern tone, courtesy of cousins and aunties back in Missouri.

Jae'cy bit her lip in contemplation, inhaled. "Juliana..." *What was her last na—?*

A flash popped up suddenly in her mind, her memory coming in clutch once again. "Pullman."

Hold music streamed into her ear without so much as a customary introduction to it. And didn't have a long life.

"It looks like the guest is temporarily out of her room—"

Jae'cy held her breath, flared her nostrils, and continued staring down her laptop screen.

"*ACT*-ually...sorry, it looks like that guest *just* checked out."

Jae'cy eyed that twenty-five-mile map pin much closer. *So, why was the VPN still showing up in this area?*

Jae'cy fluttered lightly, released her breath. "...Thank you."

But she wasn't about to adjourn just yet, definitely not. She just needed to pause, take a moment to think.

Jae'cy cut her eyes down to her phone. *Let's try another one in the area then?* Well, "Arielle" and "Smith" were both fairly common names, right? *Maybe that other guest wasn't her, and she'd decided to go to another hotel for whatever reason...*

"InterContinental. How may I assist you?"

"Can you connect me to Arielle Smith, please?" Jae'cy rose in tone, putting her acting chops more fully to work than the last call. "I tried texting her for her room number again and...no response. And I don't remember it by heart. Sorry!" She even winced for extra effect.

"Let me see if we have that guest here..." The receptionist easily spoke his own lines, with not a hint of suspicion. "Can I get your name, please?"

"Juliana Pullman."

And back to on-hold music, but this time for a bit longer. Jae'cy stared down the location map pin like a jury member or a prosecutor on a witness...

"Sorry, we don't seem to have a guest here by that name. Are you sure you have the right hotel?"

Jae'cy fiddled her hands. She wasn't sure about anything right now. "I guess not...thank you."

Jae'cy ended the call and resumed her study of the website location marker.

The next moment, she squinted.

Right there on-screen, she just noticed some wording by the location map: The estimated location refreshed every minute. That would mean that she *could* follow the geolocation pin to match Arielle's departing route from the hotel.

So, she did just that, a refresh of the page.

And *yet,* when the page, map reappeared, the pin was still in the *same exact* spot.

*So.* Jae'cy started to shape the presently slim discoveries into something with body. Perhaps this site was wonky with its location estimation. Perhaps Arielle's laptop (and the turned-on VPN on it) was still at Freehand, if she had accidentally left her laptop there or had it stolen (both highly improbable since Arielle kept her laptop on her like people did their phones). Or the site was telling a truth that Jae'cy just couldn't yet see...

...or didn't want to see.

She swallowed, eyes back on her iPhone...No, she *was* tryna see something real quick, to double-check. She dialed quickly.

*RING.*

*RING.*

*RI—*

"Uh-oh, hold on. Let me check for pigs outside. You actually, *finally* read it all?!" the woman on the other end playfully instigated.

Jae'cy sure wished that the rest of the instigations going around could be just as playful, could be about IT training guides rather than social media defamation.

"Hey, Auntie. Quick ques—"

"Me first," Loren interjected. "Are you okay?"

Jae'cy had to just bite her lip a moment before immediately speaking again. "...Can someone steal another person's VPN access?"

"Mm-kay...so you *have* been listenin' to your auntie. *And* now you've read my mind regarding this mess. What you're talking about is when someone installs malicious software on a device. A big, bad one is a keylogger that records *everything* you do, including your logins. And yes, within that, VPN info can be in the mix. And from there, they route their computer activity through that person's IP address, using it as a proxy server, which means—Hope I haven't lost you yet!" Loren pivoted for a vibe-boosting chuckle.

Jae'cy gave a low laugh back.

"So, *yes*. It means that all of the activity a schemer does will show up as coming from that person's device, to do nasty things at the expense of someone else. And honey, a schemer has been *real* nasty, okay?"

Jae'cy chuckled once again, but shakily.

"Call me if you need me, Jae Bae, hear?"

Jae'cy's mind trailed back to the one piece of a lead that had been surfacing in her mind before calling her aunt: recalling how Arielle and Breyah had computer-shared at Honest Bites once. She was perhaps not the only good actress around these parts. An infiltrator, whomever it was, was clearly lurking around.

And in order to be one, you had to be invited into someone's circle.

Or have been there for a long, long while. Trusted.

Back to her phone. And she waited for the hotel to answer again. The hotel known as...

"Freehand."

Jae'cy toyed the loose fabric of her shirt, its hanging fringe on one sleeve. "Yes...can you connect me to Ms. Breyah Wilkinson's room, please?" she inquired in the best British dialect she could muster. Breyah often used this hotel for client gigs, celeb fittings for events and such, ever since moving to San Diego last month...

Keeping up her act, Jae'cy affected a bashful, apologetic chuckle. "I forgot the room number, so sorry."

"Let me see…Your name, please?"

Jae'cy stood up from her kitchen counter stool and peered out her window blinds, for some kind of hodgepodge of words that could work…Just in time, a taxi passed bearing a portable billboard of a current local entertainment show of a vaudeville performer:

*Ed 'Swords' Vandenelzen*

"Vanda…Edwards." *Please work.*

"One moment."

She was a bit preoccupied, but if she heard this milieu of clarinets and piano keys *one* more ti—

"Sorry, but…" the receptionist returned.

Jae'cy started to sigh, both disappointed…and relieved.

"That guest is momentarily away from her room. Would you like to leave a message?"

Jae'cy froze, then pursed her lips tight. And just dazed at the location pin, feeling her eyes glaze over. She couldn't stonewall this one: She was hurt.

"Ma'am?" The front desk *had* to be growing suspicious by now.

Well, that made two of them. Jae'cy hung up. More like tapped so hard on that red button on her phone screen that she felt the dull pound of her assaulting fingertip after the fire in her veins cooled down.

In which time, she'd set up a new email account on her cell phone.

Now she had to meet someone, to present all of today's discoveries.…

The final dial. She brought the phone up to her ear. And then…

"Hey, what's your schedule like? Have time for a quick weekend trip this way? Move our meeting up with some drinks and *ninety*-degree, not eighty-degree, sun?"

♡ 43

BREYAH SASHAYED OVER WITH A FULL SERVING OF SUNNY-SIDE UP IN SHADED GLASSES, apricot eye shadow, and matching highlighted extensions.

Jae'cy looked up from her menu as Breyah continued her stroll down the host of restaurant tables to her own, tucked into a corner. She dipped down into arrival with her trademark smirk that Jae'cy always told her looked like she knew something you didn't...Like that time she hid the last free samplers for herself at Paula's fragrance launch...

...*Or* at the mall years back when she'd stashed a last of the lot Birkin bag in a cart behind Jae'cy's "granny purse," her first professional gig purchase after a cameo in Paula's music video (booked *her*self much to Paula's hard-earned surprise). Jae'cy figured if it wasn't broke, don't fix it, and Breyah figured if the Birkin wasn't detectable, don't tell and instead show the cashier. *So* Breyah.

Jae'cy sipped the lemon-wedged ice water as Breyah pushed her shades up onto her forehead, surveying Jae'cy's natural finished face and straightened hair, the inborn thickness of it rivaling a lace-front in all of its voluminous, shiny glory. But a feeble dimness in Jae'cy's eyes contrasted it.

Breyah beamed nonetheless. "*Ooh,* look at you!"

She was always that obstinately spirited, spunky friend, Jae'cy reflected as she lowered her glass and nudged up her eyebrows on behalf of her mouth that couldn't quite do the same. Always seeing that Aries fire in Breyah, but possibly blind to some other kind of smoke, ill will, within her because of it...

Breyah lowered her grin just a little. Then her eyebrows twitched. "Girl, have you been sleeping?"

"With a six-year-old who's going on *twenty*-six yet still learning how to not wet the bed or throw a tantrum over homework, I'm basically immune to that," Jae'cy stated, mentally flashing back to last night. The long twilight as she traveled the Internet webs, weaving different discoveries together.

But Jae'cy didn't mention any of that. For the first time, she wasn't speaking girl talk. Today was a conversation not between two girls but between two women. Business.

Jae'cy cocked open her laptop and unlocked it, moving to her business email inbox.

"Mommy, Cee-Cee's just tryna help get your mind off what's happenin'. That's *GOOD!*" Breyah chuckled.

Jae'cy paused there a second. Breyah blinked, grinned a bit wider...and shakier.

*Good.*

"Right now, I gotta focus," Jae'cy lightly, casually, countered as she began to head for the restroom.

"*Yesss.* Business!" Breyah perched up, already whipping out her own laptop and pulling up her own inbox.

*Business.* "Yeah, go ahead and get it going, miss." Jae'cy nodded at her laptop, for Breyah to prep her look-book of the different proposed styles she was designing for Jae'cy's upcoming photoshoot.

Breyah leaned her body immediately over the table, picking up Jae'cy's external hard drive (no, not her beloved old one) for the lookbook file dumping. "Yes, ma'am. You and your 'gotta drive miles to drop hella kilobytes into your *direct* drive because you're paranoid' behind."

"You know it," Jae'cy confirmed nonchalantly, trekking further away from the table. *But as we can both see, with all of my emails and DMs now out on front street, my trust issues are valid—technology not exempt...*

As she made her way back down the aisle of tables and diners, Breyah sprung her head up from Jae'cy's laptop. Then, milliseconds later, gave a slow, flamboyant finger snap. The two actions in the sequence looked disjointed, but Breyah's typical bombastic vocality glued it together.

"Boom, done just like *that*," she boasted. Then she began to swerve the laptop back Jae'cy's way with, it looked from a distance, all kinds of fashion idea thumbnails. "*NOW*...say it ain't the 'knit *all-BLACK* turtleneck, low rope braid with the hoops, and all things achromatic classic' for you. Too bad you don't sing, girl, or I coulda hooked you up even better than Paula."

"One sec," Jae'cy said. But as she settled back into her seat, she didn't look at what was more than likely an exceptional Sade nod for her upcoming Black fashion homage magazine feature. "Just have to check some logistics for the café..."

Even from her slightly bowed head, she could feel Breyah's sudden attention. She must've now been concerned by (not necessarily *about*) Jae'cy's still pretty soporific, toneless behavior.

Jae'cy figured, as she tapped on her new email account on her phone under their table, that Breyah was befuddled.

"You can just sit over there and look cute, admire your work some more, or whateva," Jae'cy diverted...as she spotted an email that had just landed in her inbox:

*Your Recordings Request*

"Nope, Quiet Storm. Now *I'm* going to the ladies room real quick."

With Breyah temporarily gone, Jae'cy tapped on the email on her phone. A group of attached screenshots...and one video attachment. She clicked on it.

Instantly, up came her business email inbox, how her screen had appeared when she'd turned her laptop to Breyah just before stepping away. The tactic had worked: she'd temporarily left to leave Breyah to do her thing...

...and do it she had, all soon-to-be evidenced by the pointer arrow's clicks to various emails, Internet pages, and hard drive files on the video as from the reported time of five minutes ago when Breyah had been on her laptop. Yes, in addition to the other things last night, Jae'cy had also installed a keylogger on her laptop, another Aunt Loren discovery that recorded all keystrokes and movements on computers. The new email account was the confidential place for today's recording. And now, the recording played out all of Breyah's actions:

Breyah inserted a USB drive, judging by the notification pop-up that flashed in the bottom right corner. *Okay, not too sketch*, Jae'cy judged as she watched, because Breyah had to deliver files. Then, she inserted Jae'cy's own newly bought USB drive, followed by both drive windows sharing the screen side-by-side. She highlighted file thumbnails of fashion designs, dragged, and released them into Jae'cy's drive. Okay, still expected. Jae'cy liked to keep things on her external drive, so as to keep her computer's internal storage freed up, and so, she'd asked Breyah to do as such.

Then Breyah minimized both drive windows, pulled up a new browser window: incognito. *Now*, she was getting somewhere. Right into Google Drive.

*Breyah never uses Drive, only iCloud*, Jae'cy remembered. Even more, there was no need to open up *any* window incognito if she'd already ported the files from her USB drive into Jae'cy's.

Next, Breyah entered a login that was clearly not a normal one. (*"hotgurl007"...really?*). Then all kinds of files appeared...

An old college paper, oddly enough on food chemistry...a random photo of the great Diahann Carroll (sure, why not?)...a résumé from 2010. None of which Jae'cy had saved directly on her computer *or* current USB drive…but all of which were *too* identical to her file names of the past…file names that she *did* have on her old external drive.

The drive that had been missing for the past year and some change, with only the tattered cable back in her possession.

Jae'cy didn't have much time to contemplate that as Breyah scrolled fast in the video recording, stopped, and pulled up candid photos: Arielle stepping out in a polo, a fitted cap, from the Luxe. A sunglasses-donning Jae'cy stepping out from the same in slim-cut, tapered pants tucked in open-toe booties, with the knit crop top.

The candid shots were the same exact ones that had appeared in The HollyHall Pass & their Hallway Monitor Friends' social pages.

Recollections flashed in Jae'cy's brain: A few times in the past year or two when she just *knew* she'd felt camera flashes, but not uninvited paparazzi or polite fan selfie requests. And one of those times was when she was leaving Honest Bites with Elise and…

Jae'cy gazed at Arielle outside of the Luxe…thinking about the small birthmark she had on her left temple that no one could see unless their own face was right up in hers, like hers had been when she first noticed it…at that very same hotel. And yeah, *this* shot, of *her* outside the Luxe, was another time she now recalled feeling that mysterious faint camera flash from afar, too. Camera flashes during the day…Breyah, the industry know-it-all, said it was the best time to use flash…

Jae'cy temporarily stepped out of her maze of thoughts as she watched Breyah get back to action in the recording: Another fast scroll back up, down, up, down. Breyah was searching for *something.* Going right past—*That clip of me with Mahogany!* Yep, it was the interview clip that had appeared on HollyHall Pass's IG.

Then Jae'cy watched Breyah, evidenced by the mouse icon's next movement and the subsequent new passing visuals onscreen, continue past all of the leaked and doctored messages that had appeared on social media, the latter of which were accompanied by matching InDesign or Paint files (Breyah did take graphic design classes back in high school)..
*So, just the whole library, huh? Just in case you wanted to dig back into these stories? Add to them?*

That included going past the screenshots of her real DMs with Timere and with Arielle.

Even past the fake and imposter DM screenshots…between "Taylor" and "Jae'cy"… "Arielle" saying okay to the real her to the Honest Bites location scouting and ice cream parlor invitation…from "Jae'cy" to Michi saying that she was giving Arielle a chance even though "she's awkward AF BUT also talented AF 😵"…then asking him to come over after her Honest Bites soft launch because of an odd car outside her house...*This explains all of those weird miscommunications. Why didn't I question it more?*

But before Jae'cy could answer that question, not to mention while periodically checking the direction of the bathroom..., she witnessed in the recording Breyah once again swiftly scrolling some more. Right past a clear nighttime photo of Arielle heading to a car outside of Jae'cy's house, Jae'cy standing at her doorway, and both in the clothes worn at her Honest Bites soft launch. *But she sho nuff still used that flash at night, that night, too, huh?* Jae'cy sourly smirked, flabbergasted by how long Breyah had been at work with this foolishness. It was painful to watch.

But what was even more painful was what came up next in the recording from moments ago. Breyah made another quick whip up the screen—but not quick enough that Jae'cy didn't catch one last file: a photo of Cori at what had to be six months. Jae'cy could tell by Cori's big 'fro that started blooming during that period. Jae'cy also knew that it had to be taken on her old DLSR camera from high school because she'd been too afraid to use her cell for pics at the time. Oh, the irony.

In the background of the photo was her *tattered* large external USB drive cable.

It had been the victim of Cori's terrible twos, when that former six-month-old could now move around and "play" with Mommy's coveted things. And that was when she realized one final, essential element about that photo: she'd never shared it on social media, which would've made it much easier for any random person to save it to their own devices. Instead, she had saved it to that beaten yet still sturdy external USB drive...that same drive she'd been missing for over a year...That same drive whose filenames she recalled just moments ago when she'd seen them pop up on the screen in the keylogger recording after Breyah opened that Google Drive account and the various files had looked like her own.

Even though the newer files, the leaked images, voyeuristic photos, and doctored conversations, were definitely not what had been on the old drive back before it went missing, she *knew* those other filenames. Breyah simply had just transferred all of those old drive files from one place to a backup, to this Google Drive stash, like a wire transfer to (wisely) eliminate a clear direct path to the person with the last possession: herself.

Breyah had taken her external hard drive.

And almost got away with its USB cable, too—but must've misplaced it outside of Paula's. Jae'cy revisited that fateful day in her head: She had ridden with Breyah to her mom's for Paula to watch Cori a few hours and for Paula to get some photos she wanted before Jae'cy and Breyah went to a day boat party. Then Breyah swung her back to

Paula's to pick up Cori and *for Breyah to quickly come in* and say hi to Paula as usual. Meanwhile, Jae'cy went into the den, where Elise was in a Zoom with Arielle...

Jae'cy swallowed...

"Are you ready to order, miss?" the returning waiter questioned.

But Jae'cy was too engrossed to look up, knowing her time was almost up. "Sorry, one more sec. Till my friend's back." *'Cause baby girl's about to learn her feeding frenzy is done.*

"Certainly," the voice stated, then withdrew.

Jae'cy stared at her phone, at the recording, observing the ultimate slay, the grand finale of what Breyah had done on her laptop:

The keylogger-recorded laptop screen now showed the Google Drive screen disappear. And up came a Gmail sign-in page—evident burner account based on the email address Breyah typed in—and the account's profile avatar: the same ethnically ambiguous woman from the IG fiasco.

Breyah started up an email, but Jae'cy recognized she didn't put any email address in the recipient line. So, obviously, it was something she was going to send later...after a little more thought (the best stories needed that). Then, sure enough, Jae'cy noted Breyah attach a file, reading *Sell with a Story: How to Capture Attention, Build Trust, and Close the Sale.* It was an e-book on Amazon that Jae'cy had downloaded three years ago and saved on her hard drive, when she still wasn't yet quite confident enough to begin Honest Bites.

The final nail in Breyah's coffin appeared in the email body:

*But this is what you HAVEN'T heard... Check the attachment. Looks like Jae'cy Carter has been pennin' the role to her own melodrama this whole time?! Doing the old desperate celeb trick: creating a saga for publicit*

Without finishing the message, the mouse pointer arrow, like a suspect fleeing the scene, sprinted to the Sign Out option of the Gmail burner account. Then pulled back up Jae'cy's new external USB drive's folder just before the video froze in conclusion.

As she gazed at it, Jae'cy knew Breyah's sudden rush was due to Jae'cy's return to this table.

*You know what? Lemme just...*Jae'cy sourly, angrily laughed to herself, exiting the keylogger recording on her cell phone with a quickness. She refused to give Breyah any further satisfaction, especially as Breyah was now making her way back to the table. Instead, Jae'cy went to the VPN IP lookup site on her phone, entered Arielle's VPN IP...and got the current use location in the geographic widget:

Just feet away. **CHECK THE END OF THIS CHAPTER.**

She trailed her eyes up as Breyah cluelessly tipped her head at Jae'cy's laptop screen and dramatically dropped down at the table. "Sorry, nature called! Shouldn't have done a seven-day juice cleanse that I just ended last night. THEN I got a client call. Soo...what's the verdict, trick?! And *dang!* A waiter hasn't come by *yet?*"

Jae'cy studied her quietly a second, then said, "You really think she did it?" She wanted to see how low Breyah could go right in front of her eyes just as memories flooded in her mind of the many times they'd playfully grinded at parties over their many years of friendship. *Ha...*Friendship.

Breyah's smile twitched but was resistant to fall. "I think it's not unheard of for *people like her—*"

Jae'cy subtly went tongue-in-cheek. *This girl...I have some thoughts about people like you.*

"Like, 'I see an exclusive opportunity I'd typically never be able to get my hands on, I'll take it,'" Breyah continued. "At least, that's *MY* take on it. What's your theory?"

"...That we can wrap this up."

"Everything okay?" Breyah asked, the smile sinking.

"Just have to go home and think some things over." Jae'cy stood up and vaguely detected a small, stiff rise of Breyah's chest and shoulders, and the slightest nervous smirk rising at the corner of Breyah's mouth. But just one final questioning. "...How come you didn't tell me you were already in town?"

Even given Breyah's pouchy cheekbones that always permanently made her look like a mischievous chipmunk hiding away forage, this smirk was...different. Like she hadn't concealed a chestnut or two, but the whole damn tree.

"Girl! You know I *stay* busy," Breyah retorted.

Jae'cy then nodded ever so faintly, with an internal resolve. A settling in that this was the end of their relationship, one of irreconcilable difference where one *was* too busy—busy being envious when the other was just trying to be a friend. This was why she never opened up too wide: just more opportunities for someone to take advantage...

Jae'cy sharply cut her eyes away from her inner dialogue, and this physical one. And with that, she walked away, feeling Breyah's gaze.


When she got home, she sat down at her own dining table, and typed out (in what else better way than technology) a verdict:

*At-Will Freelancer Partnership Termination*

And finally, with a *hard* click on her laptop's trackpad, delivered to the defendant that sentence.

And when she saw Breyah's name and number come up on her cell, she let it ring to silence. *All these years, Breyah? You'd been holding some type of feelings in after all these years?* Jae'cy grieved as she watched her screen fade to black. She was concerned about Breyah's mental state, but she'd done what she needed to do for right now.

And therefore, court was now adjourned with pure, quick delivery. But J Hovah didn't feel the performance was fully complete.

Her *biggest fan* wasn't there to witness it, and she wasn't talking the one who'd just lost fan club privileges…She was talking the one she hadn't talked to in many days. The one who *had* been honest to Jae'cy, every word.  Like she'd always known.

She found herself click to a page that she hadn't unfollowed: El*Word*smith.

And she wished she could've said to herself that the words there in the name were what her gaze fell on.

But that wouldn't have been honest.

♡ 44

DAYS LATER, SHE FELT EVEN MORE LIKE SOMETHING AKIN TO A STAN OR STALKER.

It happened without warning, just after she exited the top-floor elevator for the mixtape release party of a friend. In the elevator corridor, her ears were greeted by the Spinners' "Games People Play." Yes, she knew the song and the artist, thanks to Midwest summer backyard parties from Paula's roots. *DeBarge would be proud.* Jae'cy halted the thought with a stiffness.

"Cuh! I'm so glad you're bein' social *AND* a soldier against these games people are indeed playin'!"

*Juliana???* Jae'cy dipped behind an artificial plant, feeling like a mole that had invaded the trenches.

She peeked out to find Juliana leaving the restroom down at the other end of the elevator corridor, the side of the awaiting gathering…followed by Sinead…followed by Arielle.

Juliana was glancing back at Arielle. "I know you're happy about what Deejay Uncle Randy got goin' on right now instead of lettin' the younger generations, who this is for, have their party back."

Sudden quiet hit  Jae'cy's ears.

Jae'cy didn't know her fully by any means, but she did know that Juliana *always* talked. So this silence was sketchy…

"Okay…It might be the poorly mixed Cognac—or a *Maury* family plot twist in the makin'. But isn't *that*—?"

*Please don't let her see me. Pleeeease.* BUT why is *SHE HERE?!!! You've got to be kidding me.* Jae'cy wheeled around to the exit door beside her elevator, because she didn't have time to wait. .

And as she neared the door, she hoped that she'd been saved from Arielle's detection. Rushing down the four floors of stairs, she finally hit the pavement outside the venue, blinded by the August sun that struck her before she could pull down her shades.

"…You have a thing with getting confused around restroom hallways, I see. *Or* the old folks' music scared you off."

Jae'cy felt a shiver at the sound of the familiar voice, even in this sun. *Of course. She took the elevator while you took the stairs.* She turned around to the entrance to find Arielle—and her laptop peeking a bit out of her messenger bag.

Jae'cy had wanted to destress a bit after the social media fiasco, so she'd decided to come out to the party. Between Timere's public statement and her own, sent out earlier this morning, along with the email she'd sent Breyah, and sharing with her family, friends, and close business associates about her true character, this particular rumor mill wouldn't have any more fresh lies anytime soon. She could continue to just grow Honest Bites without money spent on a lawsuit. The biggest loss would be that Arielle would probably still not want to talk to her.

But now she wished she hadn't come out. Because it was also apparently a whole family affair...that included Juliana and Sinead, who must've been related somehow to her friend's DJ boyfriend (???!!). LA really was more like one degree of separation.

"...But in a minute..." Arielle segued, looked around the public outdoors that *currently* was shockingly empty. "The restroom hallway will be The *Hall* Pass," she notified sarcastically. Yet what came out of her mouth (and her hands) next was far from a joke. "And I've already made my starring role in it as 'The Hall Monitor.' 'Thief' would be two too many for a rookie like me."

And then, there appeared Jae'cy's clutch purse.

Indeed, it wasn't a punchline. It was a literal blow.

Jae'cy furtively nibbled on one of her inner cheeks as she took the item that she'd let slip out her grip somehow in the building as she'd booked it out of there.

..."Can I—?"

"Be my guest," Arielle discharged, tipping her head in the direction just behind a now-confused Jae'cy's shoulder...

...Noting an approaching athletically stacked girl in a tank and biker shorts, who then asked Jae'cy, "Cool with a photo op?"

Jae'cy and Arielle tensed up, at the girl and her lifted and ready cell phone. But then, Arielle turned away. "Nah."

"But she'll take one. She's *cool* with everything." And with that, Arielle was off down the curb.

Or not.

"JAE'CY!" A media reporter, the TMZ variety, rushed across the street with a big camera, swarming around and blocking the path to what appeared to be Arielle's navy Ford Expedition. "Arielle! Are you two...?"

"Why the hell are you facin' *ME?!!*"

Abruptly, the cameras, phones, and the bodies connected to them wavered from around Arielle, who thrust her arm in their general vicinity.

"You all know this is LA. This is probably just for her reel, and it has us all acting like *fools*. Now, go play THAT!" Then she slammed inside of her truck.

"DAMN!"

A passing guy shouted behind the cell phone screen of his BIGO LIVE broadcast he'd quickly started of Arielle zipping off.

"*Daaaaaaaamn*," the athletic girl chorused right along, wheeling her neck around to Jae'cy.

Jae'cy worked up enough energy to pull her eyes to the still-waiting cameras—then artfully dodged them, keeping control of the only thing she still could in this scenario, or ever: herself.

"Keep that crown up, queen!" the girl called as the paparazzo stepped in closer. Leaving Jae'cy to dip away into her car, with a sharp stride and stoic face.

"JAE'CY!"

"Ay, let her know what air is, homie. Social distancin'," yawned out a 6'4" security guard (whom Jae'cy had forgotten was there due to his cell phone-donning arrival then useless bystanding).

"ARE YOU GONNA TAKE IT TO COUR—?"

*Shut.*

Thankfully, her car was close, and the windows were tinted. She knew the Canon flash that had just barely bounced off her would be making its rounds, but it wouldn't be much to look at.

But just as she began to stick the key into the ignition, she paused for two things: the paparazzo slipping a wad of cash to the useless security guard. *Of course*, she snickered. A kickback for the informant who'd obviously filled him in about spotting her. Only in LA.

…And then, there came a slowly passing Ford Expedition in her peripheral. Navy.

Arielle. Who rolled down her window.

And so, she rolled down hers.

*Sigh.*

"Can I talk to you?"

It didn't matter who said it. Both wanted it.

But what came next went left.

Literally. Jae'cy rolled her eyes, rolled her windows back up, and then sharply turned her Range Rover's wheels left and vroomed right on by Arielle.

*Oh, NOW she wants to wheel back around here.* Jae'cy sneered, but the sound was lacking a bit, as she continued down the street. Frankly, not even sure what street she really was on right now anymore…*or where I'm even going??*

**KEELA BUFORD**

She flared her nostrils hard as she busted a U-turn to go back to her side of town. She was hot because she was hurt. But something about that Scorpio/Sadge mix of ego…

*Nah, she left. Obviously, not worth her time.* This queen smirked harshly.

*So, now, I just beat her to it.* And then, the feeling faded…just as fast as this "victory" had.

Because this "queen" didn't feel victorious, like she won anything. If *anything*, she just lost another diamond on her throne. What she wanted wasn't as easy to come by: internal assurance. That being the true sign of a queen—because before one could properly, rightfully oversee and maintain *her* court, her land, she had to do so first within her inner domicile.

♡ **45**

*WHY ISN'T THIS WORKING?!*

ARIELLE punched the Bluetooth button in her Expedition. She was upset, and her playlist wasn't helping to pacify her.

*WHYYYY was she there? Of all the places in LA, she had to be THERE????*

*I KNEW I should've stayed at the hotel and only emerged for tomorrow's third day of the workshop!*

*Or maybe…Juliana planned—*

Arielle slammed on the brakes at the red light, but before she could dial up Juliana to give her a piece of her mind, Juliana beat her to it with a series of incoming texts:

*A goodbye woulda been nice???*
*Especially cus that woulda been unc's cue*
*to finally turn off that old ass music*

*But GIRL was that really HER?!*
*I told you LA ain't that big*

Arielle was determining if Juliana was guilty of subterfuge when in came a new messenger:

"Marlon." Siri stated the name aloud as Arielle looked at her digital display and saw his incoming WhatsApp call.

*So my Spotify is out of order but more human interaction is on the Bluetooth menu?!*

Arielle grinned sourly as she stared at the traffic light. She knew she better answer it. But even more, she knew she wanted to answer it. A piece of home was just what she needed.

"I accept," Arielle instructed Siri.

Marlon got right to the point, with a sober gaze at her face as his own appeared on the dash display. He was sitting stationary in a freight truck, work gear on, which meant he must've been on break. "How ya holdin' up?"

As Arielle pressed the gas pedal at the change of the light, she inhaled tightly.

"I ain't heard you go that high in tone since that time I broke your favorite CD player back when we both were still living at Ma's," Marlon continued for her, commenting on her "grand exit" just seconds ago.

"Yeah, well. I wish all of this was just over a CD player," Arielle finally responded.

Marlon chuckled. A temporary lull in the early afternoon traffic allowed her to peek at him on her dashboard: his smile rescinded and a serious gaze returned. *Oh boy...*

"The only other time I've seen you be so passionate is when you were sneakin' through my music stacks back in the day. Just around the time that Dad—"

Arielle cut her gaze to the road, back to him, then back ahead as the car in front of her made a sudden stop. She was shocked that Marlon knew all of this time. But the most jarring thing was the mention of—

"Remember what Ma said? That whole unrest thing—or whatever poetry she be pullin' out that you got from her. But you know what I'm sayin'. After Dad, she was...cool."

Arielle gripped her steering wheel.

"She had to be for us. But it still impacted us."

Arielle was suddenly more on-edge than when she'd left Jae'cy, redirecting her attention to the moving traffic. But she still heard him...

"After Dad left, I figured I'd do the same in all of my relationships. Like father, like son, even if he wasn't around. I figured it was in the genes." Marlon faintly chuckled. "So when my time finally came, to be a family man, a dad. Latrina has Jada, and a month later, I was *out.* Because I was scared."

Arielle peeked at Marlon, looking right back at her.

"Scared to be hurt, EQUALLY scared to be the one *to* hurt, and almost made both happen anyway. But luckily, Trina gave me another chance. Or more like she gave me the opportunity to give myself another chance. I don't think any of us give ourselves that enough."

Marlon had never openly expressed this to her, but across gender, across age, their shared vulnerability was the same—and their hopes that they'd meet someone to help them bravely revisit it and heal it. *But...*

"You have to give yourself another chance, sis," Marlon finished Arielle's thought. "In whatever type of way that means to you, you know, as a woman. Or you might lose it for good: the passion, the fun, the love. Ight?"

Arielle had hit another pause in traffic. *So you might as well look over...*

Marlon's countenance was all the way locked in on hers, clearly a sincere need for her to respond.

"My big head just nodded."

Marlon slowly rose in a new longer, fuller laugh; Arielle weakly joined, meeting him there. *Because everything else is up in the air right now.*

"Well, gotta get back to my shift," Marlon imparted. And with that, Marlon hit Arielle with the peace sign and was out, his face disappearing. Leaving Arielle with herself, her process.

And even as the cars began moving once again, her mind was still caught in traffic, a lineup of thoughts.

She'd tried. She was upset, but in the midst of that, she'd tried. Like she had so many tries before. *So, yeah, I did leave. Because I was pissed! And I could go to her house and—ha—TRY again, but she kicked me out, right? Ma said to give her time, and now HE'S saying give myself another chance.*

Arielle cut hard onto a new street.

*So how about this? I'm gonna give myself a chance to calm the hell down and to give her and her purse ALL the time in the world.*

And the next instant, she felt her foot let up on the gas pedal.

*Maybe then she'll have a chance to see how many chances I gave.*

♡ 46

JAE'CY CURLED UP ON PAULA'S DEN COUCH across from her sweeping mother, now a half-hour later. She couldn't stop replaying the whole scene: Arielle initially whizzing off like the speed of light.

Paula brought her broom to a stop. Peered over. "She's just hurt *and* a newbie to this world. Never a good combo. Speakin' hurt like we all sometimes do, but they'll be a whole new slew for the media to feed on any day now, okay? Some will even pay the hounds for it for relevancy."

She was right, once again. In a day or two, other Hollywood personalities' DUI accidents and mugshots, baby momma drama, or controversial yet attention-grabbing social posts would be laid out on the computer and cell phone screens. Fame's trash cycle.

"And with that, we move on." Just like Paula did.

And Jae'cy peeked as her mom went back to sweeping what didn't need to be swept any longer—doing it a bit slower this time around.

*She's not gonna push…but she's waiting, Jae'cy.*

"I've moved on, too." For the first time in the conversation, Jae'cy made eye contact.

Paula peered over, placed a hand on the hip, all ears. "So, you're lettin' her go?"

Jae'cy bit her inner cheek, ruminating… "Which one?"

Paula crossed her eyebrows, clearly now truly confused but awaiting more details. Jae'cy cut her eyes away, inhaled. "Breyah's tried to re-follow me on Instagram and all of that. After I ended our business relationship…amongst other things. Be-*cause* of Instagram," Jae'cy sourly smiled. "And yeah, that means she's the latest addition to my list of subtractions," she confided low. "But that one makes sense."

"*She's* spread all of this," Paula stated. But by her age, was anything truly that surprising anymore? "Well…" She seemed to pat the floor with the broom now, like a roundabout, elusive pat to Jae'cy's arm from afar. "That's life."

Yep, another truth. A cold, hard one.

"I hate that that's the case. Her fire, I always loved it… And, you know, I've also been fooled more times than I'd care to admit," Paula confessed. "Jealousy makes people do crazy things."

"How'd you come out of it?"

Paula eyed Jae'cy out of one eye, before redirecting her gaze to the floor. "I stopped sellin' myself short. And Mister Kadeem Jackson puttin' me in my place during our very first training session also helped. Told me in so many words that my stomach was unacceptable for someone who used her diaphragm for a career. So I told *HIM* that me and my momma pouch had gained three Grammys and two Soul Train awards just fine. And *then* that's when *he* said, 'And you woulda had three *more* Grammys if you'd been workin' your instrument in a gym on a routine basis.'"

Jae'cy chuckled at Paula's tale of her and her boyfriend's direct and highly communicative start to their still direct and highly communicative relationship. But at hearing about people being direct and communicative, Jae'cy felt herself cower a bit into the couch...and not exactly over her and Breyah.

Paula's humorous scowl helped to lift Jae'cy back up. Paula looked pissed off all over again at the memory.

"But I heard him—of course, with an attitude at first," Paula admitted. "But then, with acknowledgment that I had to remove *all* nonsense from my life, including my track record with partners who didn't challenge me to challenge myself."

"So...never gonna judge someone getting rid of nonsense in their life," Paula ended. And Jae'cy peeped it, something that was hard to find from her: approval, even if it came out a bit cloaked. *Finally.*

Jae'cy twitched on a faint smile, and Paula let loose a sly smirk. In that one expression, one line, all of that was known.

But of course...

"*SO.* Back to my question."

Jae'cy rolled her eyes wearily.

"You said she came back around, so why'd YOU then decide to go?"

"Because I was mad."

"And? You both were. And you both were there, might as well finish the interaction."

"I did," Jae'cy snickered.

"By leaving."

"Mm-*hm.* Getting rid of nonsense." Jae'cy tugged at the fringe of one pillow.

Paula chuckled. Long, full. For the nonsense. Jae'cy felt herself burning all over again...but also fluttering. "...She didn't stop to talk when I asked her to."

"Has she ever done that before?"

Jae'cy quieted. Knew the truth and where this was going—even at the key moment when Arielle should've rightfully moved on, after Jae'cy's "just friends" excuse, she'd come back that very same night to make Jae'cy burn and flutter. When Jae'cy asked.

"And so, you're mad because, for the *first* time, she didn't do something *you* wanted her to do."

Jae'cy really silenced then.

"You've been like that since a kid. And being the *only* kid didn't help. Wanting what you want, and most times, I admit, getting it because I spoiled you."

*Yeah, that was the least you could do, not being here.*

"I saw how your face changed when she showed up at that party the other night. The same way it looked when you'd get a clarinet here, a pair of ballet shoes there...to only fall out of love with it in a few months."

Jae'cy started to feel herself check out a bit. *Like I always have to do...Guess the seconds before WERE too good to be true.*

"However, you're grown now. And grown women have to make grown decisions and stand by them. Not make a sudden move just because they feel some type of way."

At that moment, something compelled Jae'cy to try something new. She sullenly squinted. "...Do you always have to do that?"

Paula slowed, looked back. "What?"

"Always expecting that I won't commit to something."

"Well, if history shows you something..." Paula scoffed a bit.

"Yeah...it has," Jae'cy repeated...then averred. "I saw how Grandma sometimes would talk less nurturing and more 'real' to you and Auntie Loren..."

Paula went quiet, still retaining a held face but much too still. Too consciously self-monitoring. Not showing her cards, her pain. *Hunh, like mother, like daughter.* Arielle remembered the Everlasting Young red carpet interviewer's accurate call.

"And then, as I became a teenager, how you started talking to me." Jae'cy squinted tighter. "And I bet that's why you two never wanted to take recipes from her, too close to home."

Paula waved her off. And Jae'cy only sustained.

"But she was from a different time, a time where women of our kind had to be tougher on themselves and their kids to make it. And look..." She pointed to the fancy diamond-encrusted chandelier, the spacious room. And Paula peeped them.

"You made it, Ma. So, why can't you celebrate that and celebrate me? As I do the same?"

Jae'cy's mouth trembled, and then Paula's own did ever so slightly just before she turned her head.

"...We'll see..."

"The café has boomed, Ma. Much more than I predicted and so quickly. More and more customers by the day and media coming in to interview. And—"

"Exactly. It's still something on the uptrend: your zest for it included. But what's gonna happen once it reaches a certain, inevitable statis for a minute? Or even more, a possible dip?" Paula snickered hard. But it wasn't in mockery; it was heard in the slight crack of her voice. "Will *YOU dip?*"

Jae'cy fluttered, teary...and so was Paula.

"You don't stand by anything when it calls on you to be a bit bare and still boldly move, Jae'cy. And that's not on me. *That's*—" Paula emphasized, pointed at her. "On you."

"But it has to be on you, too. As my *mom*, right?" Jae'cy shifted into recalls of her distant and not-so-distant past. "'Are you going to pursue music like your mother?' 'Hey, Paula's daughter.' 'She think she's cute *like* her momma.'"

Paula took to folding her arms.

"By my teens, I was being judged, compared more than the freshman year high school electives I was deciding on, let alone what I wanted to do for a career after it."

"Even more reason to be your own woman," Paula countered without pause. "That's what got me through the many different stories people were tellin' about me when you and I first got to this city, you on my hip. 'She's stealing so-and-so's man for his connections to producers. She's sleeping with the producers because how *else* could she have blown up so quick?' So, I've had my woes—"

"Okay, but right now, Ma, I'm talking about ME!"

Paula quieted.

So Jae'cy continued, panting even a bit through her louder outcry. "Have you ever thought that maybe I've never trusted myself enough, *anything* enough because I've always been living up under you? Under your shine and your expectations for me *to* shine?...But so long as it wasn't more than you?" Jae'cy narrowed her glint, shining mad gander, and her trembling mouth at Paula.

And Paula rubbed her neck instantly, reflexively, like a truth target had literally just pierced her, and she couldn't ignore it.

"How can I ever stand on *that*?"

As Jae'cy awaited some kind of response, Paula still was quiet, no follow-up tough guidance per usual, no scoff, nothing. The silence was so loud. *Woah, that's a first. Nothing to say, argue, this time?*

"...When my mother was in that hospice bed at Bobby's, the last words I had spoken to her were 'Why didn't you leave Daddy when he'd finally gambled all the savings away? Or even months after he unexpectedly collapsed? You could've come and stayed with me.'"

"And like I knew she would, she said what so many other *strong*, proud women from *that* time did: 'I stand by my vows. That's what you do when you have kids.'…And she did. She *stayed*. Stayed in Saint Louis," Paula clicked her tongue, grinned sourly, but her squint into the distance sharply squeezed, like trying to capture an old memory through a cloudy lens, an old bittersweet taste…when maybe Paula had wanted *more*, Jae'cy observed. But all she could have was an old bittersweet taste—one very much unlike butterscotch…"Yep, stayed even after all those kids had moved out, on, gotten kids, standing by their own vows…"

Right then, Paula turned her head and her eyes purposefully, firmly on Jae'cy. "And so, I want the last words you speak to me on my last days to be 'I finally stood by *my* vow to myself.'" Paula studied Jae'cy. "Not turning. Not forever leaning, denying, and then secretly regretting…*Standing*."

Then she shifted her eyes away, rolled back her shoulders. "That's when nothing else from *anywhere* else but from *you* will matter. That's it, that's all…My momma duties are done for today." And with that, she turned to the deep hallway.

*Indeed.* Jae'cy sourly, dimly smiled down at the pillow she now realized she'd been holding in front of her. Shielding. Having started with Paula and ending with…

*Who?*

*When will it end?*

Almost like telepathy, Paula paused herself, just by Jae'cy on the couch. And suddenly, gently blinked.

"I called myself trying to right my unavailability by putting you in the best schools, everything you wanted to join. But still went about it the wrong way, because now, you're *still* having a temper tantrum."

Jae'cy flared her nostrils…but softly blinked herself. Again, Paula was right. Sometimes the truth, tough love hurt—everyone.

"Actually, the *BOTH* of you." Paula chuckled anew, free, lighter, less cutting and more sympathetic to these young souls still with so much life to live and learn. And love.

"I just want for you to realize that this isn't school degrees, spices, scripts, Jae'cy baby. This is a person. And if she's one you really care about, I'll tell you one thing, she doesn't like to play around. I know." Paula cocked up a brow for weight. "I've worked with her."

Jae'cy slowly rose.

"But just like jealousy makes you do crazy things, so does…"

Jae'cy pushed out a gust of air. "Yeah."

And Paula finally released the broom to a wall then the messy bun atop her head, then gave a try at a smile, smoothing out a tendril of Jae'cy's hair. "Yeah."

And what was understood didn't need to be explained.

Both making a new move: exit stage left.

$\heartsuit$ **47**

*THE FACE OF THE EARTH.*

Those were the words at the top of the page Jae'cy was reading. An apocalyptic screenplay full of highlighted dialogue and action, it was her latest gig that had just wrapped up its first of a projected sixty days of filming. Even with the mess in her private life, her agent and team had proceeded like business as usual. The show must go on, etc.

Besides, this wasn't the first time, and definitely wouldn't be the last, that a star was a victim of gossip. And as the director imparted to her with a wink before heading to his own trailer a moment ago after a "good job": "You've generated publicity. That right there should've hooked you a larger weekly cut…including of the salami."

The set's catered deli sandwiches *should've* been from Honest Bites, Jae'cy noted before stepping foot into the temporary stillness of the day's wrap-up shutdown. Temporary falls off the face of the Earth.

Things were basically back to normal: the most tantalizing paparazzi shots being filling up at a gas station or exiting Target. Placing down her script, as she began to remove her elite character's jewelry for her own more laidback medium hoops, there was a knock on her trailer door.

"Come in."

The door opened. Jae'cy casually looked over, then cracked a smirk.

Paula virtually never came to her sets, much too busy with her own stuff. Yet, here her mother was, even though Cori was her running buddy for the next two days as Jae'cy had back-to-back filming. Jae'cy quickly deduced that her little one was hanging with Elise in Paula's waiting car. But what she couldn't figure out was…

"Why am I here, right?" Paula got to it, not even sitting down. "This Saturday. Clear your schedule. Seven-thirty sharp. Dinner first, *then* conversation. Capri's."

Jae'cy temporarily lapsed…then rolled her eyes as she swapped her heels for Reeboks. "Stop playin'. Why are you *really* here, lady?"

"You're welcome." Paula held back a grin. "Love you, too." And with that, she stepped right on down the trailer steps and right back out the door.

Oh, she was *serious* serious…

Jae'cy gazed at the door, one sneaker in hand; she had gone stationary in disbelief but also stunned gratitude. Then she looked to her mirror and stared. The moment she'd wanted for the longest had finally arrived: meeting one of the culinary wizards she respected the most.

So, how come she didn't feel a smile trekking as wide across her face as she'd always imagined?

♡ 48

SHE COVERTLY FIDDLED HER HANDS, seeing the dim-lit restaurant for the first time ever in-person. Things always looked larger onscreen. She guesstimated that it followed the rule of thumb she had learned about the restaurant industry over the course of Honest Bites' conception: easily more than twelve square feet of space for every customer chair.

It wasn't overwhelmingly expansive, and the warm colors of the wall trimmings, Brazilian metal, and untreated wood art, she felt, added to its grounded feel. A relatable intimacy mixed with the cultured vibe that she had admired from afar.

Now, Jae'cy would do so face-to-face, sitting with the man *himself* to pick his brain a little. That was if she had the courag—

No, she would. She would. She was here now, no turning back.

"Carter, Jae'cy?" the hostess greeted with a polite smile and nod to the wider dining space that…didn't have a lot of people. That was a bit odd, given how popular this place was.

But Jae'cy was also happy about the quiet and figured her mom had arranged it. Just a few mostly older and foreign tourists, who provided her reassurance that they couldn't care less about her waning drama.

And then, she tallied a final head as she followed the hostess past the front-of-house kitchen: a slim, tall goateed man in chef uniform. The man himself.

Capri greeted her with a quick nod and smile from the cooking pit. "I know you want my advice, and here's tip one: give the craziest thing you see on that menu a try. Then we'll talk!" He returned his attention to the veggie sauté he appeared to have going on. Looked good, even from a distance.

Jae'cy timorously smiled then continued behind the hostess in the quiet space, strolling closer and closer to the dark rear of the restaurant— presumably to ensure Capri's comfort in conversing with her after she ate.

As the hostess came to a stop at a booth against a wall and wheeled around to her, she now clearly discerned an image just four feet in front of her: Arielle, head bent and swiftly texting on her cell phone.

"Here you are!"

Arielle lifted her head at the hostess' announcement, casually enough that Jae'cy knew she hadn't registered her presence yet…and that she wasn't expecting it.

Much like Jae'cy hadn't.

As the hostess twitchily moved her smile from Jae'cy's tightening jaw to the wryly grinning Arielle, Jae'cy had her notion confirmed. This was planned, but not by them.

Arielle remained silent, trailing her eyes down Jae'cy's collared sage pantsuit in a way that made Jae'cy quiver just the slightest.

Jae'cy sharply cut her head away from the investigation as the hostess flapped a menu awkwardly against one palm of her hand and tersely spread her smile. Then, gave a parting nod as she placed the menu on the table.

"A server will be back to get you all's requests, okay?"

Arielle blinked, turning to the hostess as she shot out a short, dry laugh. "No, actually…I'm supposed to be with another party?"

The hostess' smile became shaky as she shifted her eyes between the two diners in this reserved "party"—then pivoted around with a quickness. Out of the vicinity.

Jae'cy rolled her shoulders back discreetly, then her neck. Arielle subtly flared her nostrils as she looked glassily at the menu in front of her.

Seconds passed that felt like minutes. Neither Arielle nor Jae'cy could move their eyes or mouths.

"I have business here," Jae'cy insisted as she began to step up to the other side of the booth, directly across from Arielle, where the second of only two clear, awaiting plates rested.

"Business," Arielle proffered back. But judging by her glance at Jae'cy's sleek hair bun, all the way down to her manicured toes…

*It's obvious she wants to say something else.* Jae'cy noted it as she sat down. Then she gazed over, from Arielle's tactfully unbuttoned black satin shirt up to her ponytailed hair. *That darn ponytail…*

Jae'cy redirected her attention to her purse, setting it down beside her. *It's obvious I want to say something else, too. Actually, a couple of things…*She fixated openly on Arielle's face…while folding her arms. "So, what did you yell at the paparazzi now so they finally found some business of their own, too?"

Arielle snorted. "I see you haven't…unfollowed me yet. Unfriended? Or whatever it's called."

"Didn't want to add fuel to the fire." Jae'cy kept a poker face…but her eyelids seemed to ever so slightly twitch.

"And I'm not trying to be an arsonist now, too, so…" Arielle began jokingly, but it quickly puttered out. *Yeah, this ish isn't vibin' like it used to.…*

Although Jae'cy took to playing with the folded napkin, she wasn't playing with this moment any longer. *Since we're here...*"I just can't believe you'd help them drag on the gossip. Me secretly leaking out my own private conversations, claiming relationships, and then putting the blame on you? *Really?*" Jae'cy advanced.

*This is ridiculous. We're out here actin' like a couple. I did not step outside for this tonight...But damn,* Arielle noted, trailed down Jae'cy again even then, couldn't ignore her even with the red she was feeling inside. *She has the audacity to be looking this good.* And that just frustrated Arielle even more. "And I can't believe that *you'd* honestly believe I was the one leaking it to begin with.  Rumors? Especially on *social media?*"

"Why wouldn't I when I've only known you for...barely two years?"

"You've known someone else for what, fifteen?" Arielle countered. "And how'd that turn out?"

Jae'cy paused, then saw Arielle's face soften. "So, you knew or suspected all this time and, yet, never say anything...?"

"Why not? Isn't that what you always do?" *'Cause you know that you've always recognized Breyah's insecurities, too,* Arielle thought. *Anyone that demonstratively "loud" all of the time has to be hiding something quietly inside.*

Arielle dropped her gaze, wishing for someone or something, anything but this—but nothing was coming to save her. Her own inner kid had to fight. *Next round.*

"I *did* say something, you just didn't listen."

"You only stated that you couldn't believe it. You didn't say anything about—"

"You're *still* not listenin,'" Arielle said with a weary shake of her head. "So that's why I had to show you."

Jae'cy was confused, attention piqued. But she wasn't going to show her cards, just her steady gaze.

"I said, 'It's getting weird—'"

"*Exactly.* That's what I just said, and it's why I got—"

"No, Jae'cy. In the first post that started this whole mess. The IP address thing. The next day, in the comments, I literally typed 'It's getting weird' and added a link."

Jae'cy went speechless.

"That was me, Jae'cy. In a way, I—" Arielle stopped briefly, wryly chuckled. "'*Leaked'* it to you, the clue in the comment. The link to that next ridiculous set of rumors about you, Timere, Michi, and Taylor, and most importantly, to that truly weird commenter who was lurking under there, like she did in all of the other posts."

Jae'cy inhaled.

"You say we use too many words, right?" Arielle countered, her face suddenly tighter. Then she shrugged limply. "So…I just took action. I gave you a lead, not sure if it *would* lead to Breyah. But she was the only logical suspect in my mind. You know, keep your friends close, enemies closer. And then, there was a weird VPN message I got on my computer right after her borrowing it that time in your café. And obviously, as we both now see…"

"…Why?"

"*WHY?* Because she was—"

"No—why…for me?"

*For you?* Arielle bit her tongue, with another tired chuckle. Chewed on that question she'd been asking herself these past days, weeks, months. *Why did you fall in love, Elle? Why?* "Well," Arielle whispered. "It was for me, too. Clear my name. Finally."

*She was right, taking a stand…and it looked so good on her,* Jae'cy admitted in her mind. "I'm sorry if you didn't think I respected you…You probably think I still don't now."

"It's not that you didn't respect me. It's that you don't trust me…because you don't trust *you.* Enough to face what you want and risk being hurt again."

Jae'cy silenced.

"No, really think about this: How can I give you something when *you* don't accept what you need and want? Because I can give you something, but you wouldn't take it….I gave you something you didn't want, but that you need."

Jae'cy tensed up, mouth tight, arms folded. Arielle turned away.

"I think that makes two of us, no?" Jae'cy stated more than asked. Not flat. Not cool. But softer, even while direct.

Arielle swung her head back around. "No. You and I are *different.* Inharmonious. Because you want the comfort of what you've had in the past, the safe distance, while I wish the past had never happened at all, and so to ensure it doesn't continue to repeat itself in the present and most definitely *not* the future—"

"You want to keep a safe distance?"

Arielle maintained her stance yet clenched her fist inside her pants pocket. She hoped Jae'cy couldn't see her subtly trembling mouth.

"No, I *need* to…The only similarity between us is that neither of us can seem to crawl up out of the past. But it's for different reasons, and so, inharmonious."

Jae'cy smiled jadedly. "You know what's brave about you?" *And attractive as hell, if only you could see it.*

Arielle went still. *There's no one here to save you…*Then she laughed under her breath.

"Time and time again, even after a bad or rough conclusion comes, you're never afraid to put the self-deprecation down just a second. Pick up a pen. And see what you may uncover once again. Because who knows…maybe *this* time, you'll get a happy ending." Jae'cy didn't let up her gaze. The compliment. The directness.

Arielle was feeling cornered. Just like that fateful corner where her desk sat on that fateful day in first grade. And now, that paper, that bearing of what she so intimately felt, which was first complimented by her deceiving classmate before the classmate turned it to the rest, before things turned, was inching toward the hands of the one she'd wanted it to all along…And that was the odd thing about triggers: They came up reflexively, uncontrollably. And much like their name, they attacked…others…themselves…or most frequently, both…

"So, now Surface Level is an Aristotle-in-training…" Arielle derided, slowly looked back over. "You don't let the good ones in even when they're right *there*, right at that door, waiting. Until they realize they'll only ever get that much: the front, never what's behind it, and they finally leave."

Jae'cy's face only subtly twitched, at the nose, an annoyed scrunch but with dim eyes, and then she looked away. Arielle smiled resignedly (relieved although she didn't want to admit it) and started to rise.

"So," Arielle began to fill her in, deflected really. Because now, it wasn't Jae'cy acting cool. It was Arielle acting. "Since it looks like that tough act will continue…"

Acting like she didn't see that Jae'cy was the girl of her love song. Who was opening that paper as Arielle successfully evaded the scene this time around and… *Let's go, Elle. Let's go, let's go, LET'S—*

"How do you really know if you haven't fully listened to what *I* have to say?"

Arielle paused, gulped…then looked over her shoulder. Jae'cy subtly appeared as if about to tremble, a twitchy chew of the inner side of her cheek. *Get yourself together, J…*

"Answer this, for real: If you had known this is what the night would bring…would you still have come?" Jae'cy asked, softly, vulnerably. But clear.

"Jae'cy." Arielle grimaced faintly. "I—"

"I would've."

Arielle froze, wrestling with how her unexpected words had just made her feel. *Scared.*

Scared because Arielle couldn't predict the rest of the storyline. Unlike that day in class. This was now, not then. Wouldn't be able to envision the set, not even the lighting. These past two months had confirmed that. And unlike that day, this story was one she wouldn't be able to write herself; she'd *have* to have the other star of the show apart of it...because this was a lover, not a classmate. A lover, not a classmate...who unlike the classmate, could do so much more damage.

...*And because*...Jae'cy had amassed glossiness in her eyes that couldn't be attributed to the dim lighting...*She's crying.* It was Arielle's first time ever seeing this cool and collected woman's tears openly...The girl of her love song was supposed to smile in elation, say thank you, something, *anything* but cry. And that scared her even more than if she'd rejected. In any possibility, whether the ones she predicted in her mind or the ones that played out right in front of her, Jae'cy scared her. Her sudden heart flutter scared her. This all had to be felt, consumed, and it scared her. And so...

"...Your question was one with way too much fairytale and plot holes," Arielle barely commented, swallowed that down. "And I, too, came for business. For *real.*" *Now get outta there.*

And she did. Because all of *this* business between them was much too capricious, much like marketing, which was why she'd switched careers.

Because even still, she *still* would've come, knowing Jae'cy would be there.

Because she always came.

Because she needed to, and therefore, wanted to.

Because she would do anything.

For her.

She was going where it was safe. She was going back outside.

"Alright. You *do* that." *The nerrrrve of her.* Jae'cy watched Arielle's departure, her racing breath becoming shallower as if all of a sudden, the restaurant had become packed to the brim. Airtight.

*The nerve of me, of both of us...knowing this crazy thing we want, and too scared to try.*

Only after Arielle was out of her sight, Jae'cy slowly, soberly stood. And as she made her way past the tables, she paused briefly by Capri in the cooking pit. He shifted his observation from the swinging-shut entrance door to her. Silently.

She tried to clean up the thought-cluttered space but couldn't erase the complex gaze, glitchy blink. "Apologies, Capri. Something suddenly came up...can we reschedule? I have an idea I'd like to present that I think you might like."

Capri nodded gently. "Sure thing."

With that, she worked up a smile and headed out. To the parking lot.

*Don't even LOOK that way, J.* But she did. She wanted to, no matter her complex feelings, so she did. First, to the immediate left that Arielle had made down the street...

...Then the right...where in the dusk, three dark-toned vehicles blended together.

And she scoffed, then continued to her immediate front, to her car parked curbside...

Hey, not everything could be a sale. Especially when the parties weren't ready to buy in.

*Just plain old not ready,* Jae'cy iterated with a fold of her trembling lips that didn't match the sharpness of the words she texted Paula:

*PLZ don't pull this (stunt) again #respectfully*

She did one last scan to the left lot, Arielle not in sight, and then got in her Range Rover, for home.


* * * *

And Arielle's energy was about the same, already gone in a Lyft. While texting Juliana:

*I said no more blind dates*

And while she awaited her response, an additional text to:

*Kimesha, that was NOT a business meeting.*

And while she awaited *her* response, she got one back:

*If you know the person across from you, then it's not blind.*
*Unless y'all want it to be.*


* * * *

...One of the cars in the right lot, a Camry, rolled down its driver's window. Another, a Yukon, rolled down its rear passenger side. And then the third...

...revealed Juliana with Sinead at the wheel, looking to the Yukon.

"Welp, we struggle-bused that one, y'all!" Juliana initiated.

And Sinead incited. "Just like I did makin' my way over here on damn near E. So, I know someone's about to CashApp me forty," she yawned out. But that wasn't no sleeptalking.

"O-*KAY*?!" Passenger Paula agreed emphatically, Elise beside her in the chauffeured Yukon. "My momma duties are *TRULY,* officially done. If she don't want the help, I can't help her. Over here doin' nighttime castin' like I'm some type of agent when I have my OWN roles in the *A.M.* to fulfill. With her spoiled triflin' behind..." And with that, as she rolled up her window, she kept her mouth going.

"Thanks anyway, ladies," Kimesha sighed in her Camry.

Then her Camry followed the Yukon, and right behind, Sinead.

$\heartsuit$ **49**

*BUT I JUST DID THAT, THOUGH!* Jae'cy beamed to herself as she exited with Capri out of Honest Bites days later. The start of a menu collaboration to be revealed at both of their restaurants next year: three respective limited-time dishes, Creole meets Brazilian. Since Brazil and New Orleans shared similar cultures in the Creole populations, food included, as Jae'cy had explained to Capri just moments ago, this collaboration would be sensible and also stimulating for their respective customers.

Yes, it only made sense, much like Jae'cy had artfully pitched after carrying her most popular dish (air-fried Louisiana wings) to Capri's table and unpacking the sample (his highly acclaimed roasted chicken) that he'd brought. They'd try the other's to really uncover the shared taste and how they could blend it into a Brazilian-Creole chicken fusion remix. Then just two more new dishes to create. It would bring established epicureans with wise palates her way, to sharpen her craft, and bring him exposure to her younger generations. With the Caribbean-Creole influence at the heart of both establishments, it wouldn't be a hard stretch.

"It's gonna be a HIT!"

Indeed.

*Now, whose available seats we fillin' – and with what mutual dates accompanying us – for the celebration?*

Jae'cy's smile twitched as she received Capri's follow-up text when she arrived home. Much more unsettling and queasy than their first sit-down, which had turned out to be not *too* bad after all.

Some of the biggest uncertainties seemed to end up like that. Some.

She replied to Capri...

*You choose*
*BUT luckily we still have a whole year to decide lol*

...as she felt her shoulders stiffen at the simultaneous arrival of a Facebook video live request. From Breyah.

She had to pick a choice here, one she could stand by.

And so, she tapped.

Breyah didn't immediately say anything, only blinked quickly and nervously. The girl was so shooketh (or full of BS) that she had to speak with technology between them.

The irony.

Finally, Breyah mustered up a fidgety smile. "For the first time, there is nothing I can say that will smooth this all over with a laugh."

She was right about that at least. In the heat of their friend disagreements or mini-fallouts, regardless of who had been in the wrong, one wise-crack by Breyah a day or two later would instantly bring them back into their crazy, fun dynamic. But not this time.

"Be-*cause*..." Breyah expelled with a sigh, "I did something truly inexcusable. And I'm lucky that your cold shoulder was the extent of my punishment and consequence."

Precisely, once again.

"But that shows what a goodhearted person you are. Even though you try to act like you don't need a heart, most times."

Jae'cy only inhaled, shallow and subtle.

"And I just hope that I didn't cause that heart to slide even further back, when it deserves to be seen and shared." Breyah's face became much more serious as she looked down from the screen. "And...I know that I more than likely won't be a lucky recipient to witness it up close ever again, should you decide to bring it back out. But I do want to know this..." She peeked up. "How can we *possibly* move on from this?"

Jae'cy wanted to pick words that illustrated non-malice, yet also definitiveness. Almost like her approach with Cori. But these days, she was experiencing really new, unknown things. She could feel it, and she was liking it.

"Truthfully...the best thing, Bre, that you can do right now, not for me but for *you*? Is moving on with your life...for your own peace and a better relationship to *honesty*. Truthfully examining why we do the things we do...like I'm starting to do. And with both of our hearts on that? We'll still be riding together...just in a new way."

Breyah chewed on her bottom lip, eyes glistening.

And like a mirror, Jae'cy felt herself doing the same. A bittersweet example of close friends who had turned practically into kin. But she knew this was how it had to be, for right now. Because she had taken a stand.

And Breyah knew it, too. "Well, that's definitely a Scorpio response." She lightly, weakly chuckled.

Jae'cy smiled back softly in sympathy. "For sure. An evolving one."

"Yeah," Breyah admitted, still repentant, but with a hint of reverence. "Yeah."

And they left it at that, to embark on their journeys away from each other.

*Oh, Bre.*

*And me. But we have to live with our decisions, right?* Jae'cy rubbed the back of her neck, with a new thought, for another relationship.

♡ 50



*NOW, WHO IS THAT??*
    *...DING-DONG.*
That was the front door's repeated answer to being ignored as Jae'cy ascended from her couch and her book, after finally having some downtime. The two-month filming of *The Face of the Earth* had just concluded, and Cori was with her mom as a gift to Jae'cy for her birthday). So she'd settled down to some orange-and-cinnamon-infused mocha, her latest experiment, which had become an autumn entry at Honest Bites this season...and would possibly be in her cookbook...Her cookbook...*Butterscotch* had gone not into publication but into...hiatus. There were still some backstories to edit, with no—

She fluttered, neared the door, focusing back on the present. It couldn't be a random pop-up from Elise (she'd just stopped by with a day-after birthday gift after a Puerto Rico vacation with her girlfriend) or Paula (she'd be coming by later with Cori)—or a paparazzo (they thankfully had stopped hounding her).

She opened the door and found—

"HEY, MOMMY!" Two dark, curly pigtails came prancing in, holding a Styrofoam container.

"Aw, okay. Nothin' saved for me, huh?" Jae'cy grinned at Cori.

"Girl, I knew I shouldn't have let her have that sugary raspberry drink at the restaurant we went to," Paula greeted her.

"Why are you back so soon?"

"You should've seen how she yanked me outta MY house after makin' some pom-pom owls that *she* wanted," Paula recapped, shaking her head as Cori skipped toward the kitchen. "Said she was ready to come home."

That was...weird. Usually, Jae'cy had to physically detach Cori from Paula after hanging with her Mee-Maw. Then Jae'cy remembered, snapping a finger.

And Paula did, too, knocking her head back with a laugh. "Her show."

If there was one thing Cori didn't play about, it was this new kids' gymnastics competition series on Netflix. When it came on, everyone else was dismissed so she could give her undivided attention to it. Jae'cy was considering enrolling her in a beginner's tumbling class.

"Okay, welp," Jae'cy said. "Thanks for your services, but they're no longer needed." Paula finished and was already filing back out. "But I'll take it. Mama's got a date, which I haven't had in *weeks*. The mister is not taking a change of plans, okay?"

Jae'cy chuckled as she watched her mom disembark for her weekend of fun with Kadeem. But her laugh faltered as she shut the door.

Heading back to the living room, she was bum-rushed by Cori, tugging her to the kitchen.

"You're not upstairs?" Jae'cy furrowed her brows at this energetic girl.

"Can I have some lemon-infused ricotta with olive oil and black pepper toast?!"

"Girl, *what?!*" Jae'cy cracked up. "I don't think that's gonna taste good, Rumpa."

"Uh-*hunh!* Anything that you make with the heart."

The toast was indeed bomb, one Jae'cy had made herself before in culinary school and loved. And her grandmas' meals had always been with love. And so, although she wasn't sure Cori's kid palate would quite be in love with such a different snack…

"O-*kaaay,*" Jae'cy obliged as they landed in the kitchen.

She started to reach for her countertop jar organizers of spices and flour and—

"STOP!"

And Jae'cy definitely did so, looking over. Who did she think she was yellin' at?

"I have a recipe," Cori explained as she hopped up onto a stool at the island. "You HAVE to follow a recipe."

*Girl, I'm a chef!* Jae'cy rolled her eyes good-naturedly and folded her arms. "Then where is it?"

Cori pointed to Jae'cy's laptop on the countertop beside her. "In your email."

"Since when do you have email?"

"I sent it from my tablet."

Jae'cy narrowed one eye at Cori, opened her email on her laptop, and sure enough, she spotted an email subject line in her inbox, near the top:

*The Recipe*



*Cute.* She smiled to herself, clicked on it, but instead of a link to Food Network, the URL she spotted was—

"Cori, this is a YouTube link. You *know* what I said about being on—And hold up. Actually, I have a block on these types of videos on your tablet, so how did you—?"

"Open it, open it!" Cori interjected, biting her nails while jumping down off the stool and then bouncing on her tiptoes.

She'd let the little one off the hook this one time because she was clearly caught between a show she was yearning to go see and a hard place known as the corner of the island countertop. She looked so darn cute. *And that was part of her problem right now. With those big cheeks that she still hasn't fully grown into.* And Jae'cy kind of hoped she wouldn't. Her little Rumpa.

Jae'cy didn't want to think about that. Instead, did as told and clicked. Up popped a page of lyrics, playing on the screen to a recognizable beat.

*What in the world?* Jae'cy whipped her head over instantly to Cori, who was now hiding a grin. "Cori, this is *not* a recipe."

"I know. It's *her!*" Cori professed easily as she started to skip to the hall.

"I thought we were doing this?" Jae'cy called out.

"We are. You gotta read it first!"

The kid was right; it literally was H.E.R., the artist, and the instrumental melody was "Hard to Love." And there was a lot to read.

Jae'cy was confused…yet also intrigued. So she turned back fully to the laptop, the "recipe" playing out on the screen, though there was no lemon, ricotta, black pepper, or toast in sight.

Instead (as the words displayed on the screen):

*It started with "Scene 1,"*
*a new school Tweet, a.k.a. DM on IG,*
*subliminally*
*about something so known*
*yet so hard to achieve:*
*the perfect recipe.*
*And yet, I must admit,*
*I was Addicted,*
*and so, yet still I agreed.*

*And soon, "Beautiful" I was down*
*for whatever, any weather. Down*
*Soul For Real for just "Being With You." Down*

*for even just "Wasting Time"*
*coming over 7 Miles for some bad reality TV takes,*
*some Sebastian, Brent, or Drake,*

*but all based*
*on simply being able to "Spend Some Time."*

*Can't lie,*

*Was also down for you know what "for the sport*
*of it." Your team and mine on the court*
*on our Channel Live.*

*Nah. Skip the play,*

*the "Friendship." One wants*
*First Class treatment, wants*
*to be, what Eric says, "Organic" yet "Truly Yours" all day,*
*where you'll "Call Me Every Day" and on "Weekend Getaways."*

*Because "If Pretty Was a Person"*
*"Pretty Girl," it would be you.*
*And I want it to be "Just Us"*
*like Chris, Wale, and Frankie.*
*Yeah, "I Want To Be In Luv" like Craig G.,*
*"What More Could I Ask For" but "Magic" like Craig D.,*
*and knowin' it'll "Survive" like Kenny,*
*knowin' you'll "Never Let Me Go" like the Mac with Mickey D's?*

*Therefore, there's somethin'*
*I wanna "Start Over" like some good Musiq if you let me,*
*like a good Remix 'cause like D'*
*Angelo "I Found My Smile Again."*

*No more Changing Faces,*
*no more "Silent Treatment."*
*Let's get to The Roots.*
*"Visit Me," "143."*

*'Cause I'm sayin' like Jesse P, "Are You Missin' My Love" still, too,*
*even after falling into this Conclave "Twice' now with you?*
*'Cause out of 112 reasons not to*
*"Why Does' my mind still go back to you?*

*And it can be*
*Ideal-ly*
*"All About You" and "Sentimental" me.*
*A "One of a Kind Love" Intro-duced naturally*

*with an "Excuse Me Miss"*
*from Jay Z*
*(it's only polite) or Miss*
*"Soulstar" ('cause alil' more elevating Musiq is* **always** *right)*
*"Let Me Be the One" instead of "Passin' Me By"*
*to the Pharcyde*
*with Common words like,*
*"Well,… 'I Used To Love H.E.R.,'*
*almost like, in the words of Elzhi,*
*I've always known her*
*since back in 'Ferndale.'"*

*It's all a weird set of "Motions" that even Raheem*
*can't redeem.*
*But here's to proposing*
*that maybe*
*that all can change. Maybe*
*Elusion becoming "Reality"*
*one of these days. And finally*

*deciding on a Puma "Midnight Blue,"*
*not to*
*"Still Wonder."*
*The "City Lights," and Devin and DJ Harrison on the Spotify 1s and 2s*
*helping this room "Under the Moon"*
*with the "Girl of My Dreams" tonight to turn into*

*a "Technicolor" Sunni or Lucky Daye*
*with the best of The Ton3s, Kenyon, Malia, Stokley, and Isleys on low play.*

*And at Sevyn, we'll still be Monkey_n, "Closer" "Better" "Lazy Lovin'" inside*
*with "Good & Plenty" pillows, "Cherry Sorbet" in our "Café," and vibes*

*after being out on the surface for far too*
*long. The J. Quest Is On*
*My Mind. But it's all up to…*

*…H.E.R.*

*A perfect recipe who's "Hard To*

*Love"*

Jae'cy inhaled as the opening guitar chords hypnotically hit the air.

And most importantly,...

*"Her..."*

her voice over the track.


*"Her*
*and I have given it more than awhile.*
*It's like a business plug meets acting bug:*
*With time, I've learned more things that lead me deeper in."*
Jae'cy blinked a few times. So many thoughts were swirling around in her head. *How did she get Cori in on this?*


*"Like the way she introduces you to the new:*
*The different but perfect marriage known as lime, maple, and sweet potato.*
*Music that isn't so terrible but ight,...or maybe even kinda consumable.*
*And yeah,...asparagus, too."*


Jae'cy started to tear up beyond her control, a smile spreading across her face.


*"And does all of that magically*
*even while still working on her cocoon.*
*Does all of it magically,*
*strangely so soon*
*before anyone else ever could.*
*Which is good*
*because...*

*now I can help her work on her music game."*


Jae'cy broke out into a soft chuckle, mixing in with...her.


*"Those are the unique benefits.*

*These here were my key messages.*
*And now, I guess it's time for a positioning statement*
*on this dual auditory and visual true source of truth—*
*Instagram and Friends not included.*
*SO..."*

She paused on the track, as any MC knew to do, to sell themselves.

And Jae'cy paused her breath, just watched from her seat on the stool, at this proving- surprising mastermind on the proverbial ones and twos, who had her full attention.


*"...if her*
*favorites this sappy grit the way I heart it,*
*fully, unabashedly, boldly back,*
*then we'll both know that*
*we're both finally feeding off the same page, same vibe.*
*Lockstep..."*


The music faded out. But her voice remained.


*"And then,...she can open*
*her...*
*front door."*

And then, it was just Jae'cy, alone again in the room...eyes still on the video, the recipe...

She inhaled, then slowly rose.

Then she floated toward the front door. Inched, one step, then another.

Extended her arm, then placed her hand on the doorknob. Lightly clenched it, then twisted it, and pulled. The door opened, fully, and her arm lowered. Fully.

She blinked at the person in front of her.

Arielle, on the other hand, didn't blink. Or speak.

But they gazed, *felt*, the universal language between the two of them. At this open door.

Finally, Arielle pulled in an audible, nervous, bracing breath....

And then she extended something from behind her back. A Styrofoam food container.

Jae'cy thought over what to do with her hands. Ultimately, she knew what she wanted to do. And she knew what Arielle wanted her to do, standing there, extending herself.

Jae'cy reached out, took the container, and opened the lid. Inside was a bite-size piece of lemon-infused ricotta with olive oil and black pepper toast. Along with an actual recipe...from a cooking website. *Cute,* Jae'cy repeated, feeling a smile arise in herself.

"The lemon represents me...the chilled ricotta, you. Me, sour at first, and you, cool, trying to stay separated." Arielle stuffed her hands into her pockets. "But when mixed with, interconnecting with each other, somehow they work together."

*Em, let's try it.* Jae'cy picked up the toast and took a bite. Her eyes opened wide as her taste buds were ignited—amongst other things.

"Because what I learned from the chef is there's a first time for everything. And sometimes, it isn't bad. Just takes some time to love." Arielle held steady—so steady. She needed that statement to be true.

"No, it wasn't bad..."

Arielle busted up.

And Jae'cy chuckled low, vulnerable as the new rise in the corner of her mouth. "Nah, really...it just—"

"Had too much lemon," Arielle assumed with a nod, looking away.

"Em-mm..." Jae'cy clarified. "Not enough."

Arielle slowly looked back over to find Jae'cy's face looking serious, intentional. She'd asked for more lemon. For more.

"We'll try it again," Jae'cy concluded. Then finished the last bite.

Arielle lifted her face fully back up in response. Taking it in.

"BUT hold up," Jae'cy cross-examined now, pulling up a brow with a playful, rising grin. "I was just the first to hear your *new sound?* AND you made something with dairy in it? I'm *honored.*"

Arielle smiled, ever so lightly at first, on just one side. Then the other side lifted. And then a muffled chuckle. "Sorry to break it to you, but that was pea protein ricotta."

"Oh, well then, in that case..." Jae'cy started back up, popping her lips in affected offense. "I don't have an older sister, but I'll refer you to my older, *vegan* brother. Don't really see him a lot because he's on my dad's si—"

"And on *that* side he can stay."

Jae'cy squealed.

"Also, you don't have no brother."

"How do you know?!" Jae'cy giggled some more, a higher pitch that gradually, gracefully made its descent to home base: Arielle and her light smirk. And her attention.

"You would've told me."

Jae'cy reflexively returned to tweaking and twisting the doorknob. "...Thank you."

Arielle fully settled her grin, held her eyes. "No. Thank you." Still locked in on her, a nonverbal, visual lockstep.

There, just inside that front door. Past, present, and future all trying to see how they could co-exist.

"Looks like I missed your birthday, though." Arielle toyed with her fingers.

Jae'cy floated her eyes down to the container then to their meeting feet... "But you can always make it up to me. Plus, you said after my birthday."...Then back up. "That's what belateds are for, right?"

Arielle fluttered. Jae'cy, concealing a smile, stepped to the side, pulling the door back. For the outside to come in.

Arielle clenched her stuffed hands that were hidden in her jeans pockets. She knew they were the only part of her that she could hide, once she walked in that door.... *But you'll never know unless you...*

Arielle entered.

And *she* shut the door, just as the second mixtape song, one that hadn't been spoken or seen in the recipe lyrics but was being orated by Maimouna Youssef, greeted them:

She *stay.*

Jae'cy glanced back at Arielle with a faint furrow of her discerning eyebrows, which caused Arielle to give it all away with a simper. Jae'cy responded with a matching curl of her lip and then a roll of her eyes.

Arielle was a crafty, strategic (thanks, marketing) one: reserving the win in the trenches. The unlisted song in the "recipe," the song about staying, the deeper meaning that—Arielle hoped—this would all work out in her favor, in their favor. A plot twist in the tale to shock them both if they pedaled just a *bit* further, to the next page. That one last push...

As they reached the living room, Jae'cy lowered her arm, her hand open. "Just promise me you're gonna do somethin' beyond YouTube playlists, though, and get more into the beats."

"Promise." Arielle extended her own hand and wrapped it around Jae'cy's. Accepted those two-inch, French tip nails like they were now accepting her—even given their differences.

"Are you girlfriends *now?*" Cori asked while peering around from the staircase. 'Cause trust and believe *her* show was still just as important as this other one she'd just temporarily came down to ensure had played out according to Arielle's plan.

Arielle looked away from Cori, who looked away, too: both sets of eyes landing on Jae'cy...

"Yeah, baby," Jae'cy declared with a soft nod at Cori. Then Arielle watched Jae'cy's eyes slide over to her. "Yeah. We are."

* * * *

"Yeah, we are." Arielle filled in the next, last destination to Jae'cy, who was, in turn, filling in the dip of Arielle's free hand where another's hand should go. Like a puzzle.

Riding in the on-road Slingshot that Arielle was navigating through the late-evening traffic just outside of the Strip. Their date that had started about an hour ago and was now ending with sunset and…

"What happened to the museum and fancy dinner?" Jae'cy asked exclusively into Arielle's ear as they came to a stop at a red light.

Both eyeing it like it couldn't turn green quick enough. Arielle clutched the steering wheel, Jae'cy ran her fingers along Arielle's forearm, giving her goosebumps even though this mid-October still felt like late August.

"I think we've played it cute for long enough," Arielle lowly explained.

Jae'cy cracked a giggle aloud to their inside reference as the light turned green.

And, well…

…Hands now met Arielle's hair minutes later as Arielle's lips met the tummy.

Mole.

Waistband.

And then, in Arielle's bed…

All in.

More than enough water for Lake Mead tonight.

**ONE YEAR LATER**

*DING-DONG! DING-DONG!!*

As Arielle wiped up a spill of frappé nestled by stacks of serving cups, candy bags, and lime-infused candied yams on Jae'cy's kitchen counter, she thought she registered someone at the front door. But over the party music (kid-friendly), balloons, and child squeals, it was hard to tell.

However, not a second later, Elizabeth walked in behind Elise with (wait for it) more paper towels.

Arielle chuckled under her breath. Not at the quasi-OCD matrilineal gene, but because her mom's arms looked like they were carrying the entire Target aisle, rather than the four to five more that Arielle had requested she get.

Before Arielle could thank her mom, Elise whipped around with her own paper towel bundle and placed it on the crowded countertop. She was temporarily working part-time for Paula now, due to her debut novel finally dropping. For her first step into the world, her book marketing (with the help of some of Arielle's connections) had scored her above-average new author success, to the point where she had some solid press engagements lined up with local literary circuits. Paula's words to her right before they finalized their new work contract? "Don't get too cute."

"You know I'm almost, kinda-sorta your name twin, right? Or, like, the unofficial oldest daughter you never had," Elise proposed to Elizabeth, a hand on her hip.

The convo became null and void to the sound of Jae'cy from the other room....

"Whoever needs to hear this, a.k.a. the people in the kitchen, we're about to cut my baby's cake!"

Arielle gulped—and not in anticipation of the crowd of folks or even the yummy (vegan) chocolate whipped cream and vanilla goodness....

"*Yesss*, the finale," Elise segued, rubbing her hands together as she dipped out.

Indeed, it was an exciting day for all: For the guests, more taste-testing (this time, of Jae'cy's and Capri's three menu collaborations that were about to launch). For Jae'cy, her third year into Honest Bites (including LA Hit List and *Time Out* magazine features), along with the joint publication of *Butterscotch: On the Rocks We Dwell* and her forthcoming kid cookbook with Cori, both edited by Arielle. And for Cori, moving on to level two in her gymnastics class, and at the top of her class, while also being a seven-year-old author.

Hence, all of the balloons in this room, Elise disappearing into them. Much like Arielle wished she could.

For this morning had been an excitable undercover event, or rather decision, for her. She suddenly zapped out of her nerves just enough and quick enough to tap Elizabeth's wrist just as it was about to go into the land of balloons: the living room where Jae'cy and the rest were

Elizabeth reemerged into the kitchen, not with a question, but an instinctively answered one as she studied, read, and then deciphered her daughter's now skittish face, slightly widening eyes.

Arielle's hands got to dancing—and Bruno Mars' "Uptown Funk" that had just boomed against the walls wasn't even the reason.

She just watched, uneasily peering at Elizabeth from the corner of her eyes as her mom's eyes bulged next...

...at what was now in Arielle's hand: an open jewelry box with a ring.

Elizabeth looked back up. "You think you're ready?" She'd met Jae'cy, quickly called her the other daughter she'd never had (sorry, Elise). And then observed quietly just how much of an emotional impact Jae'cy had on the one she'd actually birthed. Knowing this other woman would have to become the main one to provide Arielle what she couldn't.

But it was up to Arielle.

Yet before a suddenly antsy Arielle could answer, before she could state that she actually was—

"*Uhhh*, we're ready!" Calling out unseen from the other room was Jae'cy once again.

"UH-oh!"

But *that* wasn't.

Bruno had left the building, the track dropping. The music stopping.

Now, a foot inside of the kitchen, was Juliana, cup in one hand, Sony ZV-1 camera on a selfie stick in the other. She had started a YouTube channel to capitalize on the five minutes of fame that had extended last year, recently having created an intimate, motivational Mixology Master Class Patreon series. Then, also pulling through the balloons, Cristal-first, came Sinead. Extending the bottle to Arielle. "Spirits from Melanie. In spirit." And then shock. "And what is THAT?"

All eyes (and camera) had turned to that ringed diamond, with an impressed head tilt from Juliana. Then they all looked over in one direction simultaneously.

With just one fur-trimmed bootie into the kitchen, stood a woman who looked to be some kind of IG model/influencer with the amount of satin and diamonds on her hands, chinchilla-ribbed turtleneck, and ears. Arielle recalled her entering some time ago with AD. But even she paused for the cause known as That Jewelry Box in Arielle's Hands.

Arielle shrugged at the woman, finally spoke. "My mom's," she uttered unconvincingly with a tip of her head at Elizabeth, who mustered a smile at the girl. "Mother's Day."

Mother's Day was four months away.

"It's like *that*, cuh?! You've REALLY made it." Juliana zoomed *all* the way in on the 1.25-carat round diamond that Arielle still couldn't believe her cheap self had acquiesced to. But the color of the diamond just looked so right. She knew it from first sight...much like she had about Jae'cy.

The chinchilla woman worked up an awkward chuckle, brought up a cocked-back thumb, pointing to the Land of Balloons. "The graduation girls have graduated to the next event: cake-cutting."

She pivoted around (*much* too quick for Arielle's liking). *She's not that excited about some chocolate frosted cake...*Then Sinead did the same. Then Juliana, but only after a hip bump that propelled Arielle into the helium madness.

When she could see again, stuffing the jewelry box away into her pocket, Elizabeth was just a bit behind her, and everyone else all around her, as she stepped deeper into the trenches of this living room. She spotted Gary, who shot up his eyebrows at her as she moved by...almost like he was seeing a new story play out, a sketch...(Not happenin'.)

*BUT is THIS really happenin'??? This wasn't supposed to happen until...*

*Until when? Until you chickened out?*

Arielle mentally hyperventilated, while more of the clueless room came into view. They didn't know what her mind was spinning about; on the outside she was trying really hard to look cool as a cucumber.

She stepped past Kimesha, who now had gained *more* clientele after Arielle's social media fiasco.

But Arielle's anxiety shot back up as she reached the table with the long sheet of chocolate alongside Honest Bites food trays, some labeled as new menu candidates (including her and Capri's creations), and hardcovers of *Butterscotch* and *Butterscotch and Hopscotch: Children's Sugary Spin-Offs* (using agave syrup ONLY) on either side of the sweet centerpiece....

...that had Jae'cy right in front of it. And Cori, who had finally stopped trying to "fly" off tables and was, instead, hitting splits in her advanced gymnastics courses. Case in point, she somersaulted perfectly into the waiting arms of Jae'cy in the tutu leotard that she had been set on wearing today.

And Paula was up there, too, on the mic. (No singing today, sorry again, Juliana. Just hosting.) And a clear-as-day engagement ring of her own on the left hand that was holding it.

*Dang, even Kadeem had kept it sane (for his own much higher budget) with fewer carats.* Arielle couldn't help but to gulp at the still modestly huge rock, while feeling the one she had hidden against the front of her thigh. She was sure that she looked like a deer in headlights as she moved further in Jae'cy's direction...

These days, Paula was trailblazing in yet her latest side venture, an already flourishing cosmetics line. Not to mention, she'd landed a spot in a Black Hollywood women celeb reality show (appropriately called *The Real Angels of LA*), as a platform to promote her businesses. Very strategic, like the boss that she was.

She looked Arielle's and Elizabeth's way, to finally get this cake-cutting going.

"Why, HELL-o!"

But before Arielle or Elizabeth could reciprocate beyond their affected sorry grins and light chuckles, Paula was already gathering everyone's attention to tutu-twirling Cori and her excited butter knife–holding hands being guided by Jae'cy into the cake.

"Mee-Maw's baby means business," Paula announced to the room.

Everyone cracked up and clapped as Cori got to adorably focused work cutting the cake into squares.

"I want to say thank you to everyone who came to celebrate with me and my bab-*ies*." Jae'cy glanced up just briefly to acknowledge the room. And Arielle.

And then the room naturally acknowledged Arielle, some comically cooing. She meekly, silently tipped her head with an awkward grin.

Next thing she knew, a plate was landing in her hand care of Jae'cy. But not without a smiling assessment. "What type of party did you all have going on in the kitchen, though? And why have you been so quiet today?"

Arielle felt her stomach drop and could barely glance at Jae'cy's awaiting countenance. Even though the cake looked good, and would undoubtedly taste good, she currently wasn't able to stomach anything but the ever-increasing nervousness that was rising within her. She was seriously considering hopping back into that kitchen for her last-ever lime yams, then scurrying back to Vegas, never to be heard from again.

"Proud of ya, Jae Bae!" Aunt Loren announced as she suddenly came up to hug Jae'cy…and also to slide her a new training guide. Because trust and believe, Jae'cy had actually finished that other one (network security and servers) after the social media fiasco.

"Me too," rejoined a man, coming up with a quick, purposely fun, rocking embrace of Jae'cy and Cori, which made them both chuckle.

A man who, Arielle nervously noted, discreetly toying with the jewelry box in her pocket, was Jae'cy's twin in facial structure and height. And that was why Arielle had instantly known he was Jae'cy's father, Jules, when they'd been fleetingly introduced in all of the day's motion. He had flown in from Houston, where Paula had once briefly lived in the late eighties during her pre-fame days.

*And now he's here. Of all days.* Arielle gulped even harder as he turned around to her with one of those naturally occurring smiles people give after swiveling around from a preceding pleasant chat. *Let's see if that face stays the same in the next moment, because today is truly the best one of any for a father's blessing.*

Arielle smiled back, yet clutched the jewelry box within the safe havens of her pocket one final time, then released it, along with a tight breath, as she took a step inward to Jae—

Up popped Tish's tapping arm on Arielle's shoulder. "Hold up."

*No, YOU hold up,* Arielle impatiently greeted back in her head to a cake-stuffing Tish. Arielle peeked over Tish's shoulder to see that Jae'cy was now caught up in conversation with some other relative anyway. And was honestly a bit relieved, too. Just for a second at least.

"When are we—?"

"I'm getting everything lined up," Arielle interjected.

Tish had been pressing her for the past month about starting some DJ sets between LA and Detroit. They'd been practicing for months now, syncing up occasionally in the other's city to do some jamming and fine-tuning the basics of the craft. Now, they both—yes, Arielle—felt that they were ready to do the thing in public.

To solidify Tish's confidence (and make her chill all the way down *because we don't need two people on-edge right now*), Arielle put on a grin that was a bit preoccupied at the moment by another, more immediate key moment she was about to bravely face.

She took another peep at Jae'cy, who looked to be wrapping up with the relative. Maybe the moment was now.

*Before you chicken out—*

"Okay, time for some congrats!" she heard Paula direct the room.

*Sigh.*

Tish's one-year-old son, Drew, suddenly tripped on nothing but his own young feet, then easily bounced right back up and toddled right on about his business to Erica.

"So...looks like his joints are pretty uncompromised," Arielle shakily smirked, trying to psych herself out of her jitters.

"Better be. His immune system, too. We give him them those turmeric elderberry gummies from Whole Foods, 'cause parents gotta work. Can't afford off-days for his sick days."

"But you can afford Whole Foods elderberry gummies." Arielle shook her head with a laugh. But it was short-lived.

"Well, apparently, you're affordin' some things, too..." Tish tipped her plate forward in the direction just behind Arielle's head.

"What did you do?" Arielle stiffly whispered.

"Wasn't me," Tish chuckled.

*Yeah, okay, Shaggy.*

Marlon stepped up right then, with his own goofy, cake-chewing face. "There you go, sis. Giving yourself a chance at something new." And again, he was damn sure not talking about her finally publicly showing her passion for beats.

Arielle slowly turned around....

*Oh, no...*

...as everyone started turning around to *her.*

*No-no-no-NOOO.*

Then Arielle looked to where Tish's and Marlon's attention had redirected.

And what unraveled was like a twisted game of Telephone, on the LCD screen mounted on the wall above the cake table. Paula panned her hand over to it like Vanna White on *Wheel of Fortune*: social media guest book entries praising new kid author/gymnast Cori and actress/chef Jae'cy on her recent Honest Bites attention in local culinary media:

*Congrats Baby Cee—and Mommy Cy!*

*You go, cuties! "Best of Level 2 Gymnasts" List?* ✓ *The LA Hit List?* ✓

*Gettin Level 2s AND Time Outs. Like mommie like mini!*

*AND momma also finna get that RING!!*

*Siiiigh.* Arielle snaked her gaze back to the room, the heads looking amongst one another, and then back to her. Who knew who the turncoat was, but Arielle was going to make it their Last Supper....

Then she detected the possible culprit: the chinchilla woman, AD's girl, discreetly bulging her eyes then dropping them to her cell phone. *Yeah...what else had you done with that device seconds ago?* Arielle just subtly pushed her tongue into one inner cheek. It was what it was at this point: The context clue had just been made public, and at any time now, Jae'cy, whose eyes were still trailing down that screen, was about to connect the dots...

Whereas Juliana face-palmed, Paula whipped her flat-ironed, layered bob over to Arielle...and then Jae'cy slowly turned her head over her shoulder to Arielle, too.

But Arielle couldn't yet reciprocate the scanning turned steady gander of Jae'cy that focused on her, even though (or especially because) she was right *there* in front of her. So she instead braved, with a twitchy, manufactured grin as her artillery, the crowd:

Cori. Now somersaulting over to...

...AD, who was working to balance a long-distance coparent rhythm with his travel-heavy ATL/LA career. But had he just given Arielle a very faint nod...of respect??? Guess, just like a true businessman, since he'd missed the opportunity, it only made sense for a rightful qualified candidate to step in.

Then Capri.

Elizabeth.

Gary, who was *really* in full attention now (and not just because Elizabeth had magically found her way over to him...).

Paula, who now promenaded over to her fiancé Kadeem to get a better front-facing view of Arielle and whatever was about to pan out...

Elise, who was taking a big bite of her big slice of cake with big eyes beside her girlfriend.

Kimesha, who, yes, had finally mastered those damn mussels.

Timere and his girlfriend.

Aunt Loren.

Jules. Whose smile was a bit less liberal and *much* more curious now.

Marlon, who, with Latrina and Jada beside him, clapped proudly.

Sinead. And Melanie, who was now there in digital spirit by way of Sinead's WhatsApp-broadcasting cell phone.

Tish, who, even with Drew in her arms, found some way to be euphemistically non-PG. Eying AI by the rim known as Jae'cy's...

backcourt. Then motioning an arm up in ball-holding arc position with a wink and grin.

And, of course, Juliana, Rashad (yep), and her Sony (yep-yep)… that then turned right to Jae'cy's face…a face that now expressed faintly widening eyes, behind an otherwise frozen countenance. Widening eyes that Arielle finally could bear to face.

Arielle smiled through her jitters. "Welp, since someone got a lead on it…"

She dipped down to one knee in front of Jae'cy and reached into her pocket as the crowd ignited, cooing or joyously whispering, or hushing (and pulling out their phones).

All the while, Jae'cy remained eerily silent. Arielle both hated and loved that about her.

And therefore…

*Woooo. Here goes.*

She pulled out the jewelry box and popped it open. *You got this, Wordsmith….* "Well, uh, as you can see," she commenced, looking up at the many recording cell phones pointed in their direction, then back to Jae'cy. Steady, deep. "Everybody else is ready. And they always have been. Even when we weren't. So, let's make this a good story for them. But ultimately, most importantly, for ourselves. One that's real, that lasts. One that started when a certain costar stepped up. And now, all I need is her to move forward. If she's ready to."

"Smooth, AI. SMOOTH!" Tish sidebarred, and the rest in the room agreed with chuckles.

Then all of the room hushed in wait…gazes back on Jae'cy. Whose face hadn't left Arielle, nor Arielle hers.

"Is she?" Arielle opened this potential new chapter.

Jae'cy took in a breath; Arielle could see her chest rise and fall. "…I don't know."

The crowd murmured, hid their collective empathetic or uncomfortable reaction as Arielle tried to hide her own. *Well, damn.*

"Because that sounds so corny."

The subsequent quiet became so unbearable that Arielle started side-eyeing those balloons…. She would give it three more seconds, and then she'd leave with the last scraps of dignity she had left.

*Whyyy did you do this so soon, Elle? Falling into that U-Haul stereotype and now I've done scared her away.*

But no. It hadn't been too soon. Arielle twisted her fingers around the still-open box, wrestling with her thoughts. Although it had been just about a solid year of an official vocalized relationship between them, the truth they both knew was that they'd been intimate for years prior. It had always been there between them, even when both wrestled with it for the longest before finally surrendering.

*So why am I still down on this knee with this ring, alone? And why is she still being fearful when we'd said we owed it to ourselves to be daring and—?*

"Corny...but fly."

Arielle blinked, speechless. Then slowly shifted her eyes back over and up.

Jae'cy revealed a smirk, one lifted corner from underneath that trademark veil.

Arielle took that special signal and outwardly, very audibly sighed, much to the enjoyment of the room, which broke out into chuckles.

Then the crowd applauded, whistled, hooted, twerked (no need to point out who). As the still-kneeling Arielle witnessed in mesmerized elation, Jae'cy, the ringleader of it all, jiggling as her veil fell...along with a light stream of tears.

*Proud of you, baby.*

And so, with confidence, Arielle lightly wiggled the ring out of the box, as everyone's eyes followed. *Please fit.*

Gently took Jae'cy's hand. Slipped the ring onto the fourth finger, just like that. *Perfect.*

Rose, with her focus intent on Jae'cy, and came to a stand, her face just inches away from the face she'd been waking up to as-of-late right here in this home. A face that looked just as beautiful bare in the morning as it did during a made-up affair, like right now. A face that she planned to wake up to many more mornings going forward.

She closed the small distance, with one full step forward. And leaned in.

And Jae'cy gave no hesitation—instead, she leaned in closer. For a kiss.

A *real*, long one.

No more waiting. Wavering. Fearing.

Both all in.

And maybe *too* much.

"Okay, remember, not everyone here is over eighteen," Paula reminded them loudly.

So Arielle took heed of her future mother-in-law and reluctantly pulled away from Jae'cy, cracking up, along with Jae'cy and the rest of the room...including Cori and her giggling friends.

Then she took Jae'cy's hand, with a peck on it. And Jae'cy smiled.

*Dang, girl, you're not so scary, after all,* Arielle thought as she dazed in full, unabashed sappiness at Jae'cy...and Jae'cy did the same, Arielle somehow knowing that she was thinking the same.

And that *was* corny.

But fly.

Indeed.

**KEELA BUFORD**
is the author of *Pride, and Joy*
(yes, the comma is intentional),
somewhat like the historical sister novel to
*The Buy-In.* She is a content specialist who
has helped many businesses in vast
industries. Her creative and screenplay
works have placed in semifinalist positions
with Stage 32, WeScreenplay, Outfest, and
IndieFEST. She currently lives in Illinois.